DANGEROUS THOUGHTS

FORTUNE CITY MAFIA
BOOK 2

EVELYN WARD

ISBN: 979-8-9910506-6-1 (Ebook)

ISBN: 979-8-9910506-7-8 (Paperback)

Cover design by Igor Andrich @igorandrichdesign

Editing by Marilyn Haynes at MH Editorial Services

www.mheditorialservices.com @mheditorialservices

Let us descend now unto greater woe;

...

And I, who stood intent upon beholding,
Saw people mud-besprent in that lagoon,
All of them naked and with angry look.
They smote each other not alone with hands,
But with the head and with the breast and feet,
Tearing each other piecemeal with their teeth.

From Canto Seven of the Inferno by Dante Alighieri

CONTENT WARNING

This is the second book in the Fortune City Mafia series—a dark, why-choose mafia romance. If you made it through the first book, we're so proud of you, you dirty little thing. But that was only the beginning of our dark tale.

Things will get worse from here.

If you haven't yet read the first book in the Fortune City Mafia series, Dangerous Men, we advise you to put down this book and start there. And if it's a bit too much for you—a bit *too* dark—please remember:

Things will get worse from here.

This book contains graphic sex scenes, torture, violence, stalking, abduction, discussion of human trafficking, voyeurism (consensual), voyeurism (nonconsensual), inappropriate behavior while covered in blood, murder, and one straight-up psychopath who would love to watch you bleed.

It also contains references to infidelity, parental death, and descriptions of domestic violence from a past relationship. Readers are advised that rape—off-page, in the past, and not involving any of the main characters—is mentioned at multiple points throughout the book.

Abandon all hope, ye who enter here.

Author's note: While some elements of this book were inspired by real events, this is a work of fiction. Any character resemblance to persons living or dead is purely coincidental.

If you or someone you know is experiencing domestic violence, we urge you to contact the National Domestic Violence Hotline: 1-800-799-7233

To all the good girls reading this
(and the bad ones too):
Don't be afraid of the dark

PROLOGUE
SIX YEARS AGO

SEBASTIAN

"You can't be serious."

Ashton's voice is shrill as he paces the room, his shoulders tight with coiled energy, muscles twitching. Alec watches him from where he leans against the wall, eyes hard.

"We can't do this," Ashton continues. He threads his fingers through his hair and tugs, pulling at the roots. "This, this is *fucked*. You can't seriously be asking us to go through with this."

"These are Dante's orders. Not mine," Alec responds coldly. "So, if you have a problem with—"

"Dante's fucking orders!" Ashton spits the words out and turns to Alec, throwing his arms wide. "Do you even hear yourself right now? This isn't... This is fucking monstrous, you know that? This is human fucking trafficking. Some of them are *kids*, for Christ's sake! You can't be serious about doing this, Alec!"

"I follow my orders," Alec reminds him. There's a sharp edge to his words, a warning of how close he is to losing his temper. Ashton doesn't seem to notice. He shakes his head with a scoff and resumes pacing.

"No. Not this time," Ashton says. "This is too much. This isn't us... This isn't you."

"*You* won't have to do anything," Alec insists. "Dante specifically requested Viper for this job and—"

"And Viper is fucking insane!" Ashton shouts, gesturing to where Viper currently lounges in an armchair, cleaning under his nails with a knife. "He doesn't understand right from wrong. He's not capable of it anymore!"

"Rude," Viper counters, pointing the knife at him.

"And you don't think it's extra fucked, to be making *him* do this? After what he's been through?" When Alec doesn't answer, Ashton turns on me, striding over to jab his finger against my chest. "And you! You're supposed to be his moral compass, aren't you? So where the hell are *you*? You know how fucked up this is. *You fucking know it.* You're supposed to tell him where the line is with shit like this. This is a big fucking line in the sand, Doc!"

I grind my back teeth together but don't say a word, not even when he pushes me again, practically shoving me, trying to get me to react. I don't. I can't. It's not my place to go against Alec's orders.

Even when I want to.

I ignore the bile rising in my throat and keep my face perfectly blank, eyes fixed above Ashton's shoulder. Because he's right. We've done a lot of horrible things, and we've broken a lot of laws together, even before we joined up with Dante and his organization. But this? This is different. This is evil.

And there's no coming back from it if we do this.

I keep my thoughts to myself as I watch Alec, waiting for his final decision. If he asks this of us, we'll do it. My brothers would go to hell and back for each other.

Only this time, it's looking like that's exactly what we might have to do.

"Sebastian follows orders," Alec tells Ashton, his biceps flexing as his arms tighten across his chest.

His words hit unexpectedly hard, and for a moment, my mask slips. Is that what I am now? A monster whose only excuse is that I was following orders?

Is that what I've become? What we've become?

We descended into hell so slowly over the years that we never even noticed until we found ourselves surrounded by devils.

"I won't do it," Ashton insists, shaking his head. "And I won't let you do it either, Alec. I won't let any of you do this. This isn't about territory or money, or...or anything. This is evil. This is wrong. And I won't let it happen."

"And what do you plan to do to stop it?" Alec asks in a low and dangerous voice.

There's nothing any of us can do, and he knows it. Dante owns us. He holds us by the leash. And when he says bite, well...

We're nothing more than his rabid dogs, now.

"I'll leave. I'll disappear," Ashton says, finally coming to a stop. He squares his shoulders and turns to stare Alec down, a determined look on his face.

"You think Dante won't find you and kill you for that?" Alec responds.

"Then let him kill me. I won't be that person. I swear to you, I would rather die than be that type of monster...than be that fucking evil."

He means it.

Viper and I exchange a look, then turn our attention to Alec.

A muscle in his jaw flexes as Alec clenches his teeth. He doesn't move.

"Did you hear me?" Ashton pushes. "I will let Dante shoot

me between the eyes in broad daylight, in front of all of you. I swear I will. This is too far. And you know it. You *fucking know it, Alec.*"

Alec's jaw clenches and unclenches as he stares at Ashton. "He won't accept a no on this, Ashton. We have no other options."

"Then we leave," Ashton says, like it's the simplest thing in the world. Like Dante would ever let us. "Then we fucking leave. We should have done it years ago. Enough is enough. Together, we can figure it out. It's not like he can chase us forever."

Alec stares him down, seconds ticking by as he realizes Ash isn't going to bend on this. Finally, his gaze moves away, brows pinched in thought. I can practically see the plan forming behind his eyes. A small, microscopic ray of hope enters my chest.

Ash was right. I am Viper's moral compass, the only one left in this world capable of stopping him from going too far. He relies on me to tell him where the line is.

But Ashton does the same thing for Alec. Ever since we were kids, he's been the one to pull Alec back from the brink, to set him on the right course.

And we've been going down the wrong course for so long now, pulled there by Dante, this might be our last chance to pull ourselves back.

After an eternity of silence, Alec finally speaks. "I have a plan," he tells us.

Ashton's posture instantly relaxes, his breath escaping in one long exhale. "Thank fucking God," he mutters.

"A plan to get us out of here," Alec continues. "To be free of him, for good."

That ray of hope in my chest grows, and I let myself

imagine it, for one glorious moment. Freedom. For all of us. A chance to escape this hell Dante has pulled us into.

But he's forgetting one big complication...

"What about Annika?" I ask.

Alec hesitates. His hand clenches, as though the weight of the ring on his finger has become too heavy.

"We can't risk it," he says solemnly. "You know he'll never give her up, even if she wanted to come with us. And if we take her from him, he'll never stop chasing us. She's a target on our back we can't afford to have."

Logically, I know he's right. It's too big a risk. There's no way in hell Dante would ever let us leave with her. Even if we managed to get away, Dante would burn this world to ash before he'd let his daughter go free.

It's the right move. Rationally, I know it's the right move.

So why does it feel like he just ripped my heart out of my chest and tore it to pieces?

1

THE NIGHT SHE FOUND OUT

SYDNEY

I AM *DRUNK*. LIKE BIKE-INTO-THE-BACK-OF-A-PARKED-CAR drunk.

Which I, in fact, did.

Thankfully, only one person witnessed it. He was just as piss drunk as me and watched as I swerved away from the completely open street toward the only obstacle within a thousand feet. *Crash.* We locked eyes after I gracelessly pulled myself back up to my feet, my ego more bruised than anything else.

"It's okay. I'm the only one that saw that," he reassured me in a stage whisper, emphasizing the words with an inebriated hiccup. How adorably cartoon-mouse of him.

"It's our secret now," I answered with a wink before biking away, a little steadier.

And it will remain our secret...unless I fucking die and it makes it to the news: "Local Idiot Bikes into Traffic Amidst Affair Scandal".

Dark thought, Sydney.

Through sheer luck, I manage to make it home in one piece,

with all three bottles of wine stuffed into my bag intact. Necessary provisions to get me through tonight, to help me mourn everything I lost in just a few short hours.

My chest and stomach hurt from crying. My hand hurts from the shattered mirror I had to clean off my bathroom floor. Something deep inside me feels like it was broken tonight.

I don't bother with a wine glass. I plop down on my couch, open a bottle, and swallow as much as I can straight from the source. Alcohol isn't going to solve anything, but at least it will dull the pain. And right now, all I want is for the pain to stop. I need something to deaden it, even a little.

It's funny, but before tonight, I never really believed those stories about people dying from a broken heart. It's unrealistic, right? And so ridiculously melodramatic to think that emotions could cause actual physical pain. People just like to exaggerate what they feel to make their love seem *more* than everyone else's. I used to roll my eyes at that sort of thing—too sentimental, too trite. Just an excuse for people to dress up their pain as something poetic.

But here I am, lifting the neck of an almost-empty bottle to my lips, feeling like I could die from this. Like this pain could actually kill me.

Breaking up with Chase felt like my heart had been broken, like it had shattered into hundreds of pieces. But this? Losing them? It feels like a gunshot, straight to the chest. And the wound gets bigger as I relive the night, over and over *and over* again.

Alec is married.

Alec has been lying to me, this entire time.

They've *all* been lying to me since the day I met them.

Another sip, that'll do the trick.

I take another long drink from my wine bottle to wash it all away. I'm reaching up to wipe the tears from my eyes with my sleeve before I remember I'm still wearing Alec's shirt. After Earl dropped me off, I threw on the first pair of pants I'd found, cleaned up the mess of broken mirror I'd left on the bathroom floor, finished off every drop of wine I'd had in my apartment, and left to get more.

I hadn't bothered changing my shirt.

It smells like him. And I hate that I love his smell. That it soothes me, even now, after everything he did to me.

I'm a fool for falling for these men when I didn't even really know them. How could I have been this stupid? After all the bullshit Chase fed me over the years, after all the healing I did after our breakup, I still ate up every single lie Alec told me like I was starving, ravenous for crumbs of his affection. How humiliating.

Only this time around, it's even worse. Because now I'm the other woman.

I'm the homewrecker.

And *there* goes the bottle. I shake the last drop out onto my tongue before reaching for the next one. On the table next to my provisions of wine, my phone lights up with notification after notification.

Ping.

Ping.

Ping.

Ashton: Hey, are you okay?

Ashton: Doc told us what happened. I need to know you're doing alright Babygirl. Talk to me.

Ashton: Pick up or I'm coming over.

I try to ignore him, but my phone starts ringing, Ashton's

name flashing on the screen. It must be the tenth time he's called since I got home.

I stare at my phone and wonder what Alec told him. I wonder how Ash is going to try to defend him, explain away all their lies.

The next time he rings, I answer.

"Sydney?" Ashton asks through the phone. His voice is a balm and a toxin all at once, and I hate that just hearing his voice makes my heart skip a beat, makes me want him. "Oh, thank God you picked up! Listen, I know what happened with Sebastian and—"

I hang up the phone.

I manage to open my next bottle of wine and take a single swig straight from the bottle before it rings again.

Ashton chuckles awkwardly when I answer. "Are you there? I think we have a bad connection. The call cut off and—"

"Did you put Chase in the hospital?" I cut in. I don't bother to hide the anger coloring my voice. I know one of them did it. I don't believe for one second this was a coincidence, not with what I know about them now. It's just a question of which one was responsible.

There's a long pause.

"Okay," Ash says, his voice unsteady. "I, uh...didn't think you'd find out this fast. Give me a second. I was just—"

And there's my answer. *Click.* But as soon as I end the call, he's calling back again.

"*What?*" I snap into the phone.

"Just let me explain," Ash starts.

Click.

My next gulp of wine is bitter and acidic on my tongue, and it sticks in my throat when I try to swallow. *Stupid Shiraz.*

I'm not sure why he would even bother trying to explain it. Nearly killing my ex can't be the worst thing he's done.

Who knows how many people Ashton has put in the hospital?

Or how many people he's killed.

When he calls again, I pick up and hiss, "*Why are you still calling me?*"

"Babygirl, what's going on? Are you drunk?" He sounds genuinely concerned, like he's worried about me. But between the pain gripping my chest, the storm of rage brewing inside me, and the copious amount of wine in my system, I can't seem to find the energy to care.

"I am *extremely* drunk, in fact. Maybe the drunkest I've ever been," I say. I'm genuinely proud of how little I'm slurring. "You've been lying to me. All of you."

Ashton takes a steadying breath. "Listen, I know Doc and Viper scared you. And there's a lot about our world you don't understand, but I—"

Click.

Nope. We're not doing that.

I'm not playing the dumb, naive girl anymore. They are dangerous, cheating, manipulative bastards. And now he wants to twist it like this is just about me not understanding their *world*? Like this is my fault? No. I refuse to be blamed for someone else's fuckups. I refuse to be manipulated by a man ever again.

When the phone rings again, almost immediately, my temper finally snaps. I'm done.

"Fuck off, Ash," I spit into the phone when I answer, without giving him the chance to speak. "*Stop* calling me. I need space. Space from *all of you*. I don't want to hear from you. I don't want to see you. I want you all to *leave me alone.*"

His quick intake of breath tells me he's going to respond, but before he can, I say, "Call me again tonight and I will block your number. Try me."

I hang up and glare down at the screen, daring him to call my bluff. This time, he doesn't call back. I wait a few more minutes before turning my phone off and tossing it across the room.

One night, I promise myself, as I swallow another mouthful of wine. I'll give myself just one night to be broken. I won't let myself fall apart like I did the last time a man hurt me. If there's anything positive that I can take from the last few months, it's that I am bigger than any relationship. No matter how much this hurts, no matter how much pain they caused me, I won't let this break me. I'm stronger than that. They *showed me* that I'm stronger than that.

So tonight, I'll wallow.

I'll feel sorry for myself.

I'll likely vomit.

But tomorrow is a new day.

———————

I DO VOMIT.

I vomit more than I thought a human body could possibly manage.

When I wake up the next morning—surprisingly still alive, unsurprisingly still a little drunk—I'm tangled in a blanket on the floor of my bathroom wearing nothing but Alec's shirt, and my chest and throat burn from my time spent retching into my toilet. The harsh sunlight streaming into my apartment is blinding, and for the first few minutes while I rise to consciousness, there's only the bright light and the intense throbbing in my skull to keep me company, before the memories from last night flood in. Then I remember why I'm lying on my bathroom floor, with the taste of vomit and wine coating my tongue.

Oh.

Right.

Men.

I groan as I peel myself off the ground, wrapping the blanket around my shoulders. The pounding in my head is like an off-tempo drum. Bed. I need bed. I need bed, and I need to never see another man again so long as I live.

Fuck Alec.

Fuck every lie he told me.

Fuck all the secrets he and his brothers kept from me.

I almost make it to my bed, and I'm just about to crawl under the sheets to sleep off the rest of this hangover, when there's a knock at the door. I freeze, cold anger flooding my veins.

If it's Ashton, I swear I might break something. Maybe something *attached* to him. But before I decide *what* exactly I might break, and whether it's his penis, a voice calls from outside.

"Syd?" The voice is chipper and muffled by the door, but distinctly feminine. And familiar. "Let me in. I brought you a bagel sandwich and some ginger ale. I heard you might need a bit of help."

Jade. I let out a shaky breath. My single ray of light in this horror show we call life.

"Don't make me go all the way home to get my spare key," she threatens. "I'll do it, but I won't be happy about it."

"I'm coming." It takes me an embarrassingly long time to shuffle to the door and unlatch the deadbolt.

Jade's eyes widen at the sight of me when I ease the door open.

"Oh," she says, taking a step back and blinking hard at my appearance. Her eyes roll over my body, from my split lip to the blanket wrapped around me, and then down to my bare feet. "Oh, Syd, you did some damage to yourself, didn't you?"

I wince, reaching up to touch my frizzy curls. They feel flat on one side, unmanageably wide on the other. "Is it that bad?"

"Well, it's not exactly *good*." She brushes past me into the apartment, scooting around the couch and dropping her hang-over haul on the coffee table. I shuffle along behind her, dragging my blanket behind me like a cape.

It's even brighter in my living room than it was in the bathroom. There was a time when I loved how much natural light this apartment gets, loved that it was sunny and bright all day. But today the sunlight feels like it might kill me. I collapse onto the couch with a groan and curl into a ball, praying for some clouds to block out the sun.

"How did you know I needed help?" I ask.

"You can thank your quiet doctor for that," Jade answers, pulling a bagel sandwich out of the bag. The smell of food nearly sends me running back to the bathroom, my stomach rioting at the idea of eating, but I know from far too many hangovers that it's the only thing that'll cure me right now. "Care to explain why a *shockingly* disheveled Sebastian was waiting outside the café when I tried to open up this morning, begging me to check up on you?"

I make a small pathetic noise and pull the blanket over my head, hiding my face. I don't want to explain. I don't want to think about him, or any of them, right now.

"Come on, Sydney, you smell like a winery, and you look like death." Jade nudges my cocooned legs with the food until I finally emerge and take it from her. "What the hell happened?"

I force myself to sit up and take a tentative bite of the bagel. I let it sit in my stomach for a few seconds before I trust myself to speak. "Well, I'm officially single again."

Jade's face falls. "Oh, shit." She drops heavily onto the couch next to me. "Why? Everything seemed so great with them!"

"Oh, so Seb didn't tell you that too? Now that the two of you are such good friends and all?" It's hard to sound angry when I'm actively trying to keep from vomiting. The words come out bratty and childish, my sarcasm flat.

"Oh, please." Jade clicks her tongue. "Don't do that. Green is a terrible color on you. You know you're my best and only friend, Syd. I wouldn't be bringing my patented hangover cure to anyone else."

I grumble an apology into my food.

"Forgiven." Jade crosses her arms over her chest, leaning back against the couch cushions. "So. Are you going to tell me what happened, or do I need to schedule a playdate with Seb so he can tell me while we braid each other's hair?"

I let out a laugh and regret it immediately when my stomach somersaults in protest. But the bagel is doing an excellent job of soaking up whatever alcohol remains in my body, and I'm starting to feel almost human again. I take another bite.

"I had a... moment with Seb yesterday," I admit. Jade inhales sharply. "It kind of freaked me out, and I ended up at Alec's apartment."

"Wait, what kind of moment are we talking about here? Your usual bickering or a *sexy moment?*" Jade asks, wriggling her eyebrows. She's been hinting that there's something between him and me for a while, and I was so insistent she was wrong. Great. Now I'm going to have to deal with her gloating about it.

"What do you think?" I ask with a side-eye glance.

"HA! I *told* you. I knew there was something there! You little vixen!" Jade squeals gleefully.

"We're all very impressed with your gift of foresight, but at the moment I am, in fact, still single, so maybe calm down the excitement," I remind her.

"You're right, you're right, sorry. Tell me what happened after."

"Funny story," I say with a caustic laugh. "But it turns out Alec has a wife!"

The moment the words are out of my mouth, a tight lump forms in my throat. The corners of my eyes prickle, and I swallow hard, fighting against the swell of tears.

Jade doesn't say anything. There's a heavy, awful silence from her. It goes on so long that I glance over at her, seeing the shock on her face, her jaw gaping. And then...

"You have got to be *FUCKING KIDDING ME!*" Jade's scream echoes through my living room. And through my skull.

I wince, dropping my bagel to cover my ears. "*Inside voices,* Jade! Please!"

Jade grabs a pillow off the couch and buries her face in it to scream. And even though the sound is muffled by the stuffing, it still reverberates painfully around in my skull, making me groan.

"Have mercy on my hangover, please," I beg with a whimper. "Are you trying to kill me?"

"I'll tell you who I'm about to kill..." Jade snarls, twisting the pillow violently in her hands.

"Yeah, I'd be happy to help you with that," I say with a dry laugh. Even though I'm only kidding, deep down, I know we wouldn't hesitate to kill for one another. And if I'm honest, a little spark lights up inside me at the idea of inflicting a bit of vengeful pain.

"It gets worse. I didn't find out until *after* the mind-blowing sex," I tell her. "Just to really twist the knife. I opened a drawer, and boom! There it was: his wedding ring and a picture of his wife. And let me tell you, she's *stunning.* Like, *movie star* stunning. *Disgustingly* pretty."

Jade shakes her head. "Syd, I'm so sorry... I don't even know what to say. I'm *furious*. I knew they were into some shady business shit, but I did *not* expect *this*."

Neither did I. I take a big breath.

"I mean, that's a part of it, too, isn't it? I went into this so blindly, trusting they were telling me the truth about themselves. Even when you warned me about them! I feel like such an idiot." I cover my face with my hands, sighing. "Was I just a joke to them? Just some side action they were toying with? I want to believe some of it was real, but how can I trust any of it now?"

"Hey, look at me." I don't. I drop my hands and glance at her out of the corner of my eye, picking up my bagel and curling my body over it. "You're not an idiot. People breaking your trust is on them, not on you."

"What's that saying? Fool me once, shame on you. Fool me twice, shame on me?" I laugh, but there's no humor in it. Only an anger so acidic it burns.

I bring the bagel to my lips again but can't bring myself to take another bite. Jade leans over the table and opens the bottle of ginger ale, pressing it into my hand.

"Drink," she orders.

I do. It's cold and crisp, and sweet enough the sugar coats my tongue.

Jade lets out a long breath and rubs a hand over her face. "Look, I'm not going to lie. You've had a shit run of men lately. But it doesn't change the fact that you're wonderful, Syd. And I wouldn't change a single thing about you." Her eyes are so sincere when she says it, there's no doubt in my mind she means it.

"Thanks." I give her a small smile. "I don't deserve you, you know?"

"No one does," Jade says sagely. "I'm perfect."

"You really are. I love you."

"To the moon and back," Jade answers. Then she shoots me a considering look. "I think at least one of them cares about you, though. I don't think your usually stoic doc is the type to show up outside of our shop like that if he doesn't care just a little. Maybe it's not all bad."

"Please tell me he isn't still downstairs," I say, my stomach sinking. I don't think I can face him right now. Not after everything that happened.

"No, he left. He just told me I should check on you, something about you maybe getting a bit too drunk last night?" Jade eyes the half-empty bottle of wine, uncorked on my coffee table, and then stares pointedly at the empty bottles next to it.

"Ash must have told him. He called me last night," I admit. I set down my half-eaten bagel, frustration welling up inside of me. Of course. I should have expected they'd share everything with each other.

"What did he have to say for himself?" Jade asks.

"I wasn't exactly in a listening mood," I say, pressing the palms of my hands to my eyes and rubbing furiously. "I can't trust a goddamn thing he says. Anything *any* of them say."

Because it wasn't just Alec. They were all lying to me. Letting me make a fool of myself by falling for them without letting me glimpse even a fraction of their real lives.

We're dangerous men, Sydney, the memory of Sebastian's voice mocks me.

Jade glances up at the clock and groans. "I have to head downstairs and open the shop." She frowns at me, taking in my disheveled and, I'm sure, pathetic appearance. "Why don't you take the day off? I don't think it'll be too crazy today, and I doubt you'll be much help today, anyway. Not in the state you're in."

She's right. And even though my guilt immediately kicks in,

I know better than to argue. "Thanks. I'm sorry I'm such a mess."

"You're *my* mess. And you'll be okay. You're going to get through this," Jade promises. "Make sure you eat every last bite of that bagel, okay?"

She gives me a long hug before she leaves.

After the door closes behind her, I fetch my cell phone and turn it back on, the screen immediately filling with missed calls and messages from Ash.

And one message from Alec.

I don't bother reading it. I furiously swipe the message away, refusing to give him the satisfaction of lying to me again.

Tell it to your wife.

2

ONE WEEK LATER

SYDNEY

Ashton: Good morning, Babygirl!

I SIGH AND SWIPE THE NOTIFICATION FROM MY PHONE screen. Not that it matters. The fact that I haven't read or responded to any of Ashton's messages since we last spoke hasn't stopped him from messaging me multiple times every day.

Or—I'm reminded when I open my door—from sending me *gifts*.

The moment I step out of my apartment, I stumble over the box of red roses sitting on my doorstep, accidentally trampling half of them in my effort to stay upright.

Shit.

This is the third time this week I've stepped on a present he's left for me. Yesterday, I almost died tripping over a stuffed dog that meekly said "I WOOF you" before nearly sending me flying down the stairs. With a frustrated sigh, I kick the box of flowers over the threshold and into my apartment, vowing to deal with them later. I wish he would stop. Or at least slow down. I have enough roses filling my apartment now to open a flower shop, and I'm quickly running out of places to put them.

I slam the door to my apartment shut, crushing another rose blossom in the doorjamb, and head downstairs to work.

I hate that I miss him. Hate that, as furious as I am, a part of me *wants* to message him back, wants to talk to him, wants to hear his side of things.

But I'm not ready for that. Not yet, at least.

The moment I round the corner to the Book Boutique and Bakery, I spot a massive stuffed bumblebee leaning against the entrance and groan.

If I thought today was going to be a flowers-only gift-barrage, I was apparently mistaken.

The two-foot bumblebee proudly wears a T-shirt saying "BEE mine", and I don't bother to collect this one as I unlock the door and speed past it into the café. I leave the gift outside, hoping someone else will pick it up and find some joy in it.

I know I won't.

By the time Jade has made me my morning caramel latte, and I'm leaning against the counter to enjoy it, there are three more messages from him filling up my phone screen.

Ashton: I have a fight coming up.

Ashton: At the Golden Rings casino.

Ashton: There's a ticket for you at will call.
Please tell me you'll come.

Swipe, swipe, and swipe.

I should have known Ash would have difficulty understanding the concept of *needing space*. But this is getting a little ridiculous.

"Which one is that?" Jade asks, glancing over from her spot

at the register and taking a sip from the coffee mug she's cradling. Her hair is a fiery red today, with bright orange tips that pair well with her neon yellow nail polish. I wonder how long this look will last before she colors it again.

"Ashton," I grumble around the rim of my cup.

"Ah." She chuckles. "The puppy dog."

Maybe a week ago, I would have agreed with her. Ashton, despite his size and muscles, comes across like a lost little puppy, doesn't he? So eager and enthusiastic. I'd let that enthusiasm sweep me right off my feet, blind to the fact that he isn't a puppy at all.

Ashton is an attack dog. Built to fight.

Built to hurt.

My thoughts must be showing on my face, because Jade sets her drink down on the counter, lips folding into a frown.

"How're you holding up today, Syd?" she asks me gently.

How can I possibly sum up all the feelings swirling inside me after the whirlwind of the last few weeks? How do I come to terms with the fact that the not one, not two, but *three* men I've involved myself with are not at all what they seemed?

That they're dangerous.

That they're liars.

That I unknowingly slept with a married man.

I feel a rage sizzling inside me, a live wire ready to set light to everything in its path. All the work I've done over the years to keep my temper in check is coming undone, and I feel like I could snap at any moment.

You could hurt them, like they hurt you, a terrible voice inside me says.

I take a deep breath, pushing that voice down as deep as I can.

"Fine," I tell Jade with a noncommittal shrug. It's the one

word in the women's lexicon capable of summing it all up. Saying everything while saying nothing at all. "I'm fine."

My phone chimes again, and I scowl at it.

"Do men not understand what 'fuck off and leave me alone' means?" I ask Jade, swiping the notification away in irritation.

"Obviously not these men," she says, sounding more amused than sympathetic.

"It's overwhelming! The constant messages, the gifts! I need a break from it all, I need space to get my head on straight and figure out what I want!" I snap. "And how am I supposed to do that with him messaging me every three goddamn seconds?" I slam my hand against the counter, jostling my coffee and making Jade's eyes widen just a fraction in surprise. Enough to make me realize... I'm throwing a tantrum in the middle of my store.

I am an ocean of calm, I remind myself, squeezing my eyes shut. I count to ten, forcing a wave of calming thoughts to wash over me.

My phone chimes again.

"I'm going to throw it at the fucking wall," I say in a voice that doesn't sound calm in the slightest.

Jade laughs.

But this time it isn't Ash trying to reach me for the hundredth time. Hell, it isn't even Sebastian, the only one of them respecting my wishes and keeping his distance.

It's Dorothy, our landlord.

> Dorothy: I wanted you to be the first to know. I signed the papers this morning, dear. The new owner will contact you soon. All my best.

Great.

Just fucking great. I'd almost forgotten with everything else going on that our building was being sold. Let's add that on top of the pile of shit I need to deal with.

I put my head in my hands and groan.

"Cheer up, buttercup," Jade says, placing a comforting hand on my back. "At least they're not still coming in here every day, right?"

It's a small sliver of comfort, but she's right. After I'd put my foot down with Ash, their presence fully disappeared from our shop. And that is something to be thankful for, even if I do miss the money they spent.

Not that we aren't doing well financially this month. Even without all three men here buying out our bakery case and Staff Picks book display, we are well on track to have our most profitable quarter ever.

I don't want to think about how much of that success is because of Ashton sponsoring a social media campaign for our store, generating more online buzz and business than I'd ever thought possible. Just one more way in which the three of them felt perfectly at ease inserting themselves into my life. I may not be angry that we're doing well, but I *am* angry that my business is now tied to them, however tangentially. If I didn't even know Alec was married, how am I supposed to know how their...*illicit activities* will affect my store? How this might come back to hurt me?

When I finally drop my hands from my face and look over at her, I catch Jade frowning at the empty table Sebastian used to sit at every day.

"Don't tell me you're missing them," I say with an accusatory tone.

"Oh, please." She shakes her head. "I miss the big tips, that's all." Her smile turns devilish as she turns to me and says, "Maybe you're missing their big, big tips too, hm?"

"Oh, shut up." I laugh, rolling my eyes. Only Jade could make such an ill-timed joke and still get a laugh out of me.

"But no, I don't miss them," Jade assures me. "I'm team Sydney all the way. And until they're back in your good graces, they sure as hell aren't in mine."

I smile. "Well, that day may never come, but I appreciate the support. Love you," I tell her. The bell above our shop door chimes as someone enters.

"To the moon and back," Jade answers with a wink.

"Please don't tell me you two *still* say that to each other?" A familiar voice asks with a chuckle. "I thought you stopped that back in high school."

Jade and I both turn in surprise, and there, standing in the doorway of our shop, holding Ash's stuffed bee...is Justin.

Jade's little brother.

I don't have time to hide my shock at seeing him before Jade is moving, racing out from behind the counter and screeching like a banshee as she barrels into his arms.

"Easy!" His laugh is low and warm as he pivots the stuffed animal away from her, protecting it from being crushed between their bodies. "You're going to damage the giant carnival gift someone left for you!"

"It's for Sydney. And trust me, she doesn't want it," Jade says, voice muffled against his shoulder as she squeezes him tighter.

"For Sydney, huh?" he asks, looking over at me and grinning. "I should have guessed."

Justin is only a year younger than us, and even though we practically grew up together, I haven't seen him in years, not since he left to get his PhD at some fancy Ivy League university on the other side of the country. But now he's here and...all grown up.

Justin was always lanky and a little awkward, built like a

fence pole. Puberty only made it worse, leaving him a little too tall and a little too thin. But now he's filled out. Broad shoulders, sculpted arms, and dark hair that flops across his brow in a way that probably breaks hearts on a daily basis.

He's handsome, all grown up and in the flesh, but to me, he doesn't hold a candle to Ashton.

Or Alec...

Stop it, I admonish myself, clenching my fists at my side. *Stop thinking about them.*

"Wait." Jade pulls back from their hug, narrowing her eyes at her brother in suspicion. "You only ever show up when something's wrong." Her voice lowers, threateningly. "What did you do?"

"What did I do? Is that the kind of welcome your most favorite little brother in the whole world deserves?" Justin asks playfully, twin dimples forming on his cheeks as he smiles down at her.

"You're my only brother, little or big. And speaking of... Did you hit *another* growth spurt?" She slaps his arm and scowls. "Unfair. How did I get stuck at 5'1" and you just keep growing? You're *hoarding* the height in this family."

"Can't help it if I inherited the tall and charming genes," Justin says with a shrug.

"Tall, sure. Charming? Questionable." She drags him toward where I'm standing at the counter. "Syd, look who came crawling back from nerd camp! And he brought you a giant stuffed animal to add to your growing collection!"

Justin sets the bumblebee on the countertop, turning his attention to me with a crooked grin. "Hey, Syd. It's been a while. You look good."

"And you look...tall," I answer, fighting to keep a straight face. "You know, for a brat."

Justin recoils. "No, don't do that to me. Don't try to bring that stupid nickname back."

"Like it ever went away. Come on, if you act like a brat for most of your life, you're going to earn the nickname. It's only fair," Jade says. He was never that bad, not really. But it only took him tattling on us one too many times for the name to stick. "But you're avoiding my question. What are you doing here?" Her grin widens, and she pokes his ribcage. "Did you graduate early, you little brainiac?"

"Close!" Justin says excitedly, matching her smile with one of his own. "I quit!"

The smile slips off my face, and I turn to Jade in shock. It takes a few seconds for her brain to catch up.

"What do you mean *you quit*? You dropped out of your PhD program?" Jade asks in disbelief. She smacks him on the arm, and when he barely reacts, she smacks him again, punctuating each word with another slap. "After *everything*? You were so close to finishing!"

"Hey, back off! Mom and Dad already gave me hell for it. I don't need this from you, too," Justin says, fending off her punches. He rubs his arm where she was hitting him, but I know it's just for show. There's no way she was doing any damage with those adorable little slaps. The physical strength of an infant, my Jade.

"You already told Mom and Dad?" Jade swallows audibly. "Yikes. How'd they take it?"

"Well, let's just say I would love to crash on your couch," he says, avoiding her eyes, a blush coloring his cheeks. "Because I am not really welcome at home right now."

Jade winces. "Fuck. I mean, yeah, of course you can crash at my place, but *fuck*. At least you're avoiding the dropout stereotype of living in your mom's basement." She says it as a joke, but there's no disguising the pity in her words.

"Somehow crashing on my sister's couch doesn't feel much better." Justin throws back his head and blows a lock of dark hair out of his eyes. "But thanks. I just need to make a little money and crash somewhere while I figure out what my next steps are. So, if you hear of any place that's hiring—"

"He could work here," I say to Jade immediately. "I mean, it's not a lot of money, but we're finally turning enough profit to hire someone. And we've been talking about needing some part-time help."

"Yes!" Jade says, clapping her hands together excitedly.

Justin doesn't look so convinced. "I don't know. I don't want to put you out and—"

"Shut up, stop acting like you're even remotely considerate, you brat. You'll take the job. In fact, you can start right now," Jade tells him, picking up a dish rag and chucking it at him.

He catches it, frowning. "Does this mean I have to call you 'boss'?"

"Absolutely you do!" she says cheerily, with just a hint of evil coloring her smile.

3

ALEC

My entire life, I've only let four people get close enough to know the real me.

The first was Ashton. After what happened with my parents, I spent years living on the streets, no better off than the rats that infest this city, fighting for every crumb of food and scrap of shelter I could find. The orphanage wasn't much of an improvement. It was kill or be killed at a place like that. At least it was for the lifers like me, the kids no one would ever want, with no hope of adoption or a happily ever after. The broken children.

Ashton was different. He wasn't broken, not fully. He got the attention the rest of us craved, landing himself a foster family after only a few months in the system.

And another after that.

And another.

No matter how many times he forced them to bring him back to the orphanage, the universe still gave him another shot.

Ashton had a thousand chances at a happier life, a life with a new family, and he turned his back on each and every one of them. Every time he left, I knew it was only a matter of time before he came strutting back through those iron gates, kicked out of another home and coming back to the only person he really cared about.

His brother.

I hated him for that. Hated the kid who blew every chance he had to get out of our prison. The kid who learned to fight young, who grew faster than any of the other orphans, who stole food whenever he could, even if it meant less for the rest of us. Hated him because he had something I so desperately wanted. He had a friend. A brother.

Family.

Sebastian was such a scrawny little thing back then, a bespectacled kid with a stutter living in his brother's shadow. Ashton did everything he could to keep them together, to keep his brother safe.

Even back then, even when I hated him, I respected that. Envied it.

And respect eventually gave way to a begrudging alliance. And then a friendship.

And then one day, I realized he had become my brother too, and when Ashton kept coming back to the orphanage, it wasn't just for Sebastian.

By the time Viper found us, the three of us were inseparable, bonded by something much stronger than blood. And Viper?

How could we not love Viper, even in the beginning? Broken, damaged Viper. The kid no one wanted, the kid who went through hell and managed to survive, the one they frequently had to chain up to keep his violent outbursts contained.

He fit right in with us.

And that's all I ever needed. Sure, I've dallied with women, even kept a few around long enough they thought we were something more than we were. But none of them came close to knowing me. None of them were anything more than a fun way to pass the time.

Until Sydney.

It's been one week since I last saw her. One week since I held her in my arms, since I felt her body shake and quiver as she came around my cock.

One week, and every second of it since she found that ring has been a nightmare.

That fucking ring. Worthless even before I took it off and shoved it in a drawer, all those years ago. It cost me everything. It cost me *Sydney*. She was finally mine—finally *ours*—and I ruined it. I wish I had done more that night to explain, to make her stay, but that look in her eyes when she left still haunts me. The pain, the betrayal.

Don't ever contact me again, she'd spat at me. And I knew she meant it, knew she'd hate me for reaching out to her again.

But that wasn't enough to keep me away.

I sent her a single message, the night she left, trying to explain everything. She still hasn't responded to it. Maybe she never read it, never will. Maybe she doesn't believe me. Maybe, maybe, maybe...

It doesn't matter. I feel lost without her. Untethered.

Ashton says she wants to be left alone. That she doesn't want to see any of us right now.

Fine. I'll give her space, give her time, give her whatever she needs, even if every second I'm not with her feels like I'm suffocating. I'll wait for her. Wait the rest of my miserable life, if I need to, until she's ready to talk. Even if there's a part of me— an unrecognizable part—that wants to go to her right now, wants to be in front of her, groveling on my knees and begging for forgiveness.

I glance over at my brothers. They look just as miserable as I do. Ashton hasn't been sleeping, has barely been showering. His blonde hair is limp and unwashed, his eyes hollow and dull. I heard from his manager that he's been missing sessions with his trainer and dropping weight. He looks about ready to shatter.

And Sebastian?

Even Sebastian looks like a ghost. There are dark shadows under his eyes, visible even through his glasses, and a coiled, almost frantic energy to the way he moves that wasn't there a week ago. A nervous tick to his muscles. As I watch, he runs a hand through his dark hair, then does it again, almost like he can't stand to be still.

He blames himself, thinks he's the reason she won't see any of us. They still don't know I'm the one who fucked it all up. They don't know I ruined everything.

More lies.

More fucking secrets.

I drop into my office chair and let the weight of it all settle over my shoulders. Every mistake I've made, every secret I'm keeping, presses down on me, pushing me closer to hell.

Sebastian glares at where Ashton sits on the couch, hunched over his phone.

"Put your phone away," he says, his lip curling. Ashton ignores him, his leg bouncing rapidly.

"Girls like jokes, right?" Ashton asks, staring down at his phone screen. "What's a good joke?"

"Knock knock," Sebastian deadpans.

Ashton types. "Who's there?"

"A pathetic loser who doesn't know when to stop."

Ashton's fingers tap audibly against his phone screen.

When they finally pause, he frowns, glancing up at his brother. "A pathetic loser who doesn't know when to stop, who?"

Sebastian snorts a laugh, shaking his head. "Christ, you are such a fucking idiot."

"Oh, I'm the idiot? You suck at jokes, you know that, Doc?" Ashton grumbles. "That one doesn't even make any sense."

"That's enough," I tell him, my voice too sharp. Both of them look at me. "Put your phone away, Ash."

"Whatever. It's not like she's answering any of them anyway," he mutters, shoving his phone back into his pocket.

"We're not here to talk about Sydney," I remind them. I can't. Even now, when I can't stop thinking about her, when she occupies my every waking thought, I can't talk about her.

Because I had her, had everything I ever wanted, and I lost it.

"We're here to talk about business," I say to the room, trying to corral the spiraling feeling inside me into something useful. "I want an update on what's going on in Empire City."

"We're losing ground there," Sebastian answers. His finger taps a rapid beat against his thigh. It's frenetic, unconscious. I doubt he even realizes he's doing it. "And there's fuck-all we can do about it unless we're willing to dedicate more of our men to seeking out the problem."

"And why aren't we doing that?" I ask with a growl.

"Because we're stretched too thin already." *Tap, tap, tap.* "And until we get that shipment of weapons from Tony, we risk being outgunned."

My jaw tightens until it hurts. "Give me some good news."

"How cute that you think I have any," Sebastian says with a brittle smile. "I'm fresh out of good news."

"Then give me the bad news."

He won't look at me when he answers. His eyes are glued to a point just to the right of my face, staring out at the city skyline through the windows at my back. "Oscuro had their liquor license pulled last night."

Fuck. The last bit of my calm evaporates, my hands clenching on my desk. Oscuro is supposed to be the cornerstone of our next phase of expansion here in Fortune City. When it opens, it will be the largest nightclub on the West Coast, nine full floors of sin operating independently, each with its own theme and catering to a different sort of clientele, ensuring that any patron who steps through those doors is sure to find something they'll enjoy.

And on the top floor? A special, VIP-access sex club designed by Francesca herself, made to satisfy any and all vices a select, approved clientele could ask for.

Oscuro is set to be my crowning achievement here, with financial projections suggesting the income it stands to generate for Sterling Enterprises could rival even our biggest casinos. And why not, when the seventh floor will have its own gambling parlor, complete with high-end poker games and roulette?

But no one will be lining up for opening night at a nightclub that can't legally serve alcohol.

"How the hell did this happen?" I demand. Sebastian's eyes flick to mine and away again. "We just got word that the liquor board approved the license last week."

"And the city council pulled it," Sebastian says grimly. "They're claiming the building isn't zoned for selling liquor."

You've got to be fucking kidding me.

A full year. A full year of land purchases, of planning and building, all of it above board. Only to be told at the last minute that this area isn't zoned for it?

"We *own* the council," Ashton says, brows drawing together incredulously. "Why would they—"

"Someone paid them off," I surmise, the words flat and cold.

Sebastian nods, just once.

"Handle this," I order him. "Find out who flipped on us."

"I already did." A dark smile twitches at the corner of Sebastian's mouth. "Viper is picking them up as we speak."

4

SYDNEY

In no time at all, Jade has trained our newest part-time employee on how to use her fancy—and shockingly expensive—espresso machine. We take turns taste-testing his creations until we're both satisfied he can properly recreate our café menu. If I'm being honest, he might even be better at making some of our drinks than I am.

"I worked for a little as a barista during undergrad," Justin explains when I tell him as much. "It's not like I'm a coffee prodigy or anything."

"You worked at a chain coffee place," Jade accuses, mouth twisting with distaste. "Hardly up to our standards."

Still, she gives an appreciative "hm" when she takes a sip from his flat white, before declaring it acceptable. My own flat white, I'm reminded, once earned a half-hearted "well you tried," and a pat on the head.

When the morning rush starts, I leave him to shadow Jade at the café and get to work replenishing our Book Boutique and Bakery end caps. An unexpected benefit of the spike in new business and online awareness has been a surge in our merchandise sales. Suddenly, Book Boutique and Bakery tote bags and T-shirts are all the rage with local bibliophiles.

Which means I'm constantly restocking our supply. Not that I mind. I settle myself on the floor next to the display, open a new box of shirts, and get to work.

See? I can do this. I can live my life without him. Without *them*.

I don't need a tall, dark, and handsome man to whisper filthy words in my ear. I don't need Alec's calm, sultry stare, the way he could mentally undress me with a single look. Or his hand around my throat, the flash of something wild in his eyes as he held me down.

I don't need Ashton, don't even remember what it was like to have him groan against my skin as his tongue circled my clit. I've forgotten it! Forgotten all about the feel of Sebastian's fingers between my legs. And Viper, holding a knife to my neck, the point sharp, dangerous...

"Uh, Syd?"

Justin's voice pulls me out of my thoughts, and I realize I'm crouched before the still empty display, a shirt clutched so tight in my hands that I've twisted it beyond recognition.

"Hey, brat," I greet him, voice dripping with feigned positivity, as I hastily shove the shirt into a box, hiding it. I don't need to unfold it to know it's likely ruined. "How's training going?"

He tips his head back and groans. "Horrible. She's a tyrant. Possibly a sadist. But at least I've passed all her tests for now." Justin motions to the boxes of merchandise around me. "You need any help with this?"

I hand him a stack of T-shirts and watch enviously as he easily reaches to place them on the top shelf. As he stretches, his shirt rises just enough to show off an unexpected set of abs, and I quickly look away.

"Do you mind if I ask you something?" Justin asks after a few minutes of quiet restocking. With him handling the upper shelves, and me stocking the lower, we're making quick progress. I never realized how much time I wasted having to carry my stepladder around the store, constantly climbing up and down to reach the higher shelves.

"Yeah, sure," I answer, focused on folding. There's a trick to getting the shirts to lay *just right*, so the logo shows best, but they still lay flat. I wrinkle my nose in concentration, trying to get it perfect.

When I glance up at him, Justin is staring down at me, looking concerned. "Are you okay?" I frown, brows drawing together, and he quickly adds, "I just mean you seem pretty down. Different from the last time I saw you."

That's the understatement of the year.

"Is it Chase?" he asks. "You don't have to go into it if you don't want to, but Jade mentioned to me that the two of you split up during one of our phone calls a couple months back."

Jesus. *Chase.* I almost forgot about my ex-boyfriend in all of this. I wonder if he's still at the hospital after what Ashton did to him. I shift uncomfortably, fidgeting with the shirt I'm folding.

"If it's any consolation, the guy was a total tool," Justin tells me.

My lips twitch into a smile. "You didn't like him either?" I ask, lifting my gaze to him.

"Hated him, more like." Justin mutters the words, almost too low for me to hear. Then he adds, "I just knew you could do better."

"Thanks," I tell him. "And I'm okay. I wasn't thinking about him anyway. It's actually... Well, I was dating someone else. After Chase."

Multiple someones.

"*Was* dating?" Justin asks, quirking an eyebrow as he glances down at me.

"It's complicated. I broke it off, just recently." I trail off, not sure what else to say. Then, clearing my throat, "So, you want to tell me why you dropped out? I thought you were enjoying studying..." My brain fizzles out. "Computers?" I guess.

Justin laughs. "Computer science," he corrects, in a patient voice that tells me he's had to explain it before. "With a focus on cybersecurity."

"Right." I nod, handing him another stack of shirts. "That. You seemed like you liked your program."

"I did. I really did." Justin lets out a long, sad breath. "Promise you won't tell Jade?"

I mime locking my lips with a key and tossing it over my shoulder.

He chuckles but runs a self-conscious hand through his hair. "I didn't really drop out. I was sort of kicked out of the program."

I reel back in surprise. Justin? Golden boy Justin, who never broke a single rule when we were kids? "Kicked out for what?" I ask.

He stretches up to add the stack of shirts to the display. "Harassing another student. And... assault."

"Assault?" I repeat, shocked. Justin is the least aggressive person I know. He was the sort of kid who caught bugs under a glass and insisted on releasing them back outside. "What do you mean assault? What happened?"

Justin refuses to look at me as he fiddles with the merchandise. "It's a long story. There was this girl. And we were friendly, but not like...friends, you know? Then last semester—"

Jade's voice from the front cuts him off. "Hey, trainee!" she shouts. "I need you up here for garbage duty!"

Justin groans and lets his arms drop to his side. "Sorry.

Duty calls. You can finish these on your own?" He waves his hand at the stack of shirts and totes that still need shelving.

I nod, distracted. As he heads back up to the front of the store, hands shoved in his pockets, I watch him, frowning.

Justin has always been the *good* kid. Always playing by the rules. He was the one who broke up fights, who tattled whenever Jade or I misbehaved.

He would never harass another student. He would never hurt a woman.

Right?

———

HOURS LATER, I'M STILL BOTHERED BY THE IDEA THAT THIS boy I grew up with might have become a man capable of things I never imagined.

But I never suspected Chase could be the man he turned out to be, did I? I didn't see the signs until it was too late, until I was already caught in his snare.

Monsters hide among us, wearing the most pleasant faces.

I wonder if Jade has the scoop about him leaving grad school yet. I wait until there's a lull in the café traffic before I head over to ask her.

"Weird question, but did your brother ever mention a girl? At school?" I ask her, leaning over the counter.

Jade glances up at me from where she's squatting on the ground, restocking the bakery case. "Sydney, I say this with all the love in the world: *Please* do not try to date my brother."

I let out a shocked laugh. "*What*? No! I'm not trying to—"

"I know he had a crush on you when we were kids," Jade interrupts. "And your children would be so cute, I would just die. But it would be like you're dating the male version of me, and that's just weird. I won't allow it."

I shake my head, still laughing. "You're insane, you know that? He never had a crush on me. Where are you even getting that?"

"Oh, please, he's liked you since high school. Even earlier, maybe," Jade insists. "I'm just saying, as much as I'd love to call you my sister, if you ended up dating him and you somehow loved him more than me? I just don't think I could handle that. That would destroy me."

"I could never love anyone more than you," I promise.

"Good," Jade says, standing up and pulling off her food-safe gloves. "Plus, the last thing you need right now is a rebound. Been there, done that. No, this time you're going to focus on you. I call it... Operation Sydney."

I quirk an eyebrow. "Operation Sydney, huh?"

"Correct. Instead of sitting around moping about assholes, you and I are going to try something new. Take some classes, learn a new hobby—"

"With what free time?" I ask. "We're always here."

"And now we have an employee!" Jade reasons. "One we can trust to handle running the store on his own for a few hours!"

The moment she says this, there's a loud crash from the back, and we both hear Justin swear.

I give Jade a deadpan look.

"I'm sure he's fine." Jade waves a hand in the air dismissively. "The point is all you've done lately is work. You need a break."

"Fine," I relent. "But let's start off with something light, okay? I don't think either of us should be learning beekeeping, or anything like that."

"You have no evidence I wouldn't be a fantastic beekeeper."

"You're allergic to bees," I remind her. "And I just think if we're doing this, we might want to start with something a little less likely to end with us going to the hospital." I chew my lip, considering our options. "Maybe ceramics? We took that ceramics class in middle school, remember? That could be—"

I freeze, eyes on a figure moving through the crowds outside. It's just a brief flash, barely enough to recognize the person weaving their way down the sidewalk. Barely enough to register the familiar sandy brown hair and tan skin.

Chase.

"Sydney?" Jade asks. "You okay?"

"Yeah," I lie. The figure is already gone, out of sight. "Yeah, I'm fine."

It wasn't him. Jade is talking, scrolling through her phone and already making a list of projects for Operation Sydney, but I'm having trouble listening.

It wasn't him, I tell myself, willing myself to believe it.

5

SEBASTIAN

I CHEW THE SIDE OF MY THUMB, BITING AT THE NAIL, lost in thought. A filthy fucking habit. But at least here, in the wet lab, I'm free to indulge in my filthy habits. All of them.

And *fuck* do I need that right now.

The man kneeling on the cold, sterile floor whimpers as Viper approaches him with a scalpel clutched in one hand. He tries to move, tries to pull away, but the restraints holding his arms above his head and attached to the ceiling stop him from going anywhere.

"I swear I don't know anything," he sobs.

Viper grabs his face, laughing, and draws the point of the scalpel over his cheek and jaw. He's not pressing hard enough to draw much blood, not yet, but the sharp tip leaves an angry red line in its wake.

"Here's the problem, Daryl," I say, chewing at my nail. "I don't believe you. And, more importantly, I don't think *he* believes you. Right, brother?"

Viper brings the scalpel up to Daryl's eye.

"No, no, no, no, no," Daryl chants, pulling ineffectively at the restraints.

Daryl is good at pretending. Better than most. But it won't take much more to break him.

"I'm going to make you look so pretty," Viper purrs. He cackles, angling the weapon closer, almost touching the man's cornea. "Give you a nice new hole to stick my dick in."

"Jesus Christ," Daryl sobs.

There's no Christ down here, I think with a chuckle. No Gods, no masters. There's just me and Viper. And whatever the fuck we want to do. Daryl will learn that soon enough. They always do.

Viper pulls his arm back, ready to strike, and, irritated, I finally intervene.

"Line, Viper," I tell him.

But Viper isn't listening. He tilts Daryl's head up, lining up the blow that's sure to take his eye, and more than likely leave our guest with an ocular lobotomy.

But we still don't have the information we need.

"So fucking pretty," Viper coos, lost in his own world. I know it's not Daryl he's thinking about, not Daryl he's imagining kneeling before him, ready to accept his gift of pain.

"Viper!" I raise my voice to a shout, glaring at him. "*LINE!*"

This time, he listens.

Viper's face goes dark, a muscle in his cheek twitching.

"Line." He repeats it in a cold voice. His fingers clench and unclench around his weapon. His face pivots to look at me, lip curling in a sneer. "You and your *fucking lines*, Doc."

He's angry, but at least this time he stops. Dropping his hold on Daryl, Viper turns and chucks the scalpel at the wall before stalking away with a roar of rage.

I sigh, unfurling myself from my examination chair.

Kneeling on the ground, knees inches from the drain in the

floor, Daryl sobs uncontrollably. I make my way over to the table, where Viper has all his tools laid out, and I pull on a pair of blue nitrile gloves.

"Sorry about him," I tell Daryl, snapping the gloves into place. I bend down to pick the scalpel off the ground and take it back to the table to spray it down with ethanol.

You have to keep a sterile torture room. That's just common sense.

We're not animals.

I keep the weapon with me, held at my side, as I advance toward Daryl.

"See, my brother isn't quite right in the head," I explain. Emphasizing my point, Viper chooses that moment to slam his fist against the wall, shattering a tile. Daryl winces, hard enough to shake the chains holding him. I click my tongue but continue. "He doesn't know where to draw the line, you know? Sometimes he doesn't notice when he goes too far."

Another fist to the wall, another broken tile.

"He'll be fine in a minute, don't worry," I assure our guest. "He just needs to blow off some steam."

Daryl's sobs are lessening, his breathing calming. That's good. We need him in a state where he can talk to us, answer questions.

"I know where the line is," I assure him, placing a hand on his shoulder. Like we're buddies. Friends. "I'm just here to make sure he does, too. You understand that, right?"

Daryl nods like my lie makes perfect sense, like he's not about to have another hole bored in his fucking skull.

I crouch down next to him, so we're face to face, and give his shoulder a squeeze. We're just friends, having a friendly chat.

"We just want some answers. We want to understand what's going on, and then this?" I gesture around at the room, at

Viper, at our tools. I look pointedly at the gouge marks in Daryl's legs, at the knife still sticking out from between his ribs. It quivers and jerks with every sobbing breath Daryl takes. "This can all stop. You can make it stop. It's just that easy."

"I don't know what you want," Daryl blubbers, voice and body shaking with the force of it. And these tears, these are real. "If I knew anything, *anything*, I'd tell you, but I don't—"

"Now that's not the truth. I thought we were getting somewhere." I start to beckon Viper over.

"Wait, wait. Just... What do you want to know?" Daryl asks.

There we go. It's starting to dawn on him that he's not getting out of this situation alive. That there's only a slow, drawn out and painful future, or a quick nothingness.

I straighten, coming to my feet.

"It's funny. You've been on our payroll for, what now? Two years?" I ask, striding over to where I keep my bag. I pull out a few papers, staring down at them. "And in all that time, we've never had a problem with you, have we?"

I think Daryl has started crying again.

"Imagine my surprise when I found out that someone on the city council—the council *we fucking own*—petitioned to have our newest building rezoned. And denied our liquor license." I flip through the pages and turn, pointing the scalpel at a scrawling handwritten signature at the bottom of the page. "That's your signature, isn't it?"

He doesn't answer through his sobbing, but he doesn't need to. I already know it is.

"Here's what I want to know." I set the papers down, spreading them out next to Viper's tools. "Who paid you off? Who's behind all of this, trying to fuck us from the shadows?"

His shoulders shake with the force of his crying. "He'll kill me," Daryl whines.

"No," I say. I gesture toward Viper with my scalpel. "*He'll* kill you. But you get to decide if it happens fast or slow."

"It's not just me. My family..." He trails off.

Interesting that this man would profess to care so deeply for his family. He would have ended up here for betraying us regardless, but he's getting the brunt of our ire because, during my digging, I discovered a rape allegation from a few years ago he made disappear. Men like this gain a modicum of power and use it to do whatever they want. Being a father doesn't absolve you of being a horrible, sexist monster of a man. But his children aren't at fault for his actions.

"We'll make sure your family is taken care of. I promise. But you need to tell us what you know. This is a one-time offer, Daryl, and it will expire in fifteen seconds."

"Fuck. I'm dead either way," he mutters, half to himself. "You promise? You'll get them out of the city if I tell you everything? You'll keep them safe?"

"I keep my promises. Speaking of which." I glance at my watch. "You have ten seconds."

We have him. From the way he slumps against his bounds, I know we have him.

"The guy's name is Dante," he says, resolve crackling. "Dante Basso."

My vision goes blank for a moment, the wet lab and everything in it disappearing. I give myself one long breath, eyes closed, to regain my hold on reality.

"Dante is dead. And you're wasting my time," I say. I wave my hand to my brother, gesturing him closer. "Break something important. Maybe that will jog his memory."

"No!" Daryl's voice turns frantic. "Wait, stop, he's not, he's—"

Viper is creeping closer.

"Maybe he's lying about his name!" Daryl screeches. "I don't fucking know! But I...I know what he's after!"

I hold up my hand to stop Viper's advance. He sways back and forth on the balls of his feet, waiting. Grinning like a kid on Christmas.

"Go on," I tell Daryl.

"There's a woman," he sobs. "Some, some fucking woman, I don't know. He's been asking people about her, her address, her friends, where she works. Having people dig through city records, anything he can find."

The room goes very, very still. I can hear my own pulse, pounding in my ears.

Viper isn't smiling anymore. He's still, far too still, staring at our guest like there's nothing else in the world right now except him.

"What woman?" I ask in a low voice, but I already know. Even before he says it, I fucking know.

"Sydney something," Daryl chokes out. "I can't remember the rest, but—but give me a minute and—"

There's no scream when I bury the scalpel through Daryl's eye all the way to the end. Just a shocked wet gurgle. And then silence, as his head pivots forward, blood pouring down his face, over his jaw and down the open wounds in his chest.

"Do whatever you want with the body," I tell Viper, removing my bloody glove with a snap. "But make it quick."

Viper doesn't laugh. He doesn't jump forward like a kid at a carnival.

Before we were having fun, but now?

Now it's fucking serious.

When he moves forward, it's with a cold, deadly fury he saves for special occasions.

My brothers think Viper needs me here to tell him where the line is. They see that as my one real job, infinitely more important than tending Ash's fight wounds and handling their books. Because I know. I can see that line, the one that separates us from the monsters, the one between good and evil.

But what they don't seem to understand is sometimes I don't give a shit about crossing it.

The scalpel comes out of Daryl's eye socket with a sickening squelch as Viper takes over with the forceps, fully removing his eye. The vitreous humor shines brightly in the fluorescent lights.

6

SYDNEY

Nine days.

It takes only nine days of nonstop texting and gifts before Ashton shows up at the bookshop in person. Honestly, I should have seen it coming. It's not like he was going to stay away forever.

I'm in the back of the store, finishing up with a customer, when I hear his voice carry across the shop, tugging at my heart and almost making me drop the stack of books I'm holding.

Shut the fuck up, heart, you dumb bitch. Get it together.

"Hey, Jade!" Ashton sounds like his usual happy, overly enthusiastic self. "How is this beautiful day treating you?"

"Oh, it's you. Great," Jade answers, voice so thick with sarcasm it's practically dripping. "I'm super. You know, I was just reading a Scientific America piece all about *space*. I don't think I can get enough of *space*. Isn't *space* just lovely?"

I sigh, placing the books down and closing up the register before heading over to save them from each other.

"Sure, I guess," Ashton answers nonchalantly, Jade's jab

going completely over his head. "That stuff is more Doc's scene, you know? He loves nerdy shit like that."

I arrive just in time to see one of Jade's trademark eyerolls. Really, it's an art form the way she does it. An art form totally lost on Ashton, who's leaning casually against the bakery case, eyes sweeping the café, looking from person to person.

Searching for me.

The effect of seeing him is instantaneous. He's breathtaking, mouth-wateringly attractive. I want to reach out and touch him, want to run my hands over those huge arms and chest. I want to kiss him, want to let him kiss me. Ashton has the sweetest kisses, so soft and slow and patient.

It's completely unfair that he's this goddamn attractive. I cross my arms, locking my hands under my elbow, and keeping my distance so there's no way I can give in to my urges and let him sweep me up and off my feet.

When Ashton spots me, his entire face lights up, his blue eyes sparkling.

"Hey, Babygirl!" His bright smile stretches from ear to ear, and he rocks forward like he can't stop himself from trying to get closer. "Look at you. You look stunning today. Did you know that?"

His eyes trail over me, heating as he takes me in.

I suppress my own eyeroll now, hating that even though his lines are so corny, I can tell he means them. He's just so *sincere*. Here I am wearing a simple gray T-shirt and jeans, and Ash somehow makes me feel like I'm in lingerie. I tighten my grip on myself.

"What are you doing here, Ash?" I ask, not bothering to keep the anger out of my voice.

His smile drops a fraction as he catches the tone.

"I thought you might want to go get some lunch," he explains, taking a step toward me. "You've got to eat, right? I could... I could go get us something and bring it back here for you. You wouldn't even have to leave."

He's so eager, watching me closely, with hope in his eyes. His fingers tap almost rhythmically against his thigh, like he's nervous.

"Gee, I don't know if she has the *time*," Jade starts, ready to launch into another tirade that he's sure not to get. I shoot her a glare, and she returns it, just as grumpy as I am. But at least she stops.

Sighing, I motion for Ashton to follow me, leading him further back into the shop and toward the back register, where there are fewer people. There's no reason for the entire café to hear this, after all.

Ash follows behind me, practically bouncing on the balls of his feet, rubbing his hands together in excitement.

I bring him nearly to the stockroom before I turn to him, taking a deep breath to center myself.

"What are you doing here?" I demand again.

"I told you, I thought we could get some lunch, spend some time together." He grins at me, but it's muted now. "I've missed you. So fucking much, Babygirl."

"Ashton. I don't need lunch," I say, my frustration seeping through, coloring my tone. "And I didn't ask you to come here."

"Right." His smile fades a little more. "You probably already ate, huh? Yeah, I uh... I should have figured, right? But that's cool. Maybe I could bring you something tomorrow? What can I bring?"

God, he looks so lost, so eager to please. I feel like I'm kicking a puppy.

"Ash..." I let out a long breath. "This isn't... I told you to *leave me alone*. I need space right now. You're not... You're not giving me any. Between this, your texts, and the gifts..."

"Sorry." He gives me an *aw shucks* smile and shrugs. "Not really great at the whole giving you space thing, huh?"

"It's not just that." I sigh, tapping my foot. "Did you hire a social media team for my business? For *my shop*?"

"Oh!" He laughs, running a hand through his hair sheepishly. "*That*. That was no problem. Our company has a whole social media division. They handle all my accounts, too, get buzz for my fights and everything. We figured, hey, what's one more account for them, right?"

I shake my head, jaw tight.

"But you didn't ask me," I insist, wishing he would get it. "You just went ahead and did it. Behind my back. You do these things behind my back, without consulting me."

Ashton flinches. "No, not behind your back," he insists. "We just figured you do so much already. And this wasn't a big deal, it took like two phone calls, max."

"That's not the point," I snap. "The point is, you did it without checking with me first. You paid who knows how much money without asking me—"

"Oh, trust me," he interrupts with a laugh. "They get paid, like, peanuts. They're mostly interns. It's a joke how little we pay them."

"That's also not the point." I put my head in my hands, feeling like I'm going to scream.

Think calm, happy thoughts.

By the time I calm down enough to peel my hands away from my face, it looks like Ash is finally getting it.

"You're still... You're still *this* mad?" he asks, sounding hurt. Which only infuriates me more. He thought I would get over Alec having a wife? Him taking it upon himself to beat the shit out of Chase? In only nine days?

"Yes!" I half-yell. But mad isn't even the right word. It's more than that. I can't seem to articulate how I'm feeling, the disappointment, the anger, the betrayal. "You guys don't listen to anything I say! You just do whatever you want without any regard to how it will affect my life. Did you ever think what it could do to my business to be embroiled with you all? I don't even understand what your company does, because you tell me *nothing*, but I know enough to know it comes with heavy baggage that I don't need."

"Oh," Ashton says. He stares at the ground, frowning.

"You need to ask me about these things," I tell him. "And you need to ask me before you just show up here. I'm at *work*, Ash. This isn't a game to me. This is my life."

His shoulders slump. "Yeah," he murmurs. "Yeah, I'm sorry, I, uh... This was a bad idea, wasn't it? Showing up here. I thought..." He laughs, and it's a hollow, broken sound. "I guess it doesn't matter what I thought."

I clench my hands at my side, fighting the urge to reach out and comfort him. A part of me wants to hug him. I want to bury my face in his neck and smell him. Let him buy me Mexican food and tell me I'm perfect. But then I remember how he put my ex in the hospital, like it was nothing. I remember all the lies, I remember how cozy he looked with Alec's wife in that photo. And all the jealousy and rage bubbles back to the surface.

I'll never again apologize for a mess I didn't create.

"You should go," I say, the words coming out harsher than I expect. "And no more flowers or gifts. Please. Just go and give me the time I asked for, okay?"

Ash nods slowly.

I can't bring myself to watch him leave. I stand there, arms wrapped around myself for a few seconds, cycling through my therapy mantras, until I finally feel calm enough to make my way back up to the front.

The shop door opens as soon as I reach the café, and for a

brief second, I think it might be Ash again, coming back and ignoring everything I just told him.

It isn't.

"Did you guys see who that was?" Justin asks, coming through the door and letting it swing shut behind him. He looks between the two of us excitedly. "That was Ashton 'The KO King' Sterling! You know, the MMA fighter?" He shakes his head in disbelief. "I can't believe it. You know I watched his debut professional fight here? And it was—why are you mouthing *shut up* at me?"

"The fact that you don't understand the implication of mouthing something is astounding," Jade snaps at him. "How are you the smart one?"

"That was my ex," I explain, trying to end the sibling squabble before it starts. I lift one shoulder in a shrug.

"That? *That's* the guy you dated after Chase?" Justin asks me, pointing out the door. "You're telling me that's the guy that *you* dumped?"

I narrow my eyes at him, setting my hands on my hips. "And what the hell is that supposed to mean?"

Justin cringes. "Sorry, that came out wrong. I just meant... He's a big step up from your last boyfriend."

"That he is," Jade agrees. "You should see her other boyfriends. They're almost as pretty as that one."

Justin's face freezes, recalibrates. "Her other boyfriends?" he repeats slowly.

"Hey!" Jade points an accusing finger at him. "We do not slut shame in this store. That's my number one rule!"

"Don't—" He sputters, motioning toward me. "Don't call your best friend a slut!"

"Why not?" Jade asks. "There's nothing wrong with being a slut. Some of the best people I know are sluts."

"You're infuriating," Justin insists. "I forgot how infuriating you can be."

Jade snorts a laugh. "Whatever, brat. You're late, by the way."

He looks down at his watch. "It's noon. You told me my shift starts at noon."

"And on time is late. Early is on time. We grew up with the same parents, but it's like you learned nothing," Jade says. She nods toward the café trash. "You're on trash duty until further notice."

"You're a dictator, you know that?" Justin mutters. But he moves toward the trash, gathering it up to take it out.

"I am," Jade agrees. "And don't you forget it."

7

ALEC

I stare out my office window at the lights of the city below me. *My* city. My empire that I built from the ground up, that I raised from nothing. I worked so hard to build a legacy that mattered here.

It was all I ever wanted. All I ever dreamed of.

But that was before her.

"So," I say, fury radiating off me, as I turn my back on the view, glaring at my brothers. "Dante is alive."

Alive, and after the only woman who matters to me.

Sebastian looks even worse today. He can't stay still, can't keep himself from shifting anxiously from foot to foot. Even Viper—knife in hand, flipping it idly as he lounges in his seat— looks on edge.

Sebastian's icy blue eyes meet mine. "Maybe," he admits.

"Maybe?" Ashton laughs from his place on the couch. For once, he's not glued to his phone. The second Sebastian called us in here to tell us Sydney might be in danger, he became laser focused. Determined. "You're in denial. You get that, don't you, Doc?"

Sebastian turns to glare at him.

"You were there that night," Sebastian reminds him. He turns that glare on me. "Both of you. He took two bullets straight to the chest. You really think anyone gets back up from that?"

"Maybe you missed," Ashton throws back with a shrug.

"I don't miss." Sebastian's voice is cold as ice.

"Yeah, well, maybe this time you did. Maybe you—"

I stop Ashton with a look. He's been in a mood all day, sulking around the house, snapping at everyone. He glowers at me but shuts up. "Did he give you any other information?" I ask Sebastian. "Anything that would confirm that it's really Dante we're dealing with?"

He hesitates. "Unfortunately," he says, choosing his words carefully. "He was...indisposed, soon after we extracted that piece of information."

Viper, lounging sideways in his chair, laughs like a hyena.

"Aren't you supposed to keep him in check, Doc?" Ashton asks, curling his lip. "Aren't you down there to stop him from taking shit too far?"

"Yeah, Doc," Viper coos, grinning from ear to ear. "Aren't you?"

Sebastian doesn't answer, but a muscle in his eye twitches. Christ.

Sometimes I think Viper might not be the only one who needs to be kept in check.

"We're getting off topic." Sebastian doesn't look at any of us as he says it. "The fact is, we don't have any real evidence Dante survived."

"Even if it's not him, *someone* is sniffing around our Sydney." I tap my finger on the surface of my desk. "Why?"

"Easy," Sebastian answers. "Because of you. Because of us."

Ashton's leg bounces with nervous energy as Sebastian

continues. "Right now, someone thinks they can get to us by getting to *her*."

And they're right.

Dante or not, that's what matters here.

"We should bring her to the compound," Ashton says quickly. "That's the safest place for her, right? We can protect her here. Keep an eye on her."

"Two problems with that." Sebastian raises a single finger—his middle—at Ashton. "One, the second we do that, we confirm to anyone watching that they were right to target her. It will only make them double down, not back off. We'd have to keep her under watch 24/7. And two." He raises his index finger. "Do you really think she'd agree to that? She won't set foot in this house right now. Not with us. She wants nothing to do with us."

"And whose fault is that?" Ashton says, glaring at his brother.

"What do you mean it would make them double down?" I press.

Sebastian adjusts his glasses before continuing. "If someone can gather intel on Sydney and leave without us interfering, it tells them one of two things. Either our position here is so weak that we can't sense a shark in our waters, or Sydney means so little to us that we wouldn't bother keeping the sharks away from her. Either way, they back off. But the second we move in, the second we protect her—he'll know we care. And that gives him all the power."

Fucking great.

"But we can't... We can't just leave her unprotected," Ashton insists, an edge of panic in his voice.

"We won't." I drum my fingers on my desk.

Never. I'll never leave her unprotected, never leave her side. Even if she hates me for it.

"Since she won't allow any of us near her at the moment, she needs better protection. Without alerting anyone to it," I tell Sebastian. "Real protection. A lot more than you leering at her from the bushes, Doc."

Sebastian shifts his shoulders back, almost imperceptibly, and his eyes dart away from mine.

"You have been keeping an eye on her, haven't you?" I ask, eyes narrowing.

A hesitation, and just a flicker of something in those cold blue eyes. Then, "No."

"You have got to be fucking kidding me," Ashton spits. "We're finally in a situation where your fucking...*proclivities* might be helpful to us, and you're not even watching her?"

"Big word for Elmo," Sebastian counters, cutting a sharp glance at him. When he looks back at me, he continues. "She asked for space. From all of us. She deserves to have that respected. So, no. I haven't been watching her. Unlike you, I've left her alone."

I slam my fist down on my desk.

Anyone else, any other person in the world, would have flinched. Hell, even Viper jumped at the noise, startled out of whatever fantasy he was lost in. Sebastian just looks slowly from my desk to my face, raising a single eyebrow.

"Keep an eye on her," I demand. "Christ, I shouldn't even have to ask this of you. Watch her, Sebastian. That's a fucking order."

There's a flash of anger in his blue eyes, invisible to anyone who doesn't know to look for it.

"And if I refuse?" he asks quietly.

This fucking asshole. This is when he decides to question me?

"Are you?" I ask in a deadly voice. "Are you refusing?"

That muscle in his eye twitches again.

"She asked for space," Sebastian repeats. "And you are asking me to violate that. After I already vio—" He stops. Takes a breath. "I'm respecting her decision by not reaching out, not *stalking* her. Unlike some of us, I have that self-control."

"What is that supposed to mean?" Ashton asks, voice sharp.

"It *means* that you are pathologically incapable of leaving her alone," he sneers. "Where were you today, huh? While Viper and I were downstairs working? Does Sterling even know that when we were dismembering the man helping to potentially *hurt* her, you were *at her place of work?*"

Ashton's jaw drops open in shock.

"The fact that you're surprised that I know that speaks volumes since you know you have a tracker on your phone," Sebastian continues, shaking his head. "You might be pretty, but goddamn you're so thick-skulled it's an embarrassment to our entire ancestral line."

Fury radiates from every muscle in Ashton's body as his fists clench.

"And how many gifts have you sent her?" Sebastian asks mockingly. "I have access to your personal accounts, don't ever forget that. I know down to the fucking penny how much you've spent on flowers."

"I sent a few roses." Ashton scoffs. "Big fucking deal."

"Two thousand eight hundred dollars' worth of fucking gifts," Sebastian counters. "Just in the last week."

"Who cares!" Ashton throws up his hands. "It's a drop in the bucket, anyway. It's not like we don't have the money!"

"They're not even her favorite flower, did you know that?" Sebastian asks, raising an eyebrow at his brother. "She likes orchids."

"She likes roses," Ashton growls.

"How would you even know what she likes?" Sebastian counters. "You never bothered to get to know her."

He's pushing Ashton too far, and he knows it. It's been a long, long time since I've had to break up a fight between the two of them. I brace myself, ready to intervene.

Sebastian takes a breath and runs a hand through his hair. "Look, I know this is difficult for all of us," he says, choosing his words carefully and turning back to address me.

"You don't know shit," Ashton snaps. "You aren't dating her, are you? You had one fucking moment with her. That's it. And remind us, how did that fucking end?"

Sebastian's jaw clenches.

"Don't think we've forgotten that you're the whole reason we're in this mess," Ashton continues. "You and *psycho* over there. You scared her, both of you."

Viper looks up as Ashton gestures toward him.

"She was scared, boss," he agrees. "So fucking scared."

"And at least *we're* respecting her wishes," Sebastian argues, gesturing between all three of us. "We're letting her set the pace, giving her time to decide what she wants."

"What she wants," Ashton sneers. "And you were so concerned with what she wants before, huh? This is all your fault!"

"You think I don't fucking know that?" Sebastian hisses.

"Ashton—" I start.

"New rule," Ashton says tightly. He points at his brother. "You don't get a say in any of this."

"And why would I agree—"

"Next rule, I don't give a shit if you agree to anything," Ashton says. "You're the reason she's not talking to us. You're the reason she doesn't trust us. So you can shut up, and—"

"At least I never lied to her," Sebastian fires back. And for a moment, my heart stops.

He knows.

"How long were the two of you planning on pretending to

be the good guys?" Sebastian asks. "Taking her on dates? Wooing her? Pretending the whole time we don't have blood on our hands?"

"Shut up," Ashton warns.

"Or what?" Sebastian mocks. His lips curve into a cruel smile. "What will you do if I don't?"

I put out my hand, halting Ashton as he stands up and takes a step toward his brother, violence dancing in his eyes.

Sebastian's lip curls. "At least I was honest with her. I may have scared her, but nothing I've ever done has been to sugar-coat who I am. And I'm the only one respecting her wishes by *staying away from her*," he says. Lost in his own world, Viper cackles. My palms are pressed hard against the desk as he turns to me. "And you want me to violate that."

He is driving closer and closer to crossing a line with me, and I don't tolerate insubordination or disrespect. Not even from my brothers.

I stand up but keep my palms pressed against the wood. I need to regain some of my control and get through this before I punch a hole in the wall.

"I don't give a fuck about your motivations right now," I seethe. Sebastian doesn't move, barely even blinks in the face of my anger. "Don't contact her, don't let her see you, *fine*. But you will keep an eye on her. That is an order. We can't be leaving her unprotected. Not if someone is after her. Do you understand me, Doc?"

He doesn't answer, not at first. He just stares at me, eyes cold. Glancing between the two of us, Viper shifts in his seat, a dog torn between two masters.

"Whatever you say, boss," Sebastian says, finally, lips pressed into an angry, straight line.

"Go." I motion toward the door, dismissing him. Viper

follows. But when Ashton moves to leave, I shake my head. "Not you. You stay."

He stops in his tracks and slowly turns back to me.

"You need to stay away from her," I warn him. "If Dante is alive and watching and Doc is right about how he'd play this, we can't bring more attention to her."

Ashton's shoulders sag. "Save your breath. She already threw me out today, okay? She wants nothing to do with me thanks to that asshole." He gestures at the door Sebastian slammed as he left. "And I can tell you right now, she wants nothing to do with you either."

"Right now, we *both* stay away from her. For her safety," I insist. "We fix this mess we're in before any of this shitstorm comes raining down on her."

It takes a while, but the words finally seem to sink in. "Fine," Ashton murmurs. "Can I go now?"

He's angry. And, childishly, he's not doing the one thing that would help him focus this anger into something useful.

"No." I lean further over my desk. "You've been missing sessions with your trainer."

Ashton stares at me like I just told him the sky is pink. "Who the fuck cares?"

"I fucking care," I snap between clenched teeth. "You're no good to me, or our company, when you're this wound up."

The look Ashton gives me lets me know exactly how little he cares about me and our company right now.

"I spoke with Jacob this morning." Ashton rolls his eyes at the mention of his manager. "And I assured him there would be no more missed sessions, no more missed weigh-ins. Is that clear?"

"Crystal," Ashton replies, tone laced with sarcasm.

I wave him toward the door, finally dismissing him. When

he leaves, my fingers twitch with the effort not to check my phone.

Maybe today will be the day she finally calls.

Just maybe.

8

SYDNEY

Fucking pottery. Of all the hobbies I could have chosen to distract myself, I picked pottery, which I'm quickly realizing I am completely inept at. It's very possible I have zero talent in any visual arts. I look over to Jade, who has already thrown a perfect vase in the time it took me to shape my glob of clay into...a different-shaped glob of clay. Fuck.

Justin has—somewhat surprisingly—been an amazing addition to the shop. Since he has no friends in the area, and no more university work to take up his attention, he's been more than happy to pick up whatever shifts we throw at him. Which is the reason I'm able to be here with Jade right now, creating monstrosities.

But it is helping. Spending time with my best friend, learning something new. It's helping me feel less alone. Less broken.

I don't need a man to feel whole. Hell, I don't even need *four* men to feel whole. I need this. I need my best friend. I need clay caked so deeply under my fingernails I'll have something to pick at for the next four days.

"Do you think mice have souls?" Jade asks suddenly. Leaning back on her stool, she stares calculatingly at the sculpture in front of her as if there were anything left to perfect. Our class instructor, Mr. Beck, is busying himself walking between students, offering gentle instruction and critique.

I tap my finger against my glob, considering the question.

"Give me more context," I say. "I want a full understanding of the question before I give my answer."

"Okay, let's say souls are real," Jade continues, placing her vase to the side and starting again with fresh clay. "And if you have a soul, you get into some kind of afterlife, right?"

"Like a heaven?" I ask.

Jade nods enthusiastically. "Right, like heaven. If you have a soul and live a good life, you get to go there. But what happens with things like mice? Do they have a soul? And if they do, are there just millions of mice running around heaven?"

"Hang on, back up a bit. How does a mouse live a good life?"

"I don't know." Jade sighs, exasperated. "Let's say our mouse doesn't fight with the other mice. Not ever. And she only steals food from the trash, right? Not from anyone who needs it. Plus, she never covets another mouse's wife or anything like that."

"An upstanding, moral mouse," I agree, nodding.

"Obviously, our mouse goes to heaven," Jade continues. "Which begs the question, is there a *mouse*-specific heaven? Because I'm pretty sure my idea of heaven doesn't include stampeding hordes of mice all over the place."

"Naturally," I agree.

"But then, where does it stop?" Jade leans forward, her attention somehow focused both on the mouse-heaven quandary and her quickly developing vase. "Are there insect heavens? Plant heavens? Do all species get their own heavens, separated but infinite worlds where all the good creatures can be happy forever?"

"There'd have to be some overlap, right?" I point out, jabbing my finger at what looks like...a bowl? Maybe? "Like, human heaven and dog heaven, those two could be the same thing."

"Right," Jade agrees. "Or like, cat heaven is probably bird hell, you know? There's obvious synergy there."

Jade finishes another amazing vase and holds it out for me to take.

"You have no faith in me," I complain, pouting. "You don't think I can finish and sell this...ashtray to a brilliant art collector?"

"I have so much faith in you! But part of that is the faith that you'll realize that you're shit at this, and you'll take this vase and quickly place it on your wheel before the instructor tries to help you and wastes everyone's time," Jade says, once again thrusting her vase at me.

"All right, class," Mr. Beck calls from the front of the classroom, clapping his hands together. "Bring your final vases up to the front next to the kiln to be fired!"

I abandon the clay frisbee I created and take Jade up on her offer of a fully fledged vase so I don't have to embarrass myself. "Thanks for helping me avoid a walk of ceramic shame. Next activity, let's pick something easier."

Mr. Beck gives our vases a nod of approval as we drop them off, and when we get back to our station, I add my misshapen lump of horrors back to the pile of unused clay. Jade walks over to the sink to wash the clay from her hands.

"Let's make you some hot cocoa when we get back to the shop," she offers. "Chocolate will help distance us from the memories of this failed experiment."

"Thanks." I smile at her and make my way to the sinks, staring out the window at the sunny afternoon. "I don't know what I'd do without you, Jade, you—"

No.

This time it's more than just a flash. I see him clearly for just a few seconds across the street. And then he's gone.

"Sydney?" Jade prompts when I stop talking. "You stopped in the middle of my praise, sweetie. You know I need my accolades."

"Sorry." I blink, my voice shaky. "I just thought…"

She turns and gives me her full attention, frowning. "What's going on? Is everything okay?"

"I thought I saw Chase," I explain, feeling a little dizzy. "Just—just for a second, on the sidewalk outside."

Jade's head whips around. She stares through the window, twisting and turning to examine every face walking by.

"Are you sure?" she asks, anger and anxiety commingling in her voice.

Sure? No, not at all. And I *want* to be wrong, but…

Something gnaws at my gut, that horrible intuition women have spent their entire lives cultivating, sharpened to a razor's edge from the anguish of navigating a world where too many people wish you harm.

"I'm not certain," I admit, chewing my lip. "But… I thought I saw him the other day, too. Outside our shop."

"And you *think* it was him, both times?" Jade stares intensely out the window as if she could will what I saw into existence.

I shake my head.

"No, I… It wasn't him," I say, letting the lie settle. "I'm just being paranoid."

Jade's lips thin into a straight line.

"Are you sure?" she presses. "Syd, you seem really freaked out—"

I shake my head, repeating the lie a little louder this time, hoping that I'll believe it too. "It wasn't him," I tell Jade, voice firm. But I can't meet her eyes when I say it. And she sees right through the lie. Her face darkens.

"Look, I know you don't want to see Chase again. I get that. But the way your face just paled at the idea of him being outside..." Jade trails off without finishing her sentence, watching me too closely. "Syd, lately I've been getting a feeling that maybe there's more to this than you've told me."

She's right. There is. But it's hard to admit that I haven't been honest with her. The one person I know would never judge me, even when I judge myself.

I swallow hard, and when I look up, Jade holds my gaze.

"You know you can tell me anything, right?" she presses.

"Of course I know that," I insist, drying my hands. But I struggle to find the words to tell her.

A long silence stretches between us as we finish cleaning up our pottery station. By the time we're finished, most of the other students have left.

"I need a drink," I say suddenly, my voice a little too loud. "Do you need a drink? I think maybe we should replace that hot chocolate idea with a really, really gin-forward glass of straight gin."

Jade's smile is only a little strained. "Yes, I need a drink. But no, I'm not drinking straight gin like a goddamn psychopath. I will drink it with vermouth and olive juice like the lady I am."

"Bail?" I ask, grinning at her.

"Bail," she quickly agrees.

Justin can handle running the store a little longer on his own while we get a drink, I reason as we stroll out of the class-room and into the sunny afternoon. Because today... Today, I need to share a long-overdue confession with my best friend. And I need to do it before I lose my nerve.

As soon as we step outside, I shiver, despite the sunny weather. Fall is just around the corner, and there's finally a chill in the air that I can feel all the way down to my bones. I know everyone loves the summer months, but nothing feels better to me than the beginning of autumn. This is the time of year I truly come alive.

There's a cocktail bar not far from our pottery class that Jade and I used to frequent all the time, and we head there without discussing it. The Twin Pines used to be our favorite place to grab a drink together after work, but we haven't been there in a while. Between my breakup, running the café, and dating a harem of men, I guess we just haven't had the time.

It seems as good a place as any to have this conversation.

When Jade pushes open the door and we step inside, it's like stepping back in time. It looks just the way I remember—upscale, but not too fancy. Quaint and charming. The sort of place that's easy to return to. It's only three pm, so the bar is unsurprisingly empty, apart from the bartender and one surly man at a table on his own, whiskey glass hovering below his mouth.

The bearded bartender looks up when we enter, greeting us with a huge smile. "Wow, ladies. I haven't seen you in a bit."

"Hey, Seamus," Jade says, giving him a toothy grin.

Seamus is synonymous with the Twin Pines, as far as Jade and I are concerned. He's been here nearly every single time we've come, and there's no quicker way to get to know someone than being four drinks deep every time you chat with them. You can thank my love of martinis for why I know that he moved here in his twenties to pursue music. Even ten years later, he still plays local shows on occasion, but he never saw any kind of real success with it. Still, he always seems genuinely happy. Affable. Far from his family and working in a job he didn't dream of doing, he's a consummate ray of sunshine. It doesn't hurt that his good looks and accent are enough to turn even the most miserly bar patron into a big tipper.

I give him a small wave and slide onto a barstool, the reality of my situation sinking in. How much do I tell her? How much detail do I go into?

How do you even start a conversation like this?

"We're going to need the absolute filthiest gin martinis you can conceive of, and we'll need you to keep them coming," I tell Seamus, a forced smile on my face.

"Sure thing," he responds. He wastes no time getting down to business, pulling down a bottle of gin, and focusing on our drinks.

I squirm on the barstool, trying to get comfortable. Jade is quiet until Seamus returns. He sets our drinks in front of us on the bar and immediately steps away to give us space.

"Syd, you're making me nervous," Jade finally says. "I think this is the longest we've ever gone without yapping."

"He hurt me," I blurt out.

Jade goes stiff on her seat.

I can't meet her eyes when I say it, so I talk to my martini instead. "Yeah, emotionally. You know that part, already, I guess. He was awful. But there was more. I thought I was hiding it so well, thought I was keeping it together, but of course you noticed. I should have known you'd figure it out."

"You're babbling," Jade whispers, putting her hand over mine to keep me from fidgeting. "Take a breath and slow down. What do you mean he hurt you?"

I take a few deep breaths before continuing.

Calm, I tell myself. *I am an ocean of calm.*

"He would get in these moods. And at first, he would just

throw things or punch a wall. Maybe even break something. But then one night, he...he slapped me. And then...it only happened a few times," I admit. My voice is so low that I'm not sure she even heard me until I glance over and see her staring at the wall, her eyes unfocused.

"Only?" Jade mutters. "There's no 'only,' Sydney. *He hurt you.*" I open my mouth to argue, but she just shakes her head. "I can't believe I didn't know this. I'm so sorry. I'm so sorry I wasn't there for you."

She turns and pulls me to her, wrapping her arms around me in a tight hug. She hugs me for all the times I was scared, all alone on the floor of my apartment. For all the times I had to lock myself in a different room to keep things from escalating. For all the times I avoided going home, wandering the city, waiting for him to calm down enough that I felt safe going back.

"It's my fault you didn't know," I tell her. "I was so embarrassed. Things were so normal at first. He made me feel so loved and then... I thought it was my fault. The first time he hit me, it was about something so stupid, I can't even remember what we were arguing about. Then he'd apologize, and he was... He would be so sweet for a while."

Jade hugs me tighter.

"I really thought I loved him, you know? I *did* love him, at the start."

"I know," Jade murmurs. "But he took that love and he hurt you with it. And that's not your fault."

We're silent for a while as she just holds me, my head on her shoulder.

"I'm sorry I never told you. I knew if I did, it would be real, and I would have to make a decision I wasn't ready to make." I pick up my head to look her in the eyes. "I need you to know that it was never about not trusting you."

Jade gives me a sad smile. "Of course I know that. I just

wish I could have done something more." The smile slips off her face. "God, I could just kill him, Syd. I wanted to kill him before I knew this, and now—"

"There's more," I say before I can change my mind. "You know about him showing up at Katie's barbecue, but he also came by the shop. And then to my apartment. He's been following me, harassing me. Seb knows, but he doesn't know the full history of what the relationship was like. He doesn't know Chase was ever violent with me. You're the only one I've told. Now I keep thinking I see him wherever I go, and I don't know if it's in my head or not."

Panic flares in Jade's eyes as she listens. "Fuck. Okay. Sweetie, we need to get you out of that apartment. If he's been harassing you, I don't think it's safe for you to be there alone."

"And where exactly am I supposed to go?" I ask. "The café is downstairs! It's not like I can disappear. He knows I'll be there. And your couch is occupied now, remember?" Jade opens her mouth to argue, but I cut her off. "It's okay. Seb has been keeping an eye on things. He knows Chase has been bothering me, and he was going to get a restraining order for me, right? I guess Ash probably knows, too, now, since he was the one who beat the shit out of him."

"I'm sorry, Ash did *what*?" Jade lets out a startled laugh. "Okay, maybe that guy is growing on me after all."

"I got the call right after I found out about Alec," I tell her, fidgeting. "It was all pretty overwhelming."

"So, Ash beats the shit out of your ex for scaring you right after you find out that your *other* boyfriend is married, but your other *other* boyfriend already knew about it," Jade summarizes, sounding partially impressed, partially shocked. It doesn't seem like the right time to bring Viper into the mix, so I let her sit with the redacted story.

"It sounds insane when you phrase it like that," I mumble.

"Not *sounds*, Syd. *Is*. Your life is basically a K-drama, I swear," she says, chuckling.

I laugh, scrubbing a few errant tears from my face before reaching for my martini.

"I just hate this," I admit. "I hate how scared Chase makes me feel. I don't want him to have that sort of power over me. I don't want to feel this vulnerable anymore."

"I know," Jade says softly. Her eyes are red-rimmed, shiny with tears.

"Thanks for listening to me. And I *swear* this is the last of my hidden confessions." I sniff. "You'll always be the love of my life, you know that? No matter what happens. I love you."

"To the moon and back," she answers, smiling. "And we'll figure this out, okay? Together."

I sigh, slumping in my seat. "I hate to say it, but it was easier when the guys were around. I felt protected. Now that they're gone?" My words fizzle out, and I shrug.

"I get it. But I'm here, and I'll support you, no matter what," Jade insists, smoothing down my hair and leaning in to give me a kiss on the top of my head. "And part of that support means doing the hard thing for you, when you can't do it yourself."

"Doing the hard thing, like...?" I trail off, watching as she downs the last of her drink.

"Give me your phone," Jade demands, holding out her hand. "Now."

I hesitate. "Who are you going to call?"

"You know who I'm going to call, Syd." She pins me with a look, hand still outstretched. "You might not be ready to talk to them, but I'm going to do what I can to help keep you safe."

I know there's no use fighting her. Sighing, I reach into my bag and pull out my phone, unlocking it before handing it to her.

"Wow, Ashton texts you *a lot*, huh?" Jade murmurs,

frowning down at my notifications. I don't answer, watching silently as she scrolls through my phone until she finds the contact she's looking for.

He picks up immediately. Something in my chest tightens when I hear his voice, faint but audible from the speaker of my phone.

"Sydney?" Sebastian asks. The eagerness in his voice catches me by surprise.

Jade makes an incorrect buzzer noise. "Wrong. Guess again."

There's a breath of a pause. "Jade," he states simply. "Is Sydney okay?"

"Sydney's fine," Jade says. "Actually, you know what? She's better than fine. She's glowing. Better than she's been in months. Single and ready to mingle!"

I snort into my drink. From across the bar, for the first time since he brought our drinks, Seamus looks over at us with interest.

"And you're calling me from her phone to tell me this... why, exactly?" Sebastian asks, voice turning cold.

"I'm calling to ask about the restraining order you promised to get for her. Remember that?"

Even over the phone, I can hear Sebastian swear under his breath. "Yes, I remember. Sorry, I've been distracted with a work situation. Let her know I'll have the paperwork finished and ready for her by the end of the week."

"Good," Jade says. "Then—"

"Is he there right now?" he interrupts. "Has he been bothering her again?"

Jade looks at me, raising an eyebrow. I quickly shake my head. He hasn't, not really. I'm still not convinced it was him I saw either time.

"No," Jade tells him. "We're just being cautious, that's all."

"Call me if he shows up again. With or without the restraining order, I want to know. Do you have my number?" Before she can answer, Sebastian continues, "Hang on, I'm texting it to you now."

A moment later, Jade's phone vibrates in her tote bag.

"Wow, that is extra creepy that you know my number," Jade says. "Stalker much?"

He ignores that. "Call me if he starts bothering her again." Then a pause. "Be honest with me, how is she doing, really? Is she okay?"

Jade chews her lip, her face tight. She looks at me, and something flickers over her face. "She's great," she insists in a too-chipper tone. "And you know what? Her ass has never looked better."

Before he can respond, she hangs up, a look of satisfied triumph in her eyes as she hands the phone back to me.

"That was mean," I say, taking it back from her. "But thanks."

"The sooner you have a restraining order against that asshole, the better," Jade tells me. "Listen, I need to use the ladies' room. Are you okay on your own for a bit?"

I nod as I watch her hop down from the barstool and head toward the bathroom. Seamus strolls over and sets a fresh martini in front of me, giving me a small smile before he leaves, tactfully ignoring the emotional mess I am.

I take a deep breath, feeling strangely relieved after finally telling Jade the truth about my relationship with Chase, like a weight has been lifted from my chest.

It's not my fault. It was never my fault, what he did to me.

I think I'm ready to close this chapter of my life, to finally put him behind me, for good. But that's difficult to do, when I still feel like he's out there. Watching me.

I chew my fingernail, staring at my drink. Did I really see

him, or am I just being paranoid? It wouldn't make sense for him to be outside our pottery class, right? He hates this part of the city, where the neighborhoods are cheaper, a little more run-down. And he would be at work right now anyway.

Wouldn't he?

There's one way to be sure. I look down at my phone, still clutched in my hand, and before I can stop myself, I'm dialing his work number, sliding off my stool and stepping away from the bar for some privacy.

I don't want to talk to him. I just want to know where he is.

I need to know it wasn't him I saw today.

"Hi! Thank you for calling Beacon Industries. How may I direct your call?" Caroline's chipper voice asks when the call picks up.

Fuck. My stomach sinks, my insides twisting unpleasantly. I didn't think this through. I can't believe I forgot Caroline was the receptionist there—the woman Chase cheated on me with.

"Hello?" she prompts before I find my voice. "Is someone there?"

I clear my throat. "Um, hi. Could I please speak with Chase Levine?"

"Oh." There's a pause. "Unfortunately, Mr. Levine no longer works here. I could connect you with Alicia Livingston. She took over all his accounts. May I ask who's calling?"

What the fuck.

What.

The.

Fuck.

Chase would *never* leave that job. His entire life revolved around this job.

"Um. That's okay. Do you know where he's working now?" I press.

There's a beat of silence. Then, almost a whisper. "Sydney?"

Shit.

I should hang up. That's what I should do. I should just hang up. I don't want it getting back to him that I was looking for him, don't want to give him any reason to think I still want him in my life. My finger is hovering over the end call button, my heart in my throat, when Caroline speaks again.

"Listen, Sydney... He's not here anymore. He's not working anywhere, as far as I know. I don't know the details—I don't *want* to know the details—but he's not welcome back here." Her voice is quiet, tentative, like she's afraid of being overheard.

"Oh. Okay, well, thank you—"

"Wait," she cuts in. "I'm so glad you called. Look, I'm sorry. You have no idea how many times I wanted to call you and tell you that." She's speaking so quickly, her words running together, like she's rushing to get them out before I can hang up. "I know it's no excuse, and I understand if you hate me, but you need to know: He lied to me. He told me that he'd been trying to break it off with you for months, but you were unstable, and he was scared you were going to hurt yourself. I didn't realize he was just a lying piece of shit until he did the same thing to me. You know he cheated on me, too? After he dumped me, I found out that he was screwing some wannabe influencer that called him 'master.'"

"Oh." I grimace. "Ew."

"Right? *Him?* Instant ick. Anyway, that's beside the point. I just feel like I owe you a huge apology for my role in this. I never should have believed anything he said about you."

"It's fine, Caroline. We're... We're good." I don't even mean to say it, but the words come out anyway.

"We are?" she asks with a sniff, voice almost inaudible.

"Yeah. Trust me, I know what a manipulative dick he can be," I tell her.

"God, he is! I wish I had never met him. I wish neither one of us had ever met him. I honestly wish he didn't have the ability to meet people at all," she says.

I laugh, surprising myself. Shit. I don't want to like her. I don't want kinship with her. But in another life, maybe the two of us could have been friends.

"Yeah." I laugh again. "He's definitely the sort of guy who should have started in prison and had to prove himself out." I take a second to collect myself. "Look, we're okay. Honestly."

"Really?" She laughs skeptically. "Thanks. I think I needed to hear that."

We awkwardly say our goodbyes, and I hang up.

He's not here anymore.

He's not working anywhere, as far as I know.

Then it could have been him outside the pottery studio. He could still be following me.

I'm shaking when I sit down, quickly gulping down half of my drink. The gin does little to calm my nerves.

"Sorry," Jade says when she comes back from the bathroom a few minutes later. "I got to thinking about you and Chase and...might have had a mini cry in the bathroom, and then my eyes got all puffy..." She shrugs. "You know how it goes."

I give her a strained smile and finish the last of my drink. Jade waves poor Seamus back over, letting him know it's safe to approach.

"Another round, ladies?" he asks, leaning over the bar to smirk at us. His beard is red, but his hair is just a little lighter, a mixture of strawberry red and blonde, all the colors shifting together in the dim lights of the bar.

"Only if you want to carry us out of here," I joke.

His smile widens. "I'd gladly carry you, Sydney," he says

with that soft lilt to his voice. He gives me a wink before turning back around to go close out our bill.

My eyes go wide, and I glance at Jade, who's stifling a laugh. Seamus returns with the check and places it down in front of us. He only charged us for one round, I notice, instead of the three that we drank.

"Um, thanks," I say awkwardly, putting my card down.

"Oh, absolutely not. This one is on me," Jade insists. "I bullied you into talking to me and made you cry. It's the least I can do." She picks up my card and flings it back in my direction before setting her own credit card on the tray and handing it back to Seamus.

9

SYDNEY

I'm still thinking about my conversation with Caroline hours later, as I pour myself a glass of wine and crawl into bed, book in hand.

It was almost...cathartic, talking to her. Hearing her side of everything, learning I'm not the only member of the *girls Chase has fucked over* club. I'm not sure I'm ready to completely forgive her, but at least I understand it better now. Of course he lied to her. That's what men like him do, isn't it? They lie. Manipulate.

Pretend they aren't married...

Stop thinking about them, I scold myself, fluffing my pillow. But the fluffing starts to feel more like punching, as my anger takes over. *Alec, Chase, all of them. Stop it.*

I prop my very well-fluffed pillow against the headboard and burrow against it until I'm comfortable, wriggling as I grab my book. I finally have some time to myself to just lie about and catch up on my reading. This is *me* time, no distractions, no thinking about *men,* nothing but me and my favorite escape mechanism.

I crack open the book and make it exactly two sentences before my mind drifts.

Does Annika know?

Nope, stop that. Gnashing my teeth together, I rearrange myself on the bed and open my book again. I am reading. That's what I'm doing. I am reading.

Filled with a violent determination, I start back at the top of the page. But my mind wanders before I even make it past the third word.

Crap.

I can't stop thinking about it. Them. Alec, with another woman. Alec, *married* to another woman.

It makes me feel sick, unwell. I can't stop picturing her perfectly manicured nails scratching down the dark skin of his back. I can't stop imagining Ash pressing into her from behind while Alec kisses her, touches her, holds her the way he held me.

It's not fair. He's not mine, never was. But the idea of him with someone else—anyone else—makes me feel sick. It makes me feel violent.

Does she know? Did he go home to her after our dates, get into bed with her, touch her?

I throw my book down, bury my face in my hands, and *scream.*

She deserves to know, doesn't she? If the positions were reversed, and I were her, I would want to know, wouldn't I? I mean, just recently, I *was* her.

Shit. Shit, fuck, goddamnit, shit.

Before I can pull myself back from the brink, I grab my phone and pull up the search engine.

Annika Basso and Mason Alexander Sterling, I type into the search bar.

Over half a million hits. My heart sinks. But scrolling

through them, I realize quickly there's plenty about Alec—article after article about him, his company, and his plethora of charity organizations—but nothing about Annika.

Annika Basso, I try searching for, instead.

Nothing. Not a single mention of her on any news site. No social media presence. No photos, no email, nothing. No way to contact her, even if I wanted to.

Confused, I try a third time: *Mason Alexander Sterling wife.*

This search yields more results, but not what I'm looking for. A few articles speculating on who he might be dating. An interview where someone asks if he's looking for "Mrs. Right or Mrs. Right Now?" A question Alec tactfully avoids answering.

I scroll farther down the page and find myself reading a scathing Op Ed piece in The Fortune City Gazette from a few years ago. A Pastor Daniel Whitmore pontificating about the "moral decay rotting Fortune City from within" and Sterling Enterprises' role in it.

"How can we trust the soul of this city to a man like that?" the article asks. "A man with no moral compass? Mason Sterling is no family man, and certainly no man of God. Why would we put so much faith in a man who treats this city like a prom date he's trying to coax into bed, and not a wife he wants to honor and protect?"

A few clicks later and I discover that despite his supposedly low opinion of the Sterling name, Pastor Daniel Whitmore was given a position on Sterling Enterprise's board of directors just a few months later. The Op Eds stop after that.

Frustrated, I set my phone aside. Even if I wanted to reach out and contact his wife, there doesn't seem to be a way to do it. It's like she doesn't exist. But I know she does. I saw her photograph, and I saw the ring. I saw the marriage certificate.

He admitted it. He admitted he was married.

After he fucked you, my mind hisses. *After he pushed you into the mattress, put his fingers in your mouth, and made you come so hard that—*

Stop.

Stop thinking about that.

But once I start, I can't stop. It's all I can think about suddenly. The way Alec touched me that night, the things he said to me. How his fingers felt inside me.

I press the heels of my hands against my eyes, willing myself to forget about them.

Seeing Ashton the other day reminded me of how much I still want them. Both of them. After he'd left, it had been impossible not to remember what it had felt like to kiss him (heavenly). Or how he'd looked naked (criminally mouthwatering). Or how he'd used those toys on me, and—

Toys.

I drop my hands from my face and creep to the edge of my mattress, poking my head over the side. The box of toys Alec bought for me is shoved underneath, untouched since the night Ashton and I...

My thighs clench involuntarily, remembering it, and before I know it, I'm pulling the box out from under my bed and placing it next to me.

I never really got a chance to look at them all individually. I take my time going through them this time, picking through the ones that look more user-friendly and leaving the rest untouched. But my fingers pause on the vibrator Ashton used on me, the one I thought was too big at first.

I trail my fingers over it, licking my lips. I can feel my pulse throbbing between my legs, remembering how he'd fucked me with it. How he'd slipped the head of his cock between my lips at the same time, teasing me with his tip.

The memory of him praising me while he fucked me with

his tongue has me lying back on my bed and spreading my legs. The guttural way he'd sworn—voice raspy and hungry, like I was giving him everything he'd ever needed—has me gripping the toy and switching it on.

There are so many settings. I flip through a few of them, perplexed by some (I'll call this one *slow-motion morse code*), horrified by others (this one will forever be known as *jackhammer turned up to 11*), until I find a soft buzz that feels... *right*.

Don't think about them, I tell myself, sliding the toy under the fabric of my underwear, and closing my eyes.

Don't think about how good it felt to have Ashton's cock in your mouth. How much you'd liked it when he slipped it deep into your throat. The way he'd looked at you when you swallowed for him. The taste of him on your tongue.

Don't think about the way Alec's hand felt around your neck. How far he'd pushed himself inside you when he came, and how you felt every twitch.

Don't think about Seb on his knees, looking up at you, tongue flat against your clit. Don't think about—

"Fuck!"

I pull the toy away and fling it away from me, furious and unsatisfied, panting for breath. I can't do it. I can't *not* think about them.

Clenching my teeth together tightly, I shove everything back into the box and slam the lid down. I push it back under my bed with more force than necessary, and pick up my book again, determined to distract myself with a good, smutty story.

But when I finally fall asleep, over an hour later, I've barely made it past the first page.

———

It starts slowly. Someone is touching me. Warm, rough hands moving up my sides and encircling my ribs. A thumb rubs against the base of my breast, almost like he's asking for permission.

I moan, desperate for more, and arch my back in answer. I'm naked. Uninhibited. And I need those hands to keep touching me more than I've needed anything before.

A mouth against my nipple, hot and demanding. A touch of teeth. Then the mouth is moving higher, kissing and biting up my chest and neck. A tongue slides over my jaw.

"Who do you belong to, darling?" Alec's voice asks, his breath a hiss against the shell of my ear.

"You," I gasp. His hand envelops my breast, thumb flicking over my hard nipple.

He's naked, too, I realize, when I feel the head of his cock nudge against my entrance. I spread my legs wider, rolling my hips to help guide him inside me. When he enters me, it's like the planets have realigned, like the universe has changed course.

We fit together in a way that's too perfect to be explained.

"Just him?" another voice asks. Familiar.

Ashton's hands are softer than Alec's, more gentle. And I can feel him behind me, suddenly, his chest against my back.

Alec's cock moves slowly inside me with deep, purposeful thrusts. It's just what I need, just what I've been craving, and it only gets better when Ashton tilts my head to the side to kiss me, tongue dancing with mine as his hands roam over my body.

More. I need more.

And just like that, it changes. I'm on my knees suddenly, Alec behind me, his hands on my hips. He's still inside me, still fucking me, but now Ashton is right there, right where I need him, kneeling in front of me with his cock in hand.

"Look how beautiful you are," Ashton praises. He rolls the

head of his cock over my lips, painting them with his precum. I moan, opening my mouth, begging wordlessly for more.

"Such a good toy." Alec's voice is breathy, uneven. His hips move harder, faster, as Ashton eases himself between my lips.

There is nothing else that exists but this. Nothing but this moment, right here, right where I need to be, between the two of them. I moan around Ashton's length, taking him deeper in my throat than seems possible, closing my eyes and focusing on the way it feels to run my tongue along the base of him.

More. I need even more.

Even before I open my eyes, I know what I'll see. There's a chair, now, not far from where Alec and Ashton pleasure me. And I know who's sitting there, watching us, even before my gaze finds his, and I stare into those icy blue eyes.

Sebastian.

He's relaxed, legs spread. He stares at me like I'm the only thing that matters—the only thing that has ever mattered. I suck harder on Ashton's cock, pussy clenching around Alec, as Sebastian watches me.

Then he raises two fingers, and gestures me toward him.

"Come," he says.

And things change again.

They're gone, Alec and Ash. And it's just me and Sebastian, his eyes flashing behind his glasses.

I don't even consider disobeying. I couldn't, even if I wanted to. I was made to please him, made to obey him. I crawl to him on my hands and knees, stopping when I reach him. He pulls me up into his lap effortlessly, spreading me open, his fingers sliding down to fill me.

"You were made for us, weren't you, Sydney?" he asks.

His fingers feel impossibly good inside of me, stretching me, curving at just the right place. It's like he knows my body better than I do.

"Our perfect, filthy girl."

It sounds like praise, the way he says it. Like a compliment. And I love it, I love hearing it, love moaning against the skin of his neck as I ride his fingers.

I'm close. So very close. His hand moves faster, touching me like he can read my mind, driving me closer to the edge.

I'm lost in pleasure, gasping his name, and I don't notice the dream has changed again until someone grips the hair at the base of my skull and jerks my head back.

Something sharp and dangerous presses against my throat.

"Scream for me," Viper hisses in my ear, drawing the knife to my pulse.

And I do.

I wake up with a scream, hands fisting my sheets, heart pounding in my chest, thighs wet.

When my fingers slip between my legs, where I'm slick and throbbing, it takes no effort at all to make myself come.

10

SYDNEY

The sweetest flowers for the sweetest girl.

I LOOK DOWN AT THE CARD, THEN AT THE LILIES ON MY bedside table, frowning. After putting my foot down with Ash, the constant barrage of red roses finally stopped. But when I tried to leave for work this morning, a bouquet of lilies was waiting for me, propped against my front door.

I study the card again, worrying my lip between my teeth. This doesn't feel like a gift from Ash. It's nothing like the other bouquets he's sent me, no box, no stuffed animal. And the card I found dangling from the arrangement doesn't contain a single pun or meme.

Could they be from Alec? I haven't spoken to him since the night he broke my heart—haven't even bothered opening the text message he sent afterward. Is this the start of a brand-new wave of guilt gifts, as Alec tries to grovel for my forgiveness?

I set the card beside the lilies and sigh. Between this new arrangement and the remaining roses, I'm running out of old pasta jars to hold all these apologies.

Maybe I should text him, even if it's just to let him know how much I despise lilies. They were my favorite flowers once upon a time.

But that was before Chase.

Lilies were his favorite way to apologize after he hurt me. Now, the smell of them makes my stomach churn, a nauseating, twisted Pavlovian response I can't shake.

I could tell Alec that. I pull out my phone, and my thumb hovers over his name.

I still hate you, you cheating bastard, but just for the record, I hate lilies almost as much.

Or maybe: *Save the flowers for your wife.*

My thumb lingers over the unopened message, only a portion of it visible.

Sydney, I should have told you—

I almost open it. But then my eyes snag on the time, and my heart flips in my chest.

Shit. I'm late. Somehow, with this newest batch of flowers distracting me, I'm *late to work*, even though I live literally upstairs. Truly an accomplishment, and one I'm sure Jade will never let me forget.

Shit, shit, shit.

I shove my phone into my pocket and rush out the door. But just as I'm sliding my key in the deadbolt to lock it, I hear something.

There's a scratching sound. I pause, tilting my head to listen. There it is again, a faint light scratching, coming from the walls.

Great. Just great. Late for work, and I might have mice.

Fantastic.

Locking my door, I shove the keys back into my bag and head downstairs to face Jade's wrath.

———

THE MORNING PASSES UNEVENTFULLY, AND THANKFULLY, Jade only teases me a little for my tardiness before tossing me a coffee. The store stays busy nearly all day, and I lose myself in the rhythm of it, bouncing from customer to customer, helping Jade when I can. I suppose that's why it takes me until nearly close to notice the change in our Staff Picks display.

There's a new section added, squeezed in next to Jade's. Justin's.

My eyes catch on one of the books. The cover shows a single lily, just like the ones now upstairs next to my bed, only these are floating in a puddle of something that looks suspiciously like blood. The contrast of the white of the flower with the shiny, almost sickeningly bright red sends a cold tendril of fear down my spine.

Feeling strangely apprehensive, I pick it up and flip to a random page.

———

Her breaths came faster then as terror gripped her all-consumingly. She thought back on all the warnings he had left her, reminding her that she would be his. That he would possess her, whether in life or death. Those thoughts intruded on every corner of her mind as she hid behind the living room couch. The images of Charles's mutilated body still flashed in front of her eyes, his intestines splayed across the linoleum, his severed tongue placed delicately on the dinner plate, as if saved for later. And as she worked to slow her breathing, to become as imperceptible as possible, she realized there was no hiding. Not here, not from him. The floral scent of the knitted blanket hanging off the back of the sofa made her think that, at the very least, she'll see her grandmother soon. These were to be her last moments, after all. The footsteps stilled as he reached her, sensing, but not yet seeing. It was her own scream tearing from her throat as his hand clasped her ankle—

"Hey! There you are!"

I let out a panicked sound somewhere between a squeal and a scream, clutching the book to my chest as I whip around toward the voice.

Justin freezes a good seven feet away, hands raised defensively. "Whoa! Sorry," he says. "I didn't mean to sneak up on you."

My chest feels too tight, my heart pounding painfully hard. "It's fine, it's not you." I hold the book up, showing it to him. "I was just reading, and—"

"Oh, that's a great one!" He steps closer, grinning. "I just added it this morning. I hope you don't mind. Jade said I should put up some of my own favorites, now that I'm officially part of the staff." He gestures at the name tag Jade has been forcing him to wear. Where it should say "Justin", it simply says "Trainee".

"I don't mind you adding books at all," I assure him. And I don't. *Really,* I don't. But I eye the blood-drenched flower on the cover, grimacing. "But is this really the sort of thing you like to read?"

"Yeah," Justin says excitedly. "That's from one of my favorite series. The *Special Agent Callahan* books." He takes the paperback from me, flipping to the first few pages to show me. There's a full list of other books there, all in the same series. "See, it's all about Blake Callahan, a forensic psychologist working with the FBI to track down serial killers."

I shift my weight from one foot to the other. "Serial killers?"

"Well, mostly serial killers. There is one where he helps track down a terrorist." Justin pulls a face. "I don't love that one. There's a lot of casual racism in the way the characters are portrayed. It's pretty gross, actually."

"You don't think these might be a little, uh, inappropriate? For the Staff Picks display, I mean."

Justin glances meaningfully at my own picks for the week, a smile curving his lips. "*Mine* might be a little inappropriate?"

I follow his gaze to one of my own recommendations, *Held Captive by the Merman*. The cover features a shirtless, finned man, clutching a barely clothed woman to his scaly chest. Her back is arched, arm thrown back dramatically.

I clear my throat. "You might have a point," I concede.

"Honestly, they're not as bad as you might think. You should try one of them. I bet you'd like them." His enthusiasm is disarming. "They're really fun."

"I don't know..."

"Come on, when's the last time you read something new?" he asks. "Just give it a try!"

It's amazing, really. He's almost as convincing as his sister. I wonder if it's genetic.

"Fine." *But not this one*, I think, setting the book back in its place on his display. "Which one should I start with?"

By the time Justin has finished, I have three Blake Callahan novels stashed behind the counter for later. And after skimming the first few pages of one, I have to admit, Justin was right.

They are really fun.

11

VIPER

Fire.

I slide my tongue over my teeth as I stare at the woman before me, with hair the color of flames. Her eyes are fierce and angry. A spark, ready to ignite a bonfire.

No. That's not the right word, is it? It hits the ear wrong. Discordant.

A spark, ready to ignite...

"An inferno," I say with a grin. That's the word.

She raises an eyebrow at me. Not scared but apprehensive. Cautious. I smile a little wider, wanting to show her my teeth, wanting to see how she reacts to a predator.

"Excuse me?" she asks, arms crossed. When I don't answer, she huffs, tapping her finger against her arm in annoyance. "Look, buddy, you're going to need to order something or get out of line. I don't have all day."

She gestures toward the menu behind her, but it's all nonsense to me. What the fuck do I know about the difference between a latte and a cappuccino?

"Coffee," I order, ignoring the board. "Black."

"Size?" she asks impatiently.

I grin. "Big."

So fierce, this little spark. Even with me towering above her, even with most people on the street actively avoiding my eyes, trying so desperately not to look at my scars, she manages to glare at me, irritation written all over her face.

As she pours my drink, I stare into the glass case next to the register, full of buttery-looking treats.

Lavender bunny macarons, says the sign next to a line of lilac-colored cookies shaped like cartoon rabbit heads. The eyes are grotesque, a caricature of innocence and joy.

I haven't eaten since the private jet that dropped me back in Fortune City this morning. Daryl's wife and children are safe and sound—as safe as any of us are in this world—stashed in a city where the weather fluctuates between hot and hotter. Somewhere they'll never be found. It hits me suddenly how hungry I am.

"Give me two of those," I tell her, tapping on the glass. She slips a little glove over her hand before she reaches into the case for them. Her gloves aren't anything like the ones Doc makes me wear. Hers are clear and loose, the plastic paper-thin.

Can't use gloves like that in the lab. They'd be torn to shreds.

"That'll be twelve fifty," she informs me, setting the cookies on a plate next to the mug of coffee on the counter between us. Steam floats up from the mug, a tendril of heat stretching out for me.

Reaching into my pocket, I pull out a handful of cash, barely looking at it. I don't care about money. That's Doc's job. Even my paycheck, ostensibly paid through Sterling's company fund for some such bullshit I'm apparently listed as doing, doesn't mean shit to me. It's all piling up in a bank account somewhere, all those imaginary dollars, ones and zeros, stored who the fuck knows where. None of it is real. None of it concrete.

I peel a bill away from the rest and hand it to her, ignoring the way her jaw drops as she takes it.

"W-wait! Your change!" she says, as I scoop up my purchases.

"Keep it," I tell her. What the fuck would I do with it anyway?

I have everything I want right now. I grin down at the little rabbit cookies, stacked so nicely on their plate.

The world isn't built for people my size. The chair I force myself into is uncomfortably small, and the table looks like I could break it if I moved too quickly. But I'm too focused on the little cookies to care.

I snap one in half and slip it into my mouth, closing my eyes as I chew. Sweet, like sugar and cream.

Just how I imagine my little rabbit will taste.

12

SYDNEY

"You're not going to believe this," Jade says with a laugh, sliding the cash register drawer closed, "but that guy over there just paid with a hundred-dollar bill."

"Did you check it?" I ask. It's rare, but counterfeit currency does sometimes filter into our store. Paying for a small item with a big bill is usually a red flag for any small business.

"Yeah," she says. "Tested it with the pen and everything. It's real. But that's not even the crazy thing, Syd. He told me to keep the change. On a twelve-dollar purchase!"

"He must have been charmed by you," I tell her. She rolls her eyes, chuckling. "Listen, I'll be in the back checking inventory for the next few hours, okay? Will you be all right up here on your own?"

"Oh, please. I'll be fine," she assures me, waving me away. "Go. Do your stock, or whatever."

"Call me if you need anything!"

Jade gives me a salute, and I laugh, shaking my head at her as I make my way to the back of the store.

The truth is I've been actively avoiding going through our inventory, but I can't put it off any longer. I used to love sorting through our new stock and setting things out, planning exactly where everything should go to create the best, most authentic, atmosphere. Used to love placing orders, picking out what newest books we should carry.

I liked that it was a task that gave me room to think, to lose myself in my own mind.

But...

Last night proved where my mind will wander if left to its own devices.

The memories, the lust, the sex.

But those never stick. Those thoughts always give way to their violence, their lies, their anger.

But are you any different?

Yes, I tell myself, taking new inventory from a box and slamming it down against the stockroom table a little too hard. I don't look at the spot where Sebastian knelt to lick me, at where I'd sat on the edge of the table and let him ravage me.

I am different.

I'm not a violent person. Not anymore. I changed. I'm better now, all those dark thoughts, those angry urges, they're gone. Now I like reality TV where the contestants bake things, I like cookies straight from the oven, and books...

Books about rough sex, that voice inside me says.

Books about violence, it whispers, insidiously creeping into my mind. *About women who kill for the ones they love, without regret. About strong, angry men, who don't stop when they're asked, who take what they want and—*

I slam a book against the table, chest rising and falling quickly. Then, for good measure, I lift it up and slam it back down again and again. I'm inexplicably angry, furious with myself, with *them...*

It takes much more than counting to ten to calm me down this time. It takes almost twenty minutes of deep breathing and quiet, happy thoughts before I feel sane again.

I take all those dark, dirty thoughts. I take the memories of Sebastian, the memories of Ashton holding that riding crop, the memories of me—violent, hateful memories—and I put them aside. I'm not ready to confront all of that.

It takes most of the morning for me to sort through the new stock, taking frequent breaks to ball up those rising feelings and shove them down again. It's not until almost eleven when my stomach starts to loudly protest how little I've eaten that I take a break.

It's unnerving how hungry being angry can make you.

Time to grab something delicious from Jade's pastry case to tide me over for the next few hours. I think I'll treat myself to something especially decadent today. A little treat, maybe a croque monsieur. Yes, that would hit the spot.

Satisfied with my choice, I close the stock door behind me and stroll through literary fiction, heading toward the front and—

I freeze, heart pounding in my chest when I see him.

Viper.

No. No, no, no.

He's standing between me and the end of the bookshelf, blocking my way, an easy, terrifying smile on his face.

He's even scarier than I remember. I'd been so surprised, so panicked in the alley, I'd never really given him my full attention.

Now, I can't pull my eyes away from him.

He's beautiful, Ashton's deadlier counterpart. There's no fooling myself that Viper's muscles are for anything other than inflicting pain. His arms are covered in scars, some unfathomably deep, forming chasms in his flesh, and some that are shiny like burns. A huge scar mars his otherwise perfect face, slashing through his eyebrow and curving over his cheek.

He's insane.

That's the only thing I can think as I meet those dark, manic eyes. There's no kindness there, no humanity. Viper's eyes are a pit full of shadows.

And, as he stares at me, they're also full of lust.

"Hello, little rabbit." He grins, and there's nothing kind about it. "I've been waiting for you to come out of your hole."

I run.

It's purely instinctual, and I take off without giving it a second's thought. I turn and run as fast as my legs will carry me, away from him, my thoughts a blur. I need to hide. I need to get somewhere safe. The stockroom door has a lock, and even though it hadn't been enough to keep Sebastian out, maybe it will work on him. Maybe I can get there, maybe I can—

Viper crashes into me from behind, lifting me off the ground as he wraps his massive arms around my body. I try to scream, but his hand clamps over my mouth and nose, squeezing my face so hard it hurts.

He's laughing.

His body shakes with the force of it, his chest shaking as he holds me. He crushes my body against him, my back flattened against his chest, and I can feel his body convulse with the force of his laughter.

"Oh, little rabbit, little rabbit," he purrs into my ear. "You can't run from me. Not ever."

His breath is warm against my skin. With one last laugh, he closes his teeth around the shell of my ear, biting hard. I squeal in pain, the sound embarrassingly high-pitched and frightened.

I can't breathe. His hand is too tight around my face, suffocating me. I panic, struggling against him, kicking my legs, but he's too big, too strong. I could thrash with all my strength and still not move him an inch.

"If you scream, I'll take your tongue," Viper whispers in my ear. I whimper, my body going stiff. He means it. I know he does. "Do you understand?"

I try to calm myself, try to count to ten, try to think happy thoughts.

In the end, all I can do is nod against his hand, lungs burning for air and my heart pounding in my chest so hard it hurts.

"Good." Viper chuckles.

And he lets me go.

I stumble, gasping for breath, momentarily stunned by the sudden absence of him. Quickly, I spin around to face him. But Viper just stands there, smiling, head cocked to the side as though watching to see what I'll do.

Like I'm a toy he's playing with. Like I'm not even a person.

Suddenly, all that fear turns into hot rage. All the times I felt powerless, all the times I felt I needed to behave. All of that comes rushing back to me. Before I realize what I'm doing, I've slapped him across the face, hard.

His head snaps to the side at the force, but the smile never leaves his lips. If anything, he looks even more amused, his tongue snaking out to run over teeth.

Shit.

Clearly, I can't fight him. That much is obvious.

Hesitant, I take a step back, away from him.

He steps forward. Just enough, like he's keeping me close.

Okay.

I let myself go still, forcing my too-tense muscles to relax, trying to calm my breathing.

"Are you going to hurt me?" I ask. My voice sounds low and

monotone in my ears. Not terrified, the way I would have expected.

Viper tilts his head a little more, dark eyes sparkling.

"Do you want me to hurt you?" he asks, sounding genuinely curious.

I don't react immediately. Stunned, I just stand there, letting the words rattle around my skull. Then, I shake my head, just barely, from side to side.

"Pity," he says, lip curling just a little, showing his teeth. "I want to hurt you, little rabbit. You'd like the things I could do to you."

I shake my head again, more forcefully this time.

No. I wouldn't. I don't want to be hurt. I don't like being hurt. That's not me. That's not who I am.

The way Viper looks at me makes me feel like a liar.

"What are you doing here?" I ask.

Viper's grin is feral.

"Someone needs to watch over you," he coos in a sing-song voice. "Keep away all the big bad wolves."

"You're here to...protect me?" I interpret, not believing the words as they fall from my lips.

But he nods, eagerly. He steps forward, again, ignoring the way my body tenses and flinches away from him, ready to run again. He reaches up and touches a lock of my hair, curling it around his finger.

"Only we get to hurt you," he promises me, like it's meant to be comforting. "No one else. Only we get to watch you bleed."

I gulp.

Slowly, he slides his fingers from my hair and over my cheek, his touch gliding over my skin and down to my neck.

"So soft," he whispers, almost reverently.

Voice a little weak, I whisper, "Don't touch me."

The change is instant.

Viper's hand freezes. His eyes jump to mine, eyes so, so cold and angry.

I gasp as his fingers wrap painfully around my jaw, twisting my face up.

"We *own you*, little rabbit," he snaps. I whimper, his hand squeezing so tight his nails are digging into my flesh. "If I want to touch you, I will fucking touch you."

He jerks my head back even more, looming over me.

"If I want to cut you and play in your blood, I fucking will. Do you understand?"

I nod, head barely moving in his grip.

"Open your mouth," he orders.

I obey without thought, jaw dropping open.

I watch in horror as Viper leans down over me, lining up his face to mine, and spits into my open mouth.

The sound that escapes me is undeniably sexual.

"Mine," Viper growls, digging his fingers into my jaw as I swallow.

"Yes," I gasp.

He watches me for a few long seconds, eyes impossibly dark, before nodding.

"Good," he tells me, letting go and stepping back.

I stumble, nearly falling, at the loss of him.

And just like that, the rage is gone, replaced with manic insanity.

"I'm inside you now, little rabbit," Viper says, tapping a finger against my lips. "Can you feel it?"

I can't speak. Can't even nod.

Then he's gone, walking back through the shop toward the café, trailing his fingertips over the spines of books and humming as he goes.

And I'm broken. Irrevocably broken.

Because there's no possible justification for why I'm wetter than I've ever been in my entire life. No excuse for the fact that I want, desperately, for him to turn back around and come back to me.

13

ASHTON

"Wʜᴀᴛ ᴅᴏ ʏᴏᴜ ᴍᴇᴀɴ Vɪᴘᴇʀ ɪs ᴛʜᴇʀᴇ?" I sᴀʏ ɪɴᴛᴏ ᴛʜᴇ phone, panicked.

"It means exactly what I just said," Sebastian replies coldly. "He's there. At the café. With Sydney."

I pull the phone away from my ear and swear, reaching up to tug at my hair. The tape wrapped around my knuckles catches on a few strands, yanking them out. Fuck. *Fuck.*

"I'm in the middle of fight training," I snap. "It's going to take me an hour to get down there. You gotta go over there, Doc. You gotta pull him out of there and—"

"No," he says brusquely.

I blink, too shocked to register the words.

"Wait, what do you mean *no?*"

"I mean *no*, I am not going over there, and *no*, I'm not going to physically pull Viper out of her café, Ashton."

Panic rises in my chest.

"But... Why the fuck—"

"She asked us to stay away from her," he tells me, voice curt. "Remember? And she specifically told me not to come.

She says it's fine. He's just sitting there, not bothering her. She only mentioned it to me so I would be aware."

He's not bothering her *for now*. Who the fuck knows how he'll act five minutes from now?

But I'm too hung up on something else he said, my mind crashing to a stop.

"What do you mean she told you? Sydney called you?"

"Texted, but yes. She sent me a message a few minutes ago to let me know he was there. And telling me not to come."

I take my phone away from my ear and touch the screen, navigating to my own messages. The conversation history with Sydney—saved as Babygirl in my phone—just shows my last six text messages to her.

All unanswered. All unread.

"She didn't message me," I say, numbly, into the phone.

"Because you are not giving her *space*," Sebastian snaps. That fucking prick. "You really think she's ready to open those floodgates by texting you?"

"I haven't been back to the café! I'm giving her space!" It's taken every ounce of my self-control, but I *haven't* been back to see her, not since Alec told me that it would just be painting a target on her back, that I could be putting her in danger. Just like Viper is now.

"It's not just being there in person." Sebastian sighs in irritation. "All you do is message her, over and over. You're not respecting what she asked of you. And if you keep it up, you're going to push her away for good."

He doesn't even know the half of it. This *is* me restraining myself and giving her space, okay? Doesn't anyone understand that? But he's right about one thing. Obviously, I'm not giving her what she wants because...

She didn't message me. She messaged *him*.

I'm squeezing the phone so hard in my hand I'm surprised it doesn't snap into pieces.

Since when is he the one who knows how to deal with these situations? Since when is he the one she's reaching out to for comfort? To save the day?

I could fucking kill him.

"Ashton?" Sebastian prompts through the phone. "You still there?"

"I fucking hate you," I snarl.

Sebastian snorts. "Like I give a shit," he says dismissively. "Listen, I'll swing by if it'll help calm you down. I won't go in, but I'll keep an eye on things, make sure Viper is behaving."

My laugh is dry. "Yeah, sure, Doc. We all know how much you love to keep an eye on things."

"Fucking asshole," he mutters before hanging up.

Right back at you, prick.

Fuck, I'm a mess. Scheduling this fight was a terrible idea, with my mind all over the place and my heart definitely not in it, but...

There's the tiniest, tiniest chance she'll come next week, right? And that tiny, insignificant chance is looking more and more like all I have left.

I roll my shoulders and think: fuck it. Training is a bust for today, anyway, and I'm not in the mood to stick around and try to fit in another workout. I pack up my shit, and by the time I've showered and changed, there's a text message on my phone from Alec, telling me to meet him at work.

I almost ignore him. My team can handle things just fine without me. But it's been a while since I've shown my face at the office, and since the alternative is to head home and eat an entire pint of ice cream all on my own, I suck it up and head downtown toward the Sterling Enterprises main building.

Before I can even fully open the door to Alec's office, he's already up and out of his chair, glowering at me from over his desk.

"We have a fucking problem," he snaps, radiating fury.

Jesus, he looks terrible. The bags under his eyes are big enough to be considered luggage, and his dark stubble is uneven on one side, like he tried to shave and gave up before he finished. Even his suit is a mess, wrinkled and unkempt, with the top button undone. And with his temper set to 100, he's a heart attack waiting to happen.

"What happened?" I ask, dropping into the chair in front of him.

"Someone hit our supplies shipment. Blew them to high hell. I've been dealing with our feds all morning, trying to keep this from escalating above their heads. Apparently, it's not easy to keep a massive explosion from the public." He slams his fist down on his desk with a snarl.

"Calm down," I say, trying to pacify him. Bad idea, I realize, when his nostrils flare and he turns that fury on me. "Whatever you did obviously worked, right? Since this is the first I'm hearing of it."

"That's not the point," he spits out. "It's him, Ashton. It's Dante. I don't give a shit what Doc thinks. I know it's him. He's here, he's fucking with my business, and he's fucking with my girl."

"Our girl," I correct. A muscle in Alec's jaw tics, and for a second, I honestly think his head might explode.

"If I had known he might still be alive, I never would have started expanding into Empire City." He swears, running a hand over his dark hair. "Doc's wrong. Dante isn't just scouting. He's ten steps ahead of where we thought he was."

"Listen, losing one shipment isn't going to ruin us. We have contingencies for this sort of shit. Which shipment was it?"

"The fucking guns we needed from Tony Delmano." He pounds his fist into the table again.

"Let me handle it," I say, taking pity on him. Jesus, I've never seen him look this bad before. "It's one shipment. I'll get in contact with everyone and let them know there will be a delay. Sure, we lost some money, but it's negligible. We can't fall apart over this."

"I'm not falling apart. I am trying to manage this before it gets bigger. Right now, it's just one shipment. And it's *one* liquor license that's been revoked, threatening to delay our *biggest opening yet*. And it's *seemingly* only one guy gathering information on Sydney. But we know what he's capable of." He's pacing now, fists clenched at his sides. "When we decided to take his territory, we didn't have anything to lose. Now we do. And he knows it."

That's the real problem, isn't it? It's not the guns, not the money we'll lose arranging another shipment. It's her. Our girl.

"I'll handle it," I tell him, standing up and moving to the exit. I pause at the door, my hand on the knob. "By the way, not to drive you fully over the edge or anything, but that little talk you had with me about staying away from Syd?" I glance over my shoulder at him, watching a vein in his forehead pulse. "You might need to have that same chat with Viper. Sooner rather than later."

"FUCK!"

I step out, pulling the door shut behind me, just in time to hear something shatter as he tosses it against the wall. A startled intern passing by in the hallway shoots me a terrified look, eyebrows lifting at the sounds of swearing coming from Alec's office.

"Mondays, am I right?" I say, shooting him a grin.

He scurries away, face pale, and I wait until he's disappeared down a bend in the hallway before I head to my own office and shut the door.

I don't come here a lot. Honestly, the whole department probably runs better without me. But it's nice to have a place where I can be alone. Where I won't be overheard.

If Dante's really back, really here sniffing around our girl, we need to know why. Need to know what his plan is, what he wants with her.

And there is someone who might know. Someone who might even be willing to help us. She tried to warn us, didn't she? When she showed up on that security footage, when she let us catch a glimpse of her, that was a warning, right? Or a sign, or *something*.

Fuck, my brothers are going to kill me if I'm wrong about this. I fish my phone out of my pocket and dial her number, hoping like hell I'm not making the biggest mistake of my life.

It rings. And rings. And rings. When the call finally goes to voicemail, there's no cheery message, no robot telling me who I called isn't available. Just a simple *click*, to let me know it's recording.

"Uh, hey," I say awkwardly, shifting my weight from one foot to the other. "It's me. Ash. Long time no see, right?" I give a hollow laugh. "Listen... I just want to talk. I just..."

Just what? I don't even know.

I take a breath. Let it out. "Just call me, okay?"

She won't, though.

I hang up and stare at my phone, guilt settling into my stomach.

"I miss you, sis," I murmur.

14

SYDNEY

AT SOME POINT DURING THE DAY, VIPER SIMPLY VANISHES. One minute he's lounging in the café, watching me and scaring our customers, and the next he's just...gone.

I spend the rest of the day on edge, wondering if he'll pop out from behind a bookshelf, wondering if he'll grab me as I come out of the stockroom and pull me back inside. But he doesn't.

The next morning, there's another bouquet of lilies waiting for me, wilted and already past their prime. I half wonder if they're from Viper when I read the note attached: *I'm watching you.*

It feels like something he might leave for me, a macabre sort of courting gift. And I catch sight of him again, leaning against the alley entrance, watching our front door, when I drag the morning's trash outside. He gives me a wild grin that makes me hurry, tripping over my feet in my rush to get back inside.

But he doesn't follow me. And he doesn't bother me again.

After we close for the night, I consider sending another message to Sebastian to let him know Viper is still hanging around. But I hesitate, fingers hovering over the screen of my cell phone.

We haven't spoken since he touched me in the stockroom. An image of him standing over me, slipping his finger into my mouth, making me taste myself, suddenly leaps into my mind.

"Lick it clean."

I navigate away from the screen, swallowing hard, my face too warm.

I open Ashton's texts instead, quickly scrolling through all the messages I've been ignoring from him. It's a barrage of "Good morning, Babygirl" messages, reminders of his upcoming fight, mentions of some sort of carnival coming to town, and...are these knock-knock jokes?

Sighing, I press the button to send my phone to its lock screen and slip it back into my pocket.

Take out. That's what I need tonight.

Nothing fixes a stressful day like curling up under a blanket with a big bowl of pho and a good romcom. A nice, normal, romantic comedy where the protagonists kiss once at the end when they finally reveal their thinly veiled feelings. A movie about regular people who do not have complex reactions to dangerous men. People who don't fantasize about being chased down by a psychopath.

There's a Vietnamese place just a ten-minute walk from my apartment that never disappoints. I grab my jacket and phone, then head out, determined to satisfy my pho craving.

The night air is chilly, colder than I expected, as I step outside. Perfect weather for pho and a movie.

A car idles in the street outside my building, one headlight cracked and broken. I spare it a passing glance, curious. Someone waiting for a friend, maybe? Still, it's odd. This block usually goes dead after dark, when our shop closes for the night. There's not much reason for someone to linger in this area. It's almost suspicious.

The second I think it, I laugh, shaking the thought away. I've been reading too many of Justin's Blake Callahan thrillers, I guess. They're fun, but they're clearly making me paranoid. Everything *means* something in those books, you know? Every little detail is a clue, and every parked car could hold a potential killer.

Real life just isn't that interesting.

Except, when I turn the corner and start making my way toward the restaurant, the car moves too. It rolls forward, stopping at the intersection. Waiting. When I continue down the block, it moves with me, not speeding up or slowing down. Just keeping pace.

Definitely weird. I pull my jacket tighter, picking up my steps, hurrying down the block. I reach the crosswalk just as the lights start to turn, the walk signal flashing red, urging me to quicken my pace.

Crap.

I break into a jog, rushing out into the street. I'm almost at the other side of the intersection when I catch sight of a pair of headlights, barreling toward me.

Double crap.

But this isn't just someone running a red light. The car is aiming right at me, speeding into the wrong lane, coming at me *intentionally*.

I barely manage to get out of the way in time, diving for the opposite curb as the car swerves toward me. Frantic, I throw myself into the doorway of the closest building, hitting the wall brick entryway hard and turning to watch as the car jumps the curb and screeches to a stop, just inches away from me.

My heart is racing. Someone is shouting. Other cars are

honking, laying on their horns. I cower there, pressed against the doorframe, gasping for breath.

The car just sits there in front of me. Waiting.

I can't see the driver clearly, not with the headlights blinding me. All I can make out is the vague silhouette of someone wearing sunglasses, a cap pulled down low to cover their face.

They almost hit me, I realize, fighting to catch my breath.

They almost killed me.

My vision goes red, and fury overtakes the fear I'm feeling. There's a loose brick from the doorway at my feet, and I don't think twice about bending down to grab it. I raise it above my head, screaming, before slamming it down on the hood of the car, over and over again.

As if that broke some kind of spell, the car jerks into reverse, tires screeching before it peels away.

Oh, fuck that. I jog forward and throw the brick I'm holding after it, missing by a mile, and then bend down to grab a rock and throw that too.

"You better fucking run!" I scream after it, wishing I had more to throw. "Coward!"

My voice sounds foreign, raw. I'm shaking, I notice. Trembling so hard my teeth are chattering.

"Miss?" Someone steps forward from the crowd of people watching. "Are you okay? Do you need me to call someone for you?"

Call someone. Yeah, I need to call someone, I need someone who can help me, who can keep me safe. My fingers fumble for my phone, and I hit the first contact my thumb finds.

"Babygirl?" Ashton's voice is bright when he picks up. "Holy shit, I'm so glad you called!"

I don't answer right away, still shaking and trying to catch my breath.

"Syd? Is everything okay?" he asks.

"Sorry," I blurt out. "Sorry I...misdialed."

I hang up before he can say anything else, staring at my reflection in the black screen. I called him. Not the police, not Jade. Him.

After pushing them all away, at the first sign of trouble, I'm calling them to save me.

Good progress, Syd. Really working hard on that independence thing, huh.

My phone pings once. Twice. I shove it back into my pocket, too overwhelmed with everything to deal with it right now. The crowd around me has grown, and suddenly I'm surrounded by concerned faces, bystanders wanting to help. Someone is already on the phone with the cops, reporting what happened. Someone else is asking if I need a ride to the hospital to get checked for injuries.

Shaken, I tell them all I'm fine. I'm okay.

But what the hell just happened? Was this a drunk driver? Someone texting while driving?

Why would someone target me?

Ping.

Ping.

Ping.

Suddenly, my appetite is gone. I abandon my quest to get food and slip away from the crowd, deciding I'd rather just go home to shower and change into my pajamas, pho be damned. And even though my nerves are frayed, and I'm still sick with fear, I manage to fall asleep almost instantly when I finally crawl into bed.

Ping.

15

ASHTON

"Answer the phone, you goddamn bastard," I growl into Doc's voicemail.

I'm going to lose my mind. After the countless messages I've sent her, Sydney finally called me. I don't think I've ever been so relieved in my whole life. And then she was gone.

Just a few words, but I heard it in her voice. She was scared. She hung up before I could get a grasp on the situation, and now I'm sitting here with seven unanswered text messages, leg shaking, and waiting for Sebastian to *answer his goddamn phone*.

I'm two seconds away from grabbing my jacket and heading over to her apartment to check on her myself when my phone finally rings.

"*Finally*," I snarl when I pick up.

"What?" He says it like it's barely a question, clearly annoyed with me. I can't say the feeling isn't mutual right now.

"Where is Sydney?" I ask.

"For fuck's sake. You have to let this go. I don't have time to keep going over this with you," he snaps. For a calm and collected motherfucker, he sure is snapping a lot these days.

"That's not what this is! Just listen to me!" I take a breath, forcing myself to calm down. "She just called me. Something has her rattled, but she hung up before I could figure out what was going on."

A pause.

"When was this?" he asks.

"Thirty minutes ago. Right around the time I started *calling you incessantly*," I tell him. "You need to answer your fucking phone once in a while, you know that?"

Another pause, the longest of my life.

"Give me ten minutes."

The click on the other end of the line is the only sign he's hung up.

Fuck. *Fuck.* In the ten minutes it takes for him to call me back, I've worked myself up even more. I've invented at least fifty different scenarios that could have happened, ways someone could have hurt her.

I'll kill him. If Dante hurt her, if he scared her? I'll kill him. I'll finish what Doc started, I'll beat him until there's nothing left for even the best doctors in the world to put back together, I'll—

I almost drop my phone when it rings in my hand, and again when I fumble with it trying to answer.

"She's home," Sebastian says, the second I answer. "And she's not hurt."

"Something scared her," I insist. She sounded terrified. "Is there anyone else with her?"

"No. She's alone, safe and sound."

He's probably right. "She's really okay?"

"She's fine."

My shoulders relax. "You're sure?"

"Ash..." Sebastian releases a frustrated breath. "I am looking at her right now. She's in bed, sleeping. She's fine."

"She's in bed?" I pause and rub the back of my neck. "And you're watching her? That is... That is fucking creepy, bro."

On the other end of the line, Sebastian swears. "*You* were the one who asked me to come and check on her!"

"Yeah, but like..." I run a hand through my hair. "Looking through her window while she sleeps? That's another level."

"I'm hanging up."

"Wait! She's...she's really okay?"

A long, irritated sigh, followed by a click as he hangs up the phone.

I try to take calm, steadying breaths, but I'm too amped to relax right now. I need to get out of here, get some of this energy out of my body. I grab my keys and head for the garage.

———

I HAVEN'T SPENT NEARLY ENOUGH TIME PREPPING FOR MY upcoming fight. I'm not too worried, but with all this excess energy and adrenaline coursing through my body, it might help to get a few rounds in. When I enter the boxing gym, it's full of people. Not exactly what I want, but beggars can't be choosers. I set up at my favorite bag, take my shirt off, and start wrapping my hands. And as much as I want to feel the pain today, I decide against bare-knuckle boxing and pull on my gloves.

I've been here for nearly an hour, working the bag like my life depends on it. But it's like my adrenaline can't be burned away. I'm still buzzing, like there's electricity in my veins.

Punch.

Sydney doesn't trust me.

Punch.

Sydney was scared.

Punch.

Dante is after her. And she won't let me near her.

Punch.

Won't let me protect her.

Punch.

Punch.

Punch.

Frustrated, I take my gloves off and throw them at the ground. Nothing is working, and I feel like I'm about to self-destruct. It's almost like the harder I go at the bag, the more I need to move. I take my headphones out and try to calm myself.

Bad idea. Without the music blaring through my headphones, I can hear the entire gym around me, including the guys behind me chatting.

"Yeah, she's a dime, bro," one of them laughs, playfully punching his friend in the arm. "Ass you could bounce a quarter off."

Gross. They're both decently big guys, with a lot of muscle. But you can tell right away that it's all for show. Vanity muscles, not the sort you build for work, for function. Those muscles are just to look pretty. Or their version of pretty, at least.

"Didn't even take me that long to bag her. You'd think a girl like that would be smarter. Like... Who gets that drunk on the first date?" the second guy jokes back. "She knew what was going to happen."

My ears perk up. Now I'm interested in the conversation.

"It's pathetic, really. But what can you expect? They're all sluts, some just hide it better."

A low laugh. "By the time we got down to it she was barely conscious. Still a decent lay, though. I'd go back for a second round."

"Her body, your choice, am I right?"

My vision is tunneling. I can barely breathe.

This guy raped someone.

And he's here, in the middle of my gym, bragging to his friend completely unconcerned that someone might overhear him. With the energy under my skin buzzing, I shove my things back in my bag and casually stroll over to them, acting like I'm just taking notice of them next to the ring.

They look up as I get close, watching me.

"Hey man, what's your name?" I ask, keeping my voice casual.

"Uh, I'm Jordan," Mr. *I'm a fucking rapist* answers.

The guy next to him sputters, eager to make friends. "Hey, man, I'm Harrison. Nice to—"

"Cool." I ignore Harrison completely, staring down Jordan. "Want to go a few rounds in the ring? I need to finish up my workout, and I could use the practice."

I'm taller, but he's wider. From his point of view, I'm sure it feels like an even fight. Jordan seems taken aback by the offer, but he looks me up and down and then agrees. He really thinks those pretty muscles of his stand a chance against me.

"Sure, dude," he says. "Let's go."

We step into the ring, Jordan laughing a bit with his buddy, not taking this seriously. Why would he?

Barely conscious but still a decent lay. My muscles flex as I stretch my arms out, eager to get started.

"Gloves or no gloves?" I ask. Technically, it's against gym rules to spar without padding. But he won't want to look scared. And these men? These are the ones who never think there are consequences to their actions. Who make shitty fucking choices.

"I'm good either way," he answers with a shrug.

Perfect.

"No gloves, it is," I say, dropping mine outside the ring, flexing my hands.

We start to circle each other, and a group of spectators gathers to watch. I can hear it when the whispers start. This fuckbag may not recognize me, but others here sure do. It doesn't take long for the word to travel through the crowd. Someone nudges his friend Harrison and says something to him. When the guy's eyes go wide, I know he knows. He moves for the ring, trying to pull Jordan back from the fight, to warn him, but I'm faster.

My first punch sends him to the ground.

He wobbles as he stands, but I let him get back up. Make him think maybe it was just a lucky shot, make him think he has a chance. Because I'm not ready for this to be over, not yet. He holds his arms up more confidently when he advances on me, fury in his eyes. I hit him harder than I should have, harder than light sparring rules dictate, and I've seen it a thousand times before. My hit embarrassed him. He doesn't want to lose face, so he'll overcompensate by getting more aggressive. He throws an uncoordinated punch at me that I easily dodge and return with a right hook to his kidney. I follow that up with a series of hits that have him back on the ground.

He stands again, still not willing to accept that he's completely outmatched, and throws a wild swing at my head. It connects, but I barely even notice.

My next punch slams into him with an audible crack as his cheekbone breaks. He howls in pain as he hits the mat.

This time, I follow him to the floor.

I'm not fucking done.

Barely conscious but still a decent lay.

I punch him over and over again, without pause. His hand is out, begging for mercy, blood dripping onto the mat. I hear more cracking, more bones breaking, fracturing.

"Stop, man." Jordan is crying. "Please, I can't take any more."

I lower my face to his. "Why should I stop? Your body, my choice, isn't that right?"

And I level a final punch so hard, he's knocked out cold.

No one says anything. The gym is silent as a fucking grave as I stand up, wipe the blood off my hands and make my way over to his friend.

"Harrison, right?" The guy nods, swallowing, a look of pure terror in his eyes. "You have five minutes to drag your friend out of here. Consider your gym memberships revoked. And if I ever see you two even speaking to another woman in this city, this will look like a warm up, you understand? Don't fucking test me. I have eyes *everywhere*."

With that, I grab my bag and head out of the gym.

And wouldn't you know it.

I'm finally feeling better.

16

SEBASTIAN

Sydney has started sleeping with the lights on.

That's new. And while it makes it much easier to watch her from my spot in the tree, it worries me.

I lean back against the trunk and try to relax my tense muscles. Ash's phone call yesterday wasn't that surprising. He has a tendency to overreact when he's upset, catastrophizing the smallest things. But maybe he was right this time. Something scared her, something we missed. She's unnerved, frightened and jittery as she gets ready for bed.

It's not exactly comfortable here, with my legs stretched out on a thick branch while I lean my back against the trunk. The rough bark digs into my shoulder blades, making me itch. But I've had much worse places to run surveillance.

I shift with a groan and lift my phone to my ear, pressing the screen to dial.

It feels like it rings forever.

"Hello?" Sydney says when she finally answers. "Seb?"

Hearing her voice is like a cold knife straight through me. I close my eyes, savoring the pain.

Fuck, I love the way she says my name.

"The restraining order was finalized today," I tell her, keeping my tone neutral. Calm. "I left all the documentation on your doorstep. It's signed already. This is just for your records."

Because I promised you I would.

Because I'd do anything for you.

"Oh!" She sounds surprised. "I, uh... I didn't even hear you. You could have knocked."

I hear her make her way through her living room and to the door. She opens it, stooping down to gather the packet I left for her.

"I didn't want to disturb you," I tell her.

After she closes and locks her door, she makes her way back to the bedroom, setting the packet down on her bed. I watch as she stares down at it, biting her nails. I have to swallow my knee-jerk reaction to tell her to stop.

I hate Alec for making me do this, almost as much as I love him for it. Because *fuck* I've been wanting an excuse, any excuse, to see her. To watch her.

Ashton was right. I'm not dating her. I'm not someone she chose, not the prince charming type like him and Alec. I'm just someone who got her off.

Once.

I have no claim to her at all. I only have this—watching her from a distance, when she doesn't even know I'm here. I let my head fall back until the back of my skull hits the tree behind me. Fuck, I'm pathetic.

"Look, at the end of the day, that restraining order is just a piece of paper," I explain. "It doesn't offer much in the way of real protection."

She chews her nails a little harder, face pinched with worry.

"I think you need some extra security, Sydney," I say, finally cutting to the chase.

"You might be right." She hesitates before continuing. "Jade wanted me to move in with her for a while. She's really worried. I think we'd both feel better if things were a bit more... secure."

"Are you considering it?" I ask, brushing a speck of dirt off my pants.

"Considering what?"

"Moving in with her?" It would make my job harder. So much harder.

After a moment, Sydney shakes her head. "No," she says into the phone. "There's no room, anyway."

Good. "If you're staying, we should really get you more security. For the shop and, uh...your apartment."

Sydney visibly tenses. "What exactly would that look like?" she asks, in a hard voice. "The security, I mean. In my apartment."

"No cameras," I insist. "Not in your home, not unless you want them. I'd like some for your store, and some basic security upgrades. An alarm package, better locks, maybe a gate for your front stairs."

At least she seems to be considering it.

"No camera in my room?" she presses. "You're not planning on spying on me, right?"

I deserve the skepticism I see on her face.

"No cameras in your home. And no spying," I promise, trying to convince myself that, technically, watching her from the tree outside her window isn't spying. Right. "Not if you don't want me to."

Tell me you want me to. Tell me you want the cameras, tell me you want me watching you.

Tell me anything.

She chews her lip.

"I don't know." She fluffs her hair nervously. "How much would this cost? It feels a bit over-the-top, and I'm not sure we can afford a full security upgrade right now."

"Sterling will pay for the entire thing," I assure her. "I can move the money around in a heartbeat. No cost at all to you or Jade."

She shifts on her feet, clearly uncomfortable with the idea.

"Sydney," I sigh. "Be reasonable. This is a drop in the bucket for him. For us. Ash spends more on hair care products than this will cost me to set up. Just let us do this for you. For my own sake of mind."

She stops shifting.

"Does he really?" she asks, interest piqued.

"Does he really what?" I ask, flicking a twig out into the dark.

"Does Ash really spend that much on hair products?" she clarifies, a small smile curving her lips.

"Christ, you have no idea." I chuckle into the phone. Sydney laughs, hand coming up to cover her mouth like she's trying to hide it. "Every month, he manages to spend a little more, too. It's a nightmare. That idiot is an incorrigible fucking narcissist."

She laughs again, and it twists something in my chest to hear it.

"So, the security?" I press.

"Yeah... Yeah, okay. You can put it up. But nothing in my apartment, okay?"

I tell myself the emotion that floods me at her acquiescence is relief, not anticipation. Not a carnal desire to watch her, whenever I want, while she's at work. Not the ephemeral joy in knowing that if I can't have her, at least I can have *this*.

Even the smartest of us lie to ourselves when we need to.

"One other thing, while I have you." I pause, not sure how to broach the subject. "Ash said you called him the other day. He was really worried about you. I just want to make sure everything is okay. Did anything else happen?"

"Oh, that. Um, it was silly. Just a traffic incident. I was a little shaken and I...I didn't mean to call him." She takes a breath. "I *shouldn't* have called him."

"You're sure everything is okay?" I ask.

"Yup." She smiles when she says it, that big fake smile she wears so poorly.

She's lying. I know she's lying.

I just need to figure out why.

17

SYDNEY

Overnight, the weather shifts. When I drag myself out of bed, the usually bright Fortune City sky is dark, full of black and gray storm clouds thick enough to blot out the sun. You can feel it in the air, that current of electricity that precedes a storm. It doesn't rain often here, but when it does, it's torrential. Months' worth of water pouring from the sky in just a few hours.

By the time I'm ready to leave for work, the first raindrops have just started to fall. I close my door, frowning up at the clouds, and estimate I have maybe a minute to get downstairs before the sky really opens up and this drizzle becomes a downpour.

The soft click of another door closing draws my attention, and I pause, keys still in hand, peering down the walkway at the empty apartment next to mine.

Someone's in there, I realize, taking a step closer. I can hear the shuffling sounds of someone moving inside, just beyond the door.

Has someone moved in? No, I'd have seen moving boxes,

wouldn't I? Maybe it's whoever Sebastian hired, coming to install the new security system. But why would they be next door? Why would they need to—

The new owners.

I let out a shaky breath and nearly laugh in relief. Of course. I'd almost forgotten about the building being sold. No one has reached out to us yet with the new lease agreement, but it would make sense, wouldn't it? They're inspecting the empty unit, probably getting it ready to rent.

I've enjoyed not having neighbors, but maybe it won't be such a bad thing to have someone living next door. There's a certain safety in it, in having someone so close by.

I listen to the sounds on the other side of the wall for a moment, unable to tear myself away. I should introduce myself, maybe bring them something later, if they're still here. A batch of Jade's cookies, maybe. She makes the greatest, most delicious chocolate chip cookies the world has ever known, topped with a sprinkle of sea salt, and made with fair-trade dark chocolate chunks. Everyone deserves to taste them at least once in their lifetime. And who knows? Maybe a delicious treat might convince them not to raise our rent by too much...

Thunder rolls in the distance, pushing away all my thoughts of chocolate cookies and new neighbors. A fat drop of rain hits the walkway next to my feet. And then another.

"Crap, crap, crap," I mutter, bolting down the stairs.

By the time I reach the street, the drizzle has turned into an all-out downpour, and I barely make it inside the shop without getting completely soaked.

There's no sign of Viper outside the shop, skulking around the alley today. I don't blame him. Who would want to be outside in this weather? But he isn't inside the shop either, I notice, after I sprint inside. I'm not sure how I know that, but I just...do. There's a tension between my shoulder blades, a fear that wasn't there before.

I'm *comforted* by knowing he's nearby, I realize.

Because he's the scariest thing out there, that dark voice inside me says. *And he's claimed you as his. He wants you. He won't let anyone else have you, won't let them hurt you.*

No one but him.

Shut up, shut up, shut up. I shake the rain from my hair, pushing those thoughts away.

Business is slow throughout the day. The weather isn't exactly welcoming, and the sheets of rain coming down keep foot traffic to a minimum. A few determined customers wander in for coffee and a pastry, but the shop feels empty and far too quiet without our usual crowd of customers. I let Justin cover the back register and take care of replenishing the shelves while I hover near the café, helping Jade bus tables and take orders.

When traffic to the café hits an even worse lull, I do my best to distract myself with all the little chores around the shop that need finishing. A stack of empty cardboard boxes from this week's deliveries needs to be taken out to the recycling, and I drag them from the stockroom toward the side exit, struggling to wrangle them all.

But something stops me as I'm about to step outside into the alley.

The narrow alley between our building and the next has always been dark and creepy, but the storm makes it even worse. Rain sluices down the sides of the buildings and pools on the concrete, thunder rumbling in the distance, but it's not the weather that makes me pause, one foot out the door.

Something is wrong.

A chill runs down my spine. I feel like someone is watching me, waiting for me. And there's a noise, barely discernible over the sounds of the storm. A rustling so faint it's almost inaudible, coming from the bins. Too deliberate to be just the rain.

Two months ago, I would have told myself it was nothing. Forced myself to laugh it off, convinced myself it was my anxieties getting the best of me, making me paranoid. But now? I glance down the dark alley and feel the hairs on the back of my neck rise.

Now, I'm learning to trust my intuition. And if my instincts are telling me something is wrong...

I take a step back into the safety of my shop and let the door close.

Backup. I need backup.

Justin is kneeling in front of one of our endcap displays, arranging some new titles, when I find him. He has an eye for this part of the business, setting up the display almost exactly the way I would. I walk up behind him and clear my throat nervously.

"Hey," I murmur, wringing my hands. He glances up, giving me his full attention. "Can you do me a favor? I think I heard something out in the alley when I was taking out the recycling. Probably nothing, but could you go check?"

"You're right, it is probably nothing," he says, turning back to his work. A spark of irritation flares to life inside me at being dismissed so easily, but before I can defend myself, he finishes placing the last book and stands, dusting his hands over his jeans. "But I'm glad you came to get me. If something feels off, then we should check it out."

"Oh," I say, stunned at his quick support. "Uh. Yeah, thanks. Oh! I left some boxes by the doors, if you could—"

"I'll grab them!" He shoots me an easy grin as he walks off, heading toward the exit.

Huh. I guess I shouldn't be so shocked, but it's nice to feel like someone takes my worries seriously.

I drift back to the café where Jade is reorganizing our mugs, clearly starved for things to do.

"I may have just sent your brother to a grisly death," I tell her when I reach the counter. I lean my back against it, frowning at the side exit that leads into the alley. Maybe I should have gone with him? "Sorry about that."

"Well, at least if he's dead, he won't be crashing on my couch anymore," Jade answers breezily.

"True," I admit. I glance over my shoulder at her. "Plus, imagine the attention you'll get now that you're an only child. And double Christmas gifts!"

Jade laughs just as the door opens, and Justin calls out, "Uh...guys?"

We both turn. He's standing in the doorway, dripping, soaked from just a few seconds out in the storm. His dark hair is plastered flat to his face, his shirt clinging to his body. And he's cradling something against his chest, hiding it, as he makes his way through the café toward us.

"Was there someone out there?" I ask, pulse skipping.

"Maybe." His brows knit as he steps closer. "I thought I saw someone, for just a second. But then I heard something digging around under the trash, and..." He adjusts his hands, to show us what he's holding.

A kitten. A dirty, sopping-wet gray kitten, cradled against his chest, with bright yellow eyes too big for its face. It peers around the café from over Justin's fingers, ears flat, and when it sees me, it lets out the smallest, most miserable mewl, showing a flash of pink tongue and tiny needle teeth.

"Ohhh!" Jade squeals, melting into a puddle. "It's a baby!"

"I checked around, in case there were any more or the mother was nearby, but..." Justin trails off, shaking his head. "I think he's all alone."

The kitten blinks at us, shivering in his arms. And despite

the mud and the bedraggled fur, it's easily the most adorable thing I've ever seen.

"Oh my God," Jade whispers, clutching at my arm and shaking me. "It's too cute, I can't take it. I'm gonna die."

"It's filthy," Justin murmurs, stroking a thumb gently down the cat's spine. "Probably starving. Do you two mind cleaning him up while I run and get supplies?"

"Of course!" Jade exclaims at the same time I mutter, "I don't know…"

Jade shoots me a scandalized look.

"I just don't think you should get attached," I try to explain. "Your apartment doesn't allow pets, remember?"

I've caught her scrolling shelter pages more times than I can count, pining over all the animals she can't have. This is a guaranteed heartbreak waiting to happen.

"But your place does," Jade quickly counters. She's right, and I'm ashamed to say it hadn't even occurred to me that I could take in a kitten. I've never had a pet before. "And besides, just because we're cleaning him up doesn't mean we're keeping him!"

"Actually, I think it's a her," Justin says, lifting the cat's tail to check. The kitten hisses and bats at him with a small paw, flashing sharp white claws and tiny pink toes. "Sorry, ma'am," he murmurs, letting her tail go.

I chew my lip. "Fine. We'll clean her up, feed her, and then take her to a shelter. But we can't keep her."

The look of glee Justin and Jade share makes my stomach drop. Conspirators. I'm surrounded by conspirators.

"We *can't* keep her," I repeat, louder.

———

We're keeping her.

While Justin runs to the closest pet store for supplies and Jade watches the store, I take my brand-new kitten into our staff bathroom and give her a bath in the sink. All it takes is some patience, a few dozen bloody scratches to my arms, and a little dish soap to reveal that her fur isn't gray at all.

By the end of her bath, I'm left holding a grumpy and very fluffy, pristine white kitten.

A pristine white kitten with a strong set of lungs.

"MEOW!"

"I think she's hungry," Jade says. The kitten squirms in my grasp, fur wet and spiky from her bath, half wrapped in a towel. The world's grumpiest burrito. She yowls again, even louder this time, throwing back her tiny head to scream her fury to the world.

Jade finishes pouring a drink for a customer and pulls out a hard-boiled egg from the fridge. I watch her cut it into bite-sized pieces before scooping it into a saucer.

"Here you go, baby," she coos, setting the saucer on the ground. The kitten nearly claws the towel to shreds in her rush to get out of my hands and down to the food.

"I don't know, Jade, can she eat that?" I ask, setting her on the ground. But apparently the *she* in question thinks the answer is *yes*. She attacks the bits of egg with an aggression that can only be described as terrifying.

Frowning, I pull out my phone and quickly search: *Can kittens have egg?*

"Kittens can have a little hard-boiled egg," the first article informs me. "As a treat."

Fine. A piece of yolk falls over the side of the dish, and the kitten quickly laps it up straight off the floor. "This is just a treat," I inform her. "Do not get used to it."

She ignores me.

By the time Justin returns—arms overloaded with shopping

bags—the egg is gone, and the kitten has fallen fast asleep on the belly of the two-foot-tall stuffed bee Ashton gifted me. I'd completely forgotten about shoving the damn thing behind the bakery counter until she pulled it out with her teeth and decided it was a perfectly acceptable bed.

"Don't worry, I got her a *real* cat bed for the stockroom," Justin assures me, unloading the bags on the café floor next to me. It looks like he bought half the store. "And another one for your place upstairs." He pauses, glancing at me sheepishly. "Just until we find her a forever home, of course."

I sigh, staring at the kitten. She's condensed herself into a tiny ball of fur, paws tucked against her belly, happily napping on Ashton's bee. When I reach out to stroke her between her ears, she purrs and rubs against my fingers. Who am I kidding? I'm never giving her up.

"And I got some different types of food. The woman at the store said we should mix water into it in case she's dehydrated. Speaking of! I also picked up a cat fountain."

"What's a cat fountain?" I ask.

"Cats like flowing water," Justin explains. "At least, that's what the woman told me. So it's best to give them a water source where the water is constantly flowing. This one looks like a little koi pond, and it's got fish painted on the bottom. Oh! I also grabbed some toys!" His grin is boyish, excited.

The kitten opens one yellow eye, ears perking up as he starts pulling out toys for her. He's already removed the tags and plastic, I notice. Baby proofed. "Since we don't know what she'll like, I got a variety and—"

The moment he pulls a small plush bee from the bag, the kitten sits upright, both eyes fixed. It looks like a miniature version of the one she's sleeping on right now.

"Oh, you like that, do you?" Justin wiggles it at her. There's a bell inside, jingling as he shakes it. "Is this a good one? A good toy?"

She trills in answer, making biscuits with her front paws. When he sets the toy down on the ground, we both move back a little to give her room to jump down and play.

She doesn't. After she navigates her way off the giant bee, she steps forward, moving on the tips of her paws like a dancer. She gives the toy a single light bop with her paw and then picks it up in her mouth.

A loud purr erupts from her chest.

"Don't you want to play with it?" Justin reaches out as if to take it from her, but the kitten scampers back, her purr morphing into a growl, back arching.

"You like bees, huh?" I muse. "Maybe we'll call you Beatrice. Bea for short."

"That's so corny," Justin groans. "Bea? Really?"

But the kitten purrs louder, falling onto her side with the bee still clamped in her mouth, and rolling onto her back.

"Okay, fine." Justin raises his hands in defeat. "Beatrice, it is."

"Hey, Justin?" I dig through one of the bags, frowning. "Did you only get toys and food?"

"Yeah? What else was I supposed to get?"

I give him a look. "A litter box, maybe?"

Justin freezes. "Crap. I'll be right back!"

It takes him two more trips to get everything we need, but by the time he clocks out for the day, Bea has everything a kitten could ever dream of.

18

SYDNEY

"Excuse me, I'm looking for a Jade Lee and a Sydney Sinclair?"

I glance up from where I'm straightening books, and peer around the shelf toward the voice coming from the café. A remarkably beautiful woman with sleek black braids and an immaculate Armani pantsuit is standing at the counter, briefcase in hand.

"Well, you're looking at one of them," Jade says with a flirtatious grin. That girl can't help herself when presented with a pretty face. It's like she was born to flirt. "And the other is in the back, if you want me to get her?"

"I'm here," I say, stepping out from between the bookshelves. I wipe my palms on my pants to dry them, suddenly nervous. "What is this about?"

"You're Miss Sinclair?" the woman asks. When I nod, she continues. "I'm here on behalf of my client, Virgil Incorporated. They recently acquired your building."

Jade blinks rapidly. "Wait, Dorothy sold the building?" she asks, frowning in confusion. "Without telling us first?"

I wince.

"She did, actually. Tell me, at least," I admit. A flash of hurt crosses Jade's face, quickly turning to anger. "I'm so, so sorry, I meant to tell you! I just let myself get so distracted lately."

The anger in her eyes dims a little. "We'll talk about it later," she says quietly so only I can hear. Crap. She's really pissed.

The woman from Virgil Inc. glances between the two of us, but her face stays perfectly professional. "I wanted to touch base with both of you about your new lease. But if now is a bad time..."

"No, now's fine," I insist, ushering her to one of the café tables. My nerves are buzzing as I sit down. "Can we get you anything, a coffee maybe?"

A soft weight lands in my lap the moment I get situated. Beatrice. She must have crept over from her bee-nest by the counter. She circles once, twice, then plops down with surprising force and stretches out across my thighs. Her purr vibrates straight through me, absurdly loud for her size.

"No, thank you, I'm fine," the lawyer insists, taking the seat across from me. She places her briefcase on the table and opens it, removing a stack of documents from inside.

Jade pulls over a seat from another table, and I stroke Bea absentmindedly, fingers trailing over her long fur. I can't seem to keep still. Jade shoots me a nervous look, and I return it with a small, hesitant smile, reaching out to squeeze her hand tightly.

"To the moon and back," I mouth at her. She purses her lips but gives my hand a small squeeze in return.

"So, you mentioned a new lease?" I prompt, trying to start us off. "Does that mean the new owner wants to keep us as tenants?"

The woman nods, still sorting through her files. "Oh, yes. The owner has insisted on some changes to your previous agreement, effective at the end of the month. You will remain on the old lease until then, at which point you—"

"I'm sorry," Jade blurts out, voice a little shrill. "Until *the end of the month*? So, what, if we don't agree to these new terms, we have less than two weeks? To be out of here?"

Bea meows sharply, like she's echoing Jade's outrage. I shift my fingers to scratch her under the chin until she tips her head back in bliss and shuts her eyes, quieted again.

The woman stops sorting, glancing up through her dark lashes at Jade. "Well, yes. I suppose that would be the case."

"That can't be legal!" Jade shouts in frustration. She levels another furious look my way. "Fuck, Syd... If you'd told me, we could have been preparing for this."

I know. I feel sick, guilt threading its way through my stomach. This is my fault. I should have told her, should have let her know the second Dorothy told me.

"I assure you, everything in this contract is legal and fully vetted. I should know, I'm the one who drafted it," the lawyer states matter-of-factly, unfazed by our in-fighting.

"But that's not enough time," I insist. It's not just the store, either. My apartment—my *home*—is part of this building. If we have to shut down, have to try and move to another location, where am I supposed to go?

Now it's Jade who's fidgeting, Jade whose leg is bouncing up and down a little too quickly under the table.

"May I suggest you read the document, before you start discussing alternative solutions?" She finally pulls a contract from her stack of papers and slides it over the table for us. I practically snatch it from her, Jade leaning over my shoulder to read.

"That is the new lease agreement," she tells us, removing a pen from her briefcase, and setting it next to me. "I think you will find the new terms to be very agreeable."

My eyes roll over the document, only taking in every other word. It's a standard agreement, almost copied and pasted from our old lease with Dorothy. I turn the page, nearly ripping it off the staple as I scan it for the information I'm looking for.

Finally, at the very bottom of the third page, I find it. Our new rental cost.

I read the number written there.

I blink.

I read the number again.

I feel rather than hear Jade's quick intake of breath next to me.

"This..." I flip back a page to read more carefully. "This must be some sort of mistake. This can't be right."

"Sydney," Jade whispers, staring at the numbers on the page.

"A mistake?" The woman raises one perfectly manicured eyebrow. "I assure you, Miss Sinclair, I don't make mistakes."

I turn to the final page, eyes wide, searching frantically for something I know I'm missing, some sort of explanation.

"But this..." I swallow. "This is *less* than we're currently paying."

A lot less, I think, but don't say that out loud. This is a better deal than I could have ever imagined for us.

Next to me, Jade lets out a bark of a laugh, quickly covering her mouth.

"It is," the woman agrees, nodding. "As I said to you before, I expect you two will find these new terms very agreeable."

"But I don't understand." Bea pokes her head above the table and stretches out one paw to smack the corner of the paper.

"Bea approves," Jade laughs, her voice shaky. "Wait, are pets allowed?"

The lawyer eyes Bea warily as she scrambles onto the table.

"There is nothing in the lease that disallows it. But"—she purses her lips together, like she disapproves—"I would recommend checking with the city ordinances about allowing a pet in any area that serves food."

I'm still too stunned by the rent cost to do anything but sit there, staring. Sighing, the lawyer takes the document from me and turns to the final page. Next to our names is a bright and friendly yellow sticker that says *sign here*. She uncaps her pen and hands it to me.

"The new owner is very motivated to keep you as tenants. Especially considering the internet buzz surrounding this location. Virgil Inc. owns the building next door as well, so it is in his best interest to keep you happy with the terms of your rental agreement, so you stay. If this business is doing well, whatever goes in next door will likely *also* do well, meaning more money for everyone. It's a win-win."

"Is this Alec's doing?" Jade murmurs to me. She keeps her voice low, but I know just from glancing at the woman watching us that she overheard. Her face is impassive, not even a flicker of recognition at the name.

"Maybe. Or Ash," I answer, my mind reeling. "But... They never said anything to me about it."

"Would they, though?" Jade asks, looking skeptical. "It's not like he asked you about the social media stuff."

She's right. I stare down at the rental agreement, my mind reeling. That's the only explanation that makes sense here, isn't it?

Do you even want to sign it if this is their doing? Do you want to be even more tied to them?

"Could you tell us anything about the new owners?" I ask, glancing up. "Give us a name, or...?"

She shakes her head, slowly.

"The owner has asked to remain anonymous," she explains,

as though this is a perfectly normal thing. "But, as I said, it's in his best interests to keep you on as tenants."

Jade raises her eyebrow at me. "Oh? It's in *his* best interests, hm?"

I let out a long breath. Yep. That definitely makes it sound like it's one of my boys.

"What do you think?" I ask Jade, frowning. "Should we sign, or...?"

Or *what?* I think to myself. What's even our alternative here?

Jade snorts and reaches for the pen. "Syd, if those men really believe your pussy is worth almost twenty percent off our rent, who the hell am I to argue?" She sets her pen on the document, signing her name in black ink.

I blush, glancing quickly at the woman as she watches Jade sign, but there's no judgment or curiosity in her eyes. She looks bored, completely uninterested in Jade's flippant comment. Jade pivots the document toward me, handing me the pen. Bea rubs against my hand as I take it.

There's a part of me that argues against signing, that doesn't like the idea of being indebted to Alec, or Ash, or any of them in this way.

But what other choice do I have?

Fuck it.

I add my own signature quickly, barely glancing at it before I hand the contract back to the woman waiting.

After she packs up her things and leaves, I look up from the copy she left with us to see Jade staring daggers at me.

"Sydney Marie Sinclair," she says with a scowl, hands on her hips.

I flinch at the anger in her voice. "Oh no, not the middle name."

"If I could add extra middle names to express how pissed

off I am, I would. How could you not tell me about this? I'm your *partner!*" Her voice breaks over the last word, her eyes starting to fill with tears.

"I know, I'm sorry." I rush to get the words out. Jade and I *never* fight. Just the idea of upsetting her makes me break out in a panic sweat all over my body.

"I need more than just a sorry, Syd. This isn't okay! How is this any different from how the guys have been treating you? You kept this from me! And you lied to me, every time you came into work and didn't tell me about this! It's self-involved and *mean.*"

My chest constricts, and I feel a round of panic sweats coming on. I didn't even think about that.

"You're right," I admit, swallowing hard. "I'm so sorry. I wanted to fix it, and I didn't want you to worry, but you're right. I should never have kept that from you. We're partners, Jade. And I *know* we're stronger together. It'll never happen again. I swear to you."

I can see her thinking, mulling over what I'm saying. After a few painful seconds, she finally sighs and says, "Fine. I forgive you. But you owe me a present."

I step forward to wrap her in a hug. "A big one," I promise.

———

LATER, AS I'M CLOSING THE SHOP FOR THE EVENING, MY phone buzzes with a text from Sebastian.

> Seb: Your new security system will be installed tomorrow. The crew has already been paid, all you need to do is let them in in the morning so they can set everything up.

I send him a quick thanks in response and gather up all my

new kitten supplies to head home. I'm stumbling up the back-stairs towards my apartment, Bea nestled safely in her new cat carrier and a lifetime supply of pet accessories in my arms, when I spot something that makes my blood run cold.

My door is open. Not wide open, just slightly ajar, enough to see inside.

It was storming earlier, and it was windy, but I can't imagine not at least *shutting* my door. I'm usually meticulous about locking it.

I keep Bea in her carrier as I do a thorough check of my apartment, searching it top to bottom, but nothing seems to be missing. Nothing has been moved or taken.

But it's strange.

Unsettling.

I spend the rest of the evening constantly looking over my shoulder, feeling like I'm not entirely alone.

19

SYDNEY

THE NEXT DAY, AS PROMISED, THERE ARE FOUR WORKMEN waiting for me when I go to open the shop. And to confirm, Sebastian sends me a text message explaining exactly what they'll be doing and why. He refers to them each by their name, instructing me to message immediately if any of them disrupt my work.

It takes them most of the day to finish the installation, but at least they keep to themselves, moving through the shop like ghosts, setting up cameras and sensors and doing their best to politely ignore me and Jade (and Bea, who not once but twice manages to make off with a spool of their wire, forcing them to chase her around the store to retrieve it).

It's a relief when they finally finish, packing up their things and taking off. A relief not because of the disruption, but because of the sudden weight that's been lifted from my shoulders, knowing that extra security is in place, and someone is watching over me and our store.

It's strangely comforting to know that. And maybe I should be second-guessing their motives. Maybe I should remember that it's a better idea to keep these men at arm's length. Maybe I shouldn't be putting so much faith in a man I know likes to... watch.

But you want him to watch, don't you? You like it when he watches you.

Nope. Not thinking about that. Definitely not today. Because today, of all days, I don't need the extra stress.

It's finally the second Friday of the month.

Book club.

I arrange the chairs hours in advance in the center of the shop, where there's a big enough gap between the aisles to accommodate everyone, and still barely manage to have everything set up by the time they filter in.

I wish I had the chance to join them tonight. Especially with the book they're discussing: *The Prince's Knife*, still one of my all-time favorites. But I've fallen behind on some of our bookkeeping and promised Jade I'd keep on top of it. So it's not until almost closing time that I manage to sneak by the group and catch a snippet of their discussion.

When I finally do, the voice I hear rising above the others makes me pause.

"See, that's what I'm having trouble with here," Justin is saying, sounding confused. "How is Malachi the hero of this story?"

I peak around the corner, to be sure, and there he is, seated in the circle of women, leaning forward with his elbows on his knees. His copy of *The Prince's Knife* is resting on his lap, and the women in the circle are giving him their full attention, excited but nervous to have a good-looking guy join the group and express an interest in their favorite books. I get it. He's cute, with his artfully disheveled pitch-black hair, and those dimples...

I can tell why these women might be in a bit of a tizzy over him.

But I've known Justin for too long, it's hard to picture him as anything but the little kid who used to give Jade wet willies and cut the power during our horror movie marathons to hear us scream. So, even though I have to admit that he's become objectively *very* attractive, I just can't separate him from the lanky brat he once was.

"Take the forest scene, for example," Justin is saying, tapping his fingers against his knee. "In what world is he not the villain here?"

"It's all about perspective," Jennifer is telling him. When he glances over at her, she shifts slightly under his gaze, touching her hair nervously. "That scene is written from Phaedra's point of view for a reason. When Malachi finds her in the forest and ties her to that tree, we know she consents. She wants him just as much as he yearns for her."

There are murmurs of agreement.

"Okay," Justin concedes. "But *Malachi* doesn't know that. He doesn't even give her a chance to consent. I mean, he only removes the gag once, and he only does it to put his dick in her mouth, so—"

Julia erupts into a shocked giggle, drowning out Justin's next words.

"Sorry." She blushes, covering her face with one hand and waving her outburst away with the other. "Nervous habit."

A few of the other women in the circle grin, blushing. It's fun reading these books, discussing them with our friends, and sharing our fantasies in a safe space together. But there's always a dynamic shift when a man enters those spaces, even when they have the best intentions. We might be able to read these books stone-faced in public, but having him here is like being caught watching porn. It shouldn't be embarrassing, but it somehow is.

And it's extra embarrassing to be discussing them in front of a man who looks like Justin. A man who could—with a few personality tweaks—be one of these characters.

"Hang on, though. He's a vampire, right?" Sarah points out. "So, he can like… smell her arousal, can't he?"

Justin goes still while the other women around the circle nod in agreement. He blinks once. Twice.

"I'm so sorry," he says with a deep breath, a pink blush spreading over his face, turning the tips of his ears red. "Did you just say he can smell her arousal? Because he's a vampire?"

Jennifer nods enthusiastically.

"That's just canon," Sarah explains, like it's the most obvious thing in the world. "Werewolves can do it, too."

"And the fae," Jennifer adds.

"That's…" Justin takes another deep breath. "That's a thing? In these books?"

"In fantasy romance? Yeah," Sarah tells him, nodding.

Justin looks like he's trying not to pass out.

"My point," Jennifer says with emphasis, "is that it was consensual. And he *knew* that."

"Consent requires a vocal yes. This?" Justin waves the book around. "Smelling her arousal? That is not vocal consent."

"It's romantic," Sarah insists with a shrug.

"It's a sex crime," Justin snaps, a brief flicker of anger crossing his face.

Oh.

That's new.

I don't think I've ever seen Justin angry before. But as quickly as it came, it's gone. He rubs his face, looking suddenly tired.

"Sorry," he murmurs. "I'm not... I'm not trying to be difficult, I promise. I'm just trying to understand."

"It's fiction," Jennifer insists. "Don't forget that it's just a fantasy. And in this world, in that moment in the woods, the reader gets a glimpse inside Phaedra's mind. And we know that she's okay with what is happening. In our world." She gestures around the circle. "In our world, we're not as safe as Phaedra. There can't be shades of gray in consent in our reality because women are inherently unsafe. We don't hold the power."

Justin is listening closely, nodding along with her words.

"What are these books really about, at the end of the day?" Jennifer asks the circle, looking around expectantly.

"Sex," Justin says immediately.

A few of the women giggle.

"Ladies?" she prompts.

Jennifer has been the de facto leader of our book club since the very beginning, but it's clear it's going to take more than just her asking to get someone to volunteer an answer. When none of the women in the circle speak, I suck in a breath and step forward.

"Power," I answer. Justin's eyes jump to mine, his eyebrows rising, but Jennifer smiles and nods for me to continue. "These books are about power. About being so strong you're almost untouchable. Phaedra has all the power with Malachi, even during that scene in the woods."

I address the whole circle, not just Justin. "The fact is, in this universe, we can trust Malachi, and characters like him, to be completely devoted to one thing only: her pleasure."

Around the circle, the women nod their heads emphatically.

"Malachi challenges Phaedra," I say, directing my answer at Justin. "But he would never hurt her. He'd burn the world down if it meant she felt safe."

"See?" Sarah grins smugly at Justin. "It's romantic."

You can see the indent on his face where he's biting his cheek to stay quiet.

I glance over at the wall clock and clasp my hands in front of me.

"Thank you so much for coming tonight, ladies," I tell the circle. "And... uh, gentleman." Justin gives me an embarrassed smile, and a few of the women laugh. "But I'm afraid we're about to close for the night. Jade has some pastries for all of you up at the front. And plenty extra for you to take home."

The group begins to disperse, chatting among themselves as they make their way up to the café. A few of them stay to thank me for hosting and put in their orders for next month's book. Jennifer gives me a big hug before she leaves, promising to message me her thoughts about the latest book in *The Prince's Knife* trilogy. When they're all gone and I'm just starting to put the chairs up, I notice one last guest who hasn't left.

Justin.

"You know, you don't have to participate in the book club. Jade and I never do," I tell him, dragging another chair toward the stack. "It's not mandatory for employees."

"I didn't think it was," Justin admits. He shifts, clearly uncomfortable. "But I also didn't think it would be..."

"All women?" I volunteer.

"Yeah." He gives me a small, uneasy grin. "I messed this up, didn't I? Made them uncomfortable?"

I snort, lifting another chair and dropping it onto the stack. "I doubt it. It'll take more than just you to make that group uncomfortable, believe me."

"Good." He blows out a breath, puffing out his cheeks, shoulders visibly relaxing.

"Did you like it?" I ask, nodding toward his copy of *The Prince's Knife*, still clutched in his hand.

Justin looks down at it, frowning. "Do you want my honest opinion?"

I nod.

"It's..." Justin looks from me to the book, and then back again, grimacing. "Sydney, this book is terrible."

I raise an eyebrow, crossing my arms lightly.

"There's barely any plot," he continues. "And the character's motivations are all over the place. In one scene, Malachi professes his undying love for her, and in the *very next scene*, he says they can't be together. And his reasoning is... It's absurd. It's infuriating nonsense. And I don't understand half the powers these people are supposed to have. There's no consistency between descriptions, either. Are his eyes piercing bright, or are they dark as a moonlit night? Because they *can't* be both."

"I see."

"Look, I know you love it," Justin tells me, brandishing the book. "But..."

I hold up my hand to stop him. "Oh no, I get it. It's certainly no Special Agent Callahan. A man who is seven feet tall, yet completely inconspicuous in a crowd. Who can tell people are lying by *microexpressions*." I arch an eyebrow. "I looked that up, you know. Pseudoscience. It's not a real thing."

"Yeah, but he—"

"Sleeps with a new woman in every book?" I offer, cutting him off. I lean my hip against the stack of chairs, giving him a look. "Most of whom he literally just rescued from almost being sexually assaulted and murdered?"

Justin stammers, his ears turning pink.

"Those books? They're male power fantasy. These books." I gesture toward his copy of *The Prince's Knife*. "They're female power fantasy. That's the difference. Maybe one day you can see past your dick-centric universe to get it."

A shocked laugh bursts out of him. "My dick-centric universe?" he repeats. "Jesus, Sydney!"

"It's true! You could stand to learn something from these books," I tell him.

"That's why I wanted to read this one," Justin admits, rubbing a hand over the back of his neck. "I'm trying to read more romance. But this stuff is *dark*. It feels, I don't know, dangerous? Like, if this is what women like..."

"Just because a woman enjoys reading about something, that doesn't necessarily mean she wants that in real life," I say firmly.

"I'm starting to get that," Justin murmurs. Then he smiles, a little warily. "Maybe tomorrow you can recommend something lighter? Help break me out of my *dick-centric* world view?"

"I'm sure I can find you something," I relent, mentally preparing a list of options for him.

He grins. "Thanks. I should head out for the night. Want me to take these back to the stockroom?"

He gestures at the stack of chairs, and I shake my head.

"No, you head home. I've got this."

We wish each other goodnight, and he gives me a dimpled smile and a wave before he disappears, heading toward the café. I heave a sigh and turn to finish cleaning up, when I walk directly into a wall.

Or at least what I thought was a wall.

20

SYDNEY

I SLAM INTO A MAN'S CHEST WITH ENOUGH FORCE THAT I bounce off, stumbling back and almost losing my balance. A long-fingered hand shoots out, catching me by the arm and steadying me.

My mouth goes dry.

Sebastian.

I forgot how tall he is. I have to tilt my chin up to look at him. When I do, he's exactly as I remember, sharp-featured and brutally handsome, cold blue eyes framed by thick glasses. But he's not looking at me. His gaze is locked over my shoulder, his expression cold.

"Who was that?" Sebastian asks in a low voice.

"Who?"

"The man you were just talking to." His hand tightens on my arm, but he doesn't seem to notice. I glance over my shoulder, frowning at where Justin just disappeared from view. "The man who's been following you around *all day*."

"He works here," I tell him, my words come out with a bite.

"I assume if you've been spying on me *all day*, you could have figured that out."

It's distracting, being this close to him. I shrug off his hold and take a few steps back, nervously fluffing my curls.

What was I doing? Right. Cleaning. Picking up after book club is all that stands between me and some takeout and bad TV, two things I desperately need right now. I force myself to turn away from him and shift my focus back to my work, grabbing another chair and adding it to the growing stack.

Sebastian doesn't say anything, but I can feel his eyes tracking me as I busy myself with my cleaning. I bend down to pick up a stray bookmark someone left behind, tossing it in the trash, trying to ignore the heavy weight of his stare.

"If you've finished interrogating me about my employees, I need to..."

"A name." It's not even a question, the way he tosses it at me. More like a command.

My teeth grind together as I turn to him with an overly saccharine smile. "Justin. His name is Justin. Would you like his social security number too?"

I let my smile drop as quickly as I plastered it on and glare at him, *daring him* to piss me off with one more question.

Still frowning at the spot where Justin disappeared, he mutters, almost to himself, "Jade's brother. Justin Lee." His brows draw together. "What is he doing here?"

He dared.

It shouldn't surprise me that he knows exactly who Jade's brother is, or that he recognized the similarities between them. But what does surprise me is the range of emotions I see darkening his face when he moves that sharp gaze toward me.

Anger. Suspicion. And...

"Are you jealous?" I ask. His expression shutters, all traces of his reaction vanishing.

"Just curious," Sebastian says evenly, reaching up to casually straighten his glasses. "The point of these security upgrades is to make sure you're safe, remember?"

"Well, Justin is safe," I assure him, bristling as I aggressively stuff the last of the group's garbage into the trash, shoving it down to get it all to fit. "I've known him since we were kids. He's just helping us out part-time here at the store to give us a break."

Sebastian makes a noncommittal noise, deep in his chest, like he'll be the one in charge of determining who is and isn't a risk to me.

"A break I think I deserve, considering the month I've had," I spit at him. At least he has the decency to look somewhat chagrined at that, eyes darting away from mine. "What are *you* doing here, anyway? I thought the installation was finished."

"It is," he admits, still avoiding my eyes. "I was just checking that all the cameras were in place and functioning correctly." He motions behind him without looking as he says it, and I follow the wave of his hand to where the nearest camera watches us, red light flashing. "Everything is working as intended."

I place the final chair on the stack and take a calming breath in, and let it out slowly, relieved to know the security system is in place. Ready. "Great," I say. "Do I need to do anything or—"

"So you never dated him?" he asks, speaking over me.

The shift in conversation is almost enough to give me whiplash. "What?" I sputter, reeling. "No! Not that it's any of your business, but he's like family." Like an annoying younger brother. Just this morning, he walked into the bakery while Jade and I were prepping to open, turned off all the lights, stole my coffee, and walked back out of the room, laughing at us.

Sebastian nods once, fingers tapping a rhythm against his thigh. "Good."

I almost can't believe it. "You actually are," I accuse him. "You're jealous."

Behind his glasses, his eyes narrow. "Don't be ridiculous," he says.

"I'm the one being ridiculous? Really?" I plant my hands on my hips, meeting his eyes with a glare. "Because from where I'm standing, it looks like you saw him on your security cameras and came running down here to question me about him. Is that not what happened?"

A muscle in his eyelid twitches. "Of course not," he insists.

I can't help it. A dark laugh slips out of me. "I don't believe you. Just admit it, Seb. Spare me the back and forth. Just admit that there's something about him that you—"

Something in his expression shifts, and his cold mask of indifference fractures. He steps forward without warning, icy blue eyes flashing with anger, closing the distance between us until he's so close his chest is almost touching mine. "You think I'm jealous?" he asks, in a low growl, staring down at me. "Of him?"

He's so close I can feel the heat coming off him. I swallow and draw in an unsteady breath. "I just think you *might*—"

"How could I possibly be jealous of a man who doesn't know how you taste?" he asks, his voice dropping to a whisper.

My body recognizes the words before my mind does, heat flooding my veins. My head empties, and I open my mouth, but nothing but a small, desperate sound comes out.

He's not finished. Sebastian leans in even closer, his face suspended just above mine. "A man who's never seen you come undone." His hand lifts, fingers curling under my chin, angling my face up until all I can see is him. "A man who's never known the pleasure of making you come. You think I could ever be jealous of a man like that?"

I can't breathe. The air between us is too charged, and my heart is beating so hard in my chest I'm sure he can feel it, maybe even hear it.

"He doesn't know what you like," Sebastian tells me softly. His thumb passes over my lower lip, eyes flashing as they flick down to watch it move over my skin. "But I do. Don't I, Sydney?"

A humiliating whimper escapes me before I can stop it. I remember it, remember the way he touched me, the feel of his tongue expertly unraveling me.

His finger presses against my lip, a little too hard. "Answer me," he orders.

"Yes," I gasp. He knows. He knows exactly what I want, what I need.

An expression I don't recognize passes over his face. His lips curve, a slow, sharp smile spreading as he drags his gaze over my face and down my body. "God, look at you," he murmurs, sounding almost awed. "You want it so badly, don't you? All it took was a few words, and you're practically begging for it."

He's right, and I hate it. My legs are shaking, and I press my thighs together desperately, trying to ease the ache building between them. I can tell from the way his smile widens that he notices.

He lets go of my chin, fingers trailing down my jaw and over my neck, threading in my hair. "I could take you into that back room right now, bend you over that table, and fuck you within an inch of your life, and you'd let me. Wouldn't you?"

"Sebastian," I plead. I don't know if I'm begging for him to stop or keep going. To make good on his promises or step away to give me space to breathe. He leans down, lowering his head until his mouth brushes my ear, and I have to bite my lip to keep quiet.

"And you'd love it," he promises, his breath a warm caress against my skin. "The things I could do to you? You'd never forget them. You'd be thinking about them every time you close your eyes."

I wet my lips without thinking. "Why don't you?" I challenge, my voice breathless. The store is closing, I can hear the last of the book club saying their goodbyes, can hear Jade gathering her things to leave. He could have me, right now, if he wanted.

He makes a sound too dark to be a laugh. "Because you wanted time. You wanted space. And that's what I'm giving you." He shifts, his lips brushing against my cheek, then the corner of my mouth, when he answers. "Tell me right now if I'm wrong, love."

His lips graze mine, and my eyes flutter shut, my head tilting back. He lingers against my mouth, a featherlight kiss. Then his tongue flicks out, tracing the edge of my lower lip, and every part of me threatens to come undone.

"Tell me I'm wrong," he repeats, voice rough, hand tightening in my hair. "Just say the word. We can go back there right now and—"

"Syd?" Jade's voice cuts through the quiet, and we both freeze. "I'm heading out! But, hey, your quiet doc is around here somewhere checking the cameras and—"

She makes a startled noise as she rounds the corner and finds us pressed against each other, his lips hovering above mine, his hand in my hair.

"Oh. You found him." Her lips press together, like she's trying not to laugh.

Sebastian lets me go and takes a step back, away from me,

all traces of emotion on his face washing away. He takes his time straightening his sleeves, adjusting the cuffs.

"Jade," he finally greets her, giving her a curt nod.

"Sebastian," she answers, dipping her chin in a mocking nod of her own.

He looks her up and down, gaze pausing on her bright red hair. "I like the new color," he says. "It suits you."

She beams at him.

When he turns back to me, I can only imagine how I must look. My skin feels flushed, my legs weak. I can feel my pulse everywhere, in my throat, at my wrists, pounding between my legs.

His mouth curves faintly. "Let me know when you've had enough space."

And then he's gone, leaving me a breathless, trembling mess in his wake, painfully aware of every place he touched me.

21

SYDNEY

"MEOW!"

"No," I protest, shaking my head. "Absolutely not."

Bea yowls again, flicking her tail.

"*That* is your dinner," I remind her firmly. "That is the *good* cat food that Justin bought for you. The expensive cat food. And that is what you're eating."

She gives the dish on the kitchen floor a disdainful sniff. For a single moment, I think I've won, and she'll at least try it. But then she lets out a low growl and starts pawing at the tile, as if to bury it.

"You're impossible!" I tell her, throwing my hands up in exasperation. "Why do you want the other stuff, anyway? This one has *real chicken* in it. See?"

I hold up the can and point at the ingredients, like that will prove something. I know she can't read, but it's the principle of the matter.

It's no use. She stares at me, unimpressed, and sits down beside her bowl, tail curling around her paws. I can tell that for her, it's the principle of the matter, too. She doesn't want any of the good, healthy food that Justin bought her. She wants the gross stuff.

"Fine!" I snatch her dish from the ground, dump the untouched food in the sink, and reach for a can of the cheap brand.

When Justin picked up supplies for her, he bought an absurd range of canned food, from the most expensive veterinarian-recommended premium stuff all the way down to the cheapest, off-brand sludge.

Apparently, Bea only wants the sludge.

"This stuff smells terrible, by the way," I mutter, spooning some into a fresh dish. But Bea seems to *like* the smell. She winds around my legs, mewing and rubbing against my ankles, begging loudly until I set the food down in front of her.

It's impressive just how adorable she is. I watch as she eats her dinner in tiny, happy bites, purring loudly with every mouthful. When she's finished licking the dish clean, she arches her back in a leisurely stretch, yawns, and then prances over to my favorite armchair, where her two toy bees are already waiting. She jumps up and takes her time circling the space, kneading the fabric and testing the stuffing before she curls up in a ball, hiding her face with her tail and instantly falling asleep.

Adorable.

I fiddle with the belt of my robe, knowing I should go to bed, too.

There's only one problem, though. My nerves are overstimulated, my body humming with leftover heat from my encounter with Sebastian. I feel hypersensitive, my skin too warm, and my lips still burn from that ghost of a kiss. Just a brush of his mouth against mine, and somehow, it's all I can feel, all I think about.

You could have him. His hot touches and his ice-cold anger. It could be yours. All four of them could be yours.

I squeeze my eyes shut. No. What I need is a little *me time.* A gratuitously smutty book, and some time alone in my bed, before I go to sleep. That's what I need.

That, and some privacy. Which I'm not entirely convinced I have anymore.

My apartment feels different, somehow. I can't shake the feeling I'm being watched. Like I'm not actually alone.

Hugging my arms around myself, I frown at my ceiling. Everything looks normal. Exactly the same.

Walking slowly around my apartment, I scan each room for changes, for anything that shouldn't be there. There's a smoke detector set into the living room ceiling, and a matching one in the kitchen. I stop beneath one, suddenly suspicious. Did they always look like that? Have they changed at all?

My fingers drum against my skin.

Only one way to be sure. I pull my cellphone out of my robe pocket and call his number before I can overthink it.

Sebastian picks up on the first ring. "I didn't expect you to fold so soon," he says, sounding smug.

I take a breath to steady myself, trying to ignore what his voice does to me. "I need you to be completely honest with me."

"Always," he answers. But I can hear a hesitation in his voice, and I wonder if he knows what I'm about to ask.

"Are there any cameras in my apartment?" I ask him, frowning up at the smoke detector. It just squats there in the ceiling, silently.

He answers immediately. "One. Outside your front door, pointed down the stairs so I can see if anyone tries to break in. That's it."

Still staring at the smoke detector like it might suddenly

move, I walk to my door and open it, taking a few steps down the stairs and then craning my head up to look. Sure enough, there it is. A camera, with a flashing red light.

It looks nothing like a smoke detector. It is, identifiably, a camera.

"Go ahead and wave, if you'd like. I can see you right now, through the video feed."

I don't wave. Frowning at the camera one last time, I walk back inside, close my door, and lock it.

The smoke detector looks very much like a smoke detector.

"And that's the only one?" I press, voice skeptical.

"I promised you no cameras in your home, Sydney," he assures me. "I kept that promise."

"Okay," I say, releasing a breath and heading back into my bedroom. I sit down on the edge of my bed and let myself fall backwards, my back hitting the mattress. "I just wanted to be sure."

"Are you disappointed?" he asks.

I blink, confused. "Disappointed?" I repeat. "Why would I be—"

"You're about to touch yourself, aren't you?" His tone is so casual, so nonchalant. Heat immediately rushes to my cheeks. "Are you disappointed I won't be able to watch you?"

"I..." I shift up onto my elbows, my mouth opening and closing as I sputter in indignation. "I wasn't going to—"

"It's ten... Hang on, let me check. Ten twenty-eight in the evening, Sydney," he informs me. "And something made you decide to call me, this late, to double-check that you had your privacy."

My cheeks are on fire. I sit up, hand clenched tight around the phone.

"In what world does that mean I'm going to...to do *that*," I snap.

"In every world where I'm not an idiot," he says, like it's obvious. "And, for the record, I am disappointed, even if you aren't." His voice drops to a purr. "You have no idea what I'd give to watch you touch yourself for me."

This time it's not just my face that flushes with blood. I swallow, mouth suddenly dry.

"Well, I wasn't going to anyway," I lie.

"Liar." Sebastian clicks his tongue. "Who would have thought our sweet little Sydney could be so dishonest."

If he were here right now, I'd slap him right in his face.

He might like that.

Maybe you would, too.

There's a rustle over the phone, like he's leaning back in a chair, getting comfortable.

"Tell me, Sydney, what exactly were you thinking about that got you so worked up, hm?"

I don't answer. With how tightly my teeth are clenched, I don't think I could even if I wanted to. I vaguely consider just hanging up.

"Don't want to tell me?" he asks. "Fine. Maybe I should guess, then, how about that?"

Another sound, like he's stretching. He sounds so relaxed, so at ease. Meanwhile, I'm nearly shaking with rage.

"Maybe you're thinking about Sterling, hm? I know you used to have your little video calls with him. I know he got to watch you fall apart. And he got to hold you down while you came underneath him." A mixture of desire and pain shoots through my chest before he continues. "Have you been playing with yourself, thinking about him? Spreading those beautiful legs wide and remembering how he made you come?"

"No," I bite out, finally able to speak. "I haven't."

"Hm. Pity," he says. "He's too predictable, anyway. Maybe you were thinking about Ashton? I bet if you called him right now, he would be there in under ten minutes, begging to slip his tongue between your legs."

He would. I slide my tongue over my lips, suddenly feeling too warm. A single phone call, that's all it would take.

"Am I getting warmer, Sydney?" Sebastian teases in my ear.

"No," I whisper. The robe around my shoulders feels too hot, the fabric too much sensation against my skin.

"So who does that leave? Maybe Viper, then?"

My quick intake of breath is loud, far too loud to go unnoticed.

"Oh." Sebastian chuckles. "Sounds like we have a winner, don't we?"

"N-no," I stutter.

"Oh, Sydney, I don't believe you. Huh. Isn't that *interesting*. You get more interesting by the day, you know that, love? It's not Sterling's control you're after, or even Ashton's tongue. You want the monster, is that right?"

"I wasn't..." My mouth is so dry as I swallow. "I wasn't thinking about Viper, I was..."

I can't say it. I bite my lip.

On the other side of the line, Sebastian goes quiet.

"Is that why you called *me*?" he asks. His voice is growing even darker, more seductive. "Why you wanted to know if I was watching you?"

I don't answer.

"Say it, Sydney. I want to hear you say it."

I can't.

Sebastian lets out a sound like a growl, low and primal. "Say you were thinking about me. Say it was my cock, my touch you were imagining. Tell me you've been wet for me since I touched you earlier."

"You..." I suck in a breath. "You could have had me, you know. When you were in the bookshop..."

There's a long pause on the other end of the phone before Sebastian speaks again.

"Let me have you now," he says. "Just like this."

I swallow.

"What are you wearing, Sydney?"

I'm standing on a precipice. And I have two choices. I can hang up and draw this line in the sand. Or...

You want it, don't you? The darkness, the anger. Want him to own every piece of you, even for a moment.

My bathrobe falls to the ground at my feet the moment I untie the belt, sliding off my shoulders with practically no resistance.

"Nothing," I tell him. "I'm not wearing anything anymore."

Sebastian's quick intake of breath is loud in my ear. "Get on your bed for me. Spread your legs," he orders.

I do it. Letting out a shaky breath, I ask into the phone, "Now what?"

Sebastian chuckles.

"You know what I love about you, Sydney?" he asks. I'm struck by just how vibrant his voice is, like this. No mask, no cold exterior. Right now, nothing but a voice in my ear, Sebastian is raw and expressive.

"No," I answer honestly.

"I love that you can follow orders, like a good little slut."

My pulse flutters, and I wait for the words to hit me, wait for them to hurt me. I wait for the shame and self-loathing to fill me.

It doesn't.

The words go straight through me, right to my core, and, surprising myself, I let out a quiet moan, loving the way it sounds when he calls me it.

"You like following my orders, don't you?" he asks.

"Yes," I whimper.

"Good. I want you to touch yourself for me. Play with those beautiful tits of yours."

I let my hand slide over my chest, cupping my breast.

"Pinch your nipple."

Biting my lip, I do as I'm told. A small sound escapes me.

"Harder, Sydney," he demands.

I do it hard enough it hurts, and I cry out, savoring the feeling.

"That's it," Sebastian hisses into the phone. "That's what you like, isn't it? A little pain with your pleasure?"

"N-No," I gasp, twisting them again. My mind conjures the memory of Viper, of his hands clasped around my jaw, forcing my head up, and I cry out, loudly.

"Don't lie to me, not when you're doing so well. You love it. I bet you're dripping wet right now, aren't you?"

"No," I say softly, shaking my head. But I am. I know I am.

"Prove it. Slide those fingers into your wet pussy and tell me you're not loving this."

I don't have to do it. I could hang up right now. But I follow his orders. I let my hand move down my body, over my hips and down until I slip a single finger over myself.

Just that touch is enough to make me cry out, arching off the bed.

"Say it, Sydney. Tell me what I want to hear."

"I... I'm wet," I admit, moving the finger in and out of myself. It's a vast understatement. To say I'm wet is like saying the ocean is wet. I'm soaking, every nerve on fire as my fingers roll over my body.

Sebastian groans on the other end of the phone. There's a shuffle of fabric, followed by a zipper, and I whimper, imagining it...imagining him touching himself with me.

"Are you fingering yourself?" he asks in a breathless voice.

"Yes," I say, gasping. My finger slides in and out of me, slippery with my cum.

"Dirty fucking whore," he grunts into the phone. "What do you think about when you're fucking yourself, Sydney? What dirty things do you imagine?"

I gasp, my hand moving faster.

"Are you thinking about what I said earlier? How I could have fucked you right then and there in the middle of your store?"

Oh God.

"Are you thinking about how all those people could have been just steps away while you felt my cock slam into you over and over and over again? One moan away from being caught like the dirty slut you are? How you wouldn't have asked me to stop, even when you were on display?"

"Yes," I gasp, fucking myself.

"Tell me what else you think about, tell me all those dirty thoughts."

"You!" I gasp, finger moving faster. "I... I'm thinking about you, Sebastian... about your fingers, and..."

There's a loud intake of breath on the other end of the line. And then silence.

My fingers still. "Sebastian?" I ask, breathless and uncertain. I start to remove my fingers. "Are you—?"

"Say it again," he breathes into the phone.

"Say what—?"

"Say my fucking name," he growls. His breathing ratchets up, and I can hear him, hear him fucking his own hand.

My fingers start to move again.

"Sebastian," I whisper into the phone.

"Again," he demands. "Louder."

"Sebastian!" I cry out.

"That's it," he grunts. "Say my name again, dirty girl. I

want to hear you say my name with those fingers buried in your pussy. I want you to scream it when you come."

"I'm close," I whimper, hips bowing off the bed, fucking myself hard.

"Fuck," he swears, grunting into the phone.

"Sebastian, I... I—"

I explode, screaming his name as I come.

On the other end of the line, I hear him swear, low and guttural, and then groan, and I know he's following me, know he's coming with me, sharing this moment with me.

There's a long silence after as we catch our breath, both gasping into the phone. I listen to him, imagining him. Cold, emotionless Sebastian, covered in his own release, breathless and spent. I imagine him flushed, his hair messy, lips parted.

And I made that happen. I broke through that mask and reduced him to this. There's power in this moment, right here. And it's all mine.

Finally, he speaks. "Sydney?" he asks softly.

I lift the phone from my ear, staring at it. I wish we'd done this through video. I wish I could see him, see the mess I've made of him.

"Syd, I—"

Whatever he's going to say, I don't wait to hear it.

I end the call.

Right now, in this moment, I have all the power. And I want to keep it that way.

22

ALEC

SEBASTIAN IS LATE.

And Sebastian is never late.

I glance at the wall clock again, frowning as the seconds tick by into minutes. On the couch, Ashton shifts nervously, his leg bouncing up and down.

"Where the fuck is he?" he asks, looking around. "It's not like him to—"

The door opens suddenly, and a flushed Sebastian ducks inside. "Sorry," he mutters, shutting the door behind him and running a hand through his hair. "I had a phone call I had to take."

He looks flustered. And flustered isn't a word I usually associate with him.

"Do you want to tell me what phone call could possibly be important enough to keep us waiting?" I ask, raising an eyebrow.

He looks at me, and I can see his mind working, can see him deciding exactly what to say and what not to say.

"I was talking to Sydney," he admits.

Ashton tenses, going still on the couch.

"Bullshit," he snaps. "No you weren't."

Sebastian doesn't say anything. But he holds my gaze, chin raised, looking almost...smug.

Oh. This wasn't *just* a phone call.

Surprised, I take in all the nuances of his appearance, noting the slight pink in his cheek, the disorder to his clothing. Sebastian is immaculate, perfectly dressed and composed.

Usually.

A small ember of jealousy burns in my gut. This is good, I try to convince myself. It means she's opening back up to us. It means we haven't lost her, not entirely, not yet. It means there's a world in which she might trust us again.

This is *good*.

I clench my hand under the desk to stop myself from punching him in the dick.

"Why would she call you?" Ashton asks, narrowing his eyes in suspicion.

"I don't think we need to discuss this," I say, trying to put a halt to a sibling fight before it begins. "We're already behind, and—"

"What could she possibly get from *you* that she can't get from us?" Ash interrupts.

"Guess she was feeling lonely," Sebastian volunteers, his mouth quirking up into the barest hint of a smile. "And looking for a little *fun*."

Great.

I let out a long, exasperated breath.

On the couch, Ashton's entire body goes tense. He looks at me, then back to his brother quickly.

"You're lying," he accuses, eyes boring into Sebastian. "Stop it. You're fucking lying just to get a rise out of me."

This time, Sebastian does smile, turning to look at his brother and grinning widely.

"Sure," he says coldly. "Whatever you need to believe, brother."

And cue the temper tantrum in three...

Two...

"Fuck!" Ashton yells, slamming his hands against the couch. "FUCK! You mother *fucker!*"

Sebastian just shrugs, still smiling.

"Ashton, that's enough," I say, holding up a hand to stop him. But I already know trying to calm him down is useless.

"No. No, this isn't happening." Ashton mutters, standing up from the couch and pulling at his hair as he paces. "Jesus Christ, what's next? Is she going to fuck Viper? Before *me?*"

"What makes you think she hasn't already?" Sebastian asks, casually straightening his glasses.

"Don't even joke about that," Ashton hisses, stepping forward. He shoves a finger against Sebastian's chest. To his credit, Sebastian doesn't move an inch. "Don't even fucking joke, you prick!"

"Who's joking? He's been spending time with her, hanging out at the shop, all alone with no one supervising. And you already know she likes a little pain." He smiles again, sharp as a knife. "Or maybe you're the only one who doesn't know that yet."

"I'll fucking kill you," Ashton spits out. "You fucker!"

"*Enough,*" I snap, slamming my palm against my desk. "Ashton, sit the fuck down."

He hesitates, torn between obeying a direct order and his brother's shit-stirring grin. But finally, he sits back down, glaring at Sebastian the whole time.

"I'm getting sick of this shit," I snap. "If neither of you can grow up and handle this like adults, I'll—"

Sebastian interrupts me with an abrupt laugh. "You'll what? Take your ball and go home?" He shakes his head, lip curling in a sneer. "When you met her, you gave her the option of picking what she wants from us. And she *is*. How do you think she'll react if you try to take that choice away from her now? Think that will go down easy with her? You're just angry that you're not the one she picked."

"Has she really fucked Viper?" Ashton asks him in a small voice, ignoring the conversation entirely. "Be real with me, bro. Has she really?"

Sebastian snorts derisively, shaking his head. "You're fucking pathological, you know that? You can't handle the possibility that she might not want *you*."

"Doc, I said that's *enough*," I snarl.

Lips pursed, he stops. But the damage is already done.

"What if she doesn't want me?" Ashton says, tonelessly, eyes fixed on the carpet.

"Jesus fucking Christ," I swear, running a hand over my face before glaring at Sebastian. "There. Are you happy now?"

Sebastian gnashes his teeth together. "Ashton, she *wants you*, okay?" he snaps. "But you keep getting in your own fucking way with her. I've been telling you—ad nauseum, I might add—to leave her alone. Let her decide to come back to you."

Ashton takes a deep breath.

I know that he's struggling with this, and he's not alone. I've done everything that Sydney has asked of us, and my phone still sits silently next to me day after day. I haven't talked to her, seen her, touched her...

And I'm fucking losing it.

To go from burying myself deep between her thighs to sitting alone at night just remembering what she tastes like is pure torture. I'm a patient man, usually. Happy to wait. But

I've never wanted anything more than to wrap my hand around her delicate neck and to hear her soft little moans while I pound into her sweet pussy. Never wanted anything more than to hold her, just one more time.

What if I never experience it again?

It's enough to drive the strongest man to the brink of insanity.

"Let it go," I tell Ash when he opens his mouth again. "I didn't call this meeting to deal with your fucking squabbling. We have a real threat to deal with. A threat to *Sydney*. Suck it up and do something useful if you really care about her."

Ashton glares at me but stays quiet.

"Give me an update on the Tony situation," I say, sitting back in my chair.

"I talked to him. We're getting a new shipment, just a little late. But there's another problem." Ashton shifts on the couch. "Someone else reached out to him, offering double what we're paying for it."

"Dante?" I ask.

Ashton shrugs. "Can't imagine it would be anyone else. No one here is brave enough to fuck with us like that. Either he doesn't have a weapons contact here and is trying to steal ours, or he's just trying to upset our supply. Either way, he's shit out of luck. Tony isn't going anywhere, and he sure as shit isn't selling to anyone but us."

"You know that for sure? Did he give his assurances?" I press.

"Boss, he's terrified of us. Remember when he watched Viper dismember that guy last year?" Ashton side eyes me. "No way he's going to fuck us over."

"Great. Let's hope he stays that way," I say. "Did he give you any information about the guys who approached him?"

Ashton shakes his head. "No, but I have a meeting with him about it tomorrow."

"Good." I turn my attention back to Sebastian. "Security on Sydney's building is installed?"

He nods. "Nothing unusual so far. They have a new employee, but I doubt he's anyone we need to worry about. There is something, though. I keep thinking about what she said a few days ago, about a traffic incident. It scared her. I want to investigate it more, check the police reports from that day. I'll update if I find anything."

"Great." I dismiss them with a wave. "And children, let's play nice. I'm sick of the bickering during these meetings."

Ash gives me a sarcastic salute as he and his brother stalk out of the room.

23

ASHTON

I can't fucking believe this. I kick a rock on the sidewalk, watching it bounce down the path in front of me. Sebastian. She's picking *Sebastian* over me.

Fuck, I want to punch something. Something with glasses.

Tony's club is just around the corner from Sydney's shop, and one of my favorite food trucks—*Sabor de Corazón*—should be parked nearby today. She'd loved the place when I'd taken her there for our date, right? Maybe I'll stop by on my way back, pick up some lunch for her. Sure, she wasn't exactly thrilled the last time I swung by her work, but she's got to eat sometime, doesn't she?

The more I think about it, the better the idea sounds. The best way to someone's heart is through the stomach. Everyone knows that. Doc would never do something thoughtful like bringing her lunch. Sure, Alec will be pissed if he finds out I went to see her, but he'll get over it. And who says he even has to find out? He doesn't need to know, doesn't—

"Ashton?"

I freeze mid-step, my foot hovering above the pavement.

I know that voice. Cold. Elegant. I recognize it immediately, and that's how I know, before I even turn around, who will be there waiting for me. Even before I see her seated at an outdoor table, head tilted to the side as she watches me, face blank.

Annika.

She's older—more woman than girl, now—her platinum blonde hair cut shorter than I remember. She sits with her back perfectly straight, hands folded on the table in front of her. She looks out of place here, with her designer dress and emerald earrings, sitting at a plastic outdoor table with graffiti drawn on it, an abandoned napkin fluttering by on the wind.

My mind turns to static, seeing her. And yeah, I should be thinking about how she betrayed us, how she nearly got us all killed. How she was like a little sister to me, before she chose her father over us. How she broke my little brother's heart, crushed it beneath her Louboutin heels like it was nothing.

I shouldn't be stepping closer to her, when she stands up. I shouldn't be reaching for her.

And I sure as hell shouldn't be wrapping my arms around her, pulling her in tight against me and breathing, "Fuck, I missed you," into her neck.

But I do.

Annika goes rigid. For a few seconds, she's nothing but stone, cold and unyielding. Then her muscles ease, her arms circle me, and she lets herself fall into the hug.

It doesn't last. She never was the touchy-feely type, on the best of days. All too soon, she's pulling back, smoothing invisible wrinkles from her ivory-colored dress, mouth twisting in distaste as she steps away from me.

"That was stupid, Ashton," she chides, her voice low but sharp. "Calling me. You have no idea if my phone is being monitored. Or what I would do. This could be a setup. I could be luring you into a trap right now."

Suddenly wary, I glance around at the crowd around us. "Are you?" I ask, not bothering to hide the concern in my voice.

Her gray eyes soften, just a touch. "No, Ash. I'm not."

"What are you even doing here?" Annika doesn't belong here, not in Fortune City. She should be home, should be back in Empire. He doesn't let her out of his sight like this.

She raises a single, perfectly manicured eyebrow. "You're the one who called me. Remember?"

"Yeah, but..." I struggle to explain. "What are you doing *here*? Right now? How the hell did you know I'd be here?"

"Oh. That." She almost smiles. A smug, pleased look settles on her face, softening her features. "I knew your little gun runner would go straight to you after he turned down our offer to buy him out. You should have a chat with him about his public email calendar. I knew he scheduled an appointment with you before you did, Ashton."

I grin. I can't help it. I'm fucking *proud* of her. "God, look at you. All grown up," I say. I like the short hair, like the way it complements her sharp features. It makes her look like someone you don't want to fuck with.

"Why did you call me?" she asks, cutting through my smile. "If Dante finds out I'm talking to you, I'll never see the light of day again."

Jesus. A heavy weight settles into my chest. "It's really him, huh?" I ask, feeling numb. "He's really alive?"

Annika gives me a scathing, almost pitying look. "Of course he is. Did you and your brothers really think you could kill the devil?"

Fuck. I drag a hand over my face. Yeah, I'd given Doc shit about it, but... I don't think I really believed it. Didn't really believe it was *him*. That he survived.

We're so fucked.

"What does he want from us?" I ask finally.

I don't expect her to answer. She proved it already, didn't she? She's on his side, not ours. But she surprises me. "What does any man want?" she asks lightly. "Power. Privilege." Her eyes darken. "Revenge."

That word hits me like a bullet. I've seen firsthand what he's willing to do to people who betray him. "He's researching someone we care about. Sending guys to look into her. We need to know why, what he's planning."

"Sydney," Annika confirms, without hesitation. Her lips purse. "You should stay away from her, Ash. For her sake."

My answering laugh sounds broken. "I don't think I can do that," I tell her honestly.

"If you care about her, you will." She tilts her chin, staring me down. "Dante is playing you all for fools, you know."

When I just stand there, not sure what to say to that, she goes on. "It's misdirection, Ashton. He'll use her to keep you distracted. And he'll keep toying with her until you're too busy watching her to see what he's really doing."

"We're not going to be distracted," I insist. "And she's safe, he can't get to her. She's—"

"He already has gotten to her," Annika interrupts, voice cold. "He has someone close to her. Watching her. He could take her at any moment if he wanted to. Don't forget who you're dealing with."

My stomach drops. "Why should I believe you?" I challenge.

Something flashes in her eyes, something that looks like anger. "I didn't have to come here and tell you this," she snaps. "I don't owe you or your brothers anything anymore."

"You kinda do, though," I remind her, a hint of the bitterness I'm feeling bleeding into my words. "After what you did to us."

Her eyes widen, and she takes a step back from me, recoiling like I slapped her. "What I did to *you?*"

"I mean..." I rub the back of my neck, unease spreading through me. "You sold us out, Annika. You told him our whole plan. Everything."

Her expression shutters. "That's what you think happened?" she asks in a low voice.

Think? No, that's what I *know* happened. No one else could've tipped him off. No one else knew the plan outside of the four of us. It had to be her. Except... The hurt buried deep in her eyes makes me hesitate. For the first time since we left Dante bleeding out on the floor, I'm not so sure.

But she looks away from me, and I could almost convince myself I imagined it.

"Let yourself get distracted by her, and you'll lose everything," Annika tells me. She motions to someone behind her—her bodyguard, Friedrich, standing up from another table, hand resting on the gun in his waistband. Fucking hell, a guy that big has no business blending in as well as he does. "Take my advice or don't. Either way, I couldn't care less."

Then she turns, red sole grinding on the gravel in one swift motion, and she's gone.

24

SYDNEY

Fucking fuck.

Whoever is sending me flowers needs to fire their florist. Immediately.

There's a new delivery waiting for me outside my apartment, propped against the door, when I leave to meet Jade for our next Operation Sydney outing, and I can tell something is wrong even before I get a good look at them. Sure enough, when I pick them up, the flowers are disgusting. Moldy and dead, the stems wilted, bugs scurrying about, climbing over the stalks.

The smell alone is enough to make me gag. And I know for a fact they weren't at my door last night when Bea and I came home from work, so there's no chance this is on me. They were delivered like this, no question.

Whatever. I'm already running late since I couldn't find a single clean pair of underwear this morning after my very hurried shower. I make a mental note to catch up on my clearly overdue laundry as I carry the armful of mold and dead flowers downstairs with me, tossing them in the alley dumpster on my way to the bus. It's not like I was going to keep them, anyway. Turns out lilies are toxic to cats, and there's no way in hell I'm letting them anywhere near my precious baby chaos demon.

I barely make it to my bus in time, but I fear the damage is already done. I'm officially running late, and I know Jade will never let me hear the end of it.

Our attempt at pottery may have been a disaster, but these little weekly outings with her have become an anchor for me. In all the chaos of my life, they're giving me something to look forward to, something that's mine.

This week, we opted to take a class at a brand-new cooking school that just opened across town, and I dramatically underestimated how long it would take to get there. The last thing I want to do is piss off Jade when we're going to be standing over open flames.

Leaning back in my seat, I stare out the bus window, watching my neighborhood blur past. We ease to a stop at a red light, and that's when I see him.

Ash.

He's right there across the street, standing on the sidewalk like fate has dropped him off just for me, and the effect of seeing him is instant and overwhelming. Something lights up inside of me, warming me. I almost tell the driver to stop, to let me out early, the need to see him so strong it's overpowering.

Maybe this is a sign. Last night, I let Sebastian in, just a little. Maybe it's time to do the same with Ashton, maybe seeing him here is the universe's way of letting me know I'm ready.

I stand up and reach for the pull cord to stop the bus before I realize he's not alone.

My heart stutters and then stops.

He's with a woman. A woman I recognize instantly.

Annika, Alec's *wife*, approaches him, her white-blonde hair fluttering prettily in the breeze. I blink, and suddenly they're hugging, Ashton wrapping his arms around her lower back, pulling her close to him, burying his face in her neck. It's intimate. Too familiar.

My whole body goes cold as I stand there, watching them. He's right there, just a pane of glass and a few feet separating us, but I've never felt further away from him.

I never pull the cord. The bus jolts forward, and we're moving with the rest of the traffic, that split second of seeing him now gone, the two of them fading into the distance behind me. After a while, I force myself to sit back down in my seat, my hands shaking.

I was right. This was a sign, after all. A sign to stop waiting, to stop hoping this was all a misunderstanding that we could eventually solve and get past. There's no getting past something like this. No future with them, when I'm the other woman.

I drag my hand over my cheek, wiping away the tears there, and force myself to stare straight ahead for the rest of the ride.

———————

"Is there a reason why we keep picking activities that you excel at but embarrass me to my core?" I ask Jade. Sure enough, I am late, and by the time we walk into the new cooking school together, most of the students have already picked their stations and gotten started.

"What makes you think I'll be any good at this?" she asks without a hint of irony.

"Jade, my love, my everything, you're literally a *baker*," I remind her.

"I get how you could come to that conclusion, but have you ever actually seen me cook?" Jade smirks. "Baking and cooking are completely different sciences! There are *rules* to baking.

Precision, measurement, finesse. Cooking is like the wild west, and it stresses me out."

"Great, so we picked something we'll both fail miserably at, then?" Today is just getting worse and worse.

"We picked this so that maybe we can actually attempt to cook for ourselves once in a while instead of gorging on takeout every day." Jade sits down at one of the open tables and pulls me down to sit next to her. "What is with you today, anyway? You're extra grumpy. Which is funny, since *I'm* the one that had to wait outside in the cold for *you* to show up."

"Sorry. I'm just having a bad day." The table in front of us is piled high with everything we'll need for class. I pull on my apron and assemble the ingredients in front of us just as the instructor makes his introductions. I try to listen, to pay attention to everything he says, but I can't focus. And I have no idea what a "roux" is, but apparently that's what we're starting with, so I guess I'll have to figure it out.

"Anything you want to talk about?" Jade whispers the question, but it's still loud enough to earn us an annoyed look from Chef Ramirez, the instructor.

"Later..." I say quietly, trying to avoid an embarrassing reprimand in front of the whole class.

We start by chopping onions, carrots, and celery into, what theoretically should be, equally sized pieces. Today's lesson is comfort foods, so we're making a traditional chicken pot pie. I focus on putting together the filling, while Jade works on the pie crust.

"Okay, so, I guess there's some baking in cooking," Jade says smugly as she puts the finishing touches on what looks like a perfect crust.

"I could kill you, you know. And I know exactly where I would hide the body," I threaten. An acrid smell fills the air around our station as the filling I'm working on starts to burn in the pot, and I frantically adjust the burners to turn the temperature down. "Do not test me."

Jade leans over and scoops a spoonful of my mess out of the pot, chewing it slowly. "Why is your chicken so rubbery?" she asks.

I point my spatula threateningly at her. "One more word and it's over, Jade. I swear."

"Okay, okay, let me see if I can help." Nudging me aside, she takes the spatula from me and scrapes the burnt bits from the bottom of my pan, adding in a little broth.

"That doesn't look better," I groan, assessing her progress.

"I doubt it's salvageable," Chef's voice announces from directly behind us, and we both startle with a squeal.

"Jesus," Jade gasps, clutching her chest. "How are you so stealthy?"

Chef harrumphs, turning up his nose as he heads toward the more promising students at the next table over.

I drop my voice to mutter, "That man is scary. How does he move so silently?"

"Definitely a spy," Jade answers, watching him closely, her eyes narrowed. "You don't move that quietly without professional training. I bet this whole place is a front."

I hum in agreement and poke at the concoction in my pot. He's right. There really is no saving this chicken. Sighing, I pick out the pieces, throwing them in the trash while Chef's back is turned. I should be vegetarian anyway. If I can't properly cook meat, maybe that's my sign I shouldn't be eating it at all. Jade glances over, noticing what I'm doing, and grins.

"Should we bail?" she asks, hopefully. "I don't think I want to eat a vegetable pie. Plus, I'm enjoying our trend of starting an activity and then just going drinking instead."

"Same, honestly." I square my shoulders and glance at

Chef. "Wait until his back is turned and let's book it?" I whisper conspiratorially.

We're out the door and halfway across the street before he starts yelling. We're probably making a bad name for ourselves around town at this rate, but by the time our ride-share drops us off at Twin Pines, we've forgotten all about our disastrous cooking class.

It's busier than it was the last time we were here, the bar nearly full when we slide into two open barstools. Along with Seamus, there's another bartender today, helping to take orders.

"Hey, Seamus," I greet him with a wave.

He glances over at us and grins. "Looks like you've decided to become regulars again," he says. "Fantastic! Two dirty martinis?"

"I think we'll do a bottle of wine today. Red?" I ask Jade.

"Red," she agrees, nodding.

"We have a Pinot Noir I'm sure you'll love," Seamus informs us, already moving across the bar to grab it, knowing we're not about to turn down one of his recommendations.

The moment he's out of earshot, Jade turns to me. "Okay, spill. Why do you look like someone kicked your dog?"

"I don't have a dog," I mutter, not wanting to get into it. I finally got my mind off seeing Ash with Alec's wife, and the last thing I want to do is remember it. "And if someone kicked Bea, I think I might murder them."

"Obviously," Jade agrees. Seamus returns with two glasses and a bottle of red, opening it for us. "But I can *imagine* what you would look like if you *did* have a dog, and someone *did* kick it. And that's how I imagine you looking right now."

"What are we imagining Sydney doing?" Seamus quips. "Loop me in. I'd love to imagine her too."

I scowl at him. "Quit it. You're both incorrigible. Can I just have my wine, please and thank you?"

"Of course, beautiful." He fills our glasses, leaving the bottle when he heads over to take orders from another group.

"God, that man could not want you more." Jade laughs, clinking her glass against mine. "Was he always this blatantly obvious with his flirting, or is this new?"

"Shut up, he wasn't flirting with me. He's just being... *English*," I say.

"Ah, yes, the English, renowned flirts of the western world." She rolls her eyes. "Anyway, he's *Irish*. The name should have been a dead giveaway."

Oh, right.

"And how is it you had four men fall madly in love with you and you *still* can't see when a man is interested in you?" Jade studies me, tilting her head. "What is it like to live in that delusional head of yours? Is it peaceful?"

"They're not in love with me. They never were," I mutter. "I don't think they ever really cared about me at all."

"What are you talking about?" Jade asks, perplexed.

I sigh, fiddling with the stem of my wine glass. Guess we're getting into it after all.

"Earlier today, I saw Ash with a woman," I admit. "Not just any woman. I'm pretty sure it was Alec's wife. They looked *cozy*." More than cozy, really. That image of them, his hand on her back, her head tucked against his shoulder, has been haunting me since I spotted them. How long did they stay like that? What happened after?

You shouldn't care, I try to tell myself. *It's none of your business.*

Not anymore.

"Shit." Jade sucks in a breath, tilting her head back to stare at the ceiling. "Is it crazy that I'd hoped that there was more to the 'Alec has a wife' story? Some explanation that would absolve him? Like, I don't know, maybe that she was dead or something. Is that horrible?"

"Trust me, that was my first question when I found his wedding ring. She is very alive, and now I can confirm that with my own two eyes." I exhale slowly, trying to sort through my feelings. "I thought when I couldn't find anything about her online, maybe she was at least far away? A monk who took a vow of celibacy, living in isolation and completely out of contact with him? But nope. She's alive, and she's here. With them."

I take a big swallow of wine.

"I'm so sorry, Syd." Jade wraps an arm around my shoulders and gives me a quick squeeze. "I know I said no rebounds, but maybe it would help if you actually tried dating again? You got out of this horrible relationship with an absolute abortion of a man and then immediately fell head over heels into a group thing. Maybe you need to just, I don't know, go on a regular date? Be a normal girl for a change?"

"I guess I could try that," I say. I know my heart isn't in it, but maybe she's right. Maybe I just need to let them go.

"Okay, great. It's settled then." Jade leans over the bar to shout, "Hey, Seamus! Wouldn't you just love to take Sydney out to dinner?"

I shoot her a horrified look before burying my face in my hands, mortified. There's no way every single person in Twin Pines didn't just hear that.

"Is she finally single?" Seamus asks, laughing. He takes his time walking over to us, grinning the whole way. "About damn time. It would be my pleasure to take her out." He glances at me, then back to Jade. "Can I say any of this directly to her, or do I need to go through you for all communication?"

"I'll allow direct communication for now. Actually, let me

just excuse myself so you two can sort out the details." Jade shoots me a wink and slides off her barstool, strolling away.

"I am so sorry," I tell Seamus. "I am sorry and embarrassed and...just sorry."

He leans closer, setting his elbows on the bar. "Don't be. She saved me the trouble of doing it myself. I've wanted to ask you out for a while, now, but you were always with that idiot boyfriend of yours."

"What makes you think he was an idiot?" I ask, smirking.

"Well, first of all, he let you go. Can't imagine a dumber move than that." He grins.

He is charming, I'll give him that. And not at all bad to look at. I brush a lock of hair behind my ear. "Well, you were right. About the idiot thing."

"Honestly, I'm surprised to hear you're not with him anymore," Seamus adds nonchalantly. "I assumed when I saw him here earlier, he was here to see you."

A cold weight drops into my stomach. "What do you mean you saw him?" I ask, fear coloring my voice. "Chase is here? Right now?"

"Yeah, at the back bar." He points over his shoulder towards the second bar, hidden behind the corner from this one. "Just saw him a moment ago."

No.

"Would you excuse me a second?" I stand up, legs shaking, and move across the room towards the second bar. I need to know if he's really here, need to confront him if he's still following me. My hand reaches into my pocket, pulling out my phone, ready to call Sebastian.

But when I turn the corner, there's no one there but a group of girls laughing around a table and two men cheersing their beers at the bar. I scan the room, heart beating painfully hard in my chest.

Chase is nowhere in sight.

Seamus is frowning, forehead creased in concern, when I return.

"I don't see him. Are you sure it was him?" I press.

He shakes his head. "No. Could have been another generic white guy, I suppose. You all right?"

I paint a smile on my face, but it's a little too wide. "Yeah, totally."

"So...about our date?" A slow, easy grin spreads over his face. "What do you say? Can I take you out?"

"Um, yeah. I'd like that," I manage to say. Truthfully, I'm barely paying attention. There's still a pit in my stomach thinking about whether that could have been Chase.

"Great! There's a hot new club opening tomorrow. I've got a friend who works there, so I'm already on the list. Care to join me?"

I should. I should want to go to a new club, with this handsome foreigner who seems to really like me. I should want to date, should be excited he's asking me.

I should leave the past behind me. Move on.

"Sounds great." I force myself to smile, my chest oddly tight. "Tomorrow it is."

25

ALEC

Oscuro. Opening night.

I roll my shoulders and straighten my spine. A soft opening, really. Only the bottom three floors will be accessible to the public tonight, while we organize the finishing touches on the rest of the building.

But it needs to be perfect. Everything tonight needs to be perfect, with so much riding on this. The board of directors is already on my ass about this venture, questioning the expense, the time and energy we've dedicated to this project. And it feels like someone has been trying to sabotage this launch at every opportunity. I'll be damned if I'm going to let them get away with it.

Behind me, Ashton stares at the security feed that dominates half the manager's office. We spent a small fortune to have extra cameras installed, last-minute, to cover every open area of the club. If someone tries anything here tonight, we'll see it.

"Have you seen Doc's new setup at home?" Ashton asks, fidgeting as he watches the monitors. The black-and-white feed shows a small but growing crowd already filling up the first-floor bar. We've limited capacity tonight to just friends and family—a short list of people known to the club's partial owners and employees—but we'll start letting in more as the night goes on.

"I've seen it," I answer. Hard to miss, now that Sebastian has converted a full room of our compound into a veritable altar to his voyeuristic tendencies. One full wall of monitors, each showing a different camera feed of Sydney's shop and the stairs leading up to her apartment.

Ashton rubs the nape of his neck, looking uncomfortable. "I'm starting to think it was a mistake to encourage this. The, uh, watching."

I turn to raise an eyebrow at him. "You've never had a problem with him watching before," I remind him.

Frankly, I've never given a shit either way, but there's no hiding that Ashton is a bit of an exhibitionist. Showing off to an audience has always been his preference, not mine.

"That's different," he grumbles. "That's just sex, you know? But watching her all day? Checking in on her while she's working?" He shakes his head. "That's not normal."

I check the time on my phone and scowl. Doc and Viper should be here by now. I want all four of us here tonight, in case something goes wrong.

"I don't give a fuck if it's normal," I assure him in a low voice. "It's about keeping her safe. That's all I care—"

No.

It's just like the first time I saw her. My eyes find her immediately on the monitors, pulled to her like a magnet.

Sydney. She's here, downstairs, at my club.

Even through the black-and-white video feed, I recognize the red dress she's wearing. It's the same one she wore the first night I saw her, bright red and skintight. My woman in red.

But I don't recognize the man with her. The man who's currently putting his arm around her, guiding her inside. Touching her so casually.

Touching my fucking woman.

From the angle of the screens, Ashton can't see her. I only realize I stopped speaking mid-sentence when he nudges me.

"Boss? What's up, what's going on?"

I'm dialing a number on my phone before the words are even fully out of his mouth.

"Doc? Where the fuck are you?" I grind out, voice lethally low, eyes fixed on Sydney through the monitors.

The roar of background noise lets me know he's on his bike, taking the call through his helmet. "Calm down," Sebastian says. "We're on our way. Traffic's brutal tonight. We just—"

"Get to the club. Now." My eyes track her figure as she moves on the screen. "Sydney is here. And she's with someone."

A pause. "Give me five minutes."

"What? Sydney's here? What do you mean she's with someone?" Ashton can't seem to form the questions quickly enough. He's up and out of the seat before I have a chance to answer.

"Sit back down," I command.

"Fuck off." His eyes roam over the monitors, searching for her. "Where is she, where did you see her?"

"I told you to sit down. We can't afford to be distracted tonight. Let Doc handle this."

"Fuck that!" Ashton briefly turns to glare at me before giving his full attention back to the video feed. "You don't make the fucking rules, you know. And you can't just keep me from her forever. I'm not about to sit here and..." The words catch in his throat when he spots her. Sydney, arm in arm with another man as he leads her to a booth, holding her hand as he helps her take her seat.

He doesn't speak. He just stares at them, mouth open in shock, hurt filling his eyes.

"Doc will handle this," I repeat. "Just calm down and—"

Too late. Ashton's already moving, barreling toward the door, his fists clenched. I barely get there in time to stop him, planting myself directly in his path. When he tries to get past me, I brace my forearm against his chest and shove him back into the room. "No. Not here, not now."

But he's not listening. His eyes are wild, unfocused, his breathing too fast. He's determined to get to Sydney.

"Move," he grunts, trying to push me out of the way. When I won't budge, he doubles down, slamming his body into mine, fighting me to get to her.

He manages to do it, too. He shoves me hard enough to make an opening, getting past me just enough to get to the door, fumbling to open it.

Fuck this.

There's only one way to stop him, one way to get him to listen when he gets like this.

Pulling my arm back, I swing, slamming my fist into his face so hard my arm shudders with the impact.

"What the fuck?" Ashton stumbles back into the room, one hand gripping his nose. His voice is high and nasal, full of shock. "Are you fucking serious right now?"

Before he can make another attempt for the door, I slam it shut and brace my back against it, my fist throbbing. It's been a long time since he and I have come to blows. I'd forgotten how much it hurts.

"I'm not doing this with you. Not tonight," I snap. "You need to calm down. Let Doc handle this. He's the one she trusts right now."

He stares at me, a deeply pained look of betrayal on his face. "What the fuck is wrong with you?" he sputters. "Don't you even care about her anymore?"

"Of course I care about her!" I shout. "What the fuck do you think I'm doing all of this for?" I motion to the room around us, to the monitors. "She's not *safe* until we find Dante and put a stop to all of this. All of this is *for her*."

"Then why won't you fight for her?" Something fractures in his expression. "You could fix this," he pleads. "Please. We have to go out there. We have to do *something*."

I don't answer him. I can't tell him that I'm the last person she wants to see right now.

When I choose silence, he keeps going. "It's not going to be just Doc out there, you know. Viper is with him. You trust *Viper* to deal with this? There will be blood!" He wipes his nose as he says it, then stares down at the splash of red on his hand. "Well, more than there already has been."

"We stay." My voice is steeled against any argument, and finally, Ash falls silent.

The minutes tick by so slowly it's painful. There are no more words between us. We both sit silently, obsessing.

Watching.

26

SYDNEY

Date night.

I can do this.

I take a deep breath, trying to steady my nerves. This is the right thing, I know it is. It's time to move on, time to let them go. I can't keep doing this to myself.

Ever since my phone call with Sebastian, I've been in a funk. Wanting more of what I can't have. More of him.

More of their hands on me, all over me, inside me.

I shake the thoughts away and refocus, my eyes adjusting to the dark of the space we're in, illuminated only by the brilliant white light emanating from the futuristic centerpiece dangling from the ceiling.

The new club Seamus brought us to is gorgeous—and shockingly massive, considering we've only seen the first floor. Everything is decorated in midnight black, the walls, the ceiling, even the floors. But there are unique textures everywhere to draw the eye, from the velvet curtains covering the walls to the polished granite countertops at the bar. The booth we're seated at has a dark rosewood table, impossibly smooth under my fingers, the kind of rich, heavy piece that screams money. Whoever designed this place must have spent a fortune decorating it.

We're lucky Seamus's buddy works the front door, because there's no universe in which I'd be considered important enough to be let in otherwise. A place like this is on a completely different level than the clubs I usually frequent.

"You okay?" Jade asks, prompting me to tear my gaze from our surroundings and look over at her and her date. Jade met Sienna online last week, and she reminds me a little of a fairy come to life, with her porcelain skin and long flowing red hair. Her lips are painted cherry red to match.

"Fine," I lie, forcing a smile.

A step is a step, and I'm managing. It's only natural that I be out here exploring all my options. Maybe someone like Seamus would be good for me. He's so...*normal*. And that's what I need, someone normal.

"Can I get you something from the bar?" Seamus asks.

"Always working," I joke, trying to sound playful. Flirtatious. It feels fake, though, and I quickly clear my throat to hide my discomfort. "Sure. Thanks. I'd love a gin martini and make it—"

"As filthy as they come," Seamus finishes for me. "Like I could forget. Anything for you two?"

"The same for us, thank you!" Jade waves him away. She waits until he's out of earshot, watching him navigate his way through the crowd, before she turns to me with a frown. "Are you sure you're okay? You look like you're in a hostage situation right now. Not having a romantic night with a man that I assume is attractive if you like that kind of...male-presenting thing."

"He is pretty hot," Sienna agrees.

"I know, I'm sorry," I say, twisting my hands together in my lap. "I'm kind of freaking out. I don't think I remember how to date. What do I even say to him?"

Jade sighs. "Syd, you've been dating three different men for the last few weeks..."

"Three? Dang girl, get it!" Sienna giggles gleefully.

I shoot her an embarrassed smile. "I haven't really been *dating* them. And with them, everything was just...easy. I never had to think about what I was supposed to talk about or do." I glance around and catch sight of Seamus making his way back with our drinks in hand. "What do I *do*?"

"Blink twice if you need me to pull the fire alarm," Jade whispers.

I make panicked eyes at her as she laughs.

"Here you go." Seamus slides our drinks over the table and slips into the booth next to me, casually draping his arm over the back of my seat. He takes a sip of his old fashioned, and I nervously choke back half my drink in one go.

"So, Seamus, I was wondering..." I hesitate, suddenly realizing that I don't know how I'm about to end this sentence. "Um, do you...have any favorite colors?"

Jade chokes on her drink, and Sienna giggles again.

A smile dances over Seamus's lips. "If I had to pick one, I guess I'd say green."

"Sorry, I don't know where that came from," I mutter. My cheeks feel flushed, and I fidget with my drink, too embarrassed to look at him.

"I don't think I've ever seen you nervous before. It's cute." He reaches out to take my hand, holding it still. "How about this? Why don't we put these drinks down and head to the dance floor for a bit? Does that sound good?"

"Oh, sure. Um, did you guys want to come?" I shoot Jade a pleading look.

She ignores it. "Nah, we're fine. We'll hold down the fort

over here," Jade—my *former* best friend—says. She raises her glass at me, grinning. "You two have fun!"

Okay. We're going to dance. I can do this, I like dancing. No problem.

While I try to convince myself this is what I want to do, Seamus pulls me to stand, holding my hand as we make our way through bodies to the middle of the dance floor. As if in a bad made-for-TV movie, the song switches from a high-tempo beat to a slow R&B melody the moment we hit the floor. And before I can even attempt to extricate myself from the situation, he pulls me closer and starts to move to the beat, hands circling my waist.

It's...nice. But that's about it. I sway to the music, trying to relax, but I don't get that fluttering dizzy sensation, that warmth under my skin, that makes it feel like if I don't get closer to him I could die. The feeling of wanting him to explore every inch of my body. It just doesn't feel like it does with... them. Like the way Alec and I danced together at the charity ball.

My breath hitches, the memory of that night so clear in my mind.

Alec pressing you against Ash as he explored your mouth.

Feeling Ash harden behind you while sweeping the hair off your neck, gently encouraging you to let Alec have his way.

And then...when you went upstairs, they laid you in front of that mirror and...

Between my legs, I throb, suddenly wet, suddenly wanting more.

Not only that, but I've started to sway deep into Seamus's arms, thoughts of Ash and Alec pushing me closer to him. My face is nuzzled into his shoulder, and when I look up, I can tell Seamus thinks this is about us. His eyes are half-lidded, fixed on my lips, his body rolling against mine. Before I can stop him, he moves a hand from my waist and gently cups my cheek, running a thumb across my bottom lip before lowering his mouth to mine for a kiss.

In any other world, it would be romantic. It would be what every girl wants—an attractive foreign man who can dance, waiting for the perfect moment to kiss her.

But I feel nothing.

Okay, that's not entirely true. I do feel his tongue slowly running along the seam of my mouth, patiently requesting I part and let him all the way in.

And I can't do it.

I pull back, shifting away from him.

"Sydney?" Seamus's hands drop away. "I'm sorry, did I misread the moment?"

"No. You didn't do anything wrong, I just..." I swallow, my heart caught in my throat. "Can we go back to the table? Please?"

Something passes over his face, a mix of surprise and concern. "Yeah, of course."

God, this is humiliating. I wrap my arms around myself as we push our way through the crowd, back to our booth, wishing I could disappear.

When I get close enough to spot Jade, I immediately notice the panic in her eyes.

And she's not alone.

I half expected to come back to find Jade and Sienna entwined in the corner of our booth, skirting the laws of public indecency. Instead, I find a terrified-looking Jade, a wary, uncomfortable Sienna, and seated next to them...

Sebastian and Viper.

Sebastian takes up a wide portion of the booth, his arms spread out on either side of him, eyes locking on me from the moment I see him, watching as we approach. Next to him,

Viper leans forward eagerly, elbows on the table, a manic look in his eyes. There's a knife standing straight up in front of him, the tip buried in the wood, and Sienna keeps glancing at it nervously.

"Hello, Sydney. We were just talking about you." Sebastian's eyes roll over me slowly before he moves his gaze over to Seamus. His jaw flexes, eyes darkening behind his glasses.

"What are you two doing here?" My voice trembles nervously, but I can't help it. Viper being *anywhere* makes me nervous, especially here, right now.

He's not smiling. Viper's face is cold, eyes merciless.

"I could ask you the same thing." Sebastian says the words to me, but his eyes stay locked on Seamus. "You see, this is *our* club. So, imagine our surprise when we saw your face pop up on the security system."

I swallow hard. I had no idea they owned this club. I just knew it was new and there was a lot of excitement about the opening. When Seamus had volunteered it as the venue for our first date, I hadn't questioned it.

Fuck. My date.

"Seamus, this, uh... This is Sebastian. And that's Viper." I point to them as if Seamus couldn't see them there. Even seated and relaxed, they emanate danger, command presence. Jade shoots me a surprised look. *This is Viper?* she mouths at me.

"Nice to meet you." Seamus grins at them, nothing but polite. He steps forward, holding out his hand for Sebastian to shake, clearly seeing him as the lesser threat. "How do you two know Sydney?"

Sebastian ignores the hand being offered to him, staring at it until Seamus awkwardly shakes it out and steps back. He wraps his arm around my waist instead, giving me a light squeeze.

That was a mistake.

A big mistake.

Sebastian's eyes land on his hand, and don't move, his muscles going tense.

"Hey," I say to Jade, my voice a little too loud. "Can you go grab another round of drinks while I talk to these two quickly? It'll just take a second."

Jade, bless her heart, jumps into action. "Of course!" She grabs Sienna's hand to pull her out of the booth and then turns to Seamus to say, "Would you mind helping us carry? This one stumbles over her feet too much for me to trust her carrying anything I want to survive."

"It's true, I'm a nightmare. Two left feet and everything," Sienna adds, not missing a beat, and I silently thank the universe for women who help women. Sienna shoots me a wink as she grabs Seamus's arm to lead him away.

He hesitates. "Are you sure you're okay here, Sydney?" he asks, glancing at the knife on the table. He looks torn between wanting to help me and wanting to be anywhere but here.

"I'm fine, I promise," I reassure him.

Sienna leads him away, but Jade stays back. She gives Sebastian a long look. "You think this is funny? Showing up here and ruining her date?"

He turns that icy glare on her. "I can't think of anything less funny right now, actually."

She snorts and turns to Viper, pointing an accusing finger at him. "I don't care how scary you are, don't fuck with her. She says stop, you stop. Got it?"

Viper stares after her when she storms away, a grim look on his face. He reaches for the knife on the table.

"Don't even think about it," Sebastian says, reaching out to yank it from the wood. He sets it down and pushes the knife further away from him, closer to me.

Viper's lip curls. He reaches for the knife again.

"Line," Sebastian tells him, tapping the table. A simple, clear command.

"Fuck you and your fucking lines," Viper snaps. But he withdraws his hand. His leg bounces with restrained energy as he glares after Jade.

"What does that mean?" I ask, frowning, glancing between them and the knife. "What did you just tell him?"

Sebastian stares at Viper, watching him closely. "Viper has problems with impulse control," he says finally. "Sometimes he doesn't know where to draw the line. When to stop."

"And you tell him when to stop?" I ask.

Viper barks a laugh. "You really think he could stop me, little rabbit?" he sneers, turning that dark, violent gaze on me.

"I remind him that he might be crossing a line," Sebastian explains. "That's all. Stopping is up to him."

I stare at the knife on the table, then follow Viper's eyeline to Jade, and then back to the knife. And slowly—too slowly—my mind connects the dots.

"You were going to hurt her," I say, my voice sounding strangely distant.

Viper doesn't answer. He just watches Jade through narrowed, dangerous eyes.

"Because she was defending me," I continue, my voice rising in volume. "Because she told you no. You were going to hurt Jade. *My* Jade."

"Sydney," Sebastian says softly.

Suddenly I'm moving closer, taking a step toward Viper, hands clenched.

"How fucking dare you," I hiss. My breathing is quick and erratic. There's a high-pitched ringing in my ears, like a scream.

Make him pay.

"*Sydney*," Sebastian says, louder this time, as I take another step.

Viper sits up straighter, attention now fully focused on me. His dark eyes sparkle in the dim lights.

"If you ever try to lay one fucking hand on her, I will... I will..."

Sebastian's hand whips out, grabbing my wrist, and I freeze.

I'm holding the knife.

I blink, staring down at it, clutched tight in my hand. I can't remember reaching for it, can't remember why I picked it up.

My gaze slides to his, intense blue eyes calm behind his glasses.

"Line, Sydney," he whispers. There's no judgment in his stare as he watches me. Then he lets my wrist go and sits back.

It's up to me to stop.

I drop the knife back on the table, yanking my hand away from it like it burned me.

Slowly, Viper stands.

"You'll what?" he asks, smiling down at me, his lips stretched too wide, as he closes the distance between us. "What will you do to me?"

I'm so angry I'm shaking from it. My muscles burn with the tension.

"Maybe I'll take *your* tongue, Viper," I snap, throwing his threat from the other day back in his face. "How would you like that?"

Viper's grin is all menace.

"Take it, then," he says.

Sebastian swears, scrambling to stand up to intervene, but it's too late. Viper grabs the back of my head and slams his lips down onto mine, shoving his tongue into my mouth.

I'm too stunned to do anything but stand there, frozen, as he rolls his tongue over mine, licking at my teeth, my gums, everything he can. It's not a kiss, it's nothing like a kiss. It's a claiming, like he's branding me.

I'm shaking and breathless when he finally pulls his mouth away, hand still gripping my hair.

He grins. Against my leg, his cock pulses, thick and hard.

"Sit the fuck down," Sebastian snarls at him.

"Would you really try to hurt me, little rabbit?" he asks curiously, fingers playing with my hair.

I glare at him. "I would. If you hurt what's mine."

"That's so fucking hot," Viper groans, pressing his hips against mine even harder.

"Viper," Sebastian snaps.

"Maybe I'd let you," he tells me, ignoring Sebastian entirely. "Maybe we could bleed together."

It's fear that sends my heart racing at those words. That makes my breath hitch.

Fear. And nothing else, I try to convince myself.

But the way Viper licks his lips, wild manic eyes staring into mine, makes me think he can see through the lies I'm telling myself. He pushes himself against me again, grinding his length into me, and I swallow a moan.

"I want to fuck you," Viper says, bluntly.

"And you can't," Sebastian tells him, spitting the words between gritted teeth. "Because you can't control yourself. You'll hurt her."

"Yes," Viper tells me, eyes sparkling with that promise.

"You're not gentle," Sebastian reminds him. "This is crossing a line, right here, Viper. Sit back down."

"I could be gentle," Viper tells me, ignoring his brother. "But you don't want me to be gentle, do you?"

God help me, I don't. I don't want him to be gentle at all.

I swallow, hard.

I want him to make it hurt.

Maybe he sees that answer in my eyes, maybe he knows

exactly what I'm thinking. My nerves are on fire, my pussy drenched with visions of what he would do to me.

Satisfied, Viper lets me go and finally sits back down, grinning at me the entire time.

Sebastian takes a deep breath. "Good. Now that we've settled that..." He turns, focusing on me. "Do you want to tell me what the fuck do you think you're doing here?" he asks, voice ice cold.

"What does it look like?" I ask firmly. I raise my chin a fraction in defiance. "I'm on a date."

"A date," Sebastian repeats, rolling the word in his mouth like it disgusts him.

Anger flares in my veins. *How dare* any of them try to make me feel guilty for going on a simple date, when they've hidden so much worse from me.

"Yes," I tell him. "A date. Is that a crime?"

"You were kissing him." He says it so softly, I almost miss it. But I don't miss the hurt in his eyes, the betrayal as he stares down at me. "You were, y-you were..." he stutters, stammering to get the words out. I've never seen him like this, so flustered, so out of control.

"He kissed me," I insist. "And I'm not the one who ruined everything! I wasn't the one who—"

Just like that, it's gone. That fragility in his face, that vulnerability. His face shutters, his expression going blank.

"You're right," he agrees. The emotional wall he hides behind rebuilds before my very eyes, shutting me out. "It's none of my business who you date. Why would it be?"

"It wasn't... It's not..." I'm trying to organize my thoughts into a coherent sentence, but I need to get it right, to dismantle those walls before they become permanent. "It wasn't about you, Seb. Or what we did, it's..."

How do I explain it? That I feel like I'm entitled to my

anger, to my rage. Just because he didn't outright lie to me doesn't mean he wasn't a part of the deception. But this date was more about Alec and Ash than it was about him.

I didn't mean to hurt him.

"I'm not trying to make excuses," I say softly. He won't even look at me, eyes fixed on the wall. "But finding out you all lied to me? Finding out Alec is married? That hurt me, Seb. I'm angry. And I don't know how to move forward with—"

His eyes snap to mine. "What did you just say?" he cuts in, voice low.

I stare back at him, confused. "About...?"

"About Sterling being married?" His gaze is so intense, solely focused on me.

"Um, you mean the reason I stopped seeing all of you?" I frown at him. "Are we not having the same conversation right now? Why do you think I've been so angry these last few weeks?"

He blinks slowly. "This whole time, all of it, it's because you think he's married?"

Throughout all of this, Viper has just been sitting with a growing smile on his face. Like this is all an amusing theatre production he's watching play out.

"I don't think. I *know*," I insist. "I saw his wedding ring. I saw the pictures with Annika. He admitted it. Alec lied to me, and you all just went along with it. I thought I was getting past it, but then I saw her with Ash, and I realized I can't do this anymore!"

I'm not even sure he's listening. His eyes are wide, his chest rising and falling with his breath. He takes a step closer to me.

"It wasn't me," he says softly, barely more than a whisper. "It was never me. Was it?"

I scoff, rolling my eyes. "Unless you're also married and keeping it from me, I—"

Viper gave me no warning when he kissed me, and Sebastian isn't much better. His hand comes up to cup my jaw, touch so delicate, and then suddenly his lips are on mine, his body pressing into me.

I melt into him.

This. This is what a perfect kiss can be. It's soft, slow, and unhurried. But I feel it in every cell of my body, touching every part of me.

It's impossible to resist, and I don't even try to fight it. I reach up, wrapping my arms around his neck, arching into him.

When he finally shifts back, I'm breathless, aching for more.

"We have to go," he murmurs, lips brushing against mine, fingers trailing over my cheek.

"What?"

But he's already moving away, hands dropping away from me. He motions to Viper, who stands, grabbing his knife. He doesn't say another word to me, doesn't even look at me. He just disappears into the crowd, Viper on his heels.

What the fuck?

I stand there for a few more seconds, catching my breath, trying to collect myself. It's worse than when he almost kissed me in my shop, a thousand times worse. I'm surprised my legs can even hold me.

It's not fair, the effect he has on me. Not fair, how much I want him.

When I finally feel like I'm back in control of my body—when I finally remember what the hell I'm doing here, in the middle of this club—I make my way to the bar to find the others. Jade and Sienna I spot immediately standing at the far end of the bar, wrapped in each other's arms. They're making out so vigorously I almost feel bad for interrupting them.

"Ahem..." I clear my throat when I walk up, trying to get

their attention as gently as possible. Jade's eyes snap open, and she pulls back immediately, untangling herself from Sienna's embrace. There's red lipstick smeared on her mouth.

"Uh, hey guys," I say, giving them an awkward wave. I look around the bar, searching for my date. "Where's Seamus?"

They exchange a look. "He left right around the time that you and Viper started making out in front of the entire club," Jade tells me.

"He was pretty disappointed. I think he really liked you," Sienna adds. Great. Just when I thought I couldn't feel worse.

"Fuck." I close my eyes and tip my head back. "This might be the worst first date in history."

"You have a tendency to be hyperbolic, but I think in this case you might be right," Jade concedes. "But forget about him for a second. Are you okay?"

"No. I'm really not." I open my eyes to look at her and have to fight against the urge to cry. "I think I need to leave. I'm going to head home."

"Oh sweetie." Jade pulls me into a hug. There's lipstick smeared on her neck, too. "Do you want me to come with you?"

"No, you two have fun. I'll be okay, I promise. I just need to get home and cry on my couch for a while. I'd rather do that without any witnesses."

We say our goodbyes, and I head back to the abandoned booth to grab my jacket, throwing one last glance at where Sebastian disappeared into the crowd.

Officially the worst first date ever.

It gets worse, though. Somehow, it gets far, far worse. Because when I get home, there's a note waiting for me on my doorstep.

And a photo of me at the club, dancing with Seamus.

I see you.

Everywhere you go.
You can't get away.
I have eyes in places you can only imagine.

I stare at the photo, my heart pounding in my chest. Ash wouldn't do this. None of my guys would do this.

Someone else left this for me.

Someone who wants me scared.

27

ALEC

Her date is leaving.

My shoulders loosen, tension draining out of me as I watch him head for the exit. Alone. But before I can fully relax, fully appreciate the relief of knowing she's not going home with him, the office door slams open.

And before I know it, I'm being lifted out of my chair by my neck and thrown against the wall.

"*What the fuck did you do?*" Sebastian shouts. He isn't small, by any means, but I'm still surprised by his strength as he wraps a hand against my throat and smashes my head back into the wall.

"Take your fucking hands off me," I command, voice lethally calm. "You're out of line."

He presses me against the wall harder. "She's with him because of *you!*" he snarls. "She's dating *because of you.*"

"She's *dating?*" Ashton asks, sounding devastated.

"You let me think it was my fault," Sebastian says. I watch the rage on his face slowly morph into betrayal. "You let me believe the only woman I've formed any kind of connection with since..." He stops, expression hardening. "You let me think I was the one who ruined this. For all of us." His grip tightens. "When you knew it was you all along."

"What the fuck are you talking about?" Ashton demands. "What the hell happened out there?"

"You." Sebastian turns on him, seething. "Don't even fucking start with me, brother. You're as bad as he is!"

"Both of you, take a breath, collect yourselves," I order, trying to regain some control.

It doesn't work. Sebastian's hand grips a little tighter, and my vision starts to tunnel.

That's enough.

I reach up and grab his wrist, twisting it, and before he can react, I've lifted him by the shirt, reversing our positions and slamming him into the wall.

"You don't get to touch me," I tell him. He glares down at me, lip curled. "If you ever put your hands on me like that again, I'll—"

Click.

My entire body goes rigid as something hard presses against the base of my skull. Something that feels suspiciously like the barrel of a gun.

"Let him go," Viper tells me, voice a low growl.

Fuck.

A slow smile spreads over Sebastian's face. Glowering at him, I suck in a shaky breath through my nose. "Tell him to drop the gun and back off," I order.

Sebastian's grin widens. "Make me," he purrs.

"Jesus fucking Christ," Ashton mutters. In my peripheral vision, I can see him pacing, hands threaded in his hair.

"Viper..." I start.

"Let. Him. Go." Viper punctuates each word by pushing the gun harder against me.

Fine. I drop my hold on Sebastian, slowly raising my hands until the gun disappears, and I feel him shift away from me.

"Someone tell me what the fuck is happening!" Ashton shouts.

Sebastian glares at me, murder in his eyes. "Sydney's dating. Moving on." He spits the words at me. "Because she found out all about Sterling's *marriage*. Isn't that right?"

I don't say a word, don't bother defending myself. They know now. There's no more hiding it.

"You're fucking kidding me." Ashton looks between the two of us, panicked. "What did you tell her?"

"She found out on her own," I admit.

"Found his ring, and a picture of her," Sebastian says. He turns to Ash. "Can you blame her for hating us?"

"No." Ashton shakes his head, again and again. "No, no, no. You explained it to her, right? You, you..." He shoves a hand through his hair, mussing it. "You told her about Annika, you explained it all to her, right?"

"I tried," I admit in a broken voice.

"What do you mean *you tried*?" Ashton's shout echoes in the small room.

"She wouldn't stay and listen!" I say. "I tried!"

"Fuck. Fuck, fuck, fuck," Ashton chants, pulling at his hair. "Why the hell didn't you tell us?"

"Because he's a fucking liar," Sebastian spits out. He looks like he might take a swing at me, hands flexing.

"We could have talked to her about it," Ashton says, his voice frantic. "We could have been making this better!"

"Don't you fucking start," Sebastian snaps at him. "You already made everything worse! When were you going to tell us you've been meeting up with *Annika*? Don't fucking deny it, she saw you two together! You fucking traitor!"

"Back up." I glare at Ash. "What the hell is he talking about?"

"Okay." Ashton takes a deep breath and holds his palms out to face me. "Don't be mad."

I'm not mad, I'm fucking furious. "Talk. Now."

"We needed information!" Ashton tries to explain. "To find out what Dante was planning! And I knew she could help! She's always known, hasn't she? What was going on behind the scenes?"

"Have you lost your fucking mind?" I fume, storming over to him. "You're going rogue and making decisions like that without running it by us first?"

"I knew you'd shut me down! Easier to ask for forgiveness than permission, right? You taught me that."

It's true. That was our motto, working under Dante, making the calls we knew he'd never agree to. Learning how to run an empire on our own.

"I'm not Dante," I tell him, speaking through clenched teeth. "We make these calls together or not at all."

Ashton shakes his head, refusing to see reason. "You wouldn't agree to it. Either of you. And I don't regret it, I don't regret contacting her. She confirmed it. Dante's back, and he's out for blood. Annika says he's using Sydney as a distraction." He inhales slowly, glancing quickly at his brother, then back to me. "There's more. I think we were wrong about her. I don't think she sold us out. She was—"

My phone rings, the sharp sound interrupting him.

"What?" I snap into it when I answer.

A crackle. Then, "Sir, we thought you should know there's been an incident."

"Spit it out." I don't have time for this. I don't have time for any of this bullshit right now.

There's a pause on the other end of the line. "We just

found a bomb on the premises. We're requesting permission to evacuate Oscuro, immediately."

—

Such a small thing to cause so much chaos. Tiny enough to fit into a backpack left near the rear door of the club, outside in the alley. Small, but powerful enough that it could have taken down the entire building.

Had we not hired the extra security, they might not have caught it in time.

I stay on the phone with Oscuro's security team as Earl drives me home, listening to every update, knowing the board will find a way to blame me for this. None of my brothers join me. None of them will even look at me when they leave.

It doesn't matter. All I can think about is her.

Sydney was there tonight. Sydney could have been in the club when that bomb went off, if we hadn't found it.

This is more than a nuisance. More than pulling a liquor license, more than siphoning off our income, more than going after our businesses.

This is war.

28

SYDNEY

FOURTEEN MISSED CALLS.

I wake up the morning after my disastrous date with Seamus to fourteen missed calls from Ashton. I half expect to open my door and find him camped out on the stairs in front of my apartment when I leave for work.

Thankfully, he isn't.

I spend the day barely going through the motions, distracted and miserable. Seamus still hasn't texted me back—not after my humiliating "Sorry I kissed another man on our date, can we still be friends?" message. I don't blame him. I wouldn't text me back either.

It's safe to assume we can effectively scratch Twin Pines off the list of bars I can show my face in ever again.

The sun is out today, one final beautiful summer's day before fall really sets in. It's the type of weather that draws people to patios and parks, not to a bookstore. The shop is quiet, just a few customers filtering in over the afternoon, and nothing to occupy my attention or distract me from my miserable thoughts.

Jade notices my mood, of course. And as always, she's determined to cheer me up.

Sliding a cookie toward me across the counter, she clears her throat. "Would you rather—"

"Not this again," Justin groans. "You're still playing this stupid game?"

"Shush," Jade scolds him. "It's not stupid, and it's not a game. It's a cognitive exercise, and you play without complaint, or you're fired, got it?"

He sighs, but doesn't argue, and she turns her attention back to me. "Would you rather..." Jade hums in thought, trying to think of an acceptable scenario. "Be able to fly, or be able to turn invisible?"

Justin leans his back against the counter and taps a finger against his lips, giving the question far more consideration than it deserves. "Fly," he says, finally. "Hands down. Who would want to be invisible anyway?"

"I don't know," I murmur, staring at the cookie Jade gave me, but making no move to eat it. Chocolate chip. My favorite. "I can see the appeal."

Justin looks at me like I've grown a second head. "The appeal? Of being invisible?" He shakes his head. "Flying is a superhero power. You could actually save people if you could fly! Being invisible is just creepy. What good could you possibly do with that?"

My phone buzzes in my pocket. I drag it out, throat constricting when I see the screen.

Incoming call: Ashton.

"No one could hide things from you," I reason, sending the call to voicemail and forcing my voice to be steady. "No secrets, no lies. Like I said, I can see the appeal."

My phone buzzes again immediately.

Ashton: 911.

Ashton: Pick up. Emergency.

Justin shrugs. "Still creepy," he says. "No offense, Syd."

"None taken," I mutter, staring down at my phone.

Another buzz.

Ashton: Please. Please pick up. I'm begging you.

"Hey, do you two mind watching the registers for a bit?" I ask. "I need to make a call."

"Yeah, no problem," Jade answers. "We're dead today, anyway." She turns her attention to Justin. "Okay, brat, would you rather..."

My phone buzzes incessantly as I make my way through the back of the store, but I manage to ignore it, gripping it tight in my fist until I've closed the stockroom door behind me and locked it.

The buzzing stops when I finally pick up. "Ash, this better be important. I'm in the middle of work and—"

"He's not married."

The words hit me so hard they knock the air out of my lungs. The phone slips in my grip, and I almost drop it. "What?"

Ashton swears. "I mean... Okay, he *is* married, technically, but—"

My temper snaps. "I'm hanging up."

"No! Wait, Babygirl, listen—please." His voice is frantic, edged in panic. "It's not real. The marriage was never real!"

"What the hell does that mean, 'not real'? I saw the certificate, Ash. Looked real enough to me."

"Look, Annika's dad... He's not a good guy. And he was

going to marry her off to someone she didn't know, send her away to another country, like Russia or something. She was young and scared and..." He stops to take a breath. "She came to Alec for help, to get her out of it. And he did. He married her on paper so she could stay. But they were never... *Nothing ever happened.* There was nothing between them, I swear it! She's like our little sister. You have to believe me."

My throat constricts. I remember the look on Sebastian's face when I confronted him—the shock in his eyes, like he hadn't even realized why I was angry.

It was never me.

On the other end of the phone, Ashton laughs, almost wild with relief. "So this was all just a huge misunderstanding! You have no idea what a weight off my chest this is. But it's okay now. You know the truth. We can go back to the way it was. I'll come over tonight and—"

"No."

The silence on the other end of the line is long.

"No?" His voice cracks. "But Babygirl—"

"Let's say I believe you," I interrupt, anger filling my voice. "And I'm not saying I *do* believe you—"

"But it's the truth!

"Even if it is true, Ash, you lied. You and Alec. Over and over again. About who you were, about her, about everything." My voice wavers, but I bite it back, forcing the steel into my words. "And when I told you I needed space to figure it out, you refused to give it to me."

"Sydney, I—"

"No." I grip the phone tighter. "I'm talking now. And you're going to listen. You haven't given me a reason to trust you. Not you. Not Alec. Neither of you. So no, Ash. You don't get to come over. You don't get to pretend this is fine. We're *not* fine."

On the other end of the line, there's only the sound of his breathing, jagged and uneven.

"Give me time," I say. "Actually give me time to think about it. To figure things out, okay?"

A long pause. Then a broken, "Yeah. Okay."

I take a shaky breath, trying to calm myself.

"Goodbye, Ash."

I don't wait to hear his answer before I hang up.

He's lying. He *has* to be lying.

But...

I stare down at my phone and open my messages. Alec sent me a text, didn't he? That night?

This time, I read it.

> The Boss: Sydney, I should have told you about Annika. I should never have lied to you. You're right to hate me. But I didn't tell you for one simple reason. We're married in name only. Annika and I have never been anything romantic. Please, darling, you have to believe me. I'll explain everything. Whenever you're ready, I'm here. I'll always be here. You're it for me.

The words blur in my vision.

I close the message and feel like my entire world has shifted.

———

I'M NOT SURE HOW LONG I STAY THERE, LOCKED IN THE stockroom, Alec's message echoing in my head.

I don't know what to believe. I don't know who to believe.

So I do the only thing I can think of. The only thing that's ever worked when I'm falling apart.

I run to Jade.

By the time I've dragged myself out of the stockroom and word-vomited every miserable detail of the call, I'm shaking, my head buzzing. Jade and Justin listen patiently while I regurgitate it all for them.

"So," Jade says carefully, when I finish. She takes a bite of the cookie I'd left behind on the counter, chewing it thoughtfully. "Do we believe him?"

"I don't know," I admit, wrapping my arms around myself. My voice is raw. "I want to. But wanting to doesn't make it true."

I reach out for the cookie, but Justin grabs it before I do and takes a huge bite, chewing like it's helping him think. "Okay, let me make sure I understand all of this." The words are muffled around his mouthful of chocolate chip sugary goodness. "You were dating this guy, right? But you found out he's married."

"Correct."

"So you end it. Totally fair. But then this other guy that you were dating calls you and tells you that the first guy...isn't actually married? That it's, what? Like a marriage of convenience?"

"Or something like it," I say.

"And the text you showed us." He nudges my phone where it sits on the counter, smearing chocolate on the screen. "Seems to confirm that the *second guy* is telling the truth about that."

"There's a third guy too," Jade adds. "But we're not supposed to talk about him. Or the fourth one, who kissed her in a club last night."

Justin chokes on the cookie, raising his eyebrows at me. I shrug.

"That's pretty much it," I say.

"When you found out he was married, he didn't try to explain any of this in person?" Justin asks.

"I wasn't exactly listening to him," I admit. "And I sort of ran out of the apartment...and... away."

Justin's lips twitch. "Uh-huh."

The tiniest smile tugs at my mouth, despite everything. "Okay, yes, guilty as charged. I'm the girl in the movie who runs away before a single sentence could likely clear up the entire situation. Shut up."

"At least you're self-aware about it," Justin consoles me.

The service bell for the back register rings, signaling we have a customer waiting.

"If you're not going to be helpful, go cover the register," Jade tells him, shoving his shoulder. He laughs and takes another bite of my cookie before leaving.

After he's gone, Jade leans in close. Her voice softens. "So."

"So," I echo.

"Do we believe him?"

Do I?

I hadn't given him a chance to explain that night. I hadn't wanted to.

"I don't know. If I'm being honest, it's not even just whether or not he's married. It's the lying. And what if this isn't the only thing he's lied about? I don't know anything about them, not really. It feels I'm sitting on the outside of their little circle," I admit. "And he has no intention of letting me in."

Jade reaches across the counter, squeezing my hand. "It's okay to take time to figure out how you feel, Syd. You don't have to figure everything out right this second."

Her steady gaze holds mine until I nod, some of the pressure in my chest loosening.

I don't have to figure it out this second. I can take my time, I can—

"Delivery!"

The front door swings open, and a man shuffles in, juggling a long, flat box. I recognize it instantly from the shape.

Great. More roses. I swallow a sigh. Ash probably ordered them the second he got off the phone with me.

The delivery guy doesn't even make eye contact with either of us. He just walks toward me, and before I can thank him, he drops the box unceremoniously on the counter, takes a photo of it with his phone, and leaves without a word. The door clicks shut behind him.

"Wow." Jade stares after him. "Rude much?"

"Maybe he's late for another delivery?" Unlike the other boxes, this one is gray, the cardboard cheap and thin. There's a card on the top, and I pluck it off, palming it. "Or he could just be having a bad day. You never know what someone else is going through when—"

I lift the lid and stop.

Stop, and stare.

I was wrong. They're not roses. Inside the box are lilies. A dozen of them.

And all of them are dead and desiccated, black from age.

My stomach twists unpleasantly as the smell hits me. Not just dead flowers, but something musky, almost cloyingly sweet when mixed with the roses. Something like *rot*.

"...Sydney?" Jade's voice comes from far away.

There's something else crammed down into the bottom of the box. I shift the tissue paper to get a better look at it. A stuffed animal. A cat. Once white, and now...

Torn up the middle, covered in dirt and grime, and...

There's something *moving inside it*. Writhing in the white of the stuffing, wriggling...

"Are those ...?" My voice doesn't sound like my own.

Jade moves before I can. She snatches the lid away from

me, slamming it back into place so hard she crushes a corner of the cardboard box.

Maggots.

The stuffed animal was full of maggots.

"Don't," she says, her voice fierce, commanding. "Don't look again."

"Was there something dead in there?" I ask. My heart is hammering in my chest. I feel dizzy.

"No," Jade says, a little too quickly. "No, it was just...it was just meat. Raw meat."

Raw meat.

My stomach churns. The smell of rot is in my nose, in my throat. My mouth fills with saliva.

Jade notices I'm going to faint before I do.

"*Fuck!*" She lunges forward, catching me by the elbows before I can collapse, easing me down onto the ground.

"Justin!" she yells. "Get back here! We need some help!"

From somewhere far away, I hear footsteps pounding closer. But I can't think. I can't even breathe.

"I think I'm going to throw up," I say conversationally.

"I think you're in shock. Justin, take that out to the dumpster," Jade barks. "Now. *Don't open it.* Just get rid of it."

From somewhere above me, I hear Justin's voice, heavy with concern. "Is she okay?"

"*Now, Justin!*"

Justin mutters something and scoops the box up. The smell shifts with it, gagging me all over again.

"Tell me there wasn't a dead thing in that box," I say in a hollow voice. I don't even care if it's the truth. I need to hear it.

"There wasn't a dead thing in that box," Jade insists, crouching in front of me. She takes my face in her hands. "Look at me, Syd. There wasn't. I promise."

I want to believe her. But the image of that gaping white cat, the pale roiling bodies inside...

"Where's Bea?" My voice comes out panicked. "Where's my cat, where's—"

I feel her before I see her. She nuzzles up against me, rubbing her head on my thigh. I scoop her up in my arms, burying my face in her fur and sobbing.

Safe. She's safe.

"Why would he send that?" Jade asks, sounding horrified. "I mean... I know you two ended things on bad terms, but Alec doesn't seem like the type to—"

"It wasn't him. It wasn't any of them," I answer, voice muffled in Bea's fur.

And it hits me then how much I know, in my heart, that they would never do something like that. Not to me. Not ever.

My hand unclenches. I realize I've been gripping something tight in my fist this whole time. The card.

Shakily, I set Bea down, and I peel it open and read it.

Flowers as sweet as you.

Justin covers my shift for the rest of the day.

But no matter how much I pace my apartment, or how many times I try to lose myself in mindless scrolling on my phone, I can't stop thinking about those flowers.

Lilies.

Only one man has ever sent me lilies. Only one man would want to hurt me like this. He warned me, didn't he? Told me he wouldn't go away without a fight.

What is it he said to me, during my date with Ashton?

You're going to regret fucking with me.

Chase. Chase is the one behind this, the one sending me these awful gifts. I'm certain of it.

I know I should be scared. I know, deep down, that fear is the right response.

But something else takes root inside me instead.

Fury.

It starts low in my stomach, molten and ugly, then spreads like fire through my veins. Rage for the years I've swallowed it down. Rage for every time he made me feel small and weak. And now, when I've moved on, when all of my thoughts don't revolve around him, he chooses to do this?

I'm not afraid, because unmasking the demon tormenting me makes him real again. And real, I can handle. Because Chase doesn't scare me anymore.

And as if he heard the realization click, my phone pings.

Unknown number: How did you like my little gift?

Another chime.

Unknown number: Don't worry.

And another.

Unknown number: I'm only getting started.

29

ASHTON

I'm not in my right mind going into this fight tonight.

Everything is fucked. I'm trying to suck it up, trying to paint a happy-go-lucky smile on my face, but nothing can distract me from how pissed off I am at Alec right now. I can't even stand being in the same room as him, can't look at him without wanting to kill him.

This morning, I caved and sent Sydney a text asking if I could see her, just to talk. I invited her to my fight again, hoping it would be low-stakes enough that maybe she'd agree to come and watch, and maybe we could chat after. My texts have all gone unanswered.

Still, there's a chance she'll show, right?

I scan the arena on my way to the locker room, looking for her, my eyes landing on every head of curly brown hair in the place. But I don't see her. Even worse, I don't see any of them.

No one is here to watch me tonight.

I've never had a fight where none of my brothers showed up to support me, but I get it. We're not exactly chummy right now. It still hurts. Their not being here reminds me of how it felt every time I was sent to live with a new foster family. It never mattered if the family was kind, or rich, or loving, or anything. It was the loneliest fucking thing in the world to be taken away from them. I hated it, hated leaving my brothers behind.

For me, it was always all four of us together, or nothing. And I guess tonight, it's nothing.

"Two-minute warning, champ," my trainer, Zach, says, snapping me out of my reverie. He takes my hands to adjust my wraps, checking the tightness. "You good?"

"Yeah, yeah, I'm fine," I murmur. I sure as fuck don't mean it.

"Get your head together. This guy is undefeated this season."

I scowl, shaking out my limbs and stretching my muscles. "He's only had five fights. That's not exactly an impressive record. Trust me, I'll be fine."

He gives me a skeptical look, but you know what? Fuck him.

I can do this. I will do this. I always do.

"Okay. Let's get out there then." Zach grabs my sweat towel and water bottle, leading me up to the arena.

The announcer's voice booms, filling the building. The crowd is wild tonight. I haven't fought in a while, and there's a palpable excitement from the spectators at seeing me back in the ring. That's what the crowd wants. They're here to see me, to see what I can do. To see me win. That's the reputation I built for myself over the years, even back in my days of underground fighting, before Dante. In my best years, no one could put up a real fight against me. And when I retired, I retired on top. That's the way to do it, the only way to go out.

But every few months, I still like to jump back into the ring to remind them I'm not just a pretty face.

I'm lethal. I'm a killer.

The crowd roars when I step into the ring. I throw a few showy punches and glance across the platform at my opponent. He's big. Bigger than I was expecting. We touch our gloves together and step back, ready for the first round to begin.

I know the moves. I know how to win. I've got this.

But when my eyes snag on a head full of brown curls in the front row, my heart skips a beat, and everything else around me disappears. Sydney?

Is that her?

Did she really come to see me?

I don't hear the bell.

And I don't see the fist coming, not until it connects hard with my jaw.

———

It's a bloodbath.

After the first hit, I can't get my footing. I'm on the ropes the whole first round, and it only gets worse in the second.

I barely get a chance to hit the guy, but he sure as fuck manages to hit me.

"What the hell happened out there?" Zach asks one humiliating loss later, holding a bag of ice to my swollen eye in the locker room. I don't have an answer for him. I stare up at the gray stucco ceiling, my back flat against the wooden bench, asking myself the same thing.

What happened?

She never came. That's what happened.

She doesn't want me anymore. That's what happened.

My eye is so swollen, I don't see the door open. I only hear it shut, and only realize Doc is there when he says, "Leave us."

Shaking his head, Zach sets the ice down on the bench next to my face. "He's all yours, man. Just go easy on him, okay?"

Yeah, right, I think, as the door closes behind him. *Fat chance of that.*

"I don't need your help," I grumble, as Sebastian sets his med bag down next to me and starts pulling out supplies.

"Too fucking bad," he says in an annoyingly even tone, snapping on a pair of blue gloves. "Hire another personal physician then."

We're quiet as he pulls out a square of gauze and applies a nauseatingly bright orange antiseptic to the cut above my eye. The smell is so strong it burns my sinuses.

"She didn't come," I murmur, voice low.

My brother's hand stills, and his eyes flick to mine. "Who?" he asks, raising an eyebrow.

"You fucking know who," I answer. I swallow hard. "I thought after she learned the truth about Annika that she'd come back."

Sebastian swears under his breath, tossing the gauze into the trash. "It's not that simple. Do you want to know why she didn't come?"

I want you to jump off a cliff, I think. *I want to drag you into the ring and beat the shit out of you.*

"Because I don't give her space? I text too much?" I glare at him, as best as I'm able. "You sound like a broken record. I get it, okay?"

"You don't get it, though. You think you can just re-insert yourself back into her life whenever you want? Without her asking for it?" He lets out a frustrated breath. "This isn't about Annika. This is about you not giving a shit about her boundaries."

"Whoa!" I sit up so fast that I almost black out, white dots forming in front of my eyes. The moment the room stops spinning long enough for me to focus, I shove a finger into Doc's chest. "Fuck you! I don't give a shit about her boundaries? That's a fucking joke coming from you, asshole!" I laugh, but there's no humor in it. "I can promise you right now, no woman has ever *cried* after I finished with her."

"Boundaries don't just exist in the bedroom. You get that, right?" Sebastian says, glaring at me. "That's your problem, Ashton. You hear 'consent' and you pat yourself on the back for understanding safe words."

"What the fuck are you talking about?" I wave my hands around. "I am the consent *king*. I have never, ever pushed a woman too far. I've always stopped when asked. And I've always listened to those *fucking* safe words."

He levels an irritated look at me. "What did Sydney first tell you? When you spoke to her that night on the phone?"

I scramble to remember, the pain in my face making it difficult. "That she was drunk," I say.

"You fucking idiot." Sebastian rolls his eyes so hard it's a struggle for me not to slap the glasses off his face. "She told you she wanted space. Maybe it was for something we didn't understand, but that *shouldn't matter*. She told you what she needed from you."

Right. Yeah, she did.

"And what did you do after she told you that?" he pesters.

"You're going to need to get to your point real fast, asshole, because your face is looking more and more punchable by the second."

"You texted her. Nonstop." Sebastian stares at me, over the rim of his glasses. "And what did you do when she didn't answer those text messages?"

"So fucking punchable right now," I remind him.

"You went over there. To her place of work. Uninvited, unwanted, and unasked." His eyes narrow at me. "Sydney put up a boundary and told you not to cross it. And you crossed it. Over and over again."

I blink. Or, I try to. I wink, I guess, my right eye too swollen to cooperate.

"Boundaries don't just exist in the bedroom, Ash," Sebastian tells me. He sounds a little sad when he says it. "She told you to stop. And you didn't listen."

The breath comes out of me so fast it hurts. It feels like I got punched in the chest. "No. That's... That's not..." I think I might pass out. "That's not true. I wouldn't, I didn't..."

Oh God.

I did.

The room tilts to the side, and Sebastian swears, reaching out to grab my shoulder. "You're hyperventilating. Put your feet on the ground, head between your knees."

I barely pay attention as he hauls me into position. There's a sharp ringing in my ears.

"Take a deep breath," Sebastian instructs me. His voice is almost soothing. He puts a hand on my back, rubbing a slow line up and down my spine.

I ignore him. "Holy shit," I mutter, staring down at the space between my feet. "I'm an asshole."

"Yeah," Sebastian agrees. But his touch is light and calming. "You really are."

I listen to him this time and take a deep breath. Then another. Slowly, the ringing in my ears starts to fade. My vision returns, and I watch a drop of crimson blood fall from my face and splatter on the floor, splashing my shoes.

"There you go. Sit back up. I need to stitch your face."

This time, I don't complain. I don't call him names or imagine punching him. I sit up and hold still while my little brother does what he does best. Patching me back up after I break.

"What am I supposed to do?" I ask him.

Sebastian's hands are steady as he breaks open a foil packet and pulls a needle attached to a long black suture out.

"Listen to her," he says. "Give her time to process. If she comes back, don't you want it to be on her terms? Not because you had to convince her?"

"Yeah." I swallow. "You're right."

He doesn't use a local anesthetic. We never have, not after my fights. When we first started out, just the four of us trying to make a living doing underground fights here in the city, we didn't have access to anything like that. By the time Doc had his license, it had become almost routine for us.

A punishment I let him inflict.

He doesn't say anything until the final stitch.

"I think she'll be back," he says softly. "When she's ready."

Fuck, I hope he's right.

30

SYDNEY

For so much of my life, my anger felt like an anchor, weighing me down, holding me back. It took so much work to bury it deep inside me, to push it down so deep there was no chance it could hurt anyone else.

Now, I feel it gnawing at my chest, wanting to be let out.

Let it out. Let it take care of Chase.

I should have known it wasn't my imagination. Chase never could stand to lose, to not get exactly what he felt he was owed. I never expected him to go this far, but I'm not that surprised. I know the kind of man he is. I saw those flashes of petty rage in his eyes for years.

He demanded I come back to him, and I didn't listen. Then he was humiliated, first by Seb and then by Ash. This is his escalation. The only thing I can't understand is what he hopes to get out of this. What is he hoping to accomplish, other than torturing me?

"No." A loud voice breaks through my thoughts. "You're not setting one *foot* in this place."

I freeze in the middle of trying to tempt Bea down from

the top shelf of our classics section—where she's managed to knock a whole row of books onto the ground—and turn toward the front of the store. I gave Jade the day off, so Justin and I are on our own today. That's definitely his voice I just heard.

But I've never heard Justin yell before.

"Look, buddy, I'm just trying to do my job, okay?" a gruff voice answers. "You can either let me in to complete my delivery, or you can take it yourself."

I manage to grab Bea as she's pawing at another book, holding her against my chest as I creep my way up to the front. When I get there, Justin is standing in the doorway of our shop, actively blocking a man from entering. I don't recognize the man, but I do recognize the box in his hands. Cheap gray cardboard. Another "gift" from Chase.

"And I already told you, you're not delivering here. Not anymore," Justin snaps. It's a shock to see Justin angry, to hear his raised voice. When the delivery guy shifts, like he's going to try to push past him, Justin thrusts out his arm and blocks the way, using every inch of his height to his advantage. "Who is sending this stuff to her?"

"Listen, man, I don't know what to tell you. I'm just the delivery guy! Just move aside and let me do my job so—"

"Delivering for *whom?*" Justin asks in a raised voice.

"How the fuck should I know! I never met the guy!" the man yells. "I just accepted the job through JobRabbit—take it up with them!"

"Where did you pick it up from? What's the address?"

"Fuck this shit." The delivery guy throws up his arm in disgust. "And fuck you. I don't get paid enough for this, even with the tip." Scowling, he turns to leave, chucking the box next to a trash can on his way down the street.

Justin doesn't move from the doorway until the guy is out of sight. Only then, when the man is long gone, does he step back inside, letting the door finally close.

Unaware of my presence, Justin pulls out his phone, and I watch him navigate to the app store, searching through the possible downloads until he finds one with a pink rabbit holding a hammer.

"What was that about?" I ask, setting Bea down on the ground. She takes off the moment her paws hit the floor, racing out of the café to cause trouble elsewhere.

Justin glances up at me and then back to his phone. "Nothing you need to worry about."

"Another box of horrors?" I joke. He doesn't return my smile.

"I didn't look inside," he admits. "But the guy mentioned JobRabbit. I've heard of it. It's an app for hiring people to do random tasks." He types away as he talks. "Maybe I can figure out where this stuff is coming from. And put a stop to it."

Justin keeps typing, face pinched in concentration.

Screw it.

"I think I know who it is, actually," I tell him. He doesn't look up, his brows furrowed as he types. "I'm pretty sure it's Chase."

I wasn't going to tell anyone my suspicions until I could get some proof, but I'm tired of feeling like I have to handle this all on my own. I could use some backup.

Justin looks up from his phone in surprise. "What? Why would Chase do this to you?"

"Because he's an asshole?" I offer. "I think when I refused to get back together with him, he took that as an opportunity to, I don't know, punish me? It wouldn't be the first time."

Justin's expression seems stuck halfway between pity and fury, but he schools himself before he responds. "Jesus. You really think he'd do something like this? The flowers, the uhhh

—" I don't make him finish his sentence, not wanting to remember the smell of rotting meat that accompanied his last delivery.

"I do," I tell him honestly. "But I'd love some sort of confirmation or proof that it's him. So if you still want to do your fancy computer stuff," I wave my hand at his phone. "I'd really appreciate it."

He smirks wide enough to show his dimples. "I'm happy to do my *fancy computer stuff*, but what's the plan in the meantime? Should we call the police?"

"The justice system isn't exactly known for taking stalkers seriously," I grumble. "I already have a restraining order, but until we have proof, I doubt the police will do anything. Not without something definitive, anyway."

I already know what my best route of protection is, and it doesn't involve anyone in a uniform. It involves four men, who I know wouldn't hesitate to step in, if asked.

They'd take care of him for you. Leave him in pieces for his family to find.

Justin sighs. "I know what you mean. About the police not helping. Even with proof, they're next to worthless." Something dark crosses over his face. "We can't just sit around and wait for him to really hurt you, though. I'm not going to let that happen. I'm not going to stand back and let another asshole get away with this. Not again."

"What do you mean, not again?" I ask, frowning.

He freezes, like he hadn't realized he said it.

"Justin?" I prompt.

He blows a lock of hair out of his eyes, refusing to look at me. "You remember that secret I told you? How I got kicked out of my grad program?"

"Yeah," I say, dread creeping into my chest. "For assaulting someone." He nods, slowly. "A woman?" I venture.

Justin's head whips up in shock. "What? No!"

"You said it!" I accuse him. "You said to me that there was a girl and—"

"And there was!" Justin shoves his phone back into his pocket. The look he gives me is heartbroken and wounded. "But *I* didn't hurt her."

"Okay." I cross my arms over my chest. "Then tell me. What happened?"

"There was a girl, and she got hurt. But she wasn't... She's not the one I assaulted." Justin runs a hand through his hair. "I was TAing a class, and there was a student who was..." he pauses, searching for the words. "Great. She was great. Maybe not the best in the class, but better than a lot of the guys in my grad courses. High marks, creative solutions when she hit coding issues, really just...great."

"And?"

Justin huffs. "And then she just stopped showing up. And when she was there, she wasn't...you know, present. Her grades dropped, her work was subpar, and I just couldn't understand what happened. So I started asking around, talking to the other TAs about it."

I wait, while he takes a deep breath.

"She was raped," he tells me.

My heart sinks. "Oh God," I whisper.

"This asshole she was dating took her to a party and—" He runs a hand over his face, looking exhausted, suddenly.

I take a step closer to him, reaching out my hand to touch his shoulder.

"She did everything right, too," Justin continues, voice dropping to nearly a whisper. "Not that there's a *wrong* way to react when something like this happens, you know? But she did everything they *say* you're supposed to do. She went to the nurse, got a physical, and reported it all to the dean and the police. She trusted them to handle it."

"But they didn't?"

Justin laughs, but it's a bitter, hateful sound. "No. They said it was a mistake. The guy was on a football scholarship, going to take them to the playoffs. They pretended to do an investigation, but it never went anywhere."

"That's horrible," I say, queasy just thinking about it.

"Yeah," Justin agrees. "I felt terrible for her, but what could I do, you know? And then one day, he shows up outside of the classroom with a bunch of his friends, calling her names. Said she was a liar, that she was asking for it. And I just lost it."

I don't see anger in his eyes when he looks at me, though. He looks embarrassed, ashamed.

"It's my fault," Justin admits. "I threw the first punch. After that, it's a bit of a blur." He laughs awkwardly. "I'd like to say I gave as good as I got, but, honestly, he kicked my ass. And the next day, they pulled my position."

"Justin, I'm so sorry."

He just shrugs.

"And I'm sorry I..." I can't even bring myself to say it. "I shouldn't have assumed you did anything to her. I just kept thinking about those books you like, and—"

Justin gives me a confused look. "What books?"

"Those detective books!" I counter, throwing up my hands. "About horrible men who stalk and torture women!"

"Jesus, Sydney." Justin shakes his head with a laugh. "Do you know why I like those books?"

"I have no idea. I read two, and they both scared the absolute crap out of me," I admit. Sure, they were fun to read, but I don't think I've ever been so frightened by a piece of literature in my life.

"You don't get it. You don't read those books for the *bad*

guys," Justin tries to explain. "I read them because the good guys always win. They always get the murderer, Syd. And they always rescue the victim." He laughs. "And frankly, those books —with their horrible men who stalk women and torture them? They're not that different from the books *you* read."

Oh.

He's not wrong.

"Wow," I murmur, leaning against the wall and letting myself slide down a few inches. "I think I owe you a massive apology."

Justin joins me, leaning back against the wall at my side. He chuckles. "Apology accepted." Then he pulls his phone back out, showing it to me. "We're going to get answers, Sydney. I promise you. We'll get proof, and we'll go to the cops, together."

I let myself smile at that. Because I believe him. "Thanks. You know I love you, right?"

"To the moon and back?" Justin asks hopefully.

"Let's not get carried away."

He laughs. We stay like that for a few minutes, quietly enjoying each other's company.

"You know what I miss?" I chew my lip, staring at the ceiling. "I miss when things were simple. Like when we were kids. Before..."

Before the accident. Before everything changed.

"I'm not sure things were ever simple," Justin admits. "I think it just feels like that when you're a kid." He glances at me, out of the corner of his eye. "Speaking of complicated... How are things going with the, uh, boyfriends?"

"They're not my boyfriends," I mutter. I take a deep breath. "And nothing's really changed. I'm still mad at them for lying to me, for keeping secrets. Even if they're telling the truth, and Alec's marriage isn't real..."

"Isn't there anyone who can verify that?" Justin asks. "I

don't know, someone you trust to tell you the truth about them?"

Is there?

"Maybe," I admit softly. Seb would, wouldn't he? He's always been honest with me. "But it's..."

"Complicated?" Justin guesses, with a lopsided grin.

I think about that kiss. How perfect it felt, how much I want to kiss him again.

"Yeah. It's complicated," I agree.

31

SYDNEY

I STARE DOWN AT THE PHONE IN MY HAND. MY OTHER hand rests on my bedspread, my fingers drumming nervously on the duvet.

Not wanting to wait any longer, I take a breath and dial.

Maybe he's still mad at me for going on a date. Maybe I'm still mad at him for *crashing* my date.

But he still picks up on the first ring, just like always.

"Good evening, Sydney," Sebastian greets me, in a voice so dark and dirty it sends a shiver down my spine. He doesn't even have the decency to pretend to be surprised by my call.

"I wasn't sure you'd pick up," I admit, drawing an idle pattern on my bedspread with my fingertip.

"Mm, why's that?"

"The other night. I just... I haven't seen you, and you haven't called." I would never have purposefully gone to *their* club, been so brazen about it. No wonder he was upset. "I wasn't sure if you'd want to talk to me after what happened."

"There will never be a day I won't want to talk to you, love." My breath catches, but he continues. "You caught me by surprise, that's all. Seeing you with another man. Him kissing you—" There's a pause on the other end of the line. "If I ever see another man's hands on you again, I can't promise it won't get violent."

My thighs clench at that, my body betraying me. Hearing him be so possessive, it does something to me. I realize I'm turned on just by the idea that he would hurt someone to keep me.

"I need to ask you something," I say, willing my voice to be steady. "And I need you to be honest with me."

"Always," Sebastian tells me.

I take a steadying breath. "Is Alec married?"

There's no pause, none at all. "Yes," he answers.

"And is she... What did it mean to him? What did *she* mean to him?"

A noise so low I can barely hear it. It might be a laugh. "Annika and Alec were never romantic. My brothers always treated her like a sister. Their marriage was never more than a piece of paper. One she asked for, for the record."

They were telling the truth. Something loosens in my chest, hearing it.

"You were surprised I knew about her," I remind him. "At the club, I mean."

There's a long pause before he answers. "I thought it was me," he says. "I thought I... I thought I scared you away. In the stockroom."

Lick it clean.

Heat floods my veins, my nerves suddenly alight. "No," I murmur. "No, I wasn't scared."

A soft laugh. "What were you, then?"

I can't answer him. I chew on my lip, pulse racing.

"You liked it, didn't you?" Sebastian teases. "You wanted it."

"Yes." My voice is a soft sound, barely audible.

"You still want me, don't you, love?"

I do. More than anything right now, I do. "Yes."

"Prove it. Tell me what you're wearing for me tonight," he says. There's something dark and dangerous in his tone, and I want more of it.

I wriggle back against my bedspread, sucking my lower lip between my teeth.

"Nothing," I lie. "I'm not wearing anything at all."

"Oh, my sweet Sydney..." He chuckles into the phone. "Tell me, why would you lie to me?"

I fucking knew it. My thighs clench involuntarily, and I ignore the throb his question elicits as I sit up.

"You told me there weren't any cameras in my apartment," I accuse, anger coloring my voice. "You *promised me*."

"And I was honest with you. There aren't any cameras," Sebastian says smoothly. He doesn't sound worried at all, completely unfazed by my anger. "Maybe I know you well enough to know when you're lying."

My heart races at what he says next.

"Or maybe I don't need cameras to see you tonight."

My eyes jump to my bedroom window. To the open curtains there. I swallow hard, but for some reason, I can't bring myself to get up and close them.

"Does that thought upset you, Sydney?" he asks. No kindness, no concern in his voice. Just a cold, almost clinical curiosity.

It should. I should be furious at him. It's the worst kind of violation, stealing away my privacy.

But my body doesn't seem to want to listen to reason anymore.

"No," I say breathlessly into the phone.

Sebastian's voice drops a little lower. "Does it frighten you?"

"Yes," I admit readily.

A dark chuckle on the other end of the line.

"That's good. You should be frightened of us. That's smart. Now..." He exhales slowly. "Tell me the truth. What are you wearing for me tonight?"

This time, I don't bother lying. "A black lace bralette," I breathe into the phone. "And matching panties."

His groan is barely audible. "I bet you look so good right now, Sydney," he purrs. "I bet you look good enough to eat."

Oh God. My hands inch down my stomach toward the waistline of my panties.

Sebastian tuts in my ear. "Slow down. What's your rush? We have all night together."

"I want it. I want you," I say into the phone before I can stop myself.

"Show me," he challenges.

I run my tongue over my bottom lip. "How?"

"Get one of your little toys. Show me exactly how much you want me."

It takes me a few minutes to find the box shoved under my bed, but when I do, I give very little thought to which toy I grab. It's my favorite, after all.

The one Ashton used on me.

"Good girl," Sebastian praises as I sit back on my bed with the toy.

"What now?"

"Show me how much you want it, Sydney. Show me how you'd treat my cock if I were there with you."

I hesitate, suddenly embarrassed.

"I'm waiting, love," he prompts me.

Screw it.

I raise the toy to my mouth and run my tongue from the

base to the tip. On the other end of the phone, Sebastian sucks in a breath.

So the quiet doctor wants to know what I'd do if he were here, in my bedroom? I'm more than happy to show him.

I let my tongue circle the tip of the toy before I bring it into my mouth, moaning as I do so. My thighs rub together as I work the toy between my lips, pulling it in and out slowly, rubbing my tongue over the base.

My mind replays that moment in the stockroom, with his hand in my hair and his fingers sliding over my soaking pussy. *Filthy girl*, he'd called me.

He has no idea how filthy I can be.

How filthy I want to be tonight.

I moan louder around the toy, pushing it as far into my throat as I can. I know he would do the same if he were here. He would force me to take every inch of him. He would stare at me with those intense blue eyes and shove his cock so far down my throat I'd choke.

"That's it," Sebastian's voice says eagerly from the phone. "Fuck, you love it, don't you? You love being a dirty whore for me."

The words send a perverse thrill through me. I groan, giving the toy one last hard suck before pulling it from my mouth.

"Are you... Are you touching yourself?" I ask, panting.

Sebastian hesitates before answering. "No," he says simply.

Oh. A wave of embarrassment washes over me, bringing an uncomfortable blush to my cheeks.

"Sydney... I'm harder than I've ever been in my fucking life right now. If I started touching myself, I wouldn't last a minute. My pleasure can wait."

I chew my lip, feeling strangely self-conscious, still.

"If you think that I'm not enjoying this, you're wrong," he

insists. "Fuck, Sydney... I'm going to be thinking about this for *months*, imagining you sucking my cock like you sucked that toy. Like the good little whore I know you are."

I need more, more of him talking just like that. I whimper, squirming on my bedspread.

"That's not all you'd do if I were there, is it?" he asks.

"No," I admit.

"I know what you really want from me. Say it."

"I... I want you to fuck me, Sebastian."

"Fuck, I love it when you say my name," he groans through the phone. And I can hear it, hear how close he is to losing it even if he's not touching himself. "Show me. Show me exactly how you want it."

I practically rip my remaining clothes off.

I can't show him exactly how I want it. Because what I want from him is what he gave me in the stockroom. I want him hard and rough. I want that fiery passion he hides away, that explosive lust.

I want him to possess me.

My vibrator is a poor substitute, unable to give me any of that. But, deep down, I hope he can see it in the way I move, the way I push the toy inside myself with a little too much force, the way I whimper and buck when it hurts.

I swallow a scream as I flick the toy to life.

"*Fuck,*" Sebastian breathes into the phone. "That's it. Show me how you'd take me. Filthy fucking girl."

I'm not gentle. I wouldn't want him to be. I cry out as I fuck myself with it, pulling it almost all the way out and slamming it back inside me.

"Put me on speaker phone," he orders. "If I were there, I wouldn't be able to resist playing with your clit while we fucked. Do it."

I fumble with the phone, hands shaking, but somehow manage to press the right button.

"That's it. Fuck, you look so good right now. My filthy fucking whore. Don't stop now, you know exactly what I want. Give it to me, love."

With both hands free, I'm able to manipulate the toy and my clit at the same time. It's wonderful, a perfect combination. It doesn't take long before I feel myself building toward release.

"S-Sebastian!" I gasp, back arching off the bed.

"Fuck yes. That's my girl. Show me how well you'd take it. Show me how much you crave my cock."

Oh God. I'm right on the edge, nerves on fire.

"Come for me, Sydney. Be my perfect little whore and come."

I'm shaking, legs trembling, fucking myself hard as the toy vibrates inside me, setting my body aflame.

"*Now*," he orders.

My body obeys him instantly, like it was waiting for his permission. I scream his name, pussy clenching down hard on the toy inside me as I arch off the bed with the force of it. It feels like it lasts forever, the pulse of the toy inside me sending me over that cliff again and again.

Sebastian's breathing is loud on the other end of the phone as I finally come crashing down, collapsing back against my bed. My body is limp, my muscles liquid, and it takes an ungodly amount of time to generate the energy to turn off my toy and slide it out of my body.

As the last of it fades, I focus on my breathing, on the thunderous beating of my heart.

I don't count to ten. I don't try to calm my body or my mind, don't try to wash away the dark with happy thoughts. For once, I let myself revel in it, feeling a strange mixture of power and shame. I let myself lie there, basking in it all.

His perfect little whore.

"Are you still there?" I ask when my breath returns to normal, and my body is my own again.

"I'm still here," he answers quietly from the phone.

I lift it to my ear, switching the audio back to normal.

"You do this every time," I say. "Wait for me to hang up. Don't you?"

The pause is long.

"I do," he admits.

I shift on the mattress, suddenly awkward. This is the first time we've actually spoken, afterwards. The first time I haven't hung up on him after taking what I want.

"Why?" I ask.

"It just feels right to be here. In case you need me."

"And if I never need you?" I ask, voice teasing.

"I'll still wait," he says. The sincerity in his voice makes my chest feel tight. "I'm a patient man, Sydney."

"But you won't wait forever." The words tumble out of my mouth before I even realize I'm saying them. There's a tremble of fear to my voice. "I keep pushing you away. All of you. And I just..."

I swallow hard. On the other end of the phone, Sebastian is silent, waiting.

"You won't wait forever," I finish.

"That worries you, doesn't it?" I can hear the frown in his voice. "Do you think we're going to disappear? That we'll get sick of waiting for you?"

I don't answer.

I can't.

On the other end of the line, he sighs. "I told you. I'm a very patient man," he says softly. His voice lowers, just an octave. "I can wait forever."

My breath catches in my throat. He sounds completely

sincere. And I believe him. In that moment, I believe he'd wait for me forever.

Fuck it.

Taking my phone, I stand, moving from my bedroom to the living room. The curtains here are open too, and I wonder if he's watching. I move purposefully through my apartment until I'm standing at my door.

I stop.

"Sydney?" he asks, voice curious. "If you're going for a walk, I'll remind you that you're nude. I can keep you safe, but I can't guarantee there won't be casualties."

He sounds so nonchalant about it, like he's joking. I doubt he is. If murdering someone were required to keep me safe, I know Sebastian wouldn't hesitate. None of them would.

Reaching up I disengage the deadbolt.

It's loud enough I know he hears it.

"The door is open, Doc," I say softly into the phone.

Silence on the other end of the line. I can't even hear him breathing.

"I've had enough space," I tell him, before ending the call.

I turn my phone off, not caring about my alarm, not caring if I'm unreachable. Turning on my heel, I head back to my bedroom and switch off the light before climbing under the sheets.

In the darkness, my heartbeat is impossibly loud.

———

IT TAKES HIM A LONG, LONG TIME TO JOIN ME.

Long enough I wonder if he even will. Maybe this is a line he won't ever cross. Maybe he's happier being my dirty little secret, impossibly cold until the sun sets and I reach out to call him. Maybe that's all he needs from me. All he really wants.

Lying in the dark, listening to the beating of my heart, I wish I could fall asleep. I want to escape into a world of dreams, forget that I'm waiting. I want to wake up to his hands on my body, his dirty words in my ear.

But I can't. I'm almost frightened, trembling with anticipation as I wait.

And wait.

And wait.

When he finally comes, I don't hear the door open. Only the heavy sound of the lock turning, followed by his steady measured steps as he makes his way to my bedroom.

This would be so much easier if I were asleep, I think, as my breathing spikes and I lie there, pretending I don't hear him.

He undresses slowly, methodically, without a single word. By the time he finally pulls back the covers and crawls into bed with me, I'm practically shaking.

Earlier, I wanted Sebastian's cruelty. I wanted that explosive rage simmering right under the surface, his demeaning words and his filthy tongue.

I don't get what I want.

He gives me something infinitely better.

Sebastian's hands are impossibly gentle as he rolls me toward him, hand cradling my cheek. His lips are feather light when he kisses me.

Underneath Sebastian's mask, there's a world of darkness. He's shown me glimpses of it, fragments. But tonight? Tonight, he shows me something even more hidden.

Softness.

He takes his time, gently rolling over me until he's settled between my legs. He waits for me to open to him, parting my lips and sliding my tongue into his mouth. He returns the gesture so softly, so sweetly, I feel every muscle in my body relax for him.

I'm already ready for him, soaking wet from my release, but still, he takes his time. Reaching down, he guides himself to my entrance, and slowly—so impossibly slowly—he pushes his way inside.

Every time I tense around him, he pauses, peppering my face and lips with those feather-soft kisses until I adjust to the sheer size of him and relax again. He's patient and unhurried, our breath mingling together as we join.

By the time our hips finally meet, his entire length buried inside me, he's shaking from the effort of it.

Then he begins to move.

I gasp as his hips roll against mine, wrapping my arms around his neck and shoulders, burying my hand in his hair. It feels like strands of silk between my fingers. He feels different inside me than any other man, an extra sensation I can't understand. It's *wonderful*. Intoxicating.

It gets even better when his hands slide down my body, one pinning my thigh higher on the bed to fuck me even deeper, and the other resting on my lower stomach. His thumb circles my clit, a light teasing pressure as he moves inside me.

Before Alec, before all four of these wonderfully dangerous men, I'd only known the barest hint of what it was to experience this sort of pleasure. Alec was the first man to fuck me—truly fuck me, possessing my body, my mind, my soul.

And Sebastian is the first man to make love to me in a way that feels like worship.

In the dark of my room, it's hard to make out his face, especially his eyes, hidden behind glasses that are oddly reflective in the dim light. But I know he's watching me, feasting on my every reaction, every breath, every sound. His entire focus is my body, his thumb pressing a little harder when I gasp, his hips moving a little deeper when I grip his hair tight. I've never felt so seen.

When the pressure between my legs begins to build to a crescendo, he suddenly rolls, grasping my hip and maneuvering me on top of him, straddling him. I take over without any pause in our rhythm, hips gliding against his, moving myself against his hand, chasing my own pleasure. My lips hover over his, not quite kissing, but close enough they can't help but touch.

"Don't stop," I whisper against his lips, my hips moving faster. I can feel it coming, that beautiful release, and I need him with me.

"Never," he promises. It's the only thing he says to me, and he says it like prayer.

My hands on his chest push a little more as I pick up speed. Sebastian's hips move with me, giving me everything I want, everything I never knew I needed.

When I come, with a gasp so soft it sounds like a song, I feel it in my every nerve. My entire body surges with it, a wave of sweet release that spirals out from my center and touches every part of me.

Beneath me, Sebastian's hips crash into mine once more and still, his head arching back on the pillow with a single breathless groan. I feel every pulse of his cock as he fills me.

Neither of us says a word after. I collapse next to him on the bed, and he gathers me against him silently, wrapping his arms around me and folding me so my head rests on his chest and our legs intertwine.

I lay against him, sheltered in his arms, and listen to the rise and fall of his breath until sleep claims me, whisking me away to somewhere else entirely.

32

ALEC

It's late. Late enough that I should have left the office hours ago. I shouldn't still be here, shifting through memos and financial projection reports, listening to the distant hum of a vacuum as the custodial staff that maintains Sterling Enterprises' head office slowly works their way through the building.

Outside the floor-to-ceiling windows behind my desk, the sky is pitch black, illuminated from below by thousands of city lights. Fortune City always looks better at night. Bright. Alive.

And I shouldn't be here.

I should be at home, back at the compound, sorting through these same reports and godforsaken memos in my home office.

But the compound doesn't feel like home right now. Not when Sebastian is never there. Not when Ashton won't even look at me. He's giving me the silent treatment, storming out of the room anytime he sees me. They both blame me for Sydney's absence, for everything that's fallen apart.

And they're not wrong. It is my fault.

I tap my finger on my mahogany desk, trying to focus on

work. The security report from the incident at Oscuro is open in front of me. Our cameras caught a single unidentified person placing the bomb outside the club's emergency exit, face obscured under a hoodie. Unidentifiable. Two more attempted attackers were discovered when all the footage from that night was reviewed, both scared off by our security team before they could gain access to the building.

I click my tongue as I stare down at the report. These weren't professionals. Dante is doing this cheap, hiring random thugs off the street. Even if we were to track one down, they wouldn't know anything about his organization that could help us. It's not hard to find people in a city like this who are desperate enough to do anything for a few hundred dollars.

I lean back in my chair and press my thumb and forefinger to my eyes, a headache brewing behind my temple.

"You're here late."

The voice grates against my nerves before I even look up, opening my eyes to glare at him.

Daniel Whitmore.

He's leaning in the doorway, all sanctimonious piety and starch. A man who's made hypocrisy an art form. Even in this city—teeming with liars and villains—Pastor Whitmore stands out above the rest.

I can't stand men like him. Religious men, who preach the good word of God on Sunday and then spend the rest of the week spitting on every ideal they claim to uphold. He reminds me of the priest who ran the orphanage where we grew up. A man who smiled and accepted people's praise and donations while he starved us. Who spoke about God while beating us with a belt.

Men like him and Daniel Whitmore are cut from the same cloth.

I lower my hand from my face. "What the fuck do you want, Daniel?" I ask.

He raises his eyebrows at my tone, feigning offense, as if my swearing wounds him. "Just checking in. Have you seen your brother lately?" he asks. He runs a hand over his hair—grey, dyed blond, and thinning even with the hair plugs.

"No." I don't trust where this is going. "Why?"

He shrugs. "I haven't seen him around the office in a while. People are starting to talk."

People like you, I think.

"Has there been a problem with my brother's work?" I press, closing the security file on my desk. "Has his team missed a deadline I'm unaware of?"

He waves the words away. "We both know his team runs perfectly fine without him." A thin smile. "Makes you wonder what he's doing to earn such a sizable paycheck."

My patience is running thin. "What do you want, Daniel?" I repeat, standing.

Daniel sucks his teeth. "Look, I'm sorry to do this to you, really I am." He's not sorry. Whatever he's here about has him practically glowing with self-satisfaction. "But I thought you should know. There will be a board meeting at the end of the week."

I blink, mentally reviewing my calendar. "No one informed me of that."

"Why would they?" he asks, grin widening. "The meeting is about you, after all."

He pauses there, savoring my discomfort.

"There's going to be a vote of no confidence," Daniel says, and my world tilts. "Too many things have been slipping through the cracks lately, and some of us aren't happy with the direction you're taking the company. Especially with this new club of yours. Something this expensive, already causing so many problems? And now there are rumors..." He tilts his head, voice dripping with false concern. "People are saying it might be involved in a sex ring."

Cold dread grips my chest. "What the fuck are you talking about?"

Daniel holds up his hands defensively. "We've been hearing things. That Oscuro is going to have a special access VIP lounge that offers...more than bottle service."

My hands tighten into fists. He doesn't understand. Men like him never do.

Sex work isn't legal in Fortune City. Not yet, anyway. Mostly because of pricks like Pastor Daniel Whitmore, preaching the idea that sex is immoral, and blocking any legislation that might challenge that.

But what we have planned for Oscuro isn't illegal. It's not Second Circle. It's a private sex club, no money exchanging hands, no sex workers. Oscuro's VIP level would be a place for consenting adults to explore their kinks and pleasure without shame.

But try explaining that to a man who thinks sex itself is a sin.

"We just can't have something like that sullying Sterling Enterprises' good name," Daniel insists. "Davidson and Smith agree with me, by the way."

I smile, but I know it doesn't reach my eyes. "That's three votes. Out of nine. You need the majority to get rid of me."

He shrugs again, unconcerned. "Richards won't like it, once he finds out. He's always complained about how much money Ashton makes, for how little he does around here. And Deskmukh will vote with him. He always does. You know how these things go, they snowball."

This mother fucker.

"You really think you can kick me out of my own company?" I ask him, my voice a low growl. "The company I built with my own two hands? When my name's on the fucking building?"

Clearly he does. There's no fear in his eyes as I stare him down. "I *am* sorry, Mason," he says again. And he at least tries to look sympathetic this time. "It's not you. It's business."

"My business," I remind him, through clenched teeth.

"I know how much you care about this company, Mason," he continues. "But we'll take good care of it. And who knows, maybe you can keep a position here. Not as CEO, obviously. But something less public."

Hubris is a funny thing. Clearly, I've underestimated Daniel. Underestimated how much he must hate me. Funny, how that hate is what might save me, that him being here, needing to rub my face in it, is all the warning I need to remind these fuckers why I shouldn't be messed with.

I pull my phone out and text the names to Sebastian.

> Whitmore, Davidson, and Smith.

> We'll need three new board members to replace them before the end of the week. And remind Richards who the fuck he works for.

"Mr. Sterling," I correct him, slipping my phone back into my pocket. I force myself to stay calm as I pull the laptop on my desk toward me, using the fingerprint access to turn it on.

"What?" Daniel asks, confused.

"My name," I explain coldly. "Not Mason. It's Mr. Sterling, to you."

His smile twists into something uglier. "For now."

A few keystrokes are all it takes to access the files I need. A failsafe, for just this sort of occasion. "Do you know what I hate about men like you, Daniel?" I ask conversationally.

He opens his mouth, but I don't give him a chance to answer.

"You're hypocrites," I tell him. "You preach good family values and look down your nose at the way other people live. You think you're virtuous, but men like you are always hiding the ugliest skeletons in your closet."

His face twists. "I don't know what you—"

I turn the laptop screen to face him and press play.

The video has no sound. It doesn't need it. The grainy footage says everything.

Color drains from Daniel's face as he watches.

"Does your wife know you're fucking her sister?" I ask. I glance at the screen, where he has her bent over a pew at his church. There's nothing arousing about it. He looks like a plucked chicken, rutting into her. The best thing you can say for it is that it's short, the whole thing lasting less than five minutes. "Or are you saving that sermon for next Sunday?"

He stammers. "This is..." He gestures at the screen, hands trembling. "This is a fake! AI-generated nonsense!"

I chuckle, the sound low and cold. "You and I both know that's not true. And it's not the only one I have. Would you like to see the rest?"

He's shaking now. Scared. Searching the deepest cavities of his mind for any excuse that would get him out of this.

"Here's what's going to happen." I close the laptop with a click. "You're going to resign from the board. Tonight, effective immediately. And you're going to get the fuck out of my city. Take your family, take your church, take whatever you need. But you're gone by the end of the week. Or this video goes to your entire congregation, including your wife."

"You wouldn't!" Daniel protests.

"Oh, but I would," I tell him, letting him see the truth on my face.

Happily.

Fuck, I *want* to do it. Men like Pastor Whitmore have had their tight grip on this city for far too long. I should have wiped him off the board years ago, instead of placating him with a position on the board.

Some problems you fix with bribery, and some with blackmail and threats. Daniel is a problem I should have just put a fucking bullet in.

It takes a moment for him to understand. For it to really sink in how completely fucked he is.

It's almost beautiful to see it.

"Where am I supposed to go?" he whispers, a noticeable tremor to his voice.

"I don't give a single fuck."

He swallows, straightens his back. "And if I don't? If I refuse to leave?"

I smile, and it feels good to watch him flinch seeing it. "If you don't leave by the end of the week, me releasing that video will be the least of your problems," I promise him.

He stares at me, pale and trembling. "My God. It's true, isn't it?" he breathes. "All the things they say about you. The things they say you've done. It's all true."

"No, Daniel," I tell him quietly. "The rumors don't even *begin* to cover it."

I let him see it, in my eyes, the truth of me. I'm not the monster everyone says I am behind closed doors.

I'm so much fucking worse.

When he finally flees my office, I check my phone. No reply yet from Doc.

Daniel didn't just decide to grow a spine. Something made him think this play would work. *Someone* made him think this play would work. And he was right. If that smug dickhead had just kept his mouth shut, if he had been able to stop himself from gloating...

I could have lost my position, my company.

Everything I've worked so hard to build.

Furious, I send another text.

> Check their financials, all three of them.
> They've been paid off.

But I already know what he'll find.

This was never about Oscuro. The club, the bomb, all these pesky little problems that just keep popping up in my businesses.

Annika was right. These were all distractions. Things to keep me occupied, to keep my attention away from the real threat.

Because Dante is coming for my empire. He's trying to take down everything I've built, push me out of my own company. And he almost accomplished it, all while I was looking exactly where he wanted me to.

A sharp knock on the door cuts through my thoughts.

"Sir?" Devon, my assistant, steps in holding a manila envelope.

I glance at the clock on the wall, noting the time. "It's too late for you to be in the office, Devon," I say. "We don't pay you enough to stay here after five. Go home."

"I will, sir. But this just came for you. It's marked urgent."

I take the envelope from him and dismiss him with a nod, waiting until he's gone before looking at it.

There's no return address on the envelope, no stamps. Just my name and scrawled above it in thick black ink: URGENT. PRIVATE.

Suspicious, I slide a letter opener under the flap and tear it open.

Distractions. That's been Dante's play this whole time.

And this is his final move, the last piece to keep me occupied while he worked behind my back to push me out of my own company.

The paper inside is glossy, and when I pull it out and flip it over, my vision goes red.

A photograph.

Of Sydney, fast asleep on her couch.

A photograph taken from inside her apartment.

33

SEBASTIAN

I wake up to the light touch of her fingertip, trailing over my skin. She's tracing my tattoos, following the geometric shapes and fractals, starting at my shoulders, then moving slowly down my chest. I keep my eyes closed and breathe deep, letting her touch explore me without alerting her to the fact that I'm awake.

It's infinitely more difficult to do when her hand drifts lower.

Opening my eyes just a fraction, I peek at her through my lashes. Fuck, I wish I were wearing my glasses. I want to see her clearly, the crisp lines of her features, not a blur of colors and abstract shapes.

I hadn't meant to fall asleep here last night. I'd planned to leave as soon as Sydney drifted off, to let her rest. But too many late nights, too much stress, too much of fucking *everything* lately, and before I knew what was happening, I'd fallen asleep with her nestled in my arms.

It was easily the best night's sleep of my life.

Sydney's breath quickens when she slowly—oh so slowly,

like she's scared of getting caught—peels the sheet down off my hips. Even with my poor vision, I can make out enough to see the way her lips part in surprise as she stares down at my cock. Her fingers pause at my hips, her gaze locked on where it lies against my stomach, already so hard it almost hurts.

"You can touch it if you'd like," I say, my voice husky, a combination of sleep and desire. Sydney yanks her hand back with a squeal, sitting up and pulling the sheets off me to cover herself.

"Sorry," she breathes, and I can't stand not being able to see her features clearly for a second longer. Propping myself up on my elbow, I lean over the bed to reach for my glasses. I find them on her bedside table, next to the vibrator she used on herself last night, and slip them on.

"Should I be the one apologizing?" I ask, a hint of amusement creeping into my voice. "For interrupting your somnophilia?"

Sydney's brows lift. "Somnophilia? What's that?"

I can see her clearly now, every perfect line of her, every color from the blush in her cheeks, every inch of golden skin that's not hiding under the sheet she has clutched to her chest. "The desire to engage in sexual activity with someone while they sleep."

Her nose scrunches adorably, and she gives me an incredulous look, her lips curving to form a smile. "That's not really a thing. Is it?"

Oh my sweet, innocent Sydney.

It's going to be such a pleasure to teach you how to sin.

"It is," I assure her, sitting up. I reach out to give the sheet she's holding so tightly to herself a light tug. She lets it fall, and it pools around her knees where she's kneeling on the bed.

Perfection. Moving closer to her, I slide my hand up her ribs. She fits my palm like she was made for me.

"What do you call it?" she asks so softly I almost don't hear her.

I follow her line of sight to my cock and quirk a brow at her. "I've never seen fit to give it a name."

"No, I mean—" She blushes harder, and makes a beautifully pitiful noise when my hand cups her breast. "The, uh. The piercing."

Oh. I glance down at the ring at the head of my cock. That.

"A reverse Prince Albert," I inform her. My thumb brushes her nipple, and her breathing stutters. They'd look good pierced, wouldn't they? With a single silver bar through each one? Just imagining it makes my cock twitch.

"Does it hurt?" she asks.

My hand drifts lower, down the plane of her stomach. Lower, until my fingers are between her legs, sliding over her clit. I shift closer to her, nuzzling the space where her jaw meets her neck.

"You tell me." My lips brush against her throat when I say it, and she swallows. "Did it hurt?"

Her gasping moan doesn't feel much like an answer. But her hips are moving, following the slow circle of my fingers, chasing my touch.

"I should shower. I need to—" Her voice breaks as I slip a finger inside her.

"No. I don't want you clean," I murmur against the skin of her neck. I want her just like this, still wet from last night, dripping from the combination of the two of us.

She squirms. "But I... I need to get to work, I—"

"No." I press my thumb to her clit, and she trembles, biting her lip to keep quiet. "I'm not finished playing with you yet."

"Oh God." Sydney's head tips back, hips bucking against my hand.

She's so easy to read, so fucking responsive to my touch.

Every breath, every movement, tells me exactly where she needs it. It's mesmerizing, fucking *enchanting*, to watch her.

"That's it," I encourage her when her breathing hitches, and her legs start to shake. "Fuck yourself on my fingers, just like that. Soak my hand like a good slut."

It takes so little to make her come. She grips my arm when she falls over that edge, shuddering against me, and it's the most irresistible thing I've ever seen. I drink in every second of it, memorizing the way her face flushes, the way her eyes go hooded, and her gaze loses focus.

"What's the record for how many times a man has made you come?" I ask. I slide my thumb off her clit, but keep my fingers inside her, slowly easing her through the aftershocks.

"W-what?" she asks, still gasping for breath.

I curl my finger, just the way she likes it, catching her around the waist when her legs shake so hard she almost falls back against the mattress. "Give me a number, love. How many times has a man made you come in one night?"

Her grip on my arm is a vise, fingernails digging into my skin. I don't mind, I've never shied away from pain. "I, I don't know," she tells me.

"Yes, you do." I slide my fingers out of her and press them against her clit, a little harder than I should, just a little more pressure than would be pleasurable. "Don't lie to me."

She gasps, but her hips roll forward, pressing against my touch. "T-two!"

Only two? A wide, feral smile spreads over my face. Oh, I can beat that. That's *nothing*.

It takes longer for her to come this time, but I'm in no hurry. I alternate between a little too light, and a little too rough, keeping her on the edge, toying with her, until finally she breaks, screaming and clawing at me. She almost falls again, but I hold her tightly against me, taking her weight. Her thighs snap together, trapping my hand against her, but I keep playing, pulling every last bit of pleasure from her I can.

She's a beautiful mess when her pleasure finally subsides. Panting, shaking against me, sweat glistening on her golden skin. My beautiful mess.

"Lie back on the bed," I order, kissing her cheek and slowly taking my fingers away. I bring them to my mouth, licking the taste of her from them. "Spread your legs for me."

I expect her to argue, but she doesn't. She's still fighting to catch her breath as she positions herself on the mattress, lying on her back and letting her knees fall open.

Fuck she's perfect. Obedient.

I take my time drinking in the sight of her, committing every inch of her to memory before I crawl over the bed, stopping when I'm kneeling between her open legs. She watches me, eyes wide, chest rising and falling with her breath.

"If you say stop, I stop," I tell her, holding her gaze. "Do you understand?"

I need her to understand. I need to know I'm not pushing her too far this time. I need to know she wants it, all of it, everything I want to give her.

Even if this is just a taste of it.

Sydney nods quickly, biting her lower lip.

I lean over her, mouth hovering over her nipple. "What do you say if you want me to stop?"

"I'll say 'stop,'" she answers.

"Good." I circle her nipple just once with my tongue before taking it in my mouth and biting down.

She gasps, hips bucking off the mattress. Her hands thread through my hair, grabbing a handful and pulling. But she doesn't tell me to stop, and when I bite her again, sliding my teeth over her sensitive skin, she yanks on my hair to pull me closer.

She's too overstimulated for me to use my fingers again so soon. I bite my way down her stomach, leaving suck marks and hickies, stopping when I'm between her legs.

Her fingers are still tangled in my hair when I lick a line up her center, pausing at her clit. She pulls away from me, just a little, when I close my lips over it, already sore. But I'm patient, unhurried. I could do this forever. I could die right now, with her taste in my mouth and my tongue circling her clit, and I would die satisfied. I have her exactly how I always wanted her —wet, dripping, sweaty, and shaking underneath me.

When she finally breaks, her hips jolt, trying to rise off the bed, and I have to pin her thighs open to keep her still. I hold her in place, not letting up, not giving her even a moment to recover, until she collapses back, gasping for breath.

Fucking exquisite.

She's liquid, body pliant and boneless, when I crawl up her body to position myself. Sydney's eyes are closed, and she's panting for breath, too lost in the aftermath of her pleasure to notice what I'm doing.

I want her to notice. I need it.

"Look at me," I demand, as I press the head of my cock against her entrance. When she doesn't react, I reach up with my other hand and grip her jaw, turning her face toward me. "Look at me, Sydney."

She listens to me, then. Her eyes open, and her lips part as she stares up at me, expression caught between fear and awe.

"That's my girl."

I slide my tip over her, wetting it, and hold her gaze. She makes a helpless little noise in the back of her throat, something between a gasp and whimper, when I pause at her entrance.

"Tell me to stop." My voice is soft. Almost gentle. "Tell me to stop, love."

She's breathing so quickly when she answers. "Don't stop. *Please*."

I took my time with her last night. She was so tight, even dripping wet. I didn't want to hurt her.

I'm not so nice this morning.

Sydney's back arches off the bed when I force myself inside her, but I keep her jaw gripped tight in my hand, holding her in place.

"Don't look away." My voice is a growl, low and guttural. "Look at me. Keep your eyes on me."

Fuck, I never want to forget this moment. Never want to forget the feeling of her cunt tightening around me, the wide, almost frightened look in her eyes as I pull out to the tip and then slam back inside of her, over and over again.

Her eyes roll back when I hit a certain spot, nails clawing at the bedspread.

"There?" I repeat the motion, dragging my piercing over that spot again, and she pulls at the sheets so hard I think she might tear them. "Right there?"

She has no words to tell me. She's incoherent, a writhing mess beneath me, drunk on the pleasure I'm giving her.

When she comes again, her whole body shakes from it, convulsing under me. Her gasps turn to a sob, overwhelmed, overstimulated.

"That's it," I praise her, fucking her through the last throes of it. "You're doing so well, such a good slut." I let go of her jaw and slide my hand down her body, pressing my palm against her stomach. "Give me one more."

Frantically, Sydney shakes her head against the pillow. She squeezes her eyes shut, and a tear slips out from between the lids, sliding down her cheek.

"You take me so well. You feel that?" I press down harder

with my palm, until I can feel my cock moving inside of her. "You feel how well I fit inside you?"

The noises she's making are the most alluring music I've ever heard, pained little gasps, breathless cries as she grips the sheets.

"Give me one more," I demand.

"I c-can't!" Sydney moans. Another tear, this time on the other cheek. Her lip quivers.

"Yes, you can. One last one for me."

Fuck. When she comes this time, she comes so hard I can barely move. Her legs grip me, her pussy shuddering around my cock. I stay buried in her, catching my breath, fighting my own release until she finally relaxes.

She feels so good. I lift her legs, hooking her knees over my shoulders, and she makes the most exquisite noises when I fuck her deep, forcing her to take all of me. But I want more. I need more from her. I reach out for the nightstand and grab her toy, flicking it on.

She cries out when I press it between us, just above her clit.

"One more," I tell her. I lean closer to her, folding her legs against her chest so I can run my tongue over her cheek, licking up the tears there.

"Y-you said that last time!" Her voice is broken, hoarse from screaming, and pitched high.

I grin, moving the toy lower. "I lied. Give me one more."

I wish I could fuck her forever. I want to spend the day buried in her, tasting her, feeling her come on my fingers and my cock. I want to see how deep she can take me into her throat, want to show her how I like it, want to know every limit she has, exactly how much she can take.

But when she comes this final time—with a sharp cry, almost like she's fighting it—I can't pull myself back from the brink. I can feel her tightening and pulsing around me, and it's too much, it's too good. My control slips and I lose myself, fucking her hard and burying myself in her as deep as I can go before I come with a pained groan, my back arching, fingers digging into her flesh.

This is the moment.

When I die, when all my sins are finally tallied and my life flashes before my eyes, this is the moment I'll want to play over and over again. Sydney, whispering my name, saying it like a prayer, as I fill her with my cum.

I don't move after. I stay there, braced over her, my arms bracketing her face, her legs over my shoulders. It takes me an embarrassingly long time to realize I'm still holding her toy, that the vibration is turning my hand numb. I flick it off and toss it onto the bed next to us.

Sydney is limp beneath me, eyes shut, lips parted, a trail of tears drying on her cheeks. She makes a sweet, plaintive noise when I pull out, and it sounds so helpless and sad it's almost enough to make me want to go again.

By the time I return with a wet cloth to clean her, she's already half asleep. My sweet, cum-drunk mess. She murmurs something as I roll her onto her side, something too quiet to catch.

"Shhhh, rest, love," I tell her, brushing the hair off her face and kissing the last of the tears off her cheek before washing them gently away with the cloth. Her curls are loose, her hair a wild halo around her, covering the pillow. "You did so well. You were so good."

I don't think she can hear me. She's unconscious before I'm even out of bed.

Whatever time her alarm is set for, she's sure to oversleep it in the state she's in. That will upset her, and we can't have that. I grab my phone from my pile of clothes and pull up my messages, briefly reading the ones I missed last night before opening a new text chain.

> Sydney will be coming in late this morning.

The text I receive back is almost instant.

> Jade Lee (the BFF): Doc?

> Jade Lee (the BFF): I'm going to need proof of life. Send me a photo so I know she's okay.

I glance over at Sydney. She's fast asleep, skin glistening with sweat. Ruined. She looks perfectly ruined.

> Trust me, you don't want that.

> Jade Lee (the BFF): EW

A quiet laugh escapes me. Setting my phone down, I start to get dressed. I keep my eyes on her as I pull my clothing on, taking my time, never looking away. I want to burn the image of her like this into my brain, I want to see it every time I close my eyes, projected against the lids.

I'm stopped on my way to the front door by a creature. A tiny, white thing that stands in the living room, barring my way.

Sydney's new cat. I've seen her on the cameras, watched as she knocked empty mugs off the café's tables, and ambushed customers' ankles. She's smaller than I expected, for the amount of trouble she causes, small enough she could fit in the palm of my hand.

The tiny kitten stares up at me with round, unblinking eyes, head tilted to the side, like she's assessing me. She's holding a toy in her mouth, caught between her teeth, but it's mangled beyond recognition, nothing more than a lump of yellow and black.

"Hello there," I say quietly.

That's her cue. She prances forward and drops the toy at my feet, then sits back and looks up at me, expectantly.

I crouch, studying the destroyed toy between us. "I've read about this," I tell her. "You're showing me you can hunt, aren't you?"

A soft purr emanates from her. When I reach out to stroke her tiny head with my thumb, her purrs get even louder, and she melts into my hand, arching against me.

"You are very brave and fierce," I tell her solemnly, stroking between her ears. "For murdering that toy."

She accepts the compliment with a pleased trill, rubbing the entirety of her body against my hand. Then she stretches her back and claws at the carpet before stalking away toward the bedroom, leaving her kill behind.

Cute.

There's a bouquet of lilies waiting on Sydney's doorstep when I step outside. I stare at them, frowning. None of my brothers sent these. They're disgusting, well past their prime, wrapped in cheap cellophane. I'm still frowning at them when an audible *click* from the other side of the walkway makes me look up, toward the second apartment next door to Sydney's.

Is someone living there now? I stare at the now-closed door, eyes narrowed. Curious that I haven't seen them on the cameras, coming and going.

Curious.

I take the lilies with me when I go. She deserves much better than this gas-station garbage.

34

SYDNEY

I'M LATE.

I am *so fucking late*.

By the time I wake up and finally turn my phone back on, it's late enough in the day that it's a miracle Jade hasn't kicked down my front door to make sure I'm not dead. The quick shower I take before leaving—*absolutely necessary* considering the state Sebastian left me in—makes me even later.

"I'm so, so sorry!" I call out the second I burst through the doors of the Bookshop Boutique and Bakery. It's nearly noon, and I've missed the entirety of the morning rush. Bea yowls indignantly from her carrier, furious at her imprisonment, until I finally set it down and open it to let her free. She immediately darts away, disappearing between the bookstacks, eager to start a new day of harassing our customers. "My alarm didn't go off this morning and—"

I stop in the middle of my explanation, because Jade doesn't *look* mad. Or even disappointed. She's behind the café counter, arms crossed over her chest, mouth twitching like she's trying not to laugh.

"It's fine," she says, not even trying to hide her grin. "You were *busy*. And Justin was here to help."

I frown, confused. "Justin isn't scheduled to work today."

"He wasn't," Jade admits. "But when the good doctor texted me this morning to explain why you'd be coming in late..."

Oh, no. He wouldn't. But Jade gives me a smug *I told you so* look.

"Please tell me he didn't actually text you," I beg.

"I really wish I could tell you that, Syd," she says sweetly, "but sadly, I am not a liar."

I bury my face in my hands and groan.

"So." Jade's smile widens. "You and Doc, huh? When did that start up again?"

"Last night," I murmur into my palms. "Or, maybe earlier? I don't even know."

"Uh-huh," Jade says, smirking.

"Hey, there's this *really* scary-looking guy hanging around the back, and—Oh!" Justin's voice makes us both turn. He freezes mid-step when he sees me, face going tomato red. "H-hey, Syd!"

"Justin may have read the messages as well," Jade informs me.

"Oh God." I drop my face back into my hands.

"It's fine." He gives an awkward laugh. "I was just, you know, *there* when she got the messages. She asked if I could come in and cover for you. No big deal."

"No big deal that he now knows your boyfriend sexed you into a coma this morning," Jade adds.

"He's not my boyfriend," I protest. "He's just..."

And there it is. The problem. I don't know what he is. Or where I stand, with any of them, anymore.

"Just the guy who sexed you into a coma," Jade finishes helpfully.

"I really don't think I need to be part of this conversation," Justin says, backing away. "I don't think I *want* to be part of this conversation."

"What were you saying before?" I ask him, desperate to change the subject. "About a scary guy?"

"I said a *really* scary guy," Justin corrects me. "I've seen him here before, a couple of times. Big dude. Like, *big* big. Buzz cut. Lots of scars."

My stomach flips. "A scar on his face?" I ask. I trace my finger over my forehead, following the familiar pattern. "Over his eyebrow?"

Justin taps his nose. "That's him!"

Viper.

Jade and I share a look.

"What was that?" Justin demands, glancing between the two of us. "What was that look? Is this guy a problem, or something? Do I need to kick him out?"

The mental image of Justin trying to get Viper to do anything is so comical I have to bite back a laugh.

"He's Sydney's *other* boyfriend, the one from the club," Jade supplies, with a devilish grin. I shoot her a murderous look, but she laughs and says, "What? He's going to find out about all of them eventually."

"Your *other* boyfriend," Justin repeats. His expression goes completely blank. "Huh."

"Do I need to repeat the shop rules?" Jade asks, voice turning hard. "In this store we do *not* slut sha—"

Just cuts her off, raising a hand to stop her from saying anything more. "Nope! No need to repeat anything. I was just...counting. We're up to four, then, aren't we? Are there any others I should know about?"

I ignore that. "Where is he?" I ask.

"Uh, classics. In the back."

"I'll handle it," I assure him, already moving. "And he's *not* my boyfriend," I add, glaring at Jade. But it sounds like a lie, even to me.

"You want backup?" Justin offers.

I think about the knife Viper pulled out at the club when Jade told him no. I swallow, palms sweaty.

Line, Viper.

"No," I tell Justin. "I think it's better if it's just me."

———

VIPER IS EXACTLY WHERE JUSTIN SAID HE'D BE—STANDING in our classic literature section, leaning against the bookshelves and reading. As I watch, he brings his thumb to his mouth and slides his tongue over it, wetting it before he uses it to turn the page.

Just talk to him. He's not that scary. Just talk to him like a normal human being. Just climb on top of him, pull his clothes off, and...

God, Syd, do you have a death wish? What is wrong with you?

I take a deep breath to steady myself.

But before I can step forward, I notice he's not alone. Bea circles his ankles, coming into my field of view. She rubs the side of her body against him, coming up on two legs to reach as high as she can.

It's...cute. Okay, more than cute. It's downright adorable. She trills musically and rolls onto the top of his boot, kicking her hind legs against him and gnawing furiously on one of his shoelaces.

Then Viper leans down and scoops her up, and my heart

leaps into my throat.

She looks so tiny and helpless in his grasp, legs dangling in the air. I can't help but step forward, ready to snatch her away if he hurts her. But he doesn't, doesn't even seem tempted to. He holds her gently, one big hand braced around her middle, and presses a soft kiss to the top of her head.

Bea purrs so loudly in response, I wonder if they can hear it in the café.

"I didn't know you liked cats," I say, a warm feeling rising in my chest.

"What kind of monster doesn't like cats?" Viper asks, murmuring the words into her fur. She kneads happy biscuits in the air, thrilled with the attention. He kisses her again and then sets her back down on the ground.

Since we adopted her, Bea has been skittish around the customers, at best. A criminal nuisance, at worst. I've lost track of the number of mugs she's broken this week, and just the other day, I swear she tried to take off with a customer's wallet. Soon we suspect she'll graduate to major felonies. I'm not sure how to feel about the way she arches against Viper's hand, begging for more attention, clearly enamored with him.

When he straightens and Bea realizes he's not offering anymore kisses, she rubs against his ankle one last time, then struts away, tail held high in triumph.

Viper's gaze is locked on me when I look at him. "Hello, little rabbit." The lazy grin that curls his mouth sends a chill down my spine.

The book he was reading is hanging loosely at his side. *The Brothers Karamazov*, I note, by Dostoevsky.

"That's a good book," I tell him, motioning toward it.

He doesn't answer. His eyes are locked on my lips.

I clear my throat nervously. "You don't have to stick around here anymore, you know." I force a smile and raise my hand to the ceiling, pointing at the camera above us. "Seb installed a, uh...a security system. To keep an eye on me."

Viper doesn't look up at the camera. His grin turns feral as he moves closer to me, and I instinctively take a step back. Then another. It's not until my shoulder blades hit the bookshelf behind that I realize he's cornered me, trapping me between him and our wide range of classic books.

"To keep an eye on you," he repeats. He keeps coming closer, until we're pressed against each other. He's huge, so big he takes up my whole field of vision, and I struggle to take a full breath, staring up at him. "And how long do you think it would take him to get here," he asks, "if you were in danger?"

I hadn't considered it. Not until now.

My pulse races. Viper leans down, his lips hovering over mine. "Do you really think he'd be fast enough to save you?"

It feels like a threat, the way he says it.

"Viper, I—"

His hand moves up toward my face so fast I flinch, my words devolving into a squeal. But he doesn't touch me. His hand stops right beside my head, the book clasped in his grasp, his eyes never leaving mine as he pushes his copy of *The Brothers Karamazov* back into place on the shelf. He leaves his hand there after, palm flat against the book spines, boxing me in.

"You're so pretty when you're scared," he coos with a wide grin, dark eyes sparkling.

I should do something. Scream. Slip under his arm and run. But I'm frozen in place, trembling, and he leans further into me, lowering his face to brush his nose against the vulnerable skin of my throat

"Viper." My breath stutters as he presses me against the shelves with his body, his hand slipping under my shirt. He makes a satisfied sound deep in his throat as his thumb grazes my ribs.

I manage to get my hands up and press them to his chest, but don't push him away. I'm not even sure I could.

Another low sound, unmistakably masculine, as his teeth graze over my pulse. He inhales deeply, nuzzling into my neck. "You smell like sex," he murmurs against my skin. His fingers tighten, nails biting into my ribs.

What was it? The thing Sebastian said to him?

"Line, Viper," I gasp, heart pounding, palms pressing into his chest.

He goes still. The hand gripping me beneath my shirt pauses.

Hesitantly, I push a little harder against him, and to my surprise, he moves back, taking a step away from me. His hand drags down my stomach before he pulls it away completely.

He's still too close, eyes narrowed as he watches me, a slight curl to his lips. I'm all too aware of all the places we're still touching. The way my chest brushes against his with every breath I take, the way his leg rests between mine.

"You can stay," I tell him. Truthfully, I don't mind him being here. It's comforting having him around, protecting me. "If you don't bother the customers. If you don't hurt—" *Me*, I almost say. "If you don't hurt anyone."

Viper hums thoughtfully. "And where's the fun in that?" His mouth curves into a manic smile that's all teeth.

The worst part is I'm not scared. Or maybe I am, but not enough. My skin is hot where he touched me, too sensitive. And despite everything—despite the giant *walking red flag* this man is, and despite the fact that I have no excuse for being this turned on after everything Sebastian did to me this morning—I want more.

There must be something deeply wrong with me. Because

all I want is to feel him touch me again. And, as if he senses it, he leans in closer, thumb brushing over the corner of my mouth.

"You can't touch me here, you can't—" I swallow hard. "Not here. Not where I work."

Viper tilts his head, studying me. Something shifts in his eyes.

"Not here," he repeats. His stare is heavy, all-consuming. I feel like a bug caught under glass. Something interesting but foreign to him. "Fine."

He pushes off the shelf and walks away, not sparing me another glance.

35

SEBASTIAN

I'M SUCH A FUCKING IDIOT.

I take off my glasses and pinch the bridge of my nose. One single check box, that's all it would have taken. A single box checked in the security software I installed, and the system would have recognized and catalogued every instance of someone entering and leaving the camera view by Sydney's door.

One single missed check box.

The box is checked now, and a few lines of code added were enough to set up a new alert, pinging me on my phone whenever a person comes into view.

But now I have hours and *fucking hours* worth of video footage to scrub through manually.

I start with last night, when she unlocked the door for me, stopping momentarily to palm my erection at the memory. I speed through the footage until I see myself walk up her stairs and disappear.

You can't see her door. Another idiotic fucking mistake, one I made intentionally to protect her privacy. One that makes me want to tear the camera off the roof with my bare hands and change the placement. I send a quick message to the team I sent to install it, instructing them to correct the positioning as soon as possible, and they message back almost immediately to let me know it'll be done within the hour.

Maybe I should have put a camera in the damn apartment after all.

Fuck. I close my eyes and let myself imagine what it would be like to have a tape of our time together. I have to adjust myself in my pants at the thought. Later, I promise myself. The next time I have her.

The video footage is set to 4x speed, but I tap my keyboard and speed through even faster. I watch. And watch. And watch.

And at just past five in the morning, I see myself appear and walk down the stairs, flowers in hand.

What the fuck?

I rewatch the footage again, slower.

I walk up the stairs.

I walk down them.

And in between, no one else appears. Between those two events, no one goes up her stairs to deliver a bouquet of lilies, no one walks through the parking lot behind her shop. But somehow, they show up at her door.

When I call my security guy, I don't bother with hellos.

"How hard would it be to alter the footage from those cameras you installed?" I ask.

"Almost impossible," they answer. "Why?"

My molars hurt from clenching them so hard. "Who could do it?"

"A securities expert," they venture, in a tone that makes me think they're guessing. "Someone with top-notch coding experience."

Someone like Jade's brother, Justin.

Two possibilities exist here. One, someone hacked my system, a system almost impossible to hack. Two, someone *somehow* bypassed the security system without showing up on my camera, and the only way that could be is if they were walking from the direction of the empty unit next door. A blind spot on my camera feed.

I sit back in my computer chair and rub my eyes, imagining all the ways I would take this faceless man apart, piece by piece, in our wet lab.

I try to search through previous video files, looking for him. If someone is staying in that unit, the fucker has to leave eventually, right? Has to go to work, has to go out, has to meet friends.

It takes me almost a full day of searching before I find *one fucking image of him.*

A dark gray sweatshirt, hood pulled up, non-descript jeans. He's carrying a paper bag full of groceries. He reaches the top of the stairs and disappears.

"Fuck." I watch the footage again. There's no frame where his face is visible.

No one lives in that unit. If someone had signed a lease, moved in their things, I would have seen it. I would have *known.*

Which means...

A knock on my security room door has me turning in my chair. Alec doesn't wait for me to answer. He just pushes the door open and storms in. Like usual.

"We have a problem," he says.

I raise an eyebrow at him. "Aside from you fucking up our lives with your psychotic control issues and lies, you mean?" I ask, my voice cold.

Alec stills, expression darkening, fist clenching at his sides.

I can tell he's biting back a lecture on "my place" and "disrespect." But the fucker deserves a little disrespect after the shit he pulled.

I wonder how he'd feel if he knew I could still smell her on my skin, still taste her pussy on my lips? If he knew I made her come more than any other man she's had before?

I turn my attention back to my screens, so he can't see the smug look on my face.

"I already solved your problem. All three board members have been replaced, and your assistant is drafting the press release," I tell him. "You won't have any issues with the newest members. We have enough on them to—"

"We have a *different* fucking problem." Alec crosses my room and tosses a photo on my keyboard.

I pick it up and stare at it.

And stare.

And stare.

It's Sydney. My Sydney. Curled on her side in a ball on her couch, face angelic in sleep.

"Where did you get this?" I ask. It's a miracle my voice remains steady.

"It was addressed to me, sent to our office," he tells me through clenched teeth. "Hand delivered, it didn't go through the mail system."

My hands are steady. My breathing is calm. No one would ever know the monster inside of me is clawing at my skin, screaming to get out.

I put the photo down.

Alec paces the room as I pull up the live footage of her shop, my heart thundering in my chest until I find her. Safe. Chasing her kitten around the café, Jade doubled over in laughter.

"I'm done waiting," Alec snaps. "And I don't give a fuck

what's going on between the four of us right now. Put it aside. Dante is escalating, and we need to bring him down. Now." He glances up at my screens and then back to me. "Where's Viper?"

"At this exact minute? No idea. You know he doesn't like to be monitored," I mutter. He was there earlier, at her shop, but I haven't seen him since.

"Ash?" Alec presses. Ashton is just as pissed at Alec as I am, maybe more. But Alec is right, our anger can wait. Protecting her can't.

"Licking his wounds, probably. Sydney is still icing him out, and he got his ass handed to him in his last fight." I shoot him a look. "I doubt he wants to see you right now. And I don't blame him."

I sure as hell haven't forgiven him yet for lying to us. For making me think this was my fault.

"Find him and get his ass back here. I don't give a shit how pissed off either of you are right now. I need all of us together on this."

"Fine," I tell him. "I have something else, too. Might be related. I found some camera footage from the 'traffic incident' Sydney mentioned." His jaw ticks at the mention of her name, body tensing, but I continue. "I don't think this was random. The car blew through a red light, and when she sprinted across the street, they went right for her, jumped the curb. It was... closer than I'm comfortable with." Close enough just remembering it makes that monster in me rise, remembering the fury I'd felt when I watched the footage I'd pulled from the city's red-light cameras. Then I remember her rage, that beautiful anger as she threw a brick after the car, and my dick throbs.

"License plate?"

"Ah, nothing." I adjust myself subtly, under my desk.

"There was no license plate visible from the cameras, and it was a black Honda Civic. Not exactly a rare car."

"I don't like it. Anything else?"

"Maybe," I admit, thinking about the unit next door. The lilies. "But I'm not sure what it means, yet. I'm looking into it."

He nods, satisfied. "Keep your eyes on her. Dante is planning something, and we can't let her get caught in the crossfire." Alec draws his shoulders back. "I'm done waiting for him to make his next move. It's time to go on the offensive."

"The offensive?" I repeat, raising an eyebrow.

"We hit him hard, where it hurts. Strike back before he can take this further, draw his focus off her."

"What are you suggesting?"

Alec's grin is dark and terrifying. "I want to take everything from him. Wipe everything he's touched off this Earth."

36

SYDNEY

FINALIZING THIS MONTH'S BOOK ORDERS TAKES ME LONGER than expected. With our new surge in business, and corresponding spike in inventory purchasing to replenish our stock, it takes me nearly twice as long as I'm used to.

I told Jade to head home early, and she dropped Bea off at my apartment so I could concentrate on finishing everything without her distracting me. Since she had to cover for me this morning, it felt like the least I could do was give her the night off to relax.

It's cool outside, with a bite to the air, when I finally finish and lock up for the night. A light breeze dances over my arms, making me shiver, as I insert my keys and turn the lock.

As I turn to leave, my eyes catch on him, and the keys slip from my hand, landing noisily against the pavement.

Viper.

He's standing at the mouth of the alley, half hidden in shadow, watching me. He's so still, so silent, I could almost convince myself I'm seeing things. But the headlights from a passing car wash over him, illuminating his dark eyes and razor-sharp smile for just a moment before casting him back into the dark, and there's no mistaking it's him.

I should run.

My legs tense, ready to bolt. He told me I can't escape him, that running is useless, but maybe I could make it behind the building, to my stairs. Maybe I could make it to the camera at my doorstep and draw Sebastian's attention, let him know the danger I'm in.

I can't bring myself to move. I'm terrified, frozen in fear.

And Viper just watches me.

Waiting.

Until finally, he turns, hands in his pockets, and disappears into the alley.

Now. Now is when I should run. Now is when I can escape.

I don't.

For no sane reason, after picking up my keys, my feet begin to carry me toward that alley. Not away, not back to safety, not into my shop to hide or up the stairs to my apartment. Towards him.

Because you want the darkness. You want the pain.

My heart is beating so fast I can hear it, echoing around me, beating so hard it hurts. The alley is pitch black, so dark I can't see my own hand in front of my face.

I don't see Viper when he grabs me. I only feel him, hard rough hands on my back, his mouth colliding with mine.

Viper doesn't kiss me. He fucks my mouth with his tongue, shoving it so deep I can't breathe. The wall of the alley hits my back, brick digging into my skin, as Viper tries to consume me.

I'm dizzy and gasping for air when he finally stops.

"No cameras here," he whispers. It's so dark I can't see his face, can't see his terrifying grin. But somehow I can hear it in his words. "Not inside your precious shop. No one to save you, little rabbit. How long do you think we have before Doc notices?"

Long enough for him to kill me, I realize in horror. Long enough for him to do all manner of unspeakable things.

Why does knowing that make me so wet? Make me want it? There's a promise of something dark and dangerous in Viper, and I want a taste of it.

Just a taste.

Crushing me against the wall, Viper lifts my thighs, forcing himself between my legs. His hands clutch at me, hard, griping at the fabric of my jeans. He runs his nails up and down my pant legs, from knees to hips. Then he grabs the front of them, unbuttoning them, and trying to pull them off.

The zipper catches and sticks. Viper growls, sounding more like a beast than a man. He pulls at the fabric like he might tear right through it.

"They're caught," I manage to gasp. "Let me just—"

I'm shoved even harder against the wall as he snarls in frustration.

"Next time wear a fucking skirt," he snaps, giving up on my legs and forcing his hands up under my shirt, grabbing at my ribcage.

He relaxes a little then, breathing a sigh against me.

"So soft," he groans. His hands grip me hard, fingernails digging into my flesh.

I whimper.

"No fucking time," he says, moving back just enough to push his pants down from his hips. His erection springs out, and he sets it against me, the base of him flat against the seam of my pants.

"Viper—"

I mean to tell him to slow down, but I can hear the need in my voice as I moan his name. I cry out as he crashes into me, slamming me back against the brick wall. He does it again and again, fucking himself against me.

It hurts. Each thrust is a bruising blow to my core, an agonizing jolt to my back. His hands pull my shirt up, nails tearing at my skin. He bites at me, teeth clamping down on my neck, my chest, my cheek.

This isn't sex. This is nothing I've ever experienced, raw and animalistic. Viper is a man possessed, completely consumed with his need to own me. To hurt me.

His hips pound against mine over and over, my legs wrapped around his middle, holding him tight against me. I lose myself in it, the pain washing over me, a thousand points of agony from his teeth, his hips, the brick digging into my back.

It's a shock when I come. I scream, half in horror, my nails digging into his shoulders and back. I fight against him, bucking off the wall, and it *hurts*. Even my release hurts, each continued thrust from him forcing another crest from me, pulling it painfully out of my body almost against my will.

Viper doesn't seem to notice what he's done, slamming himself against me, teeth moving up my jaw, until he finds my bottom lip and clamps down on it.

There's a sharp sudden pain as his teeth puncture my flesh. I cry out, struggling against him, fighting for room as my blood floods into his mouth.

With a single grunt, Viper tenses, my lip caught between his teeth. Even through my jeans I feel his cock pulse. Jets of hot cum hit my stomach and chest, coating me and my shirt.

He goes still, jaw opening just enough to release my lip from between his teeth.

My eyes have finally adjusted enough to see him in the dark. Bright white teeth now coated in red.

I don't expect the laughter. It bursts out of him, his body

shaking with it as he presses even harder against me, driving me back into the wall and ignoring my cry of pain.

"Look at what a mess you made!" Viper laughs. His eyes are manic, too wide and unfocused as he stares down at me, grinning wide enough to show off my blood in his mouth.

He reaches between us, rubbing his hand through the cum coating me.

Bringing his hand up to my mouth, he shoves his middle and index finger inside. I taste blood and salt, gagging on it as he pushes his fingers down against the back of my tongue.

My entire body throbs. My bleeding split lip, my bruised back, my cunt. I feel raw and broken as Viper fucks his fingers into my mouth, forcing me to taste him.

I moan in relief when he finally removes them. Then, almost sweetly, he lowers his face to mine and licks the blood from my chin. He laps at it like a dog, cleaning it all away.

I don't remember crying, but there are wet streaks of tears drying on my cheeks when he finally steps back to pull his pants back into place.

He takes my face in his hands, grinning at me.

"See?" he tells me, sounding so proud of himself. "Doc was wrong. I can be gentle, too. Can't I?"

I'm speechless. There was nothing gentle about what he just did to me.

But numbly, I nod.

"Doc will be looking for you," Viper tells me. He slides the pad of his thumb over my cheek, scooping up the tears there and bringing them to his lips to lick them off. "Time to go. Run back to safety, little rabbit."

Wordlessly, I do. My legs shake with every step that takes me closer to my apartment door.

37

ALEC

Making the decision isn't the hard part.

It's the hundred little steps that come after, the things that must be done flawlessly. But that's the work. That's what my brothers and I have always excelled at.

Sebastian's role comes first. His team hacks into Pastor Daniel's financial records, flagging several suspiciously large deposits before emptying the account entirely, leaving nothing behind. Tomorrow morning The Sterling Children's Foundation will be thrilled to receive an unexpected anonymous donation, generous enough to fund them through the next financial year. He does the same for the other two ex-members of the Sterling Enterprises' board of directors, tracing the bribes they all received back to a handful of shell companies routing cash through Empire City.

It takes days. But the final result is a full dossier detailing Dante's underground network, spanning the East Coast. Impressive that he was able to build so much from the shadows, without drawing our attention.

It's almost a shame to burn it all to the ground.

He could have operated for years in Empire City like this without us noticing. Maybe could have even infiltrated Fortune City—our home—and syphoned enough money out from under us to live like a king, and we would have been none the wiser. But he made one big mistake.

He threatened our woman.

Viper's role comes next. He's surprisingly calm and steady when he returns to the compound. Focused.

He leaves for Empire City the following morning.

What we need is a rat, someone with fresh intel on Dante's operation. We need to know where it's really going to hurt to hit him, where to stick the knife.

If there's one lesson the orphanage taught me, it's this: when someone pushes you down and takes your toy, you do not respond in kind.

You break their fucking arm.

That's what they don't teach you in business school. No one ever got ahead in this world by responding to an act of aggression with a proportional response. You respond with something so horrible, so devastating, that you guarantee they never look at you without fear again. You hit them hard enough others won't even consider making a move against you.

You make them fear you.

And Dante is about to be reminded why he should fear us.

Viper finds us not one, but two rats. People high enough in Dante's crew to know where he's vulnerable, but not high enough to be missed for forty-eight hours while we painfully extract the information we need.

What Viper finds confirms that Ashton was right to be worried all those years ago. Dante was only testing the waters with our little mission, the one that finally broke us, that pushed Ash too far. Turns out, human trafficking was far too lucrative for him to try just once. Our old mentor now has himself a horrible little side hustle financing the rest of his empire.

Or... He did, before today.

"FBI is moving," Sebastian confirms, after he gets the call. His voice is flat, matter of fact.

I grin.

Dante held the local police department at arm's length through a combination of blackmail and bribes, but that knife cuts both ways. There's always someone higher up the food chain to pay off or frighten, always another level of oversight.

When we worked for him, Dante taught me how to buy off police and judges. But Sebastian was the one who made sure we had our fingers in the pockets of all the major bureaus: FBI, ATF, CIA. Insurance, for just such an occasion.

All we had to do was hand them the information we gathered and pull their strings. It wasn't even hard. Our contacts at the FBI were thrilled to do it.

After all, who doesn't want to be the hero who takes down a human trafficker?

Everything that follows is surgical in its precision, as the bureau makes its move. Business associates become witnesses and dirty cops are quick to flip now that their freedom is on the line. Shell companies are frozen, bank accounts are locked, and safe houses are swept.

And piece by piece my brothers and I watch as the organization Dante built from the ground up crumbles into dust.

38

SYDNEY

I takes days for the swelling in my lip to go down. I hide it as best as I can, with cold compresses and makeup, but they can only do so much.

Jade notices immediately. I see the worry in her eyes, the way her brow furrows when I walk into our shop the next morning.

"It's not what you think," I tell her. I hate the fear in her eyes, the panic.

"Then tell me what it is," she volleys back at me.

I can't look at her when I say it. "A love bite? And please don't ask for details." I grab the coffee she has prepared for me, and hide my growing blush by spinning around, turning my back on her.

"A love bite?" She lets out a shocked laugh. "Syd, are you *kinky*?"

"I plead the fifth," I murmur into my drink.

Another laugh. "Was this the good doc's doing?"

"Goodbye, former-friend-who-asks-questions-even-though-

I-asked-her-not-to," I singsong as I make my way to the back of the store with my coffee.

She lets it go after that. Which is good, because how do I explain to her what happened to me? How do you explain something like Viper?

And how do you explain how much you loved it?

I replay those few minutes in the dark over and over in my head, staring off into space when I should be working, lost in the memory. I fill in the gaps with my own imagination, licking at my split lip and squeezing my thighs together.

How had we looked from the outside, with my legs wrapped around him and his body engulfing mine? Had his eyes been closed when he'd come? Or open, locked on mine, staring deep into my soul? Had he felt it when he'd pushed me over the edge, felt the shift in my body, the tense muscles, the tightening of my thighs around him?

Had he liked it?

Viper doesn't come back to the shop, not in the days following our encounter. I don't know if I'm relieved or disappointed.

I don't hear from any of them, actually.

Not Sebastian. Not Alec.

Not even Ashton.

I find myself missing the barrage of texts Ash was sending to my phone every day. Missing the way he wished me good morning, even when I refused to respond. He's finally doing what I asked of him, finally giving me the space I requested.

The space I needed to finally start missing him. To want him back.

Call it hypocritical, maybe. Call it whatever you want. But I find myself checking my phone every few minutes, wishing he would text again. Wishing I could see him.

Maybe what I told Sebastian was more honest than I'd realized. Maybe I really have had enough space.

When the swelling on my lip has eventually faded days later, and I've just settled down onto my couch with Bea to relax for the night, I suddenly realize I can't take it anymore. I miss him. Them.

I pick up my phone, and before I can stop myself, I send Ash a text.

Hi. Are you free?

He doesn't answer, not right away. Three dots appear and then vanish. After a few minutes of staring down at my phone, waiting for a response, I give up, my stomach sinking as I set it down beside me and pull my favorite blanket tighter around myself, finding comfort in the feeling of soft fabric against my skin.

Sebastian said he would wait forever, but maybe Ashton just isn't that patient. Maybe he got sick of waiting for me, of begging for my attention while I pushed him away.

Twenty minutes later, there's a knock on my door.

I sit up straight on my couch, turning in my seat to frown at it. A nervous apprehension crawls into my belly.

Another knock.

Shrugging off my blanket, I creep quietly to the door, hesitating with my hand over the lock. "Hello?" I call through the wood.

"It's me, Babygirl," comes the cheery answer. "Open up!"

Of course. Of course he saw my text as an invitation to come over. Sighing, I disengage the lock and ease the door open.

"Let me guess," I say, leaning against the door frame and eyeing the bundle in his arms. "Takeout?"

Ashton grins, and my heart melts a little seeing it. He has such a charming smile, even with the bruises littering his face. Fuck, I missed him, I really did.

"Actually," he says, hoisting the basket he's carrying a little higher. "A picnic. I was so excited you texted that I maybe went a bit overboard."

"You know, by *are you free*, I meant *are you free to talk*," I try to explain, eyeing the basket and frowning.

"Talks are always better in person!" he insists. "I thought, you know, maybe if you're feeling up to it, we could go to the park? Just to chat. Or...whatever you want to do. You call the shots."

It's still Ash. The eagerness, the enthusiasm, all that's exactly how I remember. But something is different. He's muted, just a little, his smile strained, like he's holding back.

"The park?" I repeat with a little laugh. I poke my head outside, looking around at the dark sky above us. "Ash, it's nearly nine. We can't just go sit in the park. It's not... It's dangerous out there at night."

He lowers the basket, studying me too closely.

"Syd." He looks a little sad as he holds my gaze. "I promise you there won't be anything in that park more dangerous than me."

There's no pride in his voice, no cocky assurances. It's just a fact. He watches me, after he says it, measuring my response.

He's not trying to hide it. Not pretending to be anything he's not. He's still Ashton. The man who put away my dishes, who tucked me into bed and kissed me on the forehead. A man with no fear of being in a park at night, because there's nothing out there scarier than him. It's up to me to reconcile both those parts of him.

Just like it's up to me to decide how much I'm willing to

forgive him, right now. To decide if I want to fight him, or fight for him.

I take a deep breath and try to tuck some of my anger away. I can't keep living in the in-between with them. It's not what I want.

"Okay," I say, hesitating in the doorway. "Let me get a jacket."

Ashton practically vibrates with excitement.

He helps me down the stairs when I get back, holding my hand to steady me while still carrying the picnic basket.

"What happened to your face?" I ask, staring up at the bruises.

"You should see the other guy!" Ashton laughs, letting go of my hand to gesture at his fading black eye. "Actually, no, you shouldn't, he looks fine. I got thrashed."

"Your fight," I say, suddenly remembering. My stomach sinks a little. "The one you were texting me about. I missed it, didn't I?"

He shrugs.

I wonder if he realizes how much he wears his emotions on his sleeve. I don't miss the hurt that fills his eyes before he tries to hide it.

"It's okay, you're not the only one," he tells me, forcing a smile. "Doc made me realize that I've been pretty unfair to you, lately. I shouldn't have pressured you so much about it."

"Maybe I can come see your next one?" I offer.

His whole face lights up when I say it.

The park is empty and dark when we arrive, but I'm not afraid at all. Ashton was right. I'm perfectly safe when I'm with him. He leads me over to a flat space of grass, under a spacious oak tree, and lays out the blanket he had tucked away in his basket. The way he heads right for it, like he knew exactly where the best place to have a picnic would be, makes me wonder how he even found out about this part of my neighborhood. How long he's been wanting to bring me here.

"I already ate dinner," I warn him, sitting down on the blanket and tucking my legs beneath me.

"Ah! I thought you might have," he says with a grin, not letting my hesitation derail his enthusiasm. "That's why this thing is packed full of dessert."

I watch as he removes package after package from his basket, laying them out before me.

"Ta-da!" he says, taking the lid off a container and holding it out for me. "Chocolate-covered strawberries! And, in case you don't like strawberries, I have a bunch of other chocolate-covered fruits, too. And some marshmallows, somewhere in here."

He goes back to digging in his basket, pulling out more items as he talks.

"Who doesn't like strawberries?" I question with a laugh, taking one out of the container and biting into it. It's divine, perfectly ripe, the chocolate just the perfect amount of bitter dark to complement the sweetness.

Ashton winces. "Well," he demurs, not looking at me. "Me, for one."

I balk, then sputter out, "What? How can you not like strawberries?"

After setting the last of the containers out on the blanket, he settles back, stretching his legs out. When he turns to look at me, his face is serious.

"They tried to kill Doc," he tells me. "So, it's personal, for me."

A small smile spreads over my face before I can stop it.

"It's true," he insists. "When we were young—and I mean, really young, I was eight, so he would have been like...five, maybe? Anyway, our mom took us to this little farmers' market."

Ashton's eyes are bright and animated with the memory. I nibble on my strawberry, listening.

"There was a guy who was selling strawberries, and they must have been a steal or something, because our mom buys four whole pints of them, right? Maybe she was thinking she'd make a pie, or some jam, I don't know, we never got a chance to find out. Because less than an hour after we get home, Sebastian gets into those strawberries and he just... doesn't stop."

I have to bite my lip to keep my expression blank as Ashton continues. He moves his hands as he talks, painting a picture for me.

"He eats all of them. All four pints, before she notices. And he's covered in strawberry stems and juice, a sticky mess. But here's the thing." Ashton pauses, dramatically. "About fifteen minutes later, he starts blowing up like a balloon."

"He's allergic?" I ask, horrified.

Ashton snaps his fingers at me. "Yep! He'd never had an allergic reaction before, not once. So mom shoves us in the car, and off we go, straight to the emergency room."

"That must have been so scary for your mom," I murmur. "And you."

"For me? Not at all." He laughs. "The nurses thought I was just the sweetest thing in the world. They treated me like a little prince. Poor Doc is stuck in a hospital bed, getting poked and prodded, and I've got his nurses bringing me ice cream and cookies. God, he was so pissed off about that."

I can imagine it. I picture a little Sebastian, perfectly put together and dour, with a little scowl on his face as he watches the nurses fawn over Ash.

"But to this day, I haven't eaten a single strawberry,"

Ashton admits. "I just can't forgive them for trying to kill him like that."

"I wonder how Sebastian would tell this same story," I say, grinning.

He sighs and reaches into a container for a chocolate-covered marshmallow. "With a lot more scowling, I bet."

That gets a genuine laugh out of me. I pick up another strawberry and take a bite. "I had an experience like that once. Well, actually, not exactly like that…"

I trail off, realizing my story isn't endearing or heart-warming like his.

"Never mind," I say, shaking my head.

"No, I want to know. I want to know everything about you. All of it." Ashton's eyes are bright and earnest as he says it.

"It's about Chase," I start, giving him room to stop me in case he doesn't want to hear about my ex. Ashton's eyes harden, but he doesn't tell me to stop. "He's allergic to nuts. He played fast and loose with it, too," I tell him. "One night we were at this gorgeous art opening, and they were passing around trays of appetizers. It was Indonesian food, and he didn't recognize the names of anything. I told him to be careful, but he ate some anyway and got sick almost immediately."

"What an idiot," Ash mutters.

"It gets worse. He also refused to carry his EPI-Pen. Like having an allergy made him look weak? It was ridiculous. I told him we should go to the emergency room, but he refused. Finally, I convinced him to let me run out and grab an antihist-amine. When I came back from the drugstore, he *screamed* at me about how long it took, said he could have died because I didn't care enough to hurry." I pull my knees closer to my chest, feeling strangely vulnerable remembering it. "He still ended up at the hospital, by the way. And he blamed me for how much it cost him."

"Wow," Ashton says, letting out a long breath.

"Yeah, not exactly a story of brotherly love. Just a dumb relationship squabble." I laugh, trying to shake it off.

"No, I meant 'wow, I wish I had hit him harder.'"

It's the first time either of us have broached the subject of him beating up Chase since *The Night of a Thousand Wines* (as I fondly named the incident). He watches me as he says it, like he's not sure how I'll react.

I give him a lopsided grin. "Honestly, I kind of wish you had too," I admit.

His answering smile is wide. "Hey, there's always next time!" He pulls out a mini bottle of Prosecco from his basket and hands me a plastic champagne flute, uncorking the bottle to pour me a drink.

"So, you and Seb are brothers? Actual brothers, I mean?" I ask, shifting the conversation back to him.

"Half-brothers," Ash corrects. "Same mom, different dads. We didn't meet Alec and Viper until after she passed."

Ashton's expression dims at that, and he picks at a container, plucking a piece of chocolate-covered pineapple out and rolling it between his fingers.

"I'm sorry," I tell him. "Do you want to tell me what happened?"

He shrugs. "Car accident," he murmurs. "Coming home from work. They couldn't find any immediate family who were willing to take us, so after it happened, we ended up at the orphanage."

"I'm so sorry."

"It's fine. Well, it wasn't, but you know how it goes. They separated us for a while, adopted us out to different families. But I kept getting into fights and getting sent back, and Seb?" He just laughs. "Seb always found out and found a way back to me. Once, he started a fire, almost burned down a school, just to get his foster family to send him back. Eventually, families stopped trying with him. Especially after the fish incident."

"What's the fish incident?" I ask.

Ashton flinches. "Well... One family that took him in lived on the water, and he found some fish that had washed up on the shore. They were already dead, but...he wanted to know how they worked, you know? So he brought them inside and tried dissecting them on the kitchen table..."

Nausea creeps into my belly, imagining it. "Oh."

"Yeah." He drains his glass and sets it aside. "They brought him back to the orphanage real fast after that. It was a whole thing. He got a new caseworker and everything. They threw around a bunch of diagnoses like conduct disorder, oppositional disorder, stuff like that. But he was just being Seb, right? It's like... like he knew even back then he'd be a doctor, taking things apart to see what makes them tick."

I take a sip from my glass. "When did you meet the others?"

"Alec was already there when we arrived," he explains. "No family wanted him. He was too smart, stubborn as fuck. Wouldn't listen to anyone because he always wanted to call the shots."

That sounds like Alec. "And Viper?" I ask.

Ashton shifts on the blanket. "Viper..." He frowns. "Viper came a little later. He, uh... the cops found him wandering the streets. When they figured out where he came from..."

He trails off and won't look at me.

"What?" I ask.

"They were already dead," he explains. "Everyone in the house, the whole family. Viper was the only survivor."

"Jesus!" I gasp.

Ashton nods with a grimace. "The whole story is pretty bad. They did some fucked up things to him. Things that break a person. I didn't know Viper before, but what he is now..." He trails off again.

I reach out and take his hand, giving it a squeeze. "What he is now is your brother," I insist.

Ashton looks at me, something bright shining in his eyes when he finally says, "Yeah, he is." He gives me a wide, happy smile.

"You love them, don't you? All of them?"

"Of course." Ash chuckles. "They're total pains in my ass most days. *Especially* these days. But, yeah, I love them. They're my family."

"That's like me and Jade. You're all lucky to have each other." I let out a breath, something loosening inside of me that's been coiled in my chest for weeks. This is what I needed from him. Honesty. He's being honest with me. Letting me in.

"Thank you," I say, breaking the silence.

"For what? The dessert?" Ashton looks at the mini feast he brought for us. We've barely put a dent in it. "This is nothing! Next time I'll bring you a whole banquet."

"No! I mean, *yes*, this is really sweet of you. The picnic." I falter, trying to explain it. "But thank you for telling me that story. It helps. Getting to know you, hearing about the four of you. I don't like feeling like I don't know you, like you're keeping things from me."

His face falls. "I want you to know everything. About us. And I want to know everything about you, too. I don't want to keep things from you, not anymore. Not ever."

"I'm still mad, you know," I say, tucking a strand of hair behind my ear, avoiding his eyes.

"You have every right to be. I'm mad at me, too. And I'm furious with Alec. And Seb for being such a fucking know-it-all."

"Ash—"

"Sorry. This isn't about me." He blows out a breath. "I just mean, I'll do whatever it takes to make this right. Saying 'I've fallen for you' doesn't even scratch the surface, Babygirl. It feels... it feels like I'm underwater, when I'm not with you. Everything is muted. I can't get a breath. And then when you're here..." He doesn't finish his sentence, but his gaze meets mine, and what I see there makes me feel too many things.

"You really hurt me, Ash," I tell him, setting my drink down on the blanket. "The lying, the secrets. And then seeing you with Annika, seeing you hugging her, I just—"

I stop, that familiar pain gripping my chest.

"You what?" Ashton asks, leaning closer to me, tracing my face with his gaze.

"I didn't like it," I admit. "I don't care if it's not a real marriage. I didn't like seeing the two of you together like that. I didn't—"

He doesn't let me finish before he grabs my face and pulls my mouth in a fierce kiss, groaning against my lips.

I mean to push him away, I do. But I pull him closer, instead, my hands clutching his shirt, all my thoughts and intentions fading away. His hands are in my hair, and he tilts my head back, angling me so that he can deepen the kiss.

"You were jealous," he murmurs against my lips. He says it like I've given him something, something special. "*Fuck*, Babygirl, you were jealous of her, weren't you?"

Of course I was jealous.

"That's so hot. That you care. That you were jealous of her. But there's no one else for me." He pulls away to look me in the eyes when he says it, hands still tangled in my hair. "No other woman exists. It's you. It'll always be you."

Then his mouth is on mine again, and this time, I open for

him, letting his tongue slip between my lips. He slides his hands over my body, pulling off my jacket and cupping my tits over my bra.

"I can't get enough of you. You're all I want. All I could ever want." My heart flutters in my chest at his words, and my thighs clench as he peels off my shirt. I can't form a response before he grabs the bottom of my bra and pulls it over my head, exposing me to the cold air.

"Ash..." I pant. I want more of him, more of *this*, but we're in the middle of the park, out in public. But then his hands are on my leggings, pulling them down my legs and tossing them aside.

"Anyone could see us," I remind him, the words coming out in a moan. He slips my panties to the side and runs his fingers over me, and there's no denying how wet I am.

"Let them watch." He groans as he eases a finger inside of me. "It'll be the last thing they ever see." It shouldn't make me wetter, hearing him threaten to kill someone just for seeing me like this, but it does. And I can't hide my body's reaction to it as his finger moves inside of me.

You'd kill for him, too.

"Fuck," he gasps as he pushes a second finger into my soaked pussy. "I've missed this."

He pulls me into his lap, fingers moving in and out of me, fucking me hard. Anyone could see me like this, naked and spread open on his lap, while he touches me. The thought should make me want to stop, but it just makes me want it more.

"Look how perfect you are," Ashton moans, eyes fixed where his fingers are stretching me open. His tongue slides over his lips, staring at me like I'm the hottest thing he's ever seen.

He's saying more, telling me all the things he wants to do to me, how he wants to see me marked, but I'm too far gone to understand half of it. His face drops to my chest, and he sucks my nipple into his mouth, swirling his tongue around it. And that's all it takes to completely unravel me. I come, shaking hard and screaming his name so loudly that if we didn't have any spectators before, we might now.

He lets me catch my breath, panting while he holds me against his chest, before he lifts me and sets me gently back on the blanket next to him. Then his mouth meets mine, his tongue sweetly caressing me, as I press myself against him. I whimper into his mouth, sucking on his bottom lip as my hands go to his belt, unbuckling it.

"You don't have to do that. I just couldn't help myself, I—" But my fingers are still moving, unzipping his pants and lowering his jeans and boxers. Before he can protest again, his hard cock springs free, the tip already glistening with pre-cum.

"Shut up," I tell him. I roll his hips, moving him until he's sitting up, and shifting so I'm kneeling between his legs. "I'm calling the shots right now." Then my mouth is on him, licking all the way up his shaft to his tip, moaning while I do it.

"Oh fuck me," he murmurs, his head falling back.

His tip is salty, nearly dripping. I take him in my mouth, sliding my tongue over him as I swallow his full length. I try to, at least. Tears sting the back of my eyes when he hits my throat, and I can't hold him there for long. Ashton doesn't move, letting me set the pace, his breathing hard, hands clenching the picnic blanket under us. It's not until I start to speed up, moving my mouth up and down over him, that he fists my hair, groaning like he can't take it anymore.

"Fuck." I take him as deep as I can again, and his whole body seizes up, flexing. "That's so good. You feel so fucking good."

I bring my hand up to join my mouth, stroking him as I pick up the pace, sucking on his head. His hand clenches in my hair, and he starts to mumble unintelligible words, his hips lifting off the blanket, thighs shaking.

I'm loving this. The feeling of him in my mouth, the way his breathing changes when I speed up. I swirl my tongue over his tip, humming my satisfaction, and that sends him over the edge.

"Fuck, Babygirl, I'm going to come," he warns me.

I don't stop. I moan around him, stroking him, loving the way he tenses, the way his cock swells even more, right before he fills my mouth, groaning my name as he comes.

When I look up at him, his eyes are wide, his breathing heavy. I look him dead in the eyes as I swallow.

—————

BY THE TIME WE'VE PACKED UP OUR PICNIC, AND ASHTON has walked me home, I've made up my mind. I'm done waiting. I'm done pretending I don't want this, don't want them.

All of them.

> I need a favor.

> Seb: Anything.

> I need to know where Alec is. Right now. I need to see him.

I bite my lip, waiting. I'm not even sure how Sebastian will react to my asking. Alec and Ashton are fine with sharing, but what about him?

What if he wants me all to himself?

Seb: He's at the house.

Seb: I just dropped you a pin. Security knows
you're on the way and will clear you.

Seb: Go get him.

39

ALEC

Days of planning, endless nights at the office, calls with various law enforcement agencies, and money exchanged under the table, all to hit Dante where it would hurt the most. And tonight, just a touch of that weight was lifted off my chest when I got the call from Sebastian's contact that everything went according to plan.

Even so, it's not over yet.

We still don't know where he is or the extent of the network he's built here in Fortune City. But with all his focus here, trying to dismantle what we've spent years building, we were able to hit him hard enough on his own turf that it'll take him a good long while before he gets back up again.

And he can't hide from us forever.

I take a sip of my coffee, eyes flicking to the kitchen clock. There's still so much to do, so many things to juggle. I doubt I'll get more than a few hours of sleep tonight.

There's a knock on the front door, a quick rap against the wood.

I consider ignoring it, taking another gulp of coffee. There's no way in hell someone got through our security gate and up to the front door of our compound unless they're meant to be here. Which means it's one of my brothers, finally coming home, or someone on the staff.

But they knock again. Louder.

Tossing my paper down in irritation and leaving my coffee on the kitchen table, I make my way over to the door.

"For fucks sake, Ash," I grumble. "I'm not making you another set of keys. You have to keep an eye on your—"

The words die in my throat the moment the door swings open.

Sydney. She's standing there in the doorway, hands clasped behind her, staring at me.

"Hi," she says, and the sound of her voice cuts through me like a knife.

I can't speak. I just stand there, staring at her like I've seen a ghost. She shouldn't be here. She shouldn't be anywhere near me. And yet...here she is.

"Well, I'm coming in," Sydney says, pushing past me. She slips through the door and into the antechamber, moving through the entryway of our mansion like she belongs here. I don't try to stop her. I couldn't even if I wanted to. My eyes follow her every step.

She belongs here, surrounded by luxury. She fits, like I made this home just for her, without realizing it.

"Holy shit!" Sydney gives a little laugh as she spins, staring at the compound around us, eyes trailing over the leather furniture and dark wood accents. "I mean, holy shit! I don't even... *Wow!*" She looks at everything, awestruck, her lips parting as she wanders through the hall. She steps past the kitchen, into our sitting room, eyes wide as she takes in the floor-to-ceiling windows overlooking the valley and, in the distance, the entire city skyline stretching out below us. The low lighting lets us see the entire cityscape, spanning as far as the eye can see.

Her astonishment is genuine, and it guts me. Because I've never let her see this side of me—never let her in.

"This might be the most beautiful view I've ever seen. I'm speechless, I can't believe you've never invited me over here before!" She turns to me then and scrunches up her nose. "I mean, maybe I can. Considering."

My body is still rooted to the doorway. My brain screams at me to speak, to say anything, but all I can do is stare at her, memorize her like she might vanish again if I blink.

And then she's walking toward me, fearless, determined, her small hand wrapping around my wrist. Her touch jolts me back into myself, grounds me. She tugs me gently toward the sitting room couch and guides me over to sit on it like she's the one in control.

"You promised me time. And I appreciate that. But now it's time for you to tell me the truth. All of it," she says, moving to stand between my legs. She looks down at me, from where I'm seated on the couch, face stern.

My voice comes out raw, strangled. "You're here."

"I am," she tells me. "Because I hate this. I hate being away from you. You fucked up, and I'm still furious at you, but..." She places one knee on the couch and slowly climbs into my lap, straddling me. A breathy groan slips out from between my lips. "I'm not ready to let this go. Are you?"

I can't look away from her. Her wild brown curls, her sweet face. She's everything.

"If this is going to work, I need you to look me in the eye and promise me I'm not the other woman," she says.

"You're not, darling," I tell her. My hands raise to her hips, gripping her like I'll fall apart without her. "You never were."

"You're married?" she asks, voice soft but deadly. Her hands rest against my chest.

I nod.

"But it never meant anything?"

I shake my head. "Nothing. It meant nothing."

Loosely, she wraps her arms around my neck, pulling me a little closer. "Why did you lie? Why didn't you just tell me?"

"I tried," I say, honestly. I grip her even tighter.

"Bullshit," she says defiantly, eyes narrowing. And I love seeing it, love seeing her stand up for herself, even against me. "It's not just about her. It's all of it. Tell me why you lied to me."

I take a deep breath, because all this time without her, I've gone over that time and time again and never got a good answer.

"I liked the way you looked at me," I finally admit. "The person you thought I was. I didn't want to lose that."

She assesses me, analyzing, looking for a lie in what I've said. But there's none to be found, because as selfish as my reasons were, that's what it boils down to.

I don't deserve her. I never have. But I wanted to be someone who did.

"Don't ever lie to me again," she insists. She shifts a little on my lap, then tentatively lowers her face to mine, pausing just before the kiss as if giving me a chance to stop her.

But when she leans in, when her lips brush mine, all my resolve shatters.

She kisses me like I'm the air she's been starving for, and I can't stop myself from answering with everything I've kept buried. My hands are on her, pulling her closer, greedy, desperate. The sounds she makes, *fuck*, I could drown in them.

Sydney rocks herself against me, my mouth devouring hers, and I know she can feel it when I harden beneath her. Everything finally feels right. I deepen the kiss, exploring her mouth with my tongue, pulling her body into mine. She breaks away from me, and I take the opportunity to flip her onto her back, pressing her against the dark leather of the couch.

Her breath stutters when my hand slides under her shirt and my fingers find her nipple. She pulls me down to her, kissing me deeply, rocking her hips up to feel every inch of me.

"I need to feel you," she pants between kisses, clawing at my shirt. "Please. Alec."

My shirt is gone before I realize I've stripped it off, and hers follows a moment later, hitting the floor next to mine. She's reaching for my belt, frantic, and I want—*fuck*, I want her more than I want anything else in this life.

But then her wrists are in my hands, pinned above her head. My other hand wraps around her throat, and I look down at her squirming beneath me, begging. "Please," she murmurs.

She's so fucking beautiful, writhing desperately beneath me. Too beautiful.

And I'm still lying to her.

"I missed your hands on me," she says breathlessly. She doesn't feel how I've suddenly stilled, how I've gone tense. "Make me forget. Make me forget everything."

Make me forget that you lied to me.

That you're still lying to me.

Because I am. She's come back, ready to forgive me, willing to lend me her trust. And I'm still lying to her. Lying to her about Dante, lying to her about the danger she's in. The growing danger I'll be putting her in if Dante sees me with her.

I kiss her once more, desperately, and then I wrench myself away. She's trembling, breathless, lips swollen from my kiss. And pulling away from her is the hardest thing I've ever done.

"I can't do this," I choke out, my voice rough. "I'm sorry. I can't. This is a mistake."

Sydney freezes, her eyes wide, confusion flickering across her face. She doesn't say anything, just stares at me like she doesn't understand why I've stopped. I reach for her shirt, wanting to cover her, to do *something* that will soften the blow, and when my fingers close over the fabric and I hold it out for her to take, I see it dawn on her.

Her lips part. "Oh," she says, taking her shirt back and clutching it to her chest. Color floods her cheeks, shame filling her eyes, and I hate myself in a way I didn't know was possible.

"I'm sorry," I say, reaching for my own shirt. "It's not that I don't want to. It's *all* I want. But I can't do this until I can be completely honest with you. You told me to never lie to you again, but there are things I can't tell you. Not yet, not if I want to keep you safe."

But she's already moving.

"Sydney, wait!"

She's scrambling to get off the couch, to get away from me. My chest seizes as I watch her pull her shirt back over her head, a noticeable quiver in her voice as she says, "You can't tell me? Or you won't tell me?"

"Red."

But Sydney is already moving past me, through the compound and towards the door.

"God. I'm such an idiot. Here I am, laying myself bare to you when it should be the other way around. *You* should have been knocking down *my* door, begging for my forgiveness. So, yeah, you're right," she says. She won't look at me. "This was a mistake."

Then she's rushing down the entryway, throwing the door open, and disappearing into the night. And I'm watching her walk out of my life once again.

And just like last time, I let her go.

I DON'T KNOW HOW LONG I SIT THERE, SINKING INTO THE couch, wallowing. The smell of her still clings to the air. Coconuts and new books.

Eventually, I hear the front door open, heavy footsteps crossing the compound and heading straight to the sitting room. Ashton drops into the couch beside me, legs spread wide, zero sense of boundaries and completely unaware of how destroyed I am right now. "Hey, boss! I need to talk to you. It's important."

We've barely exchanged two words since our blowup at the club, and I know he's still furious at me, but his timing couldn't be worse.

"I can't deal with you and your bullshit right now," I mutter. "Whatever it is, we can deal with it tomorrow."

Ashton snorts. "Great. Amazing attitude as usual. But I didn't come here to argue with you. You'll want to hear this, trust me."

I don't have the energy. "Just tell me what you want and get the fuck out," I say. My voice is biting, but it's not him I'm angry at. It's me.

What if this is it? What if she never forgives me for keeping my distance, for trying to keep her safe? What if that was the last time I'll ever see her?

"Doc found out who was driving the car that almost hit Sydney," Ashton says.

My eyes snap to him.

"Someone called the cops," he continues. "The night it happened. They took down the license plate, gave it to the operator."

"And?" I push.

"You're not going to believe this. It was her ex. Chase."

Ashton's face twists, his fist flexing on the couch. "Guess I didn't do enough to scare him off."

Her ex. Not Dante.

"We need to find him," I grind out. "Now. Call Viper, have him—"

My phone rings, vibrating loud enough on the kitchen counter to cut me off.

Sydney. Maybe it's her, maybe she's calling. Even if it's just to scream at me, to tell me to get fucked.

I bolt up from the couch, hurrying to the kitchen, ignoring Ashton as he calls out after me.

My heart sinks when I check the caller ID and see it's not her.

It's Sebastian.

"This better be important," I snap, bringing the phone to my ear.

"Is Sydney there?" His voice is frantic, pitched too high. "Tell me she's with you at the compound right now."

"No." Because I fucked up. Because I fuck everything up. "She was, but—"

Sebastian swears, cutting me off. "You need to get to her place right the fuck now. I'm too far out, and you're closer."

Fuck.

I'm grabbing my jacket and gun before he can even finish, sprinting for the door. "I'm on my way. What happened?"

"Someone broke into her place about five minutes ago," he says. "I just got the alert on my phone."

A dark, violent fury fills me. "Her ex?" I ask.

"No. The camera picked up his face, but I don't recognize him. A man, maybe six four, muscular. He's still inside. I keep calling her, but she's not picking up. You need to get there. *Now*, before she does."

My stomach drops. She would be here, safe with me, if only

I hadn't let my goddamn control issues get in the way of being with her. Instead of protecting her, I sent her running, straight into danger.

Ashton shouts behind me, demanding to know where I'm going, but I don't have time to explain. I grab the first set of keys I find and race toward the garage.

When I hit the unlock button on the keys I'm holding, Ash's yellow Lamborghini beeps.

I need to get to Sydney *now*, and if this gives Ash one more reason to hate me, so be it. This car is his baby. I've never seen him care for anything the way he cares for it—

Her, I correct myself, lifting the door and ducking into the driver's seat. The engine roars to life when I start the car. He fucking insists we call it *her.*

"I'm on my way," I tell Sebastian, throwing the car into gear and peeling out of the garage, tearing north toward Sydney's apartment.

"I sent you the security feed," he says. "Keep it open so you can get a read on the situation. He still hasn't left yet, but I haven't seen her arrive either."

"Got it."

I hear his motorcycle engine rev. "Fucking get there right now, Alec," he tells me. Then the phone clicks. He's already on the move, knowing he'll never make it before me.

I open the feed he sent, keeping half an eye on it and half on the road as I speed through the city. Her front door is shut, and there's no one there, no movement, nothing. I might as well be looking at a still image for all the good it does.

My eyes flick between the phone and the road, only looking up long enough to make sure I don't crash, when the car's Bluetooth suddenly picks up an incoming call. Ashton's name flashes across the screen.

"What the *fuck?*" he yells when I answer. "Tell me you did not just take my fucking car!"

"Sydney's in trouble," I tell him in lieu of explanation, no apology. "I needed it."

"Then why the fuck didn't you bring me?" he shouts. The speaker crackles with how loud he is. "Or take a different fucking car? You have like twenty!"

"Your feelings aren't my priority right now," I snap. "Someone needs to get to her place as soon as fucking possible. Doc is on his way, too. Meet us there, and you can be backup."

"WITH WHAT CAR?" he screams. I end the call. He'll figure something out.

I'm not used to this, this panicked, clawing fear gripping my chest. I haven't felt this way in decades. Growing up the way I did, you cope by either living in fear forever or making damn sure you never feel it again. I spent my whole life building walls to protect myself, making sure nothing could ever touch me, could ever hurt me. I did all of it so I would never be that kid cowering in a closet again. The kid who couldn't do anything when his father chased his mom through the house. Who had to listen to his mother crying, begging for the pain to end. The kid who heard the shot that ended her life, who had to testify against his own father in court and send him to rot in prison.

I've spent twenty years making myself untouchable. But she's in danger, and for the first time since I was that scared little kid, I feel it. Panic. Helpless, crippling fear, filling my veins.

Movement draws my eyes back to the camera feed.

Sydney's home.

She's home, and I'm still a few blocks away.

I tell the car's voice system to dial her number, my eyes glued to the feed. She digs in her purse for her keys, anger pinching her face, unaware of the danger she's in. Because of me. Because I broke something in her tonight and sent her straight into harm's way.

The call rings. And rings. She doesn't answer it.

"Fucking turn around," I bark at the screen. "Turn around and leave, right the fuck now!"

But she doesn't.

Her key goes into the lock. Turns. And she disappears inside.

The door closes.

She's in there, inside with whoever is waiting for her.

Every second stuck in the car becomes an eternity. I swerve into the back lot behind her building and slam the Lamborghini to a stop, not bothering to turn it off. I'm out the door before the car settles into park, racing up the stairs, my heart in my throat.

I hear a scream. Her scream.

But screaming means she's still alive.

I reach her door, only to realize I don't have keys to her apartment. So I do the only reasonable thing I can. I take three running steps and throw my body against the door, so hard it shatters, bursting open.

Sydney. She's on the floor, clutching her head. Her attacker has her by the hair, dragging her across the floor toward her bedroom.

I don't even stop to think.

I raise the gun and fire.

40

SYDNEY

My ears are ringing.

There's something warm and wet on me. Under me. On my hands, on my clothes, pooling beneath me. I try to stand, but the world tilts, the floor sliding out from under me. There's a sharp pain over my temple, and my scalp throbs from where someone had been dragging me by my hair.

Because someone...

Someone *attacked me*.

I blink hard, trying to think. I remember leaving Alec's mansion, humiliated and furious. I remember wanting to get home, to be alone. I was distracted, so caught up in my own thoughts and broken heart I didn't notice someone waiting inside my apartment until it was too late.

As soon as the door shut behind me, they were on me. A fist connected with my temple, and the world went white. I hit the ground, tried to crawl away, but someone grabbed my hair, yanked me up, and then—

BANG.

The grip on my hair vanished, and I slumped back to the floor.

The wet floor. It smells like copper, like warm pennies. I know that smell, somehow. Recognize it, but I can't—

A pair of hands cups my face, and I scream, scrambling to my feet to get away from them.

"It's me, darling. It's Alec."

The sound of his voice instantly eases something in me, and this time I don't shove him away when he reaches for me. My vision is blurred, and I have to blink hard a few times before his warm brown eyes come into focus. Then the rest of him falls into place. My Alec. Here, keeping me safe, scaring my attacker away. His eyes are dark, frantic and scared as they sweep over me, assessing the damage.

"Are you okay? How many fingers am I holding up?" he asks, voice husky. He's trying to stay calm and controlled, but there's a quiver of panic in his voice. He keeps one hand on my cheek, raising the other in front of me.

"Three," I croak. My throat feels raw. Screaming. I've been screaming, haven't I?

"Good girl."

He's so close to me, I can't see anything but him. I take a shaky step back, trying to put some distance between us. "What happened?"

His jaw tightens. There's red on him, I realize. All over his hands. I glance down at myself. There's red on me, too. All over my arms and my clothes. Why is there so much red? "Someone was waiting for you," Alec explains, voice low. "Why the fuck weren't you answering your phone?"

Because I put it on do not disturb. Because I was pissed, heartbroken, ten thousand different emotions after letting myself be vulnerable just to be told he still couldn't be honest with me.

"Gee, I wonder," I snap. My fists clench at my side. "Maybe I wasn't in the mood to chit-chat after throwing myself at you when *you* should be the one groveling."

"Red—"

"No. Forget it." My voice shakes with anger. "Why did you even come? Why didn't you send Seb or Ash? God, even Viper seems more inclined to help me at this point." His face crumples as the words hit their mark, something flickering behind his eyes, but I don't care. I went to him and put my heart on the line. And he rejected me.

"You will never let me in. I get it. Thank you for the help, and I appreciate you scaring him off, but I've had enough humiliation for today. Can you please just..." I glance past him and freeze, the words dying on my tongue as I realize what actually happened. He didn't scare away my attacker.

There's a dead body.

In the middle of my apartment. His blood soaking into my rug. One eye, unfixed, staring at nothing. His head...

Red. The red all over me, red all over my apartment, pooling under that too still man...

Blood. I'm covered in blood.

Alec catches my face in his hands again, turning my head back toward him. My eyes stay fixed on the body. "Don't look," he says sharply. "Focus on me."

"He's dead," I say, voice completely monotone.

"Sydney. Don't look at it. Look at me."

But I can't stop staring.

I should be emotional, right? I should feel something at the sight of a corpse lying on my living room floor. But I feel nothing. He broke in here to hurt me. He might have raped me, maybe even killed me.

"I'm fine," I hear myself say, voice oddly distant. But I'm

not. There's a dead body on my floor. I've never been further from *fine*. "I'm okay now. You can go."

Alec swears under his breath. "You're in shock. I'm not leaving you."

I do look away from my attacker then, and finally, a spark of emotion lights inside of me. Lights, and then catches fire.

Rage.

"You're not *leaving me*?" I repeat, glaring at him. "You haven't *been here*. You don't care about me! You can't even be *honest with me*."

I shove at his chest, but he doesn't move. He just stares at me, his jaw tight and his eyes impossibly dark. He's breathing quickly, chest rising and falling as he stares at me.

"Fuck it," he growls.

He moves before I can react. One step, then another, closing the space between us as I stumble back away from him until my back hits the wall. He stops just inches away from me, palms hitting the wall on either side of my face, boxing me in.

"You want honesty, *darling*?" he spits, towering over me.

I glare up at him, so furious I'm shaking.

"You're *all I care about*," he continues. "You're all I think about, night and day, every fucking second I'm awake. You're in my dreams. I have been *haunted* by you for the last few weeks. Everything I see reminds me of you, and every breath I take when I'm not holding you is a waste."

My breath catches in my throat. My pulse is suddenly racing again, my mouth dry. His face dips lower, his lips just above mine.

"Yes," he says. "I killed that man for you. And I would kill a thousand more just for looking at you. And do you know *why*?"

I swallow. "Why?"

His hand, still covered in blood, comes up to circle my throat lightly. He doesn't tighten his grip, doesn't squeeze. He just holds it there, fingers wrapped around my neck, eyes locked on mine.

"Because you're *mine*," he says quietly, staring into my eyes. "From the day you came into my life, until the day I die. You belong to me."

I tremble under his touch as his fingers tighten, my heart pounding in my chest. I slide my tongue over my lips.

"Prove it," I whisper.

There's no hesitation, no uncertainty. Still gripping my throat, Alec slams his lips to mine in a kiss so hungry I forget to breathe.

We fit together in a way that I've never fit with someone before. His lips against my lips, his tongue against my tongue. Our bodies recognize each other like we were made for one another.

Kissing Alec is like coming home.

"I never should have let you walk out of my penthouse. I shouldn't have let you walk out of my compound either," he says, hand moving to tug at my hair, angling my head so he can deepen the kiss. "I should keep you locked up with me so I can spend every second of my life with you."

Frantically, I pull him to me, clawing at his shirt. I can't get close enough to him. I need more. I'm running on pure adrenaline as my nails scratch down his neck. He groans into my mouth, and my self-control snaps.

I break our kiss just long enough to pull my shirt over my head.

"Red." I can't tell if he's cautioning me or begging me.

"Show me," I tell him. His eyes are fixed on my chest as I unhook my bra, tossing it aside. I reach up to run my hand over his cheek, and he leans into my touch, groaning. "Show me you care. Show me how much I mean to you."

He does.

No one has ever kissed me the way Alec does. Like he's worshiping me, memorizing the feel of my lips against his. It sets my body alight, touches every nerve that runs through me.

His fingers fumble with the waistband of my pants, and then they're gone, ripped off me and tossed away. There's still blood on me—on us—as he slides his hands up my legs, tugging my panties down until they fall at my feet, but I don't even care.

It's quick. No foreplay, no stretching me out with his fingers and preparing me for it. Alec takes his lips from mine just long enough to free himself from his pants, and then my legs are wrapped around his hips and he's lifting me up to—

I scream his name when he slams his cock into me, all the way to the hilt, shoving me back against the wall. Scream again when he pulls back out to thrust into me again. There's pain, sure—I'm stretched so tight around him, barely able to take him —but it's eclipsed by how good he feels inside me, how perfectly he hits that spot in me that makes my toes curl.

"You wanted me, Red?" Alec growls against my lips. I can't answer him, can't do anything but gasp as he moves inside of me. "Then take every fucking inch."

My first orgasm hits me so fast I'm not prepared for it. I claw at his shoulders, pulsing around him, seeing stars. Alec murmurs my name, sucking on my bottom lip and then taking it between his teeth to bite. I'm still feeling it, still riding the last waves of my pleasure and clenching around his cock, when he grips me by the hips, turns around, and drops us to the ground, laying me flat on my back.

"Mine. Every part of you," Alec mutters as he circles my throat with his hand once again.

Blood. It's all I can smell as Alec fucks me against the ground, hands grasping me tight enough to bruise. There's so much of it, on the floor, on both of us, perfuming the air. If he notices, he doesn't care.

I'm not sure I do either.

"Say it." Alec grips me tighter, hard enough to hurt. "Say it, Sydney."

I know what he wants to hear. What he *needs* to hear.

"I'm yours," I gasp. There's nothing controlled about the way he's fucking me now, nothing at all of the calm and collected Alec I'm used to. He's feral, lips pulled back from his teeth in a snarl, thrusts frantic and hard.

"Again," Alec demands. I arch my neck to give him better access.

"I'm yours!" I feel it coming this time. That tightening in my lower belly, that flutter in my legs. I moan, lifting my hips to meet his, matching him thrust for thrust.

"Don't fucking forget it," Alec snarls, tightening his grip, and I shatter.

I think I'm screaming again. I'm not sure. All I know is how good he feels inside me, all I can hear is his voice murmuring I'm good, so fucking good for him, made for him, and then he's twitching inside of me, filling me. Every pulse of his cock tears a little more pleasure from me, until I can't even remember my own name.

"Fuck." Alec is panting, holding his weight off me with one arm. He stares down at me, chest heaving. Stares at me like I'm the sun his world revolves around.

I should say something. *Get off me*, or *I love you*. His eyes flick down to my parted lips, and he leans forward like he's going to kiss me again.

And someone at the door clears their throat, loudly.

41

SYDNEY

"WELL, THIS ISN'T EXACTLY WHAT WE WERE EXPECTING TO find," Ash's voice floats toward me.

I whip my head toward the door. Ashton and Sebastian stand framed in it, staring at us. I have no idea how long they've been there, watching the two of us, and I can only imagine how I look right now, completely naked and covered in blood. Sebastian's jaw tightens as he drags his gaze over me, heating as he takes in every bare inch. Whatever he saw before they interrupted, he clearly enjoyed. But Ash looks ready to faint, his eyes a little too wide, showing too much white.

"Someone tell me how much of this blood is hers before I start to freak out," Ash says, his voice an octave too high, the words too fast, said in a panic.

"None," Alec grunts, pushing himself off me and settling back on his knees.

Heat floods my face, and I feel myself blush. I cross my arms over my chest, hiding myself, but Alec doesn't seem to care that his brothers just walked in on him while he was still inside me. He takes his time putting his cock away, zipping his pants like this isn't anything out of the ordinary. "Doc, call the cleaners. We need this mess taken care of." Alec glances at the body, then back to Sebastian. "Did you bring your med kit?"

Sebastian nods.

"Go get it."

"Oh no," Ash says, gesturing between the two of us. "We aren't just brushing over whatever the fuck this is."

"We'll discuss it later," Alec insists, standing. "Go get the fucking kit."

Seb gives me one last lingering look, eyes tracing every patch of blood on me, like he's committing it to memory. Then he takes out his cell phone, putting it to his ear as he steps outside, shutting my broken door behind him. It doesn't close all the way, and after a second, it swings back open with a soft creak.

Alec grabs a fluffy white blanket from my couch—the one I love to curl up with when I read—and tosses it unceremoniously over the dead man, covering most of him.

"Hey," I shout, indignant. Too late. Blood is already seeping through the fabric, staining it red. "That was my favorite blanket!"

"We can buy you a new one," Alec informs me. "Get up, darling. We need to get you cleaned up." He's already heading toward the bathroom when he says it. The sound of the shower turning on follows seconds later.

"Here," Ash murmurs, stepping forward. He grabs another blanket off the couch and offers me a hand. "Let's get you all covered up, okay? You're safe now, Babygirl. We've got you."

His voice is soft, worried. I let him help me up, giving him a shaky smile as he wraps the fleece blanket over my shoulders. He places a gentle kiss on the top of my head, tactfully avoiding any blood.

"Doc's going to look you over, after you get all cleaned up, okay?" Ash says, eyeing the bruise I can already feel forming at my temple. He looks like he wants to say more, but the door swings open again before he can.

"Cleaners are on their way," Sebastian says, stepping inside, his bag in one hand. "Should be an hour or so before the full crew shows up."

Ash frowns at the body. "Are we even sure he's dead? Did anyone check?"

Seb tilts his head, studying the motionless shape under my once-favorite blanket (RIP reading blankie). Without a word, he steps forward and plants his foot lightly over where my attacker's neck should be. He presses down in a single swift motion, leaning his whole weight into it.

Snap.

I flinch at the sound of his neck breaking, clutching the blanket tighter around myself.

"Jesus fucking Christ!" Ash takes a step back, jaw gaping. "Doc, what the *fuck?*"

"Calm down," Sebastian says, voice flat, expression cold. "It's a better death than he deserved, if he was still alive." He looks at me and nods toward the bathroom, his voice softening as he says, "Go ahead. We'll be waiting."

"Fucking sociopath," Ash mutters, guiding me toward the bathroom, hand warm on my waist.

Maybe I should say something. Kick them out, insist on calling the police. But I feel safe with them. Secure.

No one else can hurt me, with the three of them here. No one would ever dare.

Alec is already in the shower when Ash opens the bathroom door for me, his bloodied clothes piled on the floor.

"I'll give you two a few minutes to *clean up,*" Ash says pointedly. He takes the blanket from me and leads me into the shower, where Alec is waiting, hand outstretched to help me in. "No more funny business. We'll be waiting."

The door shuts behind him, and I'm alone with Alec once again. He's already clean, I notice as I step into the shower, all the blood he spilled washed away, down the drain. He adjusts the spray from the shower head, moving aside to let me stand under it.

I let the water wash over me, squeezing my eyes shut. Alec grabs my body wash and wordlessly starts to lather me up.

"Are you okay?" he asks. His voice is soft, hesitant, like he's not sure how I'll react.

"I... I think so," I manage to say.

Alec makes an appreciative noise in his throat as he works the soap over my skin, sliding his hands over me. He's gentle. Thorough. He takes his time, carefully washing the blood away, making sure to get all of it. When I open my eyes, the water swirling around the drain is red, quickly easing to pink.

"It's okay if you're not. You were attacked, darling," Alec says, kneading the lather into my skin. "You saw a man die."

"It's not the first time I've seen a dead body," I admit. I can see my parents' bodies right now, permanently seared into my mind. Those moments, right after the accident? I remember all of it. The blood. The sudden quiet. My mom's vacant eyes, staring straight ahead.

The water feels too cold, suddenly, and I shiver.

This was different, though. Traumatic in a different way.

"He was going to hurt me," I whisper, and saying it out loud makes it suddenly feel real.

Alec's hands pause. He maneuvers me fully under the shower spray, rinsing the soap away. "He was."

"Why?" I ask.

He's quiet, for a while. Long enough I start to think he won't answer.

"Because of me," he finally admits.

I don't know what to say to that. I look away from him, wrapping my arms around myself, squeezing myself tightly.

"This is what I wanted to protect you from," he says quietly. "There are people who would hurt you just to get to me."

I shake my head. "That's not a good enough reason, you know. That's not a good enough reason for you to keep things from me."

"You're right," he admits. His fingers trace my jaw, and he tilts my chin up, forcing me to look at him. His dark eyes search mine.

"You're still mad at me," he surmises, studying me.

"Yes, Alec." The words come out sharp. "I'm *still* mad at you. And a quick fuck isn't enough to fix that."

His hands drop away. "What is enough to fix it, then?"

I scoff, my hands tightening around me as I look away.

"Tell me." He takes a step closer to me, ducking his head under the water to catch my gaze. "What do you need from me, Red? You want me to get on my knees and beg for your forgiveness?"

"It would be a nice start," I snap, glaring at him.

He stares back at me for a long beat. And then, eyes locked on mine, he slowly sinks to his knees.

"Alec, what are you—" I start.

"I'm sorry, Sydney." His voice is low, deep. Water pours down his chest, cascading over his body. His hands come up to touch my legs, his eyes glued to mine. "I fucked up. I kept things from you. And I don't deserve your forgiveness. But I will beg for it."

I swallow hard against the swell of emotion in my throat.

"I'm sick of it," I tell him. "I'm sick of the lies. Being kept in the dark. You need to be honest with me."

"No more lies," he promises. He shifts forward, pressing a kiss just above my hipbone, then another on the other side. "I'm sorry I let this happen. I let you get hurt. And that will never happen again, I promise you that. You're mine."

"You're mine, too, you know," I whisper back. "But it has to be us. Together. You have to let me in."

His gaze meets mine, fierce and unflinching.

A knock breaks through the sound of the water.

"Hey guys?" Ashton calls, muffled through the door. "You're going to want to finish up and come see this."

42

SEBASTIAN

It wasn't hard to find the hole someone drilled in Sydney's wall. Not if you knew where to look.

That image of her in the photo—asleep and safe on her couch—has been haunting me since Alec showed it to me. Once Sydney left to clean up, I didn't waste any time tracing the trajectory, looking for where someone would have had to stand to take that photo.

The hole was easy to find after that.

A shame there's no one in the apartment next door when we break the door down. I already compiled a lengthy mental list of the things I want to do to the man who watched her without her knowing. That list grows even more depraved when we bring Alec and Sydney over and show them the space someone used to spy on her. When I see the realization hit her that someone did this, violated her privacy.

The apartment is sparsely furnished, nearly empty. Nothing but trash, some groceries, a mini-TV, and a sleeping bag tucked away in the bedroom.

The hole is bored into the wall, just above where that sleeping bag sits.

Sydney walks in like she's in a daze, blinking around as she tries to comprehend what she's seeing. Her face is blank, brows drawn together.

"You shouldn't be showing her this," Alec hisses under his breath to me. I ignore him.

She deserves to see it. She deserves to know what someone did to her.

The fear in her eyes as she walks through the apartment makes me want to hurt something. Hurt someone. But I watch that fear slowly shift to anger, then rage, when she notices a T-shirt on the floor, stooping to pick it up.

"This is Chase's," she says, voice so low we almost can't hear it. She lets the garment fall to the ground, slipping through her fingers.

My fingers twitch, itching for a weapon. That stupid mother-fucker. Ashton should have killed him when he had the chance.

"You're sure?" I ask her.

She nods. Then her eyes move to the next pile of clothing. She lifts a pair of underwear from the pile, a lacy black thong, staring at them in confusion.

"Yours?" I guess.

She gives another shaky nod and drops them. Disgust washes over her face, mixing with the rage. Her fists clench at her side, and she takes a deep breath in. For a moment, I expect her to swallow that anger again, to push all that beautiful fury down, like I've seen her do countless times before.

She doesn't.

"He was here, wasn't he?" She turns to look at me, some-thing dark flashing in her eyes. "Chase was *here*, in this apart-ment. Watching me. Going through my things."

Holding her gaze, I nod.

"How long?" Her voice cracks. "How long has he been here? Doing this to me?"

I don't have an answer for her. Days? Weeks? I'll find out when I get my hands on him. I intend to keep him alive twice that long, in our wet lab. Alive and in agony, begging for me to end his torment.

An angry tear slides down Sydney's face as she turns away from me. Alec steps forward, wraps an arm around her, and holds her to his chest. He rubs a palm over her back in calming circles.

"You're sure he's not here anymore?" she asks, voice muffled against his body. "He's really gone?"

"Positive," I assure her, straightening my glasses. I searched every inch of the place before I brought her over, to make sure it was safe.

"We'll find him," Alec promises.

She nods, face pressed against his chest. There's a single butterfly bandage over the small cut on her temple and a bruise forming under her eye. But she showed no signs of concussion, or anything more serious, during my brief examination of her after their shower. I would have taken my time and done a more thorough exam if Ashton hadn't been impatiently hovering at my shoulder the whole time, asking a thousand questions and distracting me. He'd practically shoved me out of the way when I'd finished to scoop her up into a hug.

Asshole.

"You can't stay in your place tonight," I tell her. Even if we repaired the door Alec broke down, there's no way in hell we'd let her stay there now. It's not safe, not anymore.

Sydney lets out a bitter laugh. "And where am I supposed to go? Justin is sleeping on Jade's couch and—"

"You're staying with us," Ashton says decisively. "There's plenty of room at the compound."

Sydney visibly tenses in Alec's arms.

"It's the safest place for you, darling," Alec tries to convince her, his voice soft.

"No! I'm not... I'm not just going to move in with you," Sydney tells him, pushing away from him and scowling.

Frustrated, Ashton runs a hand through his hair. "Babygirl, be reasonable. Please. Our house is the safest place in the city. And it'll be fun—like a sleepover!" He grins, excited. "You can stay in my bed. I'll even keep my hands to myself, I swear!"

She pulls back from us even further, wrapping her arms around herself, her movements stiff, and I want to slap my brother over the back of the head. Fucking idiot.

"She said she's not ready for that," I snap at him.

He glowers at me. "Does it matter? She's not safe anywhere else, and if Dant—"

"That's enough," Alec cuts him off.

But Ashton's wrong. There are other places in the city just as protected as our compound. Places that are secure. Discrete. Operated by the only person outside of our circle that we trust.

Places like—

"I have an idea," I say.

43

SYDNEY

Second Circle.

I stare up at the massive hotel, awed by the sheer size of it, as Earl steers the town car into the underground garage. He weaves smoothly through the structure before navigating to a reserved spot with Alec's name on it. The roar of an engine announces Sebastian's arrival moments before his motorcycle pulls into the space next to us. He takes off his helmet as he dismounts, shaking out his hair, before striding over to open the car door for me.

"You'll be safe here," he promises, offering me his hand to help me out of the car. The trunk closes with a dull thud as Earl pulls out my suitcase. "At least while we work out a more permanent solution."

I miss the person I was this morning, when I didn't know what it meant to pack a bag of everything you can't stand to leave behind. I reach into the backseat for Bea's cat carrier, grateful that she'd stayed hidden under my bed during the attack. I peek inside and see her calmly licking her paw, completely indifferent to the entire ordeal.

She's as apathetic about murder as you.

"What about my shop?" I ask.

"You'll have to close down for a few days." Sebastian gives me a long, measured look. "We'll reimburse you for the financial loss, of course."

My teeth grind together. "That's not the point."

"I know." He drags a hand through his hair and releases a tired breath. "I know, love, believe me I do. But it's the best we can do right now. It's not safe for you to be working there. Even with the cameras."

He's right. And I hate that he's right.

"Who was that man?" I press. "The one who attacked me?"

"As far as we know? Hired muscle." He takes my bag from Earl. I give the older man a polite smile and mouth *thank you*, as Sebastian guides me toward the elevators. "We're still working to ID him."

"But why would Chase—"

The elevator doors ding as they open, and Sebastian ushers me inside.

"I called Jade on our way over," he tells me. "She'll be shutting down the store tomorrow and coming here to spend the day with you."

"You didn't have to do that."

He shoots me a look that says he absolutely did. "I don't want you to be alone. And having your best friend here will make the transition easier."

He's right again. I do need her, right now. I need the comfort having her around will provide.

"She sounded excited," he adds. "When I informed her everything would be comped, she asked if that included room service and the minibar."

"Does it?" I ask, lifting a brow.

The corners of Sebastian's lips twitch, the ghost of a smile. "Of course."

The elevator doors open, and we step forward into a whole new world.

"Wow," I murmur, as Sebastian guides me past two armed guards standing watch near the entrance.

Luxury drips from every corner of the hotel lobby, from the deep crimson velvet of the couches to the gold-limned chandeliers and smooth marble floors. It feels lush in a way I've never experienced before, the shimmering light kept to a level just bright enough to illuminate passageways and the Botticelli beauties painted on the walls. There are no windows. No natural light. It's as if we're hidden away from the world, separate from it. It stirs something inside me.

Want. Need. Desire.

"Ah. Mr. Sterling. And Mrs. Sterling." An elegant, older woman moves forward from the ornate concierge desk to greet us. She inclines her head toward me in acknowledgement. "Welcome to the Second Circle. I'm Francesca. You'll be very well taken care of here, I assure you."

"Thank you," I tell her. "But I'm not Mrs. Ster—"

"The staff has been informed that you are here as Alec's personal guest," Sebastian says smoothly, talking over me. "They will be referring to you by our name, when not in private."

I'm not sure how I feel about that. Not sure why the idea of being called Mrs. Sterling sends a delighted thrill through me.

"Jonathan?" Francesca calls. An enthusiastic, trim man appears at her side almost instantly, clapping his hands together in excitement. "Please take Mrs. Sterling's bags and animal companion up to the penthouse and—"

"Not the penthouse," Sebastian interrupts, voice sharp as he stares her down. "Give her the Goddess Suite."

Francesca's brows rise, but she doesn't argue. "Of course. Too many memories, I presume?" She doesn't wait for him to answer. Turning back to the attendant, she says, "Run ahead and make sure the Goddess Suite is prepared for Mrs. Sterling and her incoming guest."

"Right away!"

"Penthouse not grand enough for me?" I ask in a low voice, as Sebastian leads me through a luxurious side passage toward an alcove housing more elevators.

"Nothing ever could be." He stops, and to my surprise he moves closer to me, dipping his head to press a delicate kiss to my lips.

Oh. I like this, this more intimate side of him. I slide my hand up to the nape of his neck and lean into him, savoring the feeling of his body against mine.

"Sir?"

Sebastian jerks back. We both turn.

A beautiful woman stands near the elevators watching us, her long black hair pulled into loose braids, dressed in a bright yellow crop top and a flowing bohemian skirt.

"You don't need to call me that," Sebastian says stiffly. He's tense, suddenly, shoulders drawn back.

She tilts her head in bemusement, but nods. "Of course. Mr. Sterling," she amends. Then she turns her attention to me, giving me a bright smile. "Mrs. Sterling. I'm Victoria. But you can call me Vicky. Francesca sent me to take you on a tour of our facilities and show you to your room."

"Of course she did," Sebastian mutters, adjusting his glasses. He lets out an irritated breath. "Vicky, this is Sydney. Sydney, this is my friend Vicky."

Vicky approaches me with a radiant, unabashed smile. "May I touch you?" she asks.

A bit taken aback, I nod. She wraps her arms around me in

a warm, unexpected hug. "It's good to meet you, Sydney. I promise you we'll take good care of you here." She takes my hand, tugging me toward the elevator. "Your room is still being prepared, but I have so much to show you!"

"Wait!" Sebastian says. He stands planted in the hall, back stiff and his jaw tight. His eyes flick between the two of us. Then he steps forward, taking my face in his hands, and pulls me into one last lingering, possessive kiss.

"Call me if you need anything at all," he murmurs against my lips. He presses a gentle kiss to my cheek, fingers tracing my jaw, before he forces himself to step away.

I'm blushing when he finally lets me go. Next to me, Vicky is struggling to hide her own smile as he walks off, disappearing down the hallway and out of sight.

"He likes you," Vicky says in an excited voice. "That's not like him."

No. It's not. My cheeks burn, flooded with heat. I have to clear my throat twice before I can speak again. "Are the two of you close?" I ask her.

"Oh yes. We're good friends." She gives me a playful smile, her eyes twinkling as she looks at me. "But I've never seen him look at anyone the way he looks at you."

My blush deepens, and I try to ignore it as I let her direct me to the elevators.

"This is your keycard." She presses a credit-card sized piece of black metal into my hand. It shimmers in the artificial lights. "It grants you access to every level of the hotel. There is a restaurant on level three, and a full bar there as well. There is another bar on the ground level." Vicky scans her own black card and presses a button. The elevator glides into motion. "But we advise you to use the more...exclusive one, during your stay here. The third level is off limits to anyone not staying at the hotel, but the ground floor is open to the general public. It's safer if you keep to the more protected areas."

"Are we really afraid I'll be attacked while getting a drink?" I ask sardonically.

Vicky doesn't share my skepticism, but she still smiles sweetly as she explains, "Mr. Sterling has made it clear that your safety is our top priority. And staying within the secure areas of the hotel is the best way to ensure that safety."

It's hard not to feel trapped when she says that. Like I'm being held captive.

Vicky notices. "Don't worry," she assures me, reaching for my hand to hold it again, giving it a friendly squeeze. "You'll have plenty to do in the hotel. We have a full spa, private movie theatre, 24/7 bars, restaurants and room service. Anything you could ever desire." Her smile grows. "And once the other girls hear about your kitten? You're going to make so many friends!"

44

SYDNEY

"Oh my GOD!"

I smirk as I stroke my fingers over Bea's fur. She's curled in a perfectly round ball on the massive bed, purring softly, completely unfazed by my best friend's shouting as she inspects my suite.

"They have ROBES!" Jade calls, her body half hidden in the wardrobe as she digs through it. "Sydney, have you seen these?"

I had seen them, actually, when Vicky gave me a full tour of the Goddess Suite. The name suits this space perfectly. Each of the four rooms are draped in golds and soft creams, crystal chandeliers bathing everything in a golden ambient glow. Canopies of sheer silk flow from the ceiling above each bed in delicate waves. It's decadent, fantastical. The stone floors are even heated, and covered with plush rugs that feel heavenly beneath my feet.

"Oh, they feel like *clouds*," Jade coos, pulling a robe off the hanger and rubbing it against her face. "We have to wear these later."

"There's a spa, too," I tell her. Jade's eyes flash with interest. "One floor down."

"We're getting massages," Jade says decisively. "There's no way we're passing that up."

She throws herself onto the bed next to me, the mattress bouncing with the force of it. The bed is so big, I barely feel it, but Bea opens a single eye and levels a grumpy glare at Jade for interrupting her nap.

"Thanks for coming," I tell Jade. I pull my knees up to my chest and wrap my arms around them, hugging myself. "You didn't have to shut down the store for this, you know."

"Sydney..." Jade gives me a *look*. "You were attacked. In your own home. Who cares about the store?"

I do, I want to say. I care about it.

"Besides, it'll still be there tomorrow. I'll open up on my own." Jade rolls over on the bed and reaches out to pet Bea. "Justin can help me in the morning, but we're usually slow enough that I can close on my own without any issues."

I still feel guilty, though. "I'm sure I'll only be gone for a day or so," I tell her. "But still... I really appreciate you coming."

"Like I'm going to miss the world's most expensive sleepover?" Jade jokes. "So. What do you want to do first?"

"Massages. Definitely. And then maybe grab a drink at the bar?" I hug myself tighter. "And then room service. And bad pay-per-view movies."

"Sounds perfect."

My phone chirps. I'd almost forgotten about it, and I realize I haven't paid any attention to it since Jade arrived. It's been easier to ignore it and pretend the outside world doesn't exist.

The Boss: How are you feeling, darling?

I'm okay.

> The Boss: Second Circle should have
> everything you need but if there's anything I
> can do, just ask.

I stare down at the screen, my anger bubbling to the surface.

> You could try being honest with me.

There's a long pause after I send my text. Sometimes I wish I were a more patient woman, but after everything I've gone through in the last few weeks, the least he can do is start opening up to me.

> The Boss: I will. I promise.

> Promise is just a word, Alec. I need more than
> that. You can't keep me on the outside of this.
> Not anymore. Not when it impacts me. Not
> when it gets me hurt.

He doesn't answer. With a frustrated sigh, I toss my phone into the bedside drawer and turn back to Jade.

She's sprawled on her back, lazily flipping through the hotel amenities book. "Did you know they have an in-house waxer? And they come right to your room." She lowers the book, an evil grin on her face. "Want to get matching landing strips?"

"Absolutely not," I say, collapsing next to her on the bed.

"Fine. We'll do the full Brazilian." She clicks her tongue. "But I have to be honest, I prefer having a little hair down there."

When I don't play along, she lowers the book again, frowning at me.

"Hey... You okay?" she asks.

"Yes. No? I don't know." I groan and drag my hands over my face. "I don't even know how to *be* right now. I was attacked! A man died in front of me! And I have *absolutely* no idea why any of this even happened!" I prop myself on my elbows, turning to stare at her. "And you want to know what the worst part is?"

"I feel like the 'getting attacked' part," Jade offers dryly. "Or your ex being the world's creepiest stalker."

"No." My voice drops. "The worst part is I don't feel bad that he's dead."

And when my boys find Chase? I know exactly what will happen to him. And I don't feel bad about that, either.

Jade purses her lips, considering me. Finally, she rolls onto her side to face me. "Do you remember Breanna Grant? From high school?"

"Of course." How could I forget my best friend's bully? The girl whose sole mission in life was to make Jade miserable. "Why?"

"Remember when she broke her leg in tenth grade and her parents kept her out of school for a month?"

I nod.

Jade laughs weakly, shaking her head. "I was so sure that was my fault. I used to pray every night that something bad would happen to her. Did I ever tell you that? I hated her so much."

"I love you Jade, I truly do, and I know we had that Wiccan phase in middle school, but even I don't think you could have caused her to have that skiing accident."

"Irrelevant." She waves my words away. "I *thought* I made it happen, somehow. And I felt terrible. Like, couldn't eat for *days* terrible."

"I'm really not seeing how this is supposed to be making me feel better," I grumble.

"Shush, be patient. That month she was out of school? That was the best month of high school for me." Her voice softens. "Best month for a lot of the kids she picked on, actually."

"I'm not surprised," I tell her. "She was awful."

"By the time she came back, I didn't feel guilty anymore. It felt like..." She pauses, mulling her words. "It felt like a good thing, what happened to her. Like her being hurt was a net positive for the world." Jade watches me, her expression sober, voice gentler now. "You're allowed to not mourn the people who hurt you, Sydney. It doesn't make you a bad person."

"It doesn't make me a good one either, though." I lift Bea into my lap, finding comfort in stroking her soft fur. "It's just, you still...felt something. Sometimes when I get angry, it's like the rage takes over. And I don't feel guilt or remorse. Just pure, unbridled rage. My parents tried so hard with me, but once I got to that point, all I saw was red."

"Oh, I remember," Jade says softly. "The day they died? I know you blame yourself for what happened, but I feel guilty about it, too."

"What?" I sputter. "How could it possibly be your fault?"

"How could it be yours?" Her voice cracks. "You were defending me! You heard Breanna call me...that word...and you just snapped and hit her." Jade shakes her head, eyes welling with tears. "But Syd, that was just the first time *you* heard her say it. She said that to me nearly every day at that school, and if I had just defended myself, you wouldn't have had to. You wouldn't have gotten sent to the principal's office, your parents wouldn't have been called, and none of it would have happened."

"That's not on you! I have no control over my anger. Of course I was going to defend you, but a *sane and healthy* person probably would have used words!" My throat tightens. "I felt nothing when I hit her. No remorse, no pity, *nothing*. It wasn't until the accident... It's why I don't let myself get this way anymore. I can't control it."

Jade considers me. "And that's how you feel now?" she asks. "Out of control?"

"I don't know. It's...hard to describe. But it feels like there's something wrong with me." I squeeze my eyes shut. "Shouldn't I feel bad? When I get like this, when the anger takes over, and I just"—I wave my hands through the air—"punch a bitch in the face, shouldn't I feel something, after? When a man is killed right in front of me, shouldn't I feel some sort of guilt?"

Jade squeezes my arm. "I don't think there's anything wrong with you. And I love you, no matter what. But I don't think we're going to solve everything that's going on in one night, and you're starting to spiral. I think what we need to do is have a licensed massage therapist smack the worries out of you for a bit."

"Yeah. You're right," I concede.

"As always, but I hate when you state the obvious, it's so axiomatic."

"Axiomatic?" I shake my head in disgust. "I knew I should have burned that SAT prep book of yours when I had the chance."

45

SYDNEY

THE MASSAGE THERAPISTS AT SECOND CIRCLE ARE GOOD. *Too* good.

The moment we get back to the suite, Jade collapses face-first on the bed and is asleep within seconds. Even I feel relaxed—my muscles loose and languid, my thoughts softened—something I didn't think was possible after what I went through last night.

While the dulcet sounds of Jade's light snoring fill the room, I retrieve my phone from the drawer I threw it in earlier. Alec has finally texted me back.

> The Boss: You're right. I don't want to lie to you anymore. You deserve honesty.

> The Boss: Let me take you out tomorrow.

> The Boss: Let me show you my world.

I re-read the messages twice, three times, before deciding to reply.

Fine.

His response is almost instantaneous, like he's been sitting there with his phone in his hand for the last hour and a half, waiting for me to text.

The Boss: Be ready at 7pm, Red.

I inhale slowly. His world. Maybe it should frighten me, knowing what little I do about what his world entails, but I feel something else, instead. Relief. I want to know more. To finally be let in.

My post-massage bliss is already starting to wear off, my mind quickly spiraling again. I can't sit in this room with my thoughts all on my own while Jade naps. Not tonight. I change out of the plush hotel robe and into the first dress I find shoved into my suitcase.

"I'm going down to the bar," I tell Jade. "I need a drink."

"Give me five minutes," she mumbles sleepily, rolling over onto her side and curling around Bea. She's asleep again before I even reach the door, and I'm half tempted to snap a photo of the two of them napping together. They're too cute together. My two favorite girls.

I close the door as quietly as I can.

———

THE THIRD FLOOR HOUSES THE MOST OPULENT COCKTAIL bar I've ever seen. It's in line with the rest of this hotel, but it still takes my breath away when the elevator doors slide open, and I experience it for the first time. The cherry red of the walls and floors is paired with deep brown accents and leather furniture polished to a soft sheen. The whole place makes me feel like I need a three-piece suit and a cigar to fit in.

It's busy, but not overcrowded. I take a seat at the bar, avoiding direct adjacency to anyone.

"Gin martini," I tell the bartender when she approaches. She's beautiful, just like every other woman I've seen working here so far. "Filthy, please."

It's mostly women filling up the room, I notice, as I look around. Women drinking together, women chatting around dark wooden tables, women working behind the bar. But no sooner has the bartender returned with my drink than I hear a man's voice behind me.

"Haven't seen you around here before," he says casually. "You new?"

I turn, and there's a portly man in an overly starched suit standing at my shoulder. He leans an elbow on the bar, watching me.

"I just got here, actually," I answer with a polite smile.

He tilts his head, studying me. "How are you liking it?"

"It's great. This place is..." I laugh, motioning helplessly around us. "It's indescribable."

"Hm." He chews his lip. "Listen, I've had a terrible week, so I'll cut right to the chase. How much?"

I blink. "How much of...what?"

"For the night." He reaches into his jacket and pulls out a wallet, opening it. "Two thousand?"

He looks at me expectantly, eyebrows raised. I open my mouth, but nothing comes out at first.

"Two thousand...dollars?" I manage to ask after an awkward beat of silence. "For what? What are you—"

"Matthew!" Vicky materializes out of nowhere, taking him firmly by the arm. "You wouldn't be bothering our other patrons, would you?"

The man—Matthew—frowns at her. "Other, pat—?"

"Because Francesca would not be happy to hear that," she tells him, an uncharacteristic chill creeping into her voice. "I'll tell you what, why don't you go join Melinda over at her table? She looks lonely tonight. I'm sure she would appreciate the company."

Surprisingly, he does as he's told, giving me one last glance before heading to the table she indicated.

"Sorry about that," Vicky says, giving me an apologetic smile.

"Did he... Did he think I was...?"

"An escort," Vicky finishes gently. "And yes, I think so." She gestures around. "This is where most of us meet our clients."

Us?

"Oh. So you're... Oh." I look away and take a long drink of my martini, just for something to do.

Vicky watches me thoughtfully. "Does that bother you?"

Does it? I push through my initial shock and check in with myself, weighing my thoughts and feelings.

"Honestly? No, it doesn't. Not at all," I admit. "Do you enjoy it?"

Vicky's answering smile is warm. "Most of the time, yes. There are always some clients that make it harder than others." She looks at Matthew as she says it, scrunching her nose like she's smelled something unpleasant. "But I enjoy it. And I love bringing people's fantasies to life, getting to try on different versions of myself. I don't believe we have to be just one thing in this lifetime. We are infinite, full of possibilities. And I like exploring that." She glances at me, then quickly adds, "And don't worry, Mr. Sterling was never one of the bad ones."

Mr. Sterling. Was a client of hers.

Sebastian.

"Oh," I say, my voice small.

"I should go rescue Melinda," Vicky tells me, giving my hand a squeeze. "But I'll keep an eye on you to make sure none of the other men here bother you, okay?"

"Thanks," I tell her, with a grateful smile.

My next martini arrives with a side of truffle fries, and I eat them slowly, unpacking what she just said.

I think that's why I don't notice right away when someone new approaches me. I'm distracted, untangling complicated emotions, when a new voice interrupts me.

"Is this seat taken?"

A woman, this time. I relax, happy to have a distraction.

"It's all yours," I say. I glance over just in time to see a well-manicured hand touch the bar top, as she slides into the seat to my right. "Are you—?"

I stop when I recognize her.

White blonde hair. Perfectly symmetrical features. She's so stunning it almost hurts to look at her, beautiful in a way that's sharp and cold.

"You're a very difficult woman to get alone, did you know that?" Annika asks me.

I can't find the words to answer her.

"I'll do the Yamazaki 18, neat," she directs the bartender. Turning her gaze back to me, she adds, "Make it a double."

Annika. Alec's wife. Sitting inches away from me.

Her gray eyes scan me up and down, assessing me. She's older than she was when the photo I saw was taken. Younger than me, but not by much. Her hair is shorter, and somehow her bone structure feels almost lethal in its beauty.

She looks dangerous.

I swallow dryly, suddenly self-conscious of the sundress I threw on before heading down here. Annika is the picture of elegance in her perfectly tailored ebony jumpsuit and sky-high stilettos so thin I wouldn't trust them to carry my bodyweight.

"Don't worry." She gives me a sharp smile. "You're not in any danger."

I wipe my fingers over the hem of my dress, trying to smooth out the wrinkles. "Why would I be in danger?" I laugh.

Her expression softens into something almost pitying. She signals for the bartender, and I only realize that she's ordered me another martini when it's delivered a moment later, without my asking. At least my drink of choice is more dignified than my current appearance. I touch the space between my cheekbone and eye, where I can still feel the swelling.

I take a steadying breath. "If you're looking for Ale—"

"You're exactly who I'm looking for," Annika interrupts. She takes a delicate sip of the amber liquid in her glass.

I let out a weak chuckle. "That's surprising. I figured you'd be looking for your husband."

Her hand pauses on her drink, almost like she'd forgotten. "Oh, *that*. A business arrangement, nothing more. He and I have very little to talk about these days."

"You're still wearing a ring," I point out. A blue sapphire glitters on a platinum band around her finger, sparkling in the dim lights of the bar.

"It keeps the men away," Annika admits, turning her hand to admire it. "Most of them, anyway."

"Mace keeps them away, too," I murmur into my drink. She laughs at that, the sound light and musical.

"No, I wanted to talk to *you*," Annika says. "Woman to woman."

"Is this the part where you warn me away from them?" I joke.

This time, she doesn't laugh. She watches me like she's evaluating me, waiting for me to make my next move.

"It is smart of them to put you here," she comments, motioning around us. "It's secure. Safe."

A shiver rolls down my spine.

"You should stay for a bit." She says it conversationally, but there's something in her tone that puts me on edge. It sounds like friendly advice, but it feels like a threat.

"That's the plan," I tell her, taking a long drink from my martini.

"Good."

My muscles tense, anger creeping into my veins. "Not to be rude, but I've had a really shit few days, and this is not the conversation I thought we'd have if we ever met." I turn to glare at her. "What is this? Are you trying to tell me to stay away from them? Or are you marking your territory?"

She scoffs. "Please. Marking my territory? The possessive big brother schtick isn't exactly my type." She shoots me a look. "Men like them? You should stay away from them. They'll chew you up and spit you out."

"And why would I believe you?" I challenge.

"Because they did it to me," she says, a bitter undercurrent to her tone.

I glance at her ring again. "You said it was a business arrangement."

"The marriage? It was." Her finger traces the rim of her drink. "There was never anything between Alec and I, Sydney. Nothing like that, anyway."

"Then what—"

"Is sex the only type of relationship you respect?" She levels her icy gaze at me. "The only way you can conceive of being close with a man?"

"What?" I draw back, offended. "Of course not!"

"You make it sound like that's the case," Annika tells me. She brings the glass to her lips, but pauses there, before drinking. "They were my family. The only family that I ever loved. And they left me, like I was nothing." With a single graceful movement, she drains her glass.

There's pain in her voice, hidden beneath the ice. When she sets her glass back on the bar, she sets it down a little too hard.

"I hope they don't do the same to you," she says, rising to leave.

"Wait!"

Annika pauses a few feet away from me before turning back. She takes a step toward me.

"You can return this to my 'ex,'" she says, pulling the sapphire ring and matching band from her finger and placing them in front of me on the bar. "Tell him I signed the paperwork this morning. I've kept my side of our deal."

46

SYDNEY

"Divorced." It's not even a question the way Jade says the word around a mouthful of pancakes the next morning.

"That's the implication," I answer with a sigh. House cleaning delivered a fresh stack of plushy white robes last night, and I'm very seriously considering stealing one when I finally leave. I'm getting far too used to this level of comfort, and I'm not sure I'll be able to give it up.

"I swear, I need a TV-style recap at the beginning of every day to remember everything that happened in the last episode of *Sydney and Her Mysterious Men*," Jade chuckles.

I throw a pillow at her, nearly toppling her pancakes over onto the bedspread.

"You should have woken me up," she scolds, pointing a syrup-coated fork at me accusingly.

"Oh please." I snatch the syrup away from her and pour it over my own pancakes. After a moment's hesitation, I pour some over my eggs as well. "You were knocked *out* when I left. There was no way I was getting you down to that bar short of dragging you there. And nothing even happened. She just kind of...warned me about them."

There's a veritable buffet's worth of breakfast spread across the bed between us. Jade scowls and leans over to pluck a piece of bacon off my plate.

"Still," she says. "I don't like that she managed to get to you, here. Isn't the whole point of this"—she gestures at the suite around us with her bacon strip—"to keep you safe? How the hell did she just waltz in to meet you at the bar?"

"She had a key card," I explain. "So she must be staying here. And the staff was watching out for me. I just don't think... I don't think they saw her as a potential threat. I don't either, honestly. She was...well, 'nice' isn't the right word, but I really think she was trying to look out for me."

Bea hops up on the bed for the hundredth time since room service delivered our food, determined to steal something. I pause midbite to scoop her up and place her gently back on the floor. I should probably call down and ask for another portion of food for her. Whatever it was the kitchen prepared—which they assured me was kitten safe—she ate it up like she was starving.

There's a soft knock on the door, and Jade stops chewing, mid slice of bacon.

"It's Vicky!" a bright voice calls from the hall. "You have a package!"

My stomach drops. Jade and I exchange a nervous look, before I climb off the bed and hurry to the door.

Maybe she was right to be worried. If Annika could get to me here...

Could Chase? Could one of his *gifts*?

But the box Vicky is holding when I open the door to let her in isn't the cheap gray cardboard I've come to expect from

Chase's deliveries. It's black velvet, topped with an elegant silver ribbon.

Expensive.

"Mr. Mason Sterling dropped this off for you at the front." Vicky grins, showing off the box. "Where do you want it?"

"Put it on the cuck chair," Jade says, pointing to the armchair in the corner, awkwardly facing the bed.

"That's not what it's called," I protest, but Vicky giggles.

"We call it that, too," she confides, shooting Jade a wink.

And Jade...

My Jade *blushes*.

For a moment, I'm sure I must be seeing things. My Jade doesn't blush. She's unflappable. A shameless flirt, sure, but she does it with a swagger that's all confidence.

But right now, her cheeks are a rosy pink, and a half-eaten strip of bacon hangs out of her mouth as she tracks Vicky across the room, watching as she sets the box down.

That's...different. New.

Choosing to ignore it for now and making a mental note to follow up on this later, I cross the room to Alec's gift. The box is even prettier up close.

"I've been asked to deliver a message with it," Vicky informs me, grin widening.

I nod, urging her to continue.

"He requests you wear it tonight. If you find it acceptable." Bea circles her ankles, mewing for attention, until Vicky reaches down to scoop her up, rubbing their noses together. "Hi, little baby! Aren't you just the cutest?"

Bea purrs as if it say, *yes, yes I am*.

"If it's more sex toys, you might want to tell him to cool it," Jade advises me as I untie the ribbon. "You're going to run out of room for them in your apartment if he keeps this up."

Vicky giggles again, and the pink on Jade's cheeks spreads up to the tips of her ears.

Okay, she and I are going to need to have a serious talk later about whatever is happening between her and Vicky. I shoot her a befuddled look before I lift the lid, pushing tissue paper away to reveal the contents of the box.

It's a dress. Jade draws in a quick breath as I pull it out and hold it up in front of me.

A *designer* dress, I realize, peaking at the delicately embroidered label inside.

"It's gorgeous," I breathe, running my fingers over the midnight black silk. It's short, barely long enough to reach past the top of my thighs. The shockingly high neckline comes up to clasp almost like a collar. And the back? I turn the dress in my hands. Nearly nonexistent, dipping all the way down to the hips.

"This must have cost a fortune," Jade murmurs, getting up and stepping closer to rub the fabric between her fingers. "Oh my God, Sydney, I think he had this custom made."

I don't doubt it. It's beautiful, like a work of art.

"Are you going to wear it?" she asks, as though there were any question at all.

"Of course," I say. "I may be pissed off, but I'm not stupid."

"Looks like there are shoes, too." Jade rummages through the box and pulls them out, holding them out for me to take. Sleek high heels, with ankle straps that mimic the collar of the dress.

"You're going to look stunning," Vicky says warmly. She sets Bea down, giving her one last stroke, all the way down her spine. Bea makes a happy chirping noise, and Vicky laughs. "Not you, baby. You already look stunning."

"She likes you," Jade tells Vicky.

"Of course she does. I'm very good with pussy," she replies with a smirk.

Jade's face turns scarlet. I think she's stopped breathing.

Holy shit, what is happening to my Jade?

I cough pointedly. "Have the two of you officially met yet?" I ask. "Vicky, this is my best friend, Jade. Jade, this is Vicky."

Jade holds out her hand to shake. "Charmed."

"Likewise," Vicky answers, ignoring the hand and pulling Jade into a hug instead. I guess that's her signature greeting. Jade looks like she might be short-circuiting, her eyes too wide.

Mid-hug, her phone chimes, and she pulls away. "Oh crap," Jade murmurs, checking it. "That's Alec's driver. He's taking me to the shop today, and he's already downstairs." She stuffs another piece of bacon in her mouth as she gathers up her things. "You want me to take custody of our child for the day?" she asks me, pointing at Bea.

"No, that's okay. I've got her." Bea has become a minor celebrity, according to the plethora of comments flooding our bookstapix account. Apparently, having a bookstore cat is all the rage, even if she does spend half her time hiding from people, and the other half actively tormenting them. "I think I could use the company today."

"Looks like you're living large today, you little menace," Jade tells Bea, booping her on the nose. Then she points at me. "You! Text me. And send me a photo of that dress before your date, okay? And you!" She faces Vicky, flustered but smiling. "It was a genuine pleasure."

"Don't be a stranger," Vicky purrs.

———

The dress fits perfectly, almost like it was tailored to my exact measurements.

Are designers really that good? Or does Alec know me so well, all my curves and swells, that he could tell them my exact measurement, down to the centimeter?

Somehow, I wouldn't put it past him.

I spend most of the day waiting for my date, and by the time it rolls around, I'm nervous. Anxious to see him, to know what he has planned to show me. I leave my hotel room a little early, giving Bea a kiss on her fuzzy little forehead and reminding her that she's not allowed to scratch the furniture. She ignores me, of course.

Even though I'm early, Alec is already waiting outside the hotel. I spot him immediately, leaning against the door to his town car, staring down at his phone.

His eyes come up the moment I step outside, drawn straight to me. It's like he could feel it, could sense I was near.

It's magnetic, this pull between the two of us.

Those dark eyes flare when he sees me, his gaze heating. But he doesn't move. He slides his phone into his pocket and waits for me to come to him. Patiently.

Like he's waited for me this whole time. His whole life.

I'm still apprehensive as I take a step towards him. But it's hard to hold onto my anger when he's in front of me like this. His perfect chiseled jaw, his deep brown eyes beckoning me.

He's dangerous. In so many ways.

I take another step.

His lips curve into a smile. I'm wearing the dress—the perfect, beautiful dress he had made for me—but he doesn't even look at it. His eyes are locked on mine, and I feel like we're the only two people in the world.

I take another step, and he finally moves forward to meet me, pulling me into a kiss that steals away every coherent thought in my head.

It's everything, whatever this is that exists between us. And

I hate that it's so delicate right now, that I'm still not sure if I can trust him.

When he breaks our kiss, he pulls back just enough to meet my eyes.

"I've missed you so much," he tells me in a deep voice. His finger strokes my cheek, gliding across my face to tuck a lock of hair behind my ear.

I can't say it back. But I know he can see it, in my eyes.

"Come," he says, opening the car door and gesturing me inside. His hand rests on the small of my back, warm and steady as I climb inside. "I have a surprise for you tonight."

He settles into his seat, and I let myself relax against him. We fit so perfectly together, me tucked under his arm, his hand on my leg.

"Thank you for the dress," I say softly, running my fingers over the hem. "It's beautiful."

"I'm glad you like it." He gives my leg a light squeeze. "It suits you."

He's not wrong. Even I can admit I look phenomenal in it. Jade's response to the photo I texted her was a series of heart emojis and crying faces that filled up my entire phone screen, and somehow perfectly encapsulated how I felt wearing it.

"But, for the record," he adds. "The dress is for your comfort, not mine. You could wear a paper bag tonight and still be the most beautiful woman in the building. I simply didn't want you to feel underdressed."

I wriggle against him.

"So, where are you taking me?" I ask, finally giving in to my curiosity.

"Somewhere I doubt you've ever been," he replies cryptically. "I want to show you a little of our world, Sydney. My world. And I think you'll like it."

———

The Golden Rings casino is nowhere near as large as Sterling Silver, Alec's pride and joy, but it's every bit as glamorous. I stare up at the glittering facade as Alec helps me out of the car, looping his arm around my waist. There's no question in anyone's mind about our relationship to one another, as he stoops down to plant a kiss on my hair.

Alec holds me like his queen, like he wants to show me off.

The town car pulls away as soon as we exit, making room for another vehicle to pull up to the waiting valet. Unlike the last time Alec brought me to one of his casinos, he doesn't guide me toward the main entrance and into the casino itself. Instead, we slip past the crowds and toward an auxiliary building, off to the side, where a line of people waits to be let in, already stretching around the block.

"Mr. Sterling!" a man greets us, waving us over to a side door. "And Mrs. Sterling, welcome!"

I glance at Alec, expecting him to correct the man.

He doesn't.

I'm reminded that I have his *actual* wife's ring, hidden in my suitcase back at the hotel right now. I wonder what he would say if he knew. But I'm not giving up any of my secrets until I start to get some of his.

"Jacob, good to see you," Alec says pleasantly, letting go of my waist for the exact length of time it takes to shake the man's hand. He returns that hand to my waist so quickly I barely note its absence. "Sydney, this is Jacob. He manages most of the talent we showcase here at the Golden Rings."

I don't have a chance to ask what "the talent" entails before Jacob reaches out, taking my hand and giving it a gentle shake.

"Not most." He chuckles. "Just a select few, really. But I do manage the talent I'm sure you're here to see tonight."

Who? I wonder. But before I can ask, he's gesturing us forward, and we're moving again.

"Follow me," Jacob says, pulling us away from the line and crowds and toward a nondescript but guarded door. The giant of a man standing in front of it doesn't even hesitate before opening it, giving Alec a nod in greeting as we follow Jacob inside.

"We had your private box stocked with food and refreshments for tonight," Jacob says as we trail behind him. The hallway he takes us down is decorated in deep purples and silvers, incredibly ostentatious. "You should have everything that you need, but don't hesitate to ring the bar if there's anything you're missing."

"And the staff is aware I've requested privacy?" Alec asks.

"Absolutely," Jacob answers without hesitation. "They know to keep their distance unless asked. And security knows to keep the other private boxes clear. Except for your list of acceptable visitors, of course."

"Of course," Alec says with a smirk.

Jacob stops at a set of elevators and grins at me. "I hope you enjoy the show, Mrs. Sterling," he says pleasantly. "It's a pleasure to have you here."

———

ALEC'S PRIVATE BOX HAS A LONG BLACK LEATHER COUCH, two tables stacked with food and beverages, and a wet bar.

It also has one full wall made entirely of glass, with a handrail guard separating the room from the window, and an expansive view of the fighting ring below.

I can't help but feel a little disappointed. I'm not sure what I expected, where I'd hoped Alec might bring me tonight, but to a professional fight? That's not what I had in mind.

I try to disguise my disappointment by hiding my face from him, going straight to the window, and staring down at the crowds of people filtering in, filling rows upon rows of seats. I put my hands on the guard rail and lean forward just a little, watching all those thousands of faces below me.

Alec's phone rings before he has a chance to join me. I expect him to silence it, but to my surprise, he answers.

"What do you need, Tony? I'm busy tonight," Alec snaps into the phone, not bothering with a greeting. I can't hear what's being said on the other side, but my ears perk up when I hear Alec again. "Then verify the number of guns that were in this shipment. If there's a discrepancy, call Sebastian with the precise amount, and we will sort it out."

He doesn't say goodbye. He just ends the call and comes to stand next to me, his hand on the rail close enough that he can stroke my pinky with his.

"Guns?" I ask, raising an eyebrow, wondering if he meant for me to hear or not.

Alec gives me a long look before he nods. "I told you I'm done with secrets," he says softly. He slips his hand over mine, entwining our fingers.

Maybe it should bother me. Maybe he's right to be worried that learning more about his world might drive me away. But I saw him murder a man in cold blood for hurting me. Trafficking guns feels light in comparison.

"I've never been to a fight before," I admit, changing the subject. Truthfully, I've never wanted to see one, never had the slightest inclination to watch grown men hurt each other for sport.

"I'm not surprised," Alec tells me. He turns to watch me, and I can't bring myself to look at him. I concentrate on the people below us as, one by one, all the empty seats begin to fill. "This isn't something you would seek out on your own, is it?"

I shrug. "No," I answer honestly. "No offense, but it seems a bit boring to me."

Alec makes a small affirmative sound deep in his throat. "I think you might enjoy it," he tells me smoothly. "If you give it a chance."

I hum in answer, a noncommittal noise. Smirking, Alec plants a kiss on my hair and moves toward the wet bar. He returns with a flute of champagne for me, and a glass of something dark and golden for himself.

"So, how does this work?" I ask, figuring I might as well put in the effort of feigning interest.

"There will be two fights tonight," Alec informs me, sipping his drink. "The first will be a warm-up. An opening act, if you will. Two good fighters, decent but not great, to get the crowd going."

"I see," I say, frowning at the ring below us. Great. So, I have to watch more than one of these. Maybe I should be drinking an espresso martini to keep myself awake.

"Each fight consists of three rounds, with a break between them," he explains. "The rounds last for five minutes, or until a fighter taps out. Or is unable to continue fighting."

I take a sip of my drink, trying to look interested.

When I lower my glass, Alec is watching me with a playful smile on his face. "Lend me a little trust tonight, Sydney," he murmurs. He glides a finger over my arm, raising goosebumps on my skin.

Licking a drop of champagne from my lower lip, I nod.

I'M ON MY SECOND GLASS WHEN THE FIRST FIGHT STARTS.

The announcer steps into the ring, listing the stats and credentials of the first round of fighters. The crowd cheers wildly as the men enter and tap their hands together, dipping their chins to one another.

When the bell rings, Alec moves to stand behind me, placing one hand on either side of mine on the guard rail.

They circle each other for a few seconds, and when the first punch lands, I wince. Not at the violence of it, but the surprise. It's fast. Much faster than I expected.

The next hit makes me jump, my muscles tensing. But I'm ready for the one after that. And the one after that. Excitement pools deep in my belly, growing as I watch.

To my untrained eye, the fighters feel evenly matched. For every hit that sends one reeling, another is returned with equal force. It's mesmerizing, enticing.

I can't bring myself to look away.

"How are you liking the fight?" Alec asks, in a voice I wouldn't call gentle.

"I like it. I... I think I might like it too much," I confess, letting the truth sink in. My eyes are glued to the men circling each other, testing each other's weaknesses. I can see the crowd cheering in my peripheral vision, excitement growing as another punch lands hard.

To my surprise, Alec laughs.

I glance over my shoulder at him. "I'm not kidding. What kind of person am I becoming?" I shake my head. "Who likes this sort of thing?"

"Oh, darling." He chuckles darkly behind me. "You're not *becoming* anything. It's already who you are, who you've always been. And you're not alone. This country was built on violence. Our economy practically runs on it."

I chew my lip at that, not liking the way it makes me feel. When I turn away from him, he reaches out, taking my jaw in his hand.

"Sydney." Alec's voice is much darker now, the grip on my jaw tight. "You will let yourself enjoy this tonight. For me."

Swallowing, I obey, turning back to the fight.

Alec holds my head in place, fingers digging a little hard into my skin. His breath is warm against my cheek when he bends down to speak.

"Watch, Sydney. Don't assume morality. Don't fight who you are. Simply watch."

I do.

"Violence is never pretty," Alec tells me. In the ring, the fighters towel off their sweat, gulping down water before pouring some over their faces and chests. "But it can be beautiful."

When the bell rings again, I move a little closer.

I wouldn't call it beautiful, no. But it's powerful to watch them. They move so quickly, muscles flexing and rolling as they circle one another.

I lick my lips. When I bring my champagne glass up to drink, I realize I've somehow already finished it. Alec takes it gently from my hand and leaves to get me another.

The third round is the most brutal. Maybe they were holding back, drawing the match out for the crowd.

But the moment the bell sounds, they come together in a flurry of blows. It's raw and violent, it's chaos of movement and skill, and I watch the entire thing with my heart in my throat, leaning over the railing to get closer to the action.

I don't notice Alec's hand trailing up my leg under my dress until he reaches my hip, fingers slowly sliding over the bone and down to press against me through the fabric of my panties.

I gasp, hips rolling against his touch reflexively.

"What do you think, Red?" Alec asks, voice a dark and dangerous purr against my neck. He presses a soft kiss to my shoulder, his fingers dipping under the seam of my underwear to touch me. "Are you enjoying this?"

I'm wet, I realize. His finger slides through it, pausing to circle my clit as I watch the fight below.

Breathlessly, I nod.

"I think you'll like the next fight even more," he teases. In the ring, a final punch is thrown, hard enough it throws the other man back into the ropes, where he sinks down to his knees.

The bell rings, the match ended.

With a growl, Alec spins me around, pressing me back against the guard rail and gripping my hair tightly, holding me in place to kiss me. I groan into him, reaching up to pull him closer.

Down in the arena, the crowd is cheering loudly as the announcer calls the winner. There will be a break between fights, he broadcasts, urging the audience to hurry back to their seats for a show they won't want to miss.

But I'm too lost in Alec's touch and kiss to notice any of it.

When he finally pulls away from me, his eyes are so dark and unhinged it's almost frightening.

"On your knees, darling," he says, stepping back from me, his hand going to his pants.

I sink down into the plush carpet, obedient, as Alec makes swift work of his belt, reaching into his pants to pull his hard cock out and stroke it for me.

His hand threads into my hair, pulling me close as I stare up at him.

"Open wide," he says.

I groan, opening my mouth and taking him between my lips. It's a stretch getting my mouth around him, my hands coming up to grip his thighs, but I manage.

The first time I'd had Ashton in my mouth, he'd taken full

control, holding me in place and fucking me. Alec's control is different, more subtle. Hands buried in my hair, he directs me forward, pushing me onto his cock until it hits the back of my throat. He shudders, thigh muscles twitching under my hands, and then he's pulling me back, sliding out of my mouth until my lips are just over his tip, then doing it all again.

I hold his gaze the entire time.

He moves me slowly, gliding himself deeper, and then back out. I move my tongue as he directs me, rubbing against the base of him, delighting in the way his muscles twitch when I do, the way his eyes flutter closed.

I barely register the sounds of the crowd, the voice of the announcer as he welcomes the next fighters—the headliners—but Alec does. His eyes flick to the window, and he stops, pulling my mouth away.

"Come on, darling. You don't want to miss this."

He takes my hands in his and lifts me, turning me effortlessly until I'm facing the ring again. This time, when he positions himself behind me, placing my hands on the guard rail and bending me forward at the waist, there's no question as to what he's planning.

The air in the room is cold on my skin as Alec flips my dress up over my hips and peels my panties down, lifting my feet to remove them.

I almost forget about the fight, with my eyes closed and his hands sliding up my legs, but I remember in time to open them and see the headliners enter the ring.

My quick inhale of breath has nothing to do with Alec's fingers, sliding over my drenched core, and everything to do with the fighter who steps forward, head held high.

It's Ashton.

I had a suspicion he'd be the one fighting tonight. But seeing it is something different entirely.

The crowd roars as he steps into the ring, raising his hands above his head and grinning at them like a star. On the other side of the ring, his opponent scowls, lip curling at the showboating, but Ashton clearly couldn't care less. This is his arena, his dominion.

I swear his eyes land on our private box, and he grins even more.

Seeing him makes me shift back more against Alec's hand, searching for friction, because Ashton?

Ashton is beautiful.

Wearing just a pair of fighting shorts, he looks like he's been sculpted for just this moment. He stretches, pulling at his wrists to stretch out his arms and shoulders, and shaking his limbs out, hopping from foot to foot.

Alec's hand disappears briefly, and when it returns, he's pressing his cock against me, sliding it through my drenched pussy.

"Do you want me to wait?" he asks, breathless.

I shake my head violently, eyes glued to the fight.

Alec makes a sound like a laugh in answer. "Hold on tight," he advises, gripping my hip in one hand and positioning himself with the other.

The bell rings the exact moment Alec thrusts inside me. My scream is lost in the deafening noise from the crowd as the fight begins.

Alec was right. The other fighters were nothing, nothing at all, compared to this.

Ashton moves like a jaguar, all toned rippling muscle and grace as he circles his opponent. He's patient, calm, moving on the balls of his feet as he waits for the first strike.

Buried to the hilt inside me, Alec waits too, fingers digging into my hips through the fabric of my dress.

The first punch is a doozy, coming at Ash so quickly I can

barely see it. But he does. He darts to the side, easily avoiding it, and answers with a hit that lands squarely on his opponent's jaw.

Alec leans his whole body over me, hands grasping mine on the rail, and gives a derisive snort.

"He doesn't stand a chance," he tells me. "Not against Ashton, not tonight. Watch him, darling. He was made for this."

I clench around him, his cock buried inside me, and am rewarded with a low groan.

It's easy to see what Alec means. Ashton's opponent is a top-notch fighter, maybe one of the best. But Ashton? Every move he makes is like water: fluid and precise. He dances around the ring, every hit, every dodge, done with an unfathomable grace.

It's a pleasure to watch him fight.

By the end of the first round, Ashton has only taken a single hit. He looks fresh as a daisy.

His opponent is already swaying on his feet, one eye so swollen it's practically shut.

And I'm not much better.

Alec refuses to move, and I'm writhing against him, trying to shift my hips enough to make him fuck me. It's a terrible torture, having him so still inside me.

"Please, Alec," I beg. I worry my bottom lip between my teeth and rock back against him, but his body is so hard against mine, so immobile, it doesn't accomplish anything but frustrating me further. I let my head fall forward, groaning.

"Please what?" Alec asks, sounding impossibly calm. His cock twitches inside me, and I moan shamelessly, trying to arch against him. "Tell me what you need, darling. Use your words."

"Fuck me," I plead. "Alec, please."

"Is this what you want?" Alec asks, moving his hips back just a fraction of an inch and then slamming forward.

I throw back my head and scream. "Yes!"

He does it again. And again. By the time the bell sounds to announce the next round, he's fucking me hard, hips slamming against me, and I can't keep quiet. I pray this box is soundproof, because no way I can stop myself from screaming every time Alec hits that perfect spot inside me.

Down in the ring, I swear Ashton's eyes are glued to our box, his attention entirely on us. So much so that he takes a hit, not making any move to avoid it as it crashes into his jaw.

Alec's hand releases mine and slides down to touch me, his palm pressing against my clit and fingers spread on either side of my pussy while he fucks me.

The fight doesn't last more than a few seconds after that.

Ashton slams against his opponent like a tidal wave, hitting him again and again, pestering him with shots and forcing him back against the edge of the ring until, finally, he lets his guard drop for a split second.

The uppercut Ashton hits him with is almost hard enough to lift him in the air. He sways for a moment, looking stunned, before he falls down to the mat at Ashton's feet.

Alec's hand grips me tighter, and he brings the other up to my neck, wrapping his fingers around my throat. I let him know exactly how much I love it, gripping the rail so hard I'm afraid I might bend the metal and screaming his name.

ALEC

IT'S INCREDIBLE TO WATCH HER COME UNDONE.

Sydney throws her head back to scream, arching against my chest as I slam into her. I tighten my grip on her throat and am rewarded with her clenching around me.

She's so perfect. Even the way her pussy squeezes around my cock is perfection. I've never felt anything better in all my life.

"Do you understand now?" I ask her, angling her head back down, forcing her to watch the ring where Ashton is holding his hands high above his head in victory. "This is our world."

She swallows hard, throat constricting under my hand, but I thrust into her again until she's screaming even more.

"It's full of blood and violence," I tell her. "And it could be yours, Sydney. It could be all yours."

She's so close. Her legs are trembling around mine, and I'm positive I'm the only thing keeping her on her feet right now. I press my hand harder against her clit, tightening my grip on her throat.

I'm not going to last much longer. It's been a fight not to

come since the second I entered her, since the moment I felt how drenched she was.

She was made for this. Made for us. And it's time she realizes it, embraces it.

"You'd be a queen," I tell her, slamming into her over and over. I don't know if the words are a promise to her, or to myself. Because I want it, I want it more than I've ever wanted anything. "*Our* queen."

"Yes!" she gasps, hips moving back to take me.

Fuck. She's too tight around me, and I can't slow down. I groan, slamming into her again and again, because I can't hold back a second longer.

When she comes, I instantly follow her, each of us screaming the other's name. She grips me like a vise, but I fight through it, burying myself as deep inside her as I can as I come.

It's a fucking miracle I'm still standing, after.

I don't want to pull out. I want to stay like this forever, inside her.

But I still have one more thing to do.

She whimpers when my cock slides out of her, and I plant a soft kiss on her cheek in apology.

"Stay right there," I order. "Don't move."

I'm not sure if she can. Her arms shake where she's gripping the railing, her legs trembling from holding her own weight.

I take my time, tucking myself back into my pants and arranging her dress just so. I gather the skirt up over her hips, kneeling down to watch my cum slide out of her, dripping down her thighs.

"You're so fucking beautiful, you know that?" I tell her, reverently.

I slide my phone out of my pocket and raise it, taking my time getting the angle just right.

"A-Alec?" Sydney asks. Her voice is shaky, raw from screaming.

"One more second, darling," I assure her, snapping the photo.

I pull up my contacts and quickly send it off to all three of my brothers.

Ours. And now, I think she's finally ready to accept it.

She lifts her feet obediently when I tap her ankles, sliding her panties back on and over her legs.

"I... I need to clean up," she complains, wriggling as I pull them over her hips and back into place.

I chuckle, scooping her into my arms so I can carry her over to the couch.

"Oh no you don't," I tell her, holding her against my chest. "I like knowing I'm dripping down those pretty thighs. You're going to keep it there for me."

Her eyes flare with lust as she bites her lips, staring up at me. I wonder if I could make her come again, so soon. But she must be famished, maybe dehydrated. She needs to eat and rest. With the fight over, I have all the time in the world to take care of her and pamper her. I intend to spend the rest of my life pampering her.

It's only fair I start right away.

48

ASHTON

The crowd loves me.

The roar of the audience is deafening as I hop out of the ring, grabbing a towel from Jacob. Behind me, Sven's manager is calling the medic over, trying to get his fighter to sit up.

I almost feel sorry for him.

It's bad form to end the fight so early, just barely past the minute mark of the second round. But how was I supposed to know he couldn't take that hit?

"That was brutal," Jacob says, shaking his head. But he's grinning. "I'd rather you'd waited for the third round, but—"

"Listen to them!" I laugh, motioning toward the stands and making my way down the narrow path out of the arena and back to the dressing rooms. "They *loved it*. Third round knockout is predictable. No one saw this coming."

Not even me.

"All the same," Jacob says, following me into my dressing room. I glance in the mirror, looking for any damage from the hits I took, but it looks like I lucked out tonight. Nothing but some minor swelling.

Which is a relief because Doc appears to be AWOL again tonight. Prick.

I'm reaching for my towel when I see my phone light up with a text and scoop it up instead. Speak of the devil and he shall appear, or some shit.

But the message isn't from Doc at all.

"I've got another potential fight lined up, if you're interested," Jacob is saying. "I know, I know, you're retired. But the crowd loves you, man, you heard them out there, they—"

"Sure," I say, not listening at all, as I stare down at my phone. "Whatever you want, man. Listen, I need the room. Right now."

Jacob pauses. "Right now, as in—"

"Right now, as in right this second, yes," I answer, adjusting my towel to cover my stiffening cock, and shooing him toward the door.

"Oh. Uh, sure, whatever you need," Jacob says, heading toward the exit. "I'll, uh, I'll get that fight set up for you then, okay?"

I nod, eyes glued to my phone, not paying him the slightest attention.

The door shuts behind him, but I'm mesmerized, staring at the photo Alec sent us.

I had thought, just for a second, I'd seen her face up in our private box. But I've been seeing her face everywhere, awake, in my dreams, everywhere I look. I figured it was just wishful thinking.

But I recognize the view from this picture. She's here, right now, up in our private box.

She came to see me fight.

My hands are shaking a little as I zoom in.

Fuck. She looks so good bent over, ass in the air like that.

I'm jealous as fuck looking at the cum dripping out of her, knowing it's Alec's.

Asshole, I think, gripping the phone.

There's a chance they're still here, a chance they haven't left yet.

I grab my towel and bar of soap and practically run to the shower.

———

It's the fastest shower of my life, and I am absolutely sure I missed a button while putting on my dress shirt, but I'm outside the door to our private box in a record eight minutes.

Sure, Jacob is going to give me hell for missing the post-fight press briefing. But there's no way I'd be able to answer a single question from any of them, not tonight. Not knowing she's here.

"Knock, knock," I say cheerily, pushing the door open. I don't wait for their answer, and part of me is hoping to catch them in the middle of round two.

Sadly, I don't.

Alec looks up from his spot in the corner of the couch with mild irritation, but no real surprise in his eyes. It figures. If he'd really wanted to keep me out, he would have taken me off the approved visitors lists.

He could have waited to send that message until their date was over, but he didn't. I meet his eyes and know exactly what he's thinking.

Ours.

She's curled up against him, head resting back against his chest, seated on the couch between his open legs. Alec has one leg propped up next to him and a glass of whiskey in his hand.

His free hand is stroking up and down her arm, gently, and she's melting under the attention.

They're cuddling.

I don't think I've ever seen Alec cuddle.

"Rise and shine, darling," Alec purrs, giving her shoulder a light squeeze. "Look what the cat dragged in."

Sydney sits up, clearly awake, and looks around. My heart skips a beat when her eyes land on me.

"Hey, Babygirl," I say, giving her a soft smile. "I didn't know you were coming tonight."

She smiles at me, and it's the sweetest thing I've ever seen. "Ash," she says excitedly. "You were *incredible*."

My face hurts from the size of the smile that stretches over my face. "Really?" I press, stepping forward. "You enjoyed it?"

"Oh yes, she did. Sydney found your fight to be *very* enjoyable," Alec says, hiding his growing smile behind his glass. Instead of agreeing, Sydney's eyes go wide, a blush creeping over her face.

Huh. I've known a lot of women who find watching MMA at least a little arousing. Who would have guessed our sweet Sydney would be one of them?

I slide onto the couch next to her, and she moves a little to make room for me. She pulls her legs up closer to her body, tucking them against herself, and that won't do at all. She deserves to be comfortable.

I reach out and take her legs, draping them over my lap instead.

She wriggles a little as I run my hands over the smooth skin of her shin and up to her knees.

"Did it get you a little excited?" I ask.

Sydney bites her lip and doesn't answer me. So fucking adorable.

"You can come watch me anytime, you know that?" I

assure her, sliding my hand a little higher. "And if it gets you excited, I can always help with that. I would *love* to help with that."

Her breath hitches as my hand creeps higher, but she keeps her legs tightly pressed together.

I pause, my hand on her thigh. "Is... Is something wrong?"

"I, uh..." She shakes her head and leans back against Alec, looking up at him pleadingly.

"You can tell him," Alec prompts.

Sydney shakes her head again.

"Tell me what?" I ask, glancing between the two of them.

Alec's hand reaches down to touch her thigh, tapping it once with his fingers, like a command.

Sydney finally lets her legs fall open.

Curious, slide my hand between her legs, up her inner thigh and...

Oh.

"You're dripping," I observe with a light chuckle.

'It's not... It's not *me*," Sydney insists, throwing another quick look up at Alec.

Of course it isn't. I know exactly who it is from that photo.

Taking her ankle, I maneuver it to the other side of me on the couch, so I'm between her open legs.

"He can be a real asshole, can't he?" I ask her with a sympathetic chuckle. I push her dress up a little higher. "A real possessive mother fucker."

"Watch it," Alec growls.

"But I don't mind," I assure her, leaning down and kissing a line up her thigh. "It doesn't bother me at all."

When I get to that wet part on her leg, I drag my tongue over it, lapping it up.

Sydney gasps, writhing back against Alec. Her mouth is open in pure disbelief when I look up at her.

It's just cum, right? Honestly, I've never seen what the big fucking deal was, why everyone's so freaked out by it.

Licking my way up her leg, I pause at her soaking wet panties, glancing up her body to make sure Sydney is watching.

She is. Her eyes are wide as I peel the fabric to the side and run my tongue through all the mess Alec left behind.

"See, darling?" Alec coos to her while she whimpers, grinding back against him. "Ashton knows how to treat his queen."

Queen? I pause, the flat of my tongue against her, and glance up.

She does look like a queen right now, doesn't she? In a dress I know Alec probably had commissioned just for her, sitting spread-eagled in a private box that cost a fortune, with the city's two most desired men at her beck and call.

Yeah. Queen. I like that.

Hail to the mother fucking queen.

I grin, lapping eagerly at her. It's better now that I can taste just her. She tastes so fucking good, so sweet against my tongue.

I should draw it out, make it last. It feels like forever since I've been able to taste her, and I want to take my time. But the second I find a rhythm and she reaches for me, burying her hands in my hair, all rational thought goes straight out the window.

I don't *want* to make her come. I *need* it. I groan against her, sucking and licking at her clit, following every cue she gives me to deliver exactly what she needs. All too soon, she's arching back, tugging at my hair as she grinds against me. And then—

Her thighs close around my ears, holding me in place when she comes. I ride it out with her, happily letting her pull me against her, hands gripping her hips to urge her even closer.

It's spectacular. With her, it always is.

Hail to the mother fucking queen.

49

SEBASTIAN

Killing him is a long time coming.

My muscles tense when I spot him leaving his building. He takes his time, slowly walking down the busy street, and I follow, keeping my head down and blending into the crowd. I've made an art form out of it, being invisible. It started as self-preservation, a way to stay under the radar and keep safe. Now it's the most useful tool in my arsenal.

Sydney is at risk, and it's past time I do something about it.

My Sydney.

Maybe before I could have waited. I could have played it safe and cautious, planned this out perfectly so there would be no risk, no chance of something going wrong.

After the other night, that's all gone out the fucking window. Fuck the risk, fuck taking my time and generating a plan. Sydney is in danger. And the only thing in the entire fucking world right now is keeping her safe.

Because she's finally mine. Ours.

I'd imagined a thousand times over exactly what I was going to do to her when she'd unlocked her door and invited me in. And she'd shown me that night that it's what she wanted from me. She'd wanted me raw and vulgar. She'd wanted me to order her, force her to do the things she's only dreamed of doing, take away all that hesitation and doubt.

And I was ready to do it. I was ready to fuck her until it hurt, ready to force her down onto my cock until she gagged. I'd wanted to make her touch me, make her rub her hand over the piercing on the head of my dick and imagine how it would feel inside her.

But then I'd touched her.

And everything changed.

She looked so perfect, lying there, leaning her face into my palm. Like an angel. So exquisite, and so beautiful, and I'd never wanted anyone more in my life.

I'll never forget the sounds she made as we touched. Soft, breathless gasps, each one like a prayer. I'll remember every single one until the day I die, the sweetest music I've ever heard.

I was transfixed by her, mesmerized by her touch.

I've never felt anything like that before.

And now?

Now I'll do everything in my power to protect her from scum like this.

He's easy to follow. Most people are. Keeping my head down so he won't recognize me too soon and only looking up to keep my eyes on him, I begin to close the distance between us.

The sun has set, and though there are people on the streets around us, the crowds are growing smaller and smaller.

By the time I'm right behind him, reaching out to grab his shoulder, there's no one else around but me. No one to save him.

"Remember me?" I ask, feeling a surge of pleasure at the way his face falls in recognition. At the fear that fills his eyes.

Chase Levine did nothing to deserve a woman like Sydney. And so long as he is alive, she will never know peace.

Killing him is a long time coming, and I hope to make his death as slow and painful as possible.

"No one will help you if you scream," I assure him, digging the barrel of my gun into his spine as I grip his shoulder tightly. From the pathetic little noise he makes, he knows it's true. I glance quickly toward the street as my car pulls up to the curb. Pressing the gun into him a little harder than necessary, I steer him toward it. "Nod once if you understand me."

He nods quickly, head bobbing up and down.

"Good," I say, reaching around him to open the car door. "Get in. You and I need to have a little chat about boundaries."

———

I've just gotten him situated in the wet lab when my phone beeps, a sharp alarm.

It's not a tone I recognize.

Frowning, I pick it up, opening the alert from my security app.

Smoke alarm.

And another.

And another.

Fear grips my heart as I pull up the video feed, pulse pounding in my ears as I watch the flames surge and grow.

As I watch Sydney's building catch fire.

50

JADE

I SIGH, STRAIGHTENING FROM BEHIND THE BAKERY counter and finally—*finally*—letting myself stop and rest for a second.

It's not *impossible* for me to run the shop all on my lonesome, even with the deluge of new customers Syd's boy toys have magically summoned out of thin air for us. Hell, it's not even all that difficult.

But it's lonely. I miss my Syd when she's not here. I miss our little furball, attacking my feet.

What's the point of making the best damn pastries in the city if my best friend isn't around to scarf them down with me at the end of a long workday? If she isn't here to gossip with me over some fresh shortbread?

Whatever. Just means more stale cookies for me to eat for breakfast tomorrow, I suppose. I shouldn't complain. It's about damn time that girl got out and did something fun for a change.

Fuck, I could kill Chase for what he did to her. Not just the obvious things, the cheating, the systematic abuse, the stalking, but the little things too. He made her feel so small, so insignificant for so long, that she started to believe that was who she really was.

Now, finally, the Sydney I knew for so long before that dickhead showed up is coming back. And if it takes four different boyfriends to make that happen, who am I to judge?

Maybe together the five of us can convince her to make a habit of this. She could start taking a night off every week, have some time for herself, go on real dates with them. It wouldn't be so bad to run the shop on my own for a few hours every week, not if it meant Sydney got to enjoy her life a little more.

Satisfied with that idea, and thinking I might just text Doc about it, I gather up the very last of the leftover pastries and start to box them up. I'm just slotting the last croissant into place when the bell above our shop entrance chimes, and the door opens.

Frowning, I turn. I'd locked the door when I'd closed earlier... Hadn't I?

I don't recognize the man who walks inside, which makes me think he's never been a customer here before. A man like that stands out. Draws attention.

"Sorry, but we're closed," I say loudly, narrowing my eyes at him.

He's older, maybe in his fifties. With a silver and wood cane in one hand, he steps slowly into the café, leaning heavily on the cane for support. His hair is slicked back, a golden blond just turning silver at the temples. He's built like an athlete just past his prime.

He looks like trouble.

"A pity," the man says with a tsk. He smiles at me, but it doesn't reach his eyes. "I've been meaning to stop by sooner. I'm looking for Sydney, actually. I went by her apartment, but she doesn't seem to be home."

"Sydney's not here right now," I tell him, taking a cautious step out from behind the counter, closer to him.

"More's the pity." He lets out a long, tired breath. "Do you know where she is, dear?"

My hackles raise at anyone, let alone this stranger, calling me *dear*. I don't try to hide my reaction as I shake my head. "No. I don't," I say firmly. "And I don't want to be rude, but you need to leave. We're closed. That door should be locked, and—"

Still smiling that empty, blank smile, he opens his hand, holding it out to show me a set of keys nestled in his palm.

"Perks of ownership," he tells me, as I stare down at them.

"Wait... You're the new owner?" I ask, confused. He certainly looks rich enough. But does that mean it wasn't one of Syd's boys who purchased our building?

"I have that pleasure, yes." He chuckles, and the sound of it sets my nerves on edge and makes the hair on the back of my neck rise. Something's wrong, something doesn't feel right about any of this. Moving the keys to his other hand—the one holding his cane—he stretches his hand out to me, inviting me to shake it.

"You can call me Dante, dear," he says.

It's rude to leave him standing there, with his arm outstretched, leaning heavily on his cane, but I can't bring myself to reach out and touch him. I'm frozen, something that feels an awful lot like fear creeping up my spine.

But then he shifts a little, and his leg shakes. He winces, as though in pain, doubling over and dropping his keys to the ground in the process. "Ah!" he cries out, hunched over himself. The cane shakes under his weight.

Fuck. I'm an asshole.

"Here," I offer, stepping forward and bending down to pick up his keys from where they've landed. "Let me get those, I—"

At least I block the first hit.

The moment I bend over, Dante raises his cane and brings it down hard, aiming for my head. I manage to get my arm up just in time, screaming as the blow connects with bone.

The pain is unbearable. I crumple to my knees, cradling my arm against my chest and sobbing. Frantically, I try to get up, to scramble to my feet.

I can't move fast enough to block the next blow. It takes me hard on the side of the head, and everything goes fuzzy as I hit the ground.

It takes a while for me to lose consciousness. And before I do, I recognize the smell of gasoline.

And smoke.

51

SYDNEY

Sandwiched between Ashton and Alec in the back of their town car, I let myself smile. This is where I belong. With them.

Together.

I curl against Ashton's side, running my hand over his arm. "Can we swing by my apartment quickly?" I ask. "I need to grab some more clothes if I'm being kidnapped for much longer."

I'd been in a daze when I'd packed, grabbing things and shoving them in my suitcase without much thought. I miss my favorite sleep shirt and could use more than just one pair of jeans.

"Of course. We can stop by on our way to Second Circle," Alec assures me. He leans forward, tapping the divider that separates us from the driver. When it opens, I hear him speaking softly to Earl, telling him to take a detour to my address.

"You better have a big bed in your suite, Babygirl," Ashton

murmurs into my ear, running his hand up the bare skin of my leg. "Because it's going to be a tight fit with the three of us."

"We're not sleeping over," Alec warns him, settling back into his seat. But he's smiling, looking more relaxed than I've ever seen him. He stretches his arm behind me, fingers idly playing with my hair. "And if we are, you're sleeping on the couch."

"Who said anything about sleeping?" Ashton asks with a flirtatious wink.

I laugh, shoving him playfully, but that only makes him move closer. He lifts my legs and sets them across his thighs, pulling me toward him until I'm practically on his lap.

Alec snorts, shaking his head.

"I missed you," I admit, staring into Ash's bright blue eyes. And I did. I missed this feeling I get when I'm with him, like I'm safe, like nothing could ever hurt me. It's even stronger now, after seeing him in the ring and watching him fight. My fierce protector.

"I missed you too, Babygirl." He shifts forward until our foreheads are pressed together. "Every single fucking second we're apart."

We're almost home, back to my place, and I can't wait to grab the few things I need and leave quickly, so I can get them up to my hotel room. Just the thought of what the three of us could do together has me excited, wriggling in my seat.

Ash notices. Of course he notices. His eyes sparkle, and his hand moves higher up my leg, fingers trailing over the seam of my panties.

"Maybe we should get some of your toys," he says softly, fingers teasing. "I have something I want to try with you..."

Alec's phone vibrates against my hip, and he swears softly as he fishes it out of his pocket. Ash takes the opportunity to kiss me, tilting my chin up and pressing a soft, chaste kiss on my lips that has me pressing against him hungrily.

Traffic is a nightmare tonight. Earl pulls the car over to the side of the road to let a fire truck pass by, the sirens blaring. Another one follows, right on its heels.

"Doc?" Alec says into the phone. "This better be good. We're on our way to—"

He stops mid-sentence, his body going stiff.

"Say that again," he says quietly.

Another high-pitched whine from a firetruck as it races down the street. And now that I'm paying attention to them, I realize I can still hear the others, like they haven't gone far at all. Like they're just around the corner...

"Alec?" Ashton asks, frowning. "What's going on?"

Alec's face is hard, his jaw tight. "We're almost there. Get here *now*," he barks into the phone.

The sirens are so, so loud suddenly.

"Sydney." Alec looks at me, eyes too soft, voice too gentle.

"What's wrong?" I ask, feeling the panic set in. "What's going on?"

So, so loud, I can't hear anything else. There's nothing but the sirens.

Alec doesn't answer me.

No.

No, no, no.

Somehow, I already know, without him saying a word.

The sirens are deafening, and as we turn the corner, our car stops, blocked from moving forward. My block. We're on my block. Frantically, I dive for the door handle, almost falling over Ashton in my haste to get out onto the street, ignoring him as he tries to stop me. There are barricades set up around my building, but I push them away, running, running...

"Jade!" I scream. I'm looking around at the crowd, eyes searching for her bright red hair, for her wide smile.

"*JADE?*"

There's no answer.

Before me, my store—my *home*—is an inferno.

52

VIPER

THE FLAMES ARE SO BRIGHT.

So beautiful.

They twist and curl, reaching up for the stars, hungry and alive. The heat of it burns my skin, even from here.

Doc gets here the same time I do, ditching his motorcycle so fast it crashes to the ground, his helmet quickly joining it. Our rabbit is running straight for the fire, screaming, determined to get inside. He catches her before she can reach the door, arms locking around her waist, lifting her clean off her feet.

But she doesn't stop. She fights him, struggling in his hold, screaming her friend's name. "JADE!"

Her Jade, I remember. The one she'd kill for. The one she'd die to protect.

It's not fair, I think, watching the flames spread and grow, devouring the top floor of her building and moving down. Her screams belong to me.

My brothers are preoccupied. Doc holding her back, the others shouting, trying to calm her down, trying to keep her safe. That's their job, not mine.

My job is different. Always has been.

I move past the chaos and toward the building, snatching a bottle of water from a waiting paramedic, and opening it with my teeth, spitting the cap onto the ground. The poor bastard does nothing to stop me, flinching away from me as I tear off my shirt and upend the bottle over it, soaking it. Not a perfect solution, but it'll do.

Perfection is the enemy of progress, and all that.

A cop steps in front of the door as I approach, hand outstretched like he thinks that he can stop me.

"Sir, you can't go in there, you need to go back behind the barrier and—"

I look at him. Just look, until he steps aside, Adam's apple bobbing as he swallows.

Rolling my shoulders back, I tie the wet shirt around my face, covering my nose and mouth, before I walk into hell.

The smoke hits me instantly, making my lungs seize, thick enough I can taste it through my makeshift mask. It tastes like gasoline, igniting a memory lodged deep in my consciousness, one I like to keep buried. Someone used an accelerant, wanted this building and everything in it to burn.

The smoke's too thick to stay standing. I drop to my hands and knees, crawling low. You can't see in a fire, can't rely on your sight. You have to move by touch. I keep my eyes closed, moving quickly, feeling my way through the building, mapping it to my memory.

The floor is hot beneath my palms, the fire roaring around me. My skin sizzles and blisters when I brush a fallen beam. I push it aside, ignoring the pain.

She has to be in here. Somewhere. Her Jade.

I reach forward, feeling through the darkness. My fingers trace a shattered piece of a coffee mug, a fallen chair, and then...

Something slick. Viscous.

A pool of blood on the ground, the feel of it familiar under my hands.

Interesting. I rub it between my fingers.

Someone *was* here. Someone got hurt.

Something cracks above me. A rush of searing heat follows as the ceiling splits apart and starts to give way. I roll, barely making it out of the way as a beam breaks off, falling to the café floor and exploding in a shower of debris and charcoal.

The air is changing. Thicker now, hotter. I keep moving, ricocheting off a wall, fumbling for a way out. I can't breathe. Can't see, can't figure out which way is out, which way is back to safety.

This would be when most people panic, when their lungs start to blister, when the idea of their mortality goes from an eventuality to an actuality.

But death and I are close friends. Kindred souls. I don't panic. I just keep going.

The world is a blur of heat and smoke, the wall unending under my palms. I feel around, making my way around the perimeter, searching, feeling, and—

Glass. My fingers touch glass.

I throw myself against it, again and again, ramming my shoulder against the window.

It shatters in a burst of cold air and pain, and I stumble out through the opening, hitting the ground hard. Yanking the shirt from my face, I suck in a lungful of air. It burns going down, and my chest convulses, coughing until I taste blood.

People are shouting. Running toward me.

"Sir! Oxygen, now!" a medic says, grabbing hold of me and pressing a mask against my face.

I snarl, pushing him away. "Don't fucking touch me."

The world is spinning. I manage to crawl forward a little

more, slumping back against the side of an ambulance, chest burning as I cough. Every breath hurts.

"I've got him," a familiar voice says. Calm. He's always so fucking calm, on the outside, when we're not in the lab. "Viper? You with me, brother?"

I blink through the haze, willing my eyes to focus. "Hey, Doc."

Then another coughing fit takes me, and I sink back into my dark place, closing my eyes and letting the world fade around me as the bookstore burns.

53

SYDNEY

I HATE HOSPITALS. THE LAST TIME I WAS HERE AT
Fortune City Emergency and Critical Care, it was to watch my
grandmother die. The time before that? My parents.

Every time I'm here, someone dies.

The waiting room chair digs into my back, no matter how I
sit. It's hopeless. It's like these seats were designed to be delib-
erately uncomfortable. I slump forward instead, elbows on my
knees.

Across the room, Alec and Seb are arguing, their voices
pitched low. I can only catch fragments of their conversation:
not safe anymore... the compound... our only choice...

I barely listen. Barely care, even though I know they're
talking about me.

The doctors are with Viper now, examining him. They said
the main concern is smoke inhalation and some second-degree
burns to his hands and arms, but I don't trust it. Something is
wrong, I can feel it. I just know it.

I've called Jade at least forty times in the few minutes it

took to follow the ambulance over here, but she hasn't answered. And Justin's phone is going straight to voicemail.

I stare down at my phone, feeling broken, empty. Gone. Everything I've built, everything I sacrificed for. It's all gone, burned down to ash.

How could this happen?

"She was probably gone for the day, right? It was already late," Ash says from the seat next to mine, trying to sound reassuring. His hand settles on my back, his touch soothing and sweet.

"Maybe." My voice sounds weak, disconnected from my body. "But I... I left her there with so much work. What if she was still in there?" I can't shake the feeling that something is wrong. Jade never ignores my calls. Never.

Alec and Seb finally stop arguing and come join us. Neither one of them looks happy.

"Viper is positive there was no one inside the café," Sebastian says, watching me a little too closely. "He swears she wasn't there."

But he had blood on his hands, I almost say.

And none of the doctors know why. Or where it came from.

"What if she's hurt?" I ask, for what feels like the thousandth time.

"She could have been taken to another hospital," Alec reasons, pulling out his phone. "I'll have my assistant call around, check every medical center and urgent care in the city. If she was hurt, we'll find her."

I don't answer. I dial her number again without offering a response.

It rings.

And rings.

And then—

"Hey."

I suck in a breath, almost dropping the phone in shock. "Jade?" I'm out of my seat in an instant, a laugh bursting out of me. "Oh my God, you have no idea how happy I am to hear your voice. Are you okay? Are you—"

"I'm fine." Her voice is monotone. Flat.

"The shop, Jade. The shop is gone." The words catch in my throat. It still feels unreal, feels like a nightmare. "There was a fire, and I thought... I thought you were still inside. You're sure you're okay?"

"That's crazy," she says. Too calm, the world's biggest under-reaction. But I'm just so relieved to hear her voice, to know that she's not dead in the alley or trapped in a corner of the shop Viper missed. "But no. I'm fine."

Then why weren't you picking up?

"Thank God," I say with a shaky laugh. "I'm okay, too. But Viper got hurt. I'm with them now, we're at the—"

"Listen, I'm in the middle of something," she interrupts, talking over me. "Can I call you back?"

"Oh. Yeah. Yeah, of course. I'm just glad you're okay. I was so worried." I take a breath, trying to calm down. "We'll talk later, okay? I love you."

There's a long pause. Too long.

"I love you, too," she says. And the call disconnects.

"See?" Ashton grins, his expression smug. "She's fine! Just like I told you she'd be!"

But I don't really hear him. I stare at the ground, heart stuck in my throat. It takes me a few seconds to pinpoint it, to realize why my chest is suddenly so tight.

I love you, too.

"Something's wrong," I say softly.

"I'll say," Ashton mutters. He stands with a groan, stretching his arms over his head. "This place doesn't even have vending machines, you know that? You think the cafeteria is still open? I need, like, a gallon of coffee. And a dozen donuts."

"No." I shake my head, tears welling in my eyes. "Something is wrong with Jade."

Seb looks over sharply, eyes narrowing. "What do you mean?" he asks.

"That wasn't—" I stumble over my words, trying to explain. Trying to put it into words they'll understand. "Something is wrong!"

I love you...

... to the moon and back.

I blink, and the floodgates open. Tears stream down my face.

"I think..." My voice breaks. "I think Jade is in danger."

EPILOGUE
DANTE

No warning.

After all the money I sank into informants—all the careers I supported and financed through the Empire City Police Department—you'd think someone would have had the decency to warn me before the FBI raided the first of my warehouses back in Empire City.

They didn't.

Everything that happened after was pure chaos. A blur of phone calls, shouted orders, and frantic updates as my men on the ground scrambled to move product to safer locations, to reach our contacts in the city government, to figure out what the fuck was happening.

Then another warehouse was hit.

And another.

It's almost poetic. I'd worked so hard to keep Alec's attention focused on Sydney while I dismantled everything he's built in this godforsaken city, and while I was distracted, he pulled the same trick on me.

I'm almost proud.

In just over a day, I lost seventy percent of my entire organization. Seventy percent of what I've spent the last few years rebuilding from ashes. All that remains are my offshore accounts and foreign investments.

The offshore accounts, and this—what little I've managed to take control of here in Fortune City. Thirty percent of my organization and a handful of warehouses, a few defunct businesses, and two decrepit old mansions north of the city border.

No matter. Empires can be rebuilt.

But they won't be able to put their woman back together after I get a hold of her.

It was a mistake, bringing her ex into this. Chase was more of a liability than an asset. For a man who said he knew his ex inside and out, better than anyone, he sure failed to get into her head. All those scare tactics of his were more appropriate for a haunted house. Dead flowers? Notes? A small near miss in a shitty car? This is all I get after the heavy sum I paid for his services? What a waste of time and money.

Embarrassing.

Not that the professionals I hired were any better. Rocco never checked in after breaking into her apartment. I wouldn't be surprised to find out he's currently rotting in a shallow grave.

Fine.

It just goes to show that if you want something done right, you have to do it yourself.

I glance over at the girl slumped in the chair. A pity Sydney hadn't been at work tonight. But no matter, this one makes an effective plan B.

"Good," I tell her, after I take the cell phone from her ear and end the call. I give her an affectionate pat on the head, like a dog. She flinches and jerks away from me. There's blood in her hair, staining the dyed red a deep crimson. And the way she's cradling her arm against her chest tells me it's broken. "You did good."

There are tears streaming down her face when she raises her head to glare at me.

It will take them a while to realize she's missing. Enough time to sow discontent between them all. Enough time for me to get Annika out of here, to send her back to Empire City, where she'll be safe.

But once they realize I have Sydney's little friend?

Ah.

That's when the real fun will begin.

WANT MORE?

Sydney's story will continue in Dangerous Deeds, Fortune City Mafia book three

If you enjoy dark fantasy, be sure to check out The Broken Blade trilogy, starting with The Queen's Blade by Evelyn Ward

For release announcements, sneak peeks, and bonus content visit our website at evelyn-ward.com and follow us on social media:

instagram.com/evelynwardbooks
tiktok.com/@evelyn.ward.books
amazon.com/stores/Evelyn-Ward/author/B0D932HHG9
facebook.com/328082750395931

ABOUT THE AUTHOR(...S)

Tragically, there is no Evelyn Ward. Or, if she does exist, she did not write this book.

The real authors are two best friends, who clearly need more personal boundaries. As always, we'll call them M & K.

K is a resident of New York City, and an all-around bad bitch who gains power by collecting shitty people's tears. She makes the plot work, adds copious amounts of trauma and tension, and doesn't laugh *too* much when she has to read an intensely spicy scene, knowing full well her co-author probably Did That Thing.

And to our family and friends who may be reading this, neither of us has ever done *anything*, let alone that thing you're thinking of, let alone with multiple partners, and we certainly wouldn't do it again, if given half a chance and a few glasses of wine.

We swear.

M is a resident of Seattle, WA, and full-time evil scientist. She hyperfixates on a scene to the point of obsession, re-reads the draft until words lose all meaning, and desperately needs to find a few new synonyms for male genitalia that don't make her cringe. She has failed in every attempt to shock her co-author, but she will keep trying.